Anna's Song

Anna's Song

Cries from the Earth, Book 1: A Time Travel Saga

BRENDA GATES

First Edition

ISBN 978-1-7325602-0-8(paperback)
ISBN 978-1-7325602-1-5 (ebook)

https://gatesgalwrites.wordpress.com

DEDICATION

Most things in life are not accomplished in isolation. Thanks to my husband, who bought me a laptop and told me to "just do it." His encouragement, belief in me, and pride in what I was doing pushed me forward. Thanks to my kids—you inspire me to keep working at my dreams because I would never want you to give up on yours. Thanks, Mom, for coming over and washing dishes so I could get upstairs and work without feeling guilty. Thanks to my writing group, you saw my writing at its worst and still wouldn't let me give up. And thank you to some special ladies who let me pick their brain on things related to being identical twins. I can't wait to see what God will do in your lives. Most of all, thanks to the One who made my imagination and gave me the desire to create something from nothing.

MIRROR, MIRROR

BEFORE I FELL THROUGH the water, I thought I was crazy.

"Hey, doc, you know that sister of mine everyone presumes dead? She's alive just like I said. Yes, sir. Saw her yesterday, in my bathroom mirror."

"Of course, you will 'see' Adeline in the mirror," my imaginary psychiatrist replies, chuckling like it's some private joke. "After all, you do look alike."

Adeline is my twin sister. Identical in every way except for a birthmark, a scar, and some serious leg muscles.

I run when I'm upset, and I've been running a lot. You see, ten months, eleven days, and somewhere between twelve and sixteen hours ago, Adeline disappeared.

The first time I saw my missing sister, I had just gotten out of the shower, and the mirror was all misty. Opening the door to let some of the extra moisture dissipate, I glanced up, and there she was, staring back at me through the myriad droplets on the glass. For a moment, I thought it was my own reflection, but her hair was dry, and, suffice it to say, we weren't exactly in the same state of dress. She looked as astonished as I felt, and when the mirror cleared, she was gone.

With my heart pounding something awful, I staggered to my room and collapsed on the edge of my bed, forcing myself to take slow, deep breaths, and thinking I had seen a ghost. But she was no ghost. You can't be a ghost if you're still among the living.

People keep saying she's dead. I know better.

There's this thing about twins. We know stuff about each other in ways most singletons can't comprehend. Adeline and I never feel each other's pain. When she broke her arm, mine felt fine. When my appendix ruptured, she didn't writhe in bed. We don't read each other's thoughts, but we often perceive what the other is thinking. We aren't much alike, outside of appearances. Still, I can always tell my sister *is*, in the same way I know I *am*. I can sense her heart beating as sure as I sense my own. I feel her soul the same way the first violinist can feel the music playing around her. We gave up trying to explain this to people. It's like pointing out a complex harmony to someone who is tone deaf. I hear her in my very bones.

The next morning, there in the mist of the mirror, she stands. I blink hard, trying to keep myself calm, and raise my right hand in a stiff wave.

"It's just me," I whisper to the image in front of me. Maybe, if I say it enough, my imagination will back off. "It's just my reflection."

She raises her right hand. Her right, not the mirror image of mine, and wiggles her fingers in a tentative wave. I open the door and run.

Determined to never look in the mirror again, I ignore the crushing tension in my chest, squeezing me until I want to weep, or scream, or both. Instead, I go about singing at the top of my lungs until the neighbor's dog yowls in protest, and all crawly creatures evacuate the region.

Okay, I exaggerate. I do that a lot.

Then I run like twenty times around the block.

Three days pass, and my nails are nubbins, the neighbors are complaining, and I do what any sane person does to relax. Take a bath. A nice, long, hot bath. It works. It works so well I forget not to look in the mirror when I get out.

There she is, looking down at me like she's looking down a well. Her hair is pulled back tight against her scalp and into a bun. What? Adeline isn't vain, but this is beyond even her lack of style. The phantom image laughs and lifts up a newspaper. The paper's name, underlined three times, catches my eye. It's not one I'm familiar with. In the corner, the date is circled. Beneath the two, penned in my sister's meticulous handwriting, is a message. I lean in closer, rub my eyes, and read it again.

This can't be real.

She shrugs and fades along with the tiny droplets, leaving me in stunned silence.

Standing there like someone super glued my feet to the floor, I stare at the mirror. My true reflection is all that remains, eyes large, gripped with the fear of seeing "her" again, and terrified that I may not.

The harsh jangle of the phone jerks me back to the present. No one calls me except for telemarketers and political fundraisers. I let the answering machine respond.

"Hi! You've reached the Johnson sisters. Please leave a message." Adeline's voice echoes through the room, a voice that once filled every day of my life.

I will never change that recording.

"Miss Johnson, this is Sergeant Bowman. Could you—"

I grab at the phone before he can hang up. "Yes, this is Anna Marie. Any news?"

"No. I'm sorry." The voice on the other end hesitates. "Anna Marie? Could you come by the office? Perhaps in the morning? We need to discuss a few things."

"I'll be right over." I hang up before he has a chance to protest. Already I'm pulling on a pair of jeans. Grabbing the first t-shirt I find, I wiggle it over my head and rush out the door. My flip-flops thump, thump, thump as I run across the front porch, down the stairs, and to my car.

Adeline. She's out there somewhere. I have to find her.

I park in front of the handicap sign—it's the only vacant spot close to the front door of our diminutive police department. Inside, Officer Walker glances up and clears his throat. Not making eye contact, he busies himself rearranging files in the cabinet. Sergeant Bowman is at his desk, and by the slump of his shoulders I know I will not appreciate what he has to say.

Coldness grips my stomach. I clench my fists and march to the chair in front of his desk where I've sat on so many visits before. I notice my shirt is inside out. Doesn't matter. Nerves make my legs tingle and burn as they bounce in agitated excitement. An overwhelming urge to run hits me, but I don't. I need to know what he knows.

Three folders are laid out on the desk in front of him. Adeline's is open, pages dog-eared and worn. Her high school graduation picture, a staple puncturing top and bottom, smiles from the upper left corner. Adeline Johnson, age 18, DOB 1/31/1995. Missing 8/21/2013. Every report, every picture inside is burned deep into my memory.

The other two folders sit alongside my sister's. I glance at them, then look away. My heart is cold as stone. These belong to our parents. They left us, and I'm to blame.

Sofia Johnson, age 27, DOB 9/27/1974 Missing 9/11/2001. Case unresolved.

Roger Johnson, age 34, DOB 12/10/1968. Missing 10/12/2002. Case unresolved.

We were seven when Mama left, eight when our father followed suit.

"Thank you for coming." Sergeant Bowman pulls at his collar and glances up at the clock like he wishes he were anywhere but here.

Our eyes lock for a brief moment before he looks away.

"I wish I had better news. You know I spent hours on your sister's case, particularly in light of similar reports about your parents." He closes Adeline's folder, rests his hands, palms down, over the top. His little finger is blocking her face.

I want to reach over and move his hand.

"The fact is, we have no clues about what happened to your sister. The more time that passes, the less likely we are to find any. The case is cold, Anna, and I can't in good conscience spend more tax dollars without a lead."

I'm shaking my head. *No. No. Please.* Ringing echoes in my ears, and I compel myself to breathe. I stare at his Adam's apple. It slides down below the rim of his collar and up again as he swallows. Behind us, the drawer on a file cabinet slams shut.

"I'm sorry, Hon." The Sergeant rearranges his collar once more. "The department is calling off the investigation."

I blink, my vision narrowing.

"You can't do this." My voice breaks.

This man knows my sister. We went to school with his children. He always bought way more Girl Scout cookies from us than any two-man police department could eat. How can he give up? "You don't under-stand. She's out there!"

I'm standing now. "Sir, I've borrowed against the house. Every penny I make goes to searching for Adeline. I have nothing left. You gotta help me find her!"

"Anna Marie, she likely drowned. You know that. The underground caves, perhaps. No one knows, but her body—"

"No!" Tears will not flow. Crying is for the weak. I see nothing but my anger, my frustration.

Why doesn't anyone understand? Adeline is every bit alive as I am. She needs me. I have to make him listen.

It's not my fault the Sergeant has a real letter opener out on his desk. I mean, really, someone who deals with criminals for a living should know better, even if we live in Po-dunk, Missouri where nothing ever happens. Except to my family. When my vision clears, we both stare at the wavering letter opener embedded deep into the wood of the desk. Blood oozes from the webbing between the Sergeant's thumb and fore-finger where I nicked it.

Uh-oh.

Strong hands grab me. Officer Walker is twisting my arms behind me, pulling me away. I struggle, kicking, writhing, trying to get free.

"No!" I moan, my knees giving way as my energy evaporates into despair. "Please. She's alive. I still feel her."

SOMEONE AS CRAZY AS ME

OUR POLICE STATION IS reminiscent of the Andy Griffith Show. Small and backward. Two wood desks sit in the middle of the room, the blood now wiped clean from the surface of the one with the puncture wound. The letter opener is conspicuously missing.

File cabinets line the side walls along with a counter that serves as a kitchenette, complete with microwave and coffee pot.

I'm in one of two cells at the rear of the room. Cold cinder blocks comprise the outer walls. Bars form a protective barrier front and center. I stand, fingers gripping the smooth steel, staring at my stark surroundings.

Daylight's last beams streak through the windows, making dust particles dance like they're excited to see night coming on.

"Sorry, Tia Lupe," I whisper, pressing my forehead against the cold metal. "Maybe if you hadn't died on us, matters would be different. Ever think of that?"

The words are seconds out of my mouth, and I feel guilty. Looking up at the ceiling, I make the sign of the cross. "No disrespect, Tia, but it's tough doing this all by myself."

My great aunt doesn't answer.

"*Ora,*" she used to say, "*pray when you got troubles. El buen Padre te ama.*" The Good Father loves you.

Yeah. Right. If my own father couldn't love me, it's not likely some God up there in the sky cares either. I tried the prayer bit when

Adeline first disappeared, even going without food for a couple days. No one listens.

Lying down on the bench that seconds as a cot, I unfold the thin blanket Sergeant Bowman handed me before he locked up and headed home. Clasping my hands behind my head, I stare up at the darkening shadows stretching across the ceiling. Dread weighs me down. What have I done? If I'm not free to look for Adeline, who will?

I close my eyes. *If* God exists, it's clear He doesn't like me much, but surely He likes Adeline.

"Help me find her," I say to the great nothingness around me as I drift off to sleep.

I startle awake as the front door crashes open, and the lights burst on.

"Get your sorry self in here, Mr. Reddington." Officer Walker's voice is unmistakable.

George Walker, aka Georgie. I never liked him much. That's okay. He doesn't like me either. We had one too many run-ins in grade school, and despite him being three grades ahead of me, I generally wound up being the one on top with him crying to a teacher for help. He learned to leave Adeline alone, but he was a reluctant pupil.

"I apologize once again, sir." The voice that answers is deep. A touch of southern drawl adds an odd charm to it. "I did not realize you were an officer of the law."

"Oh, sure. Tell me one more time who you thought I was." Georgie's tone mocks.

Guarding my eyes from the harsh overhead lights, I watch from my silent corner. Whoever this Mr. Reddington is, he's a big man. An old-fashioned wool coat hangs across his shoulders. One arm rests in a sling.

"I thank you for taking me to the physician. I am much obliged."

"Save it, General Custer." Georgie slaps the fingerprint pad down on the desk.

"Do you refer to Brigadier General Custer? I am not he. Sir, I am Jacob Reddington, of Saint Louis."

I'm leaning up on my elbow trying to get a better look. This one is either drunk or way off his rocker. Perhaps a night in jail will turn out interesting after all.

Georgie is snickering as he grasps Jacob Reddington's hands. Pressing each fingertip in turn against the ink pad, he rolls them across the sheet of paper. I study my hands. Blotches of black ink still line my fingernails.

The guy looks like he stepped straight out of an old western movie, complete with broad, muscled shoulders, and black boots. Blond hair, pulled back into a ponytail, rests on the collar of his shirt and thick leather boots point from beneath loose slacks. Reddish whiskers are trimmed into a bushy handlebar mustache. I don't normally like guys with ponytails, but the look fits this fellow. The mustache? That's a bit of overkill.

He observes the fingerprinting with intense curiosity. "What does this do?"

Georgie snorts. "We'll put this in the computer, and by tomorrow we'll know who you really are and if you have any outstanding warrants."

"This computing person can get all that information from some black smudges?"

"Your fingerprints, Custer. By your fingerprints. And it's a computer, not a person."

"Georgie," I call out from my dark corner, "you forgot to give him his phone call. And his Miranda rights. You read him his rights?"

"I can make a phone call? On a telephone?" Jacob's eyes sparkle.

"Well, you sure ain't gonna make it from something else." Georgie glares at me like he did in grade school whenever he got in trouble and I was involved. "You have the right to remain silent. Anything—"

"I would like to make a phone call. On the telephone, please. I know a number to call."

Georgie's brows go up. He purses his lips in a fake whistle, looks at me, and his finger traces a circle in the air near his temple.

"Phone is right there," he points at the bulk on the desk.

Jacob studies the phone. "Sir, would you be so kind as to instruct me on its use?"

Georgie sneers and hands Jacob the hand piece. "Okay, Custer. You speak in this end, listen on the other. Think you got that?"

Staring at the hand piece, Jacob's voice is hushed. "I speak into this device, and the person hears me in their own location?"

"Yes, you speak into the device, and they hear you," George mimics

Jacob's gentle drawl, rolling his eyes. "Here, give me the number. I'll punch it in for you."

Jacob rattles off a number, then holds the phone to his ear. A smile spreads across his face. "It says, 'leave a message at the beep.'"

"It's your one phone call." George lifts his shoulders. "Use it or lose it."

Jacob nods and begins speaking. "My name is Jacob Reddington, and I am... Where am I again, sir?"

"Monroe County Jail."

"I am detained at the Monroe County Jail. I have a letter for you from your sister." Jacob waits with the phone in hand.

"There is no reply," he says after a long silence. "Are you sure he can hear me?"

"You got voicemail." Georgie takes the receiver from Jacob's hand and hangs it up. "That's your one phone call. Time to lock you up."

"Come on, Georgie," I say, "help the guy out. Jacob, you should ask for a lawyer."

"That will not be necessary. The woman who gave me the telephone number said I should wait. Her brother will assist me."

Georgie is snickering as he leads Jacob into the cell adjacent to mine, tosses him a blanket, and locks the door. "Watch out for the girl next to you. She's meaner than she looks."

I give him the glare.

He ignores me. "You two have a pleasant night. We'll be back to check on you in a few hours."

The lights go out. The front door slams shut, and a key turns the lock.

Jacob sits on his bench, rubbing his hand across his forehead like he's trying to force his brain to think. He hasn't even looked in my direction.

"You should have asked for a lawyer," I say.

Jacob startles. Glancing my way, he leaps to his feet like his seat caught fire.

"I beg your pardon, Miss." His hand moves to his head as if he's tipping a hat, and he bows ever so slightly. "I forgot my manners."

This guy is weird. He's peering through the bars in my direction, his head cocked to the side, eyes squinting like he's trying to figure out something.

"I am sorry, Miss, but have we met?"

"Oh, brother. Not that line." I pull my blanket closer around my shoulders. The room is getting colder as the night progresses. "I don't think so, General Custer."

"Why do people keep calling me that? I am not General Custer." Jacob extends his hand through the bars toward me. "Name is Jacob. Jacob Reddington. Are you sure we are not acquainted?"

"Not in this life."

From where I lie, I can just reach his outstretched hand. I give it a shake, not sure why I bother. The guy doesn't smell like alcohol. That leaves drugs. Or insanity.

"You are cold," he says as I pull my arm back under my covers. "Please, take my blanket. I have a coat. It will suffice."

Normal me would scoff at a guy offering me his blanket, but I *am* cold, and more than that, it's an excuse to get a better look at this man. Instead of reaching for it, I stand and take the few steps toward him. He looks like a movie star. I rack my brain, trying to think which one. Thor? A young Brad Pitt?

As I approach, he looks at me and swallows hard, blinks and swallows again, kinda like my reaction when I first saw Adeline in my mirror. It may be the poor lighting, but I think the guy is going all pale. I run my hand through my hair—it must be pretty bad. I've made guys cringe before, but this is different. Like I'm some sort of specter. Handing me the blanket through the bars, his fingers touch mine. His hand trembles.

Drugs. Definitely drugs.

"It *is* you." There is awe in his voice, like he's just seen an angel.

But I'm no angel.

I grasp the blanket close to my chest and scrunch up one eye, frowning my most sarcastic expression. "Yeah, it's me, and I don't know you. Stop staring. You don't look too great yourself."

It's a lie. He looks amazing.

His face reddens. My stomach does this weird little flutter bit. Something is wrong with me. This is not how I react to men. Especially weird men. It's annoying, but I can't help the double take.

There's a ruggedness about him. His weathered skin is tanned dark enough to make his blue eyes uncanny. His worn-out clothes are thread-bare. Homeless? A clean homeless person. His eyes remind me of the neighbor's son's when he returned from Iraq, eyes belonging to some-one much older, someone wizened by a lifetime of hard experiences. But Jacob's eyes are not the eyes of a man gone mad.

I turn away, wondering what my eyes say about me.

"What happened to your shoulder?" I ask, scurrying back to my shadows and spreading the extra blanket across mine.

"I was shot."

"Seriously? So, how exactly did you go about getting shot?"

He sighs. "Let us just say someone I used to work with tried to take something very precious to me."

Jacob is staring at some point way past this room, some memory that turns his eyes dark.

"Did you get it back?"

His eyes narrow, and he looks at me with an odd expression.

"Yes."

"Well, I hope it was worth it. I mean, getting shot over it and all. You coulda been killed."

"Yes. It was worth more than I knew." The way he looks at me makes me squirm. It's not like he's being inappropriate, but just, well, like he knows something about me. Like he knows *me*.

"Does it hurt much?" I ask.

"It is a mere flesh wound. I told the lawman as much, but he insisted on taking me to the hospital. They cleaned it and put the bandage on. I have experienced worse."

"Yeah, well, Georgie is on a first name basis with the nurses at the hospital. You part of a gang?"

"No, Miss." He hesitates, staring at his boots. He extends his fin-gers wide, balls them into fists, then relaxes them once more. "I was in the war."

"Oh, that explains it."

Another veteran losing touch with reality.

"What'd you do? To get arrested?" I ask, not sure why I care.

"I was asleep on a bench. The lawman awoke me. I thought he was a confederate soldier, and I wrestled him to the ground."

Nightmares. Maybe PTSD. I feel for him, but still. This is hilarious. I smother a laugh in my blanket. Poor George. Wrestled to the ground even as an officer of the law.

"Confederates. Wow. Keep telling people that, and you'll get yourself committed to the mental hospital."

Jacob doesn't answer.

The wall clock ticks. He stretches out on his bench. Time spreads past us.

He interrupts the silence. "Pardon my intrusion, Miss, I did not get your name."

"Anna Marie Johnson. And no, we haven't met."

"Of course, you are right. We have not met until now. It is a pleasure meeting you, Miss Johnson." His voice rolls, like a smile lurks behind it. Charming, but this 'Miss' business is irritating.

"Stop calling me 'Miss.' It's Anna Marie. Just Anna Marie."

Jacob sits up, almost falling off his bench. "You are married?"

"No." Like that will ever happen. "I'm not married. It's just weird—you calling me 'Miss.' It's like I'm at a job interview or something."

He sighs and lies back, the smile returning to his voice. "What did *you* do, Just Anna Marie Johnson, to find yourself detained in jail?"

"Stabbed the Sergeant."

"What?"

"With a letter opener. He wouldn't listen to me."

"Why?"

Maybe it's because he's as out of place here as I am. Maybe it's the dark corner that I hide in and the bars that separate us. Maybe it's been so long since anyone cared. I don't know what possesses me, but I tell Jacob everything. I tell him about my sister, her disappearance, my searches. I tell him about seeing her in the water droplets on my mirror.

And I watch his reaction.

I have shared this story with no one. The expected laughter doesn't come. Instead, he leans forward, listening. I tell of my frustration with the sergeant and about losing my temper. I explain how I know Adeline is alive.

He listens. Even more amazing, he believes me.

"The world does not always work the way we think it should. I have seen things I never thought possible and are likely inexplicable. I do not believe you are delusional, Just Anna Marie."

He's quiet for so long I think he's finished. Then, in a voice soft and tentative, he speaks once more. "What if—what if your sister is trying to communicate with you? Not just from somewhere else, but from *some when* else?"

I snort and glare at him. Next, he's going to be telling me he got here riding a flying saucer.

"Yeah, right, General Custer. Like time travel is a thing. You'd have to be deranged to believe that."

Why do all the decent men have something wrong with them? Like being touched in the head.

He's quiet for so long, I'm sure he's asleep. I roll over and study him. He's unusual, to say the least. What's his story? And why do I care? I should have kept my secrets to myself. *Trust no one.* That's my motto. People care one minute, and they're gone the next.

I close my eyes. Relax. In the quiet, somewhere in that space between waking and sleeping, I think Jacob whispers, "It is true, Just Anna Marie. It happened to me. I traveled near one hundred fifty years. I came through water."

The guy is definitely crazy. Maybe as crazy as me.

As I doze, I listen for Adeline. She is a familiar, sweet melody running through the chaos of my life. She sounds like the rich, soothing tones of a cello. I almost cry.

"That's pretty, Anna Marie." Mama sits on the carpet with Adeline and me, sewing miniature outfits while we play with our Barbie dolls. We have the best dressed Barbies of all the girls at school. "I don't recognize the melody."

"Oh, that's me." Adeline doesn't look up from where

she's changing the dress on her doll. "That's the song I am in her head."

"Really?" *Mama puts down the outfit she's stitching and studies me.* "You hear Adeline like a song?"

I shrug. "Yeah."

I know it's peculiar, but that's the way the world is to me.

"Do I have a song?"

I nod. Mama's is harder to mimic. It's higher and faster. I hum it to her, and her eyes shimmer.

"Does everyone have a song?"

"No." *This is my private world. I'm not sure how to talk about it.* "Most people are silent. Other people sound alike, and I ignore them. They're boring."

The way Mama gazes at me makes me warm inside, and her and Adeline's songs weave together in ways that make me want to breathe in deep. If I were a bird, I would fly for the joy of it. Together their songs are twice as beautiful.

"What of yours? What does your song sound like?"

I tilt my head to one side, not sure how to answer. Sometimes I think I hear myself as the echo of a piano whose player is exploring and playing with notes. I shake my head.

"I don't have a song," *I say.* "It isn't silent, but the song isn't there yet."

Mama is hushed for a long time. Her brows draw close. She tucks a strand of hair behind my ear, and her fingers linger, warm and gentle against the side of my face.

"What about Daddy? What does his sound like?"

I look at her out of the corner of my eye. "Daddy doesn't make music."

"Oh." *She chews her lip. I can tell she's thinking hard, trying* to understand. I love that about Mama. Most people don't try to figure me out. "Do you hear music anywhere else?"

"Yes!" This is so exciting, because I only recently discovered it. Maybe I can teach Mama and Adeline to hear the music too. It must be so lonely to live in a quiet world. "Some places have special songs. Like at chapel at school. Sometimes, when they read the stories out loud, the chapel is full of sound—like lots of voices all singing different melodies, but they go together just right. I asked Adeline and the girl next to me the first time it happened, but they couldn't hear it. Adi says their ears don't work like mine, or maybe they don't know how to listen."

"How do you do that? How do you listen?"

I shrug. "I just close my eyes and listen. You should try. You have to be all still inside, and that's when it sounds the clearest."

There are tears in Mama's eyes, and I'm afraid I said something wrong. I'm not good at words. I say things wrong a lot, and people get upset.

"I'm sorry, Mama. Is it bad?"

"Dios Santo, no, my love." She reaches both hands and cradles my cheeks.

When she smiles, her music plays louder and faster. She draws me close, and my face gets lost in her hair. She smells clean, like fresh cut flowers.

"It is good. It is a very good thing. God has given you a precious gift."

Tonight, wrapped in the double blankets, I sleep deep and dream of women in long linen dresses with collars buttoned close around the neck. Their hair is combed into buns pulled back so tight it wipes out their wrinkles. I dream of young men with handlebar mustaches riding tall and proud in uniform, carrying muskets and a Union flag. I dream of mirrors talking, telling me to read the paper.

MYSTERIOUS BENEFACTOR

"I THOUGHT YOU DIDN'T HAVE friends."

The front door swings open and crashes against the doorstop. With a start, I slip off my narrow bench and land on the floor, my bum making a thumping sound against the linoleum tiles.

"Good grief, Georgie. Good morning to you too." I rub my back side and pull myself to my feet.

Jacob is sitting on the side of his cot, watching me. He looks way too chipper for a guy who spent the night in jail. "Are you all right, Just Anna Marie?"

I grunt. My teeth feel like scum, my hair feels like mice nested there through the night, and I'm starving.

Georgie jangles his keys and saunters our direction. He unlocks Jacob's cell, then frowns as he inserts the key into mine.

"I thought you didn't have friends," he mumbles again as he unlocks my cage.

"What?" I don't understand what he's grumbling about or why he's unlocking my door.

"Bail's paid for both of you," he says.

"You don't have to look so glum." I'm as surprised as he is. In fact, I think it's a mistake, but I will *not* argue with him. "Think of it this way. You won't have me around to converse with for the rest of the day."

The doors creak as he pulls them open. Jacob stands, massaging the back of his neck.

"Let me get your stuff from the safe, and after you've signed the papers, you're free to go. Your ride is waiting outside, Mr. Reddington."

Hurrying out of the cell before Georgie has second thoughts, I follow to the safe. It's a two-by-two box bolted to the floor next to the filing cabinets. He punches a code, swings open the door, and reaches in. The first envelope contains my cell phone, with license and credit card tucked into a little pocket glued to the back, and my car keys. That's all I brought with me.

"Who...?" I'm confused, and I glance at George, then the door, making a mental calculation of how long it would take me to bolt outside. Not that it would make a difference. It's a small town. Everyone knows me. "Who covered bail?"

"Beats me," Georgie shrugs.

I know he hates seeing me get off this easy. Hey, I'm not out of the woods yet.

"Ask Mr. Reddington here. Same guy who covered his covered yours. Paid cash. I wasn't given a name. Apparently he knows the judge and got his okay."

Jacob's eyes widen. His mouth opens, then spreads into a wide smile as our eyes meet. He shakes his head. "My friend's brother?"

"I thought you two didn't know each other."

"We don't." I wrap my arms around myself and hold tight. Giddiness and panic are warring inside. I don't like what I don't understand. And I don't like being obligated to anyone. But I need to get out of here.

The envelope containing Jacob's belongings is larger than mine. Two leather-bound books tied together with a ribbon slide neatly onto the desktop, the pages of both dog-eared and worn. A water stained cloth that looks for all the world like oiled skin is folded in a neat square and lies on top of a brown bag that looks like a small version of what the Pony Express riders used to carry. Boy, when Jacob decides to do the Civil War reenactment thing, he goes all out. The final item is a compact tin. It's dinged and scuffed, but the lid twists off easily when Georgie opens it.

"Well, look at these. Are these balls homemade? Lead?" He lifts one out of the tin and turns it in his palm, inspecting it from every angle.

"Yes, sir." Jacob frowns. "The powder is in the pouch. Not sure if it be of any use. Seems some moisture got into the tin at the spring."

"Where's the gun?" Georgie's eyes narrow as he opens the pouch and removes a pinch of black powder.

"Fellow that shot me took it, sir. I was really sorry to lose the piece. She was a fine weapon."

"Aw, man. Why didn't you say as much when I arrested you? Blast it, but I got to fill out more paperwork. What kind of gun?"

"Colt 1860, Army issue revolver."

"And it works?"

"Yes, sir! I maintain it myself."

Georgie's expression lights up. He looks like a kid who's discovered ice cream for the first time.

"Sweet! Those were .44 single action six shooters, right? Is it true they were accurate up to a hundred yards?"

"If you are very good. Most practiced soldiers can hit their target at seventy-five under ideal conditions. The battlefield, however, rarely provides ideal conditions."

I roll my eyes. This conversation could go on for hours.

"Can I go?"

Georgie doesn't even look at me. He's twirling the dark gray ball between his fingers. I want to remind him that if it's lead, he doesn't want to go handling it like that. What's Jacob doing with lead bullets? Shooting vampires? Wait, no. That would be silver bullets. Maybe the lead is what's wrong with Jacob's head.

I get a dismissive nod and a wave of the hand, and I bolt for the door like it was me shot from some chamber.

A silver Toyota parks beside my car with a petite blonde in the driver's seat. She smiles at me as I pass. Jacob's ride? A strange pang surges through me.

My car is where I left it. I say a few choice words under my breath and pull the parking ticket off my windshield, letting my breath out through my teeth. Officer George Walker. He's the only one that could be so petty. I'm so hot with temper, I hardly notice my air conditioning isn't working as I drive home.

Mature trees line the street I live on. Well-kept yards sit in front of simple bungalow style homes. Mine stands out, not for the beauty of the home, though it is beautiful in its own way, but because the grass is tall and crowded with weeds. Some rose bushes and a few brave flowers defy the tufts of grass choking the once prized flowerbeds. A window shutter hangs askew, and the peeling paint around the picture window is a pitiful cry for attention. I shrink a little bit inside and park my well-worn vehicle on the road in front of the house.

The concrete steps leading to the porch are solid, as are the wrought iron railings. Two rockers sit vacant and staring at each other. We used to play out here while Tia sat and visited with a neighbor. The chairs are well made. A bit of cleaning, and the porch would once more be inviting. Not everything is falling apart.

Opening the door, my hand hits the light switch. Nothing. I move the switch up and down. Click, click is the only response. What did I expect after not paying the electric bill for the last three months? I drop my cell phone on the counter and check the fuse box just in case, flipping each breaker back and forth. It's useless.

I straighten up. This will not stop me. Everything I earn goes to cover food, gas, and the search for Adeline. I'll just have to live like they did before electricity. Kind of like glorified camping.

I lean over and pick up the mail scattered across the floor in front of the door and sort through it. Bills, bills, and more bills. I toss them into the trash without opening them. There's a letter from the college. I lost my scholarship when I didn't show up for classes last fall. I toss the unopened envelope on top of the bills. There's the usual junk mail. "Win a cruise for two!" "Vote for Paul Moore! He understands the working class." All trash. A letter from the bank has "Final Notice: Open Immediately" stamped across the front. My heart sinks, and I tear it open, dreading what I'll find.

Foreclosure notice.

I stare at it, willing the words to change. I've failed everyone.

"I'm sorry, Tia. I thought I'd have Adi back by now."

Tia would get it. I know she would. As much as she loved her home, she'd have refinanced for every penny the place was worth if it helped find my sister. But I haven't found Adeline, and now I've lost our home.

Habit draws me to the answering machine, and my finger hovers over the black button. No blinking light. No light at all. A tremble of panic shivers through me. Adeline's voice. It's in that machine. She's gone—the voice is gone. Will it be there still when the power returns?

Pulling a chair from the table, I collapse and bury my head in my hands. *Think, Anna Marie. Think.* What do I do next?

"Twenty-eight, twenty-nine, thirty." My muscles throb and burn with the final push up. A week has passed since my overnight in jail.

"Some guy is here, says he has something for you."

I scowl at my co-worker and migrate to the squat rack. He knows I don't like my routine disturbed.

"One, two—"

"Just sayin'. My shift is over in five, and I didn't want to leave without telling you. Says his name is Jacob."

Halting, I glance at the clock and reach for the towel. My co-worker laughs.

"That's a first. Hey, guys, Anna quit her routine early. To talk with a dude."

I swat him with my towel, but we both know I'm only half joking. When your family has a history of disappearing, you take your fitness seriously.

I find Jacob sitting alone in the remote corner that holds the pitiful selection of books the fire department dares call a library. Immersed in an ancient volume of the Encyclopedia Britannica, he doesn't notice my arrival.

"Hey." I use the tail of my towel to wipe sweat from my forehead. "They replaced those eons ago with the internet."

He jumps to his feet, a hand rising to his forehead as though tipping a hat. I lean my head back to peer up at him. He's smiling so big his mustache almost turns upward. It's such a boyish expression, I smile back. Smiling is foreign. I wipe it clear.

"Miss Anna Marie!" He takes my hand like he intends to kiss it. Maybe he plans to bow over it.

Either way, ain't gonna happen. I yank my hand from his grasp. "Uh, sorry. No hand kissing."

I glance at the guys at the back table. They look away. I can hear the gossip already. Agreeing to meet Jacob here was a mistake. I clutch my keys and turn to leave.

"Forgive me, Miss Anna Marie. I have a lot yet to learn about this time. I meant no offense."

Is he for real? I glance back over my shoulder, then face him. Crossing my arms so my hands tuck safely out of kissing range, I study this strange man. His hair is secured at the nape of his neck. A jagged scar outlines the base of his jaw, and multiple small scars cross his forearm. Whatever life he's lived, it's been rough. Blue jeans and t-shirt conform to his shape like custom clothes. He looks tough enough to come out on top in an alley fight, but there's a gentleness and confidence in his demeanor. Jacob knows who he is and is at peace with it. Too bad he's crazy.

"You are really weird," I tell him.

"So I am beginning to understand."

"You have something for me?"

He looks down at the encyclopedia in his hand, like he's considering what to say next. His mustache twitches.

"You should shave that." I have this dreadful habit of blurting out what I'm thinking.

Jacob's brows draw together, one rising higher than the other, giving him a comical, questioning look. "What?"

"The mustache. You should shave it. It hides your dimple. You have a great dimple." Good grief. Did I say that out loud?

He grins wide.

"If you insist, Just Anna Marie. Consider it done." He glances around the room.

Two men sit at the table playing a game of chess. The kitchen is behind them, and behind the kitchen is the exercise room where I've been for the past hour.

"So you are employed at this facility?"

I nod. He better not say anything about this being a man's job. I'm as good as any of them. Better, if muscle mass is left out of the equation.

"They provide a marvelous library."

"Right." I release a surprised cough. "The whole thirty-two volume set of encyclopedias, and five Louis L'Amour's. Extensive. What is it you needed to give me?"

"A friend of my employer sent this." Jacob withdraws an envelope from his pocket. My name is scrawled across the front. No return address fills the corner.

"Who's this from?" I turn the envelope over. The writing is unfamiliar. "I did not ask."

I tear it open, and a receipt flutters to the ground. I know the logo. First Bank and Trust. The company that issued the foreclosure notice on Tia's house. My hands shake as I retrieve the paper. Am I being evicted already?

"Paid in full." I blink and read it again.

What? How? My whole insides quiver. I turn the receipt over. The back is blank except for a blurred image made with black ink and a rubber stamp. A shiver tickles my spine. I recognize the image from my days in Catholic School, back when Mama was still with us. The stamp depicts Saint Pancras, a long legged boy with arms outstretched. The patron saint for children and my personal, long forgotten, saint.

I swallow and gaze up into Jacob's eyes. "Who sent this?"

Jacob's brow rises, his mustache dips. "I do not know."

"What did he look like?"

He shakes his head. "I received it anonymously. I never saw the sender. Is it good news, Just Anna Marie?"

"Yes," I whisper, hugging the receipt to my chest. I blink tears away. I can't get emotional right now. My own Saint Pancras. I thought he was nothing more than a childish fantasy. "Yes, it is. Jacob? Tell your boss I have to meet the person who sent this."

"Mona, look!" Adeline points to Daddy's car parked in the driveway. "Daddy's home early! Maybe he found Mama!"

Her door is open almost before Mona can shift into park, and we both tumble out the door, running to the house. Running to Mama. I'm the fastest and reach the door first, shoving it open so hard, it bangs on the opposite wall.

"Mama?" We call out together, but then as one we freeze.

A man is in the living room facing Daddy. They stand, not like men in a friendly conversation, but as men do when they want to fight. Daddy is a head taller, but he's the one looking pale and frightened. Nothing scares Daddy, and this makes me nervous. When the stranger turns to face us, he breaks out into a wide smile. He doesn't look dangerous. In fact, he looks like Mama. Jet black hair and eyes just as dark.

"Look at you two." He pronounces 'you' like 'jew.'

He moves our way and kneels in front of us, cupping one hand on Adeline's chin and the other on mine—just like Mama does when she wants us to pay attention to something she's saying. "Mira que grande estan. You've grown so much. Are you well?"

I glance at Daddy. He says nothing, so I nod.

"Are you here about Mama?" I ask. Maybe he's with the police.

His eyes grow even darker. "Yes, M'ija. I got people looking for your Mama. In between time, I be your own Saint Pancras. Do you know who he is?"

Adeline's eyes widen. "The saint for children. We read about him in school this week. You're Saint Pancras?"

"Only for you two. I have eyes and ears everywhere. If you are hurt or afraid, call for me, and I will send help. Entienden? You understand?"

I don't say anything. I'm watching. Something isn't as it seems.

He's looking at Daddy, not us, as he speaks, and Daddy's neck is red like it gets when he's mad.

"Ain't nobody gonna hurt you, or they will be very, very sorry." He stands and nods at Mona, who hovers behind us. "You. You watch them good. I got eyes and ears."

Our saint has poor grammar.

And his help over the years is no better.

FAMILY SECRETS

THE POWER IS BACK, and so is my sister's voice inside the bulky, black answering machine. Aside from layers of dust, Tia's house is as it always has been. Dishes, washed and set on a rack to dry, wait to be put away. The phone book is open on the counter beneath the old avocado green rotary phone that hangs on the wall. Tia never felt the need to replace something that worked 'perfectly fine,' and Adeline and I never got around to getting rid of it when she was gone. A variety of fruit magnets decorate the refrigerator, a single photograph stuck proud between a faded strawberry and what I think is supposed to be an apple.

I reach up a tentative hand toward the photograph. It's from our high school graduation. Adeline and I stand on either side of Tia, wearing goofy faces while embracing our great-aunt and waving our caps above our heads in triumph. Tia Lupe beamed. She never attended high school, but now 'her girls' were on their way to college. Standing tall, not leaning on her cane, the tilt of her head speaks of pure pride.

Two months later, she passed to 'that other place' while Adeline and I were moving into our college apartment. For once, this loss wasn't my fault. She was just old, and her heart napped at the same time she did. Knowing what happened has its own strange consolation.

I remember the first day we came to live with Mama's aunt. Daddy had been missing for days. Mona cried and hugged us tight, explaining that the judge wanted us with family, and Tia Lupe was our closest known relative. It was awkward at first, the way Tia fussed over us. That grew on me after I got to know her and realized she honestly meant it.

Our room is still as it was before Adeline left. A poster of Michael Phelps, Adeline's hero, hangs on the wall above her bed, and her swim medals line the window ledge. My side of the room brandishes posters and bulletins featuring Itzhak Perlman, Hilary Hahn, and Sarah Chang.

I run my finger across the dust on the end table. Adeline. I write her name in bold block letters across the table's surface. *Where are you?*

From the corner of my eye, I notice something out of place. I glance down where the quilt doesn't quite cover the head of the bed. Just a tiny black edge peaks out at me from between her mattress and box springs. A notebook. I know it's Adeline's. She must have filled out hundreds of similar notebooks over the years. Mama used to journal, and Adeline takes after her. It's as though I hear my sister calling me, I want to read it so badly.

"Open it," she seems to say. "You know you want to."

My fingers shake as I tug the book from its resting place. I run a hand over the black and white striped cardboard cover. Inhaling deep, I open it.

Taped on page after page of the notebook is a collection of newspaper articles and other family documents. There's a copy of Mama's birth certificate and one of a woman I don't know. Isabella Garcia.

Reading through Mama's documents, I discover Isabella Garcia de DeSanto is my grandmother, and a man named Pedro DeSanto is Mama's father. My grandparents are strangers to me. As far as I know, we never met, and Mama never discussed them. There's a lot Mama didn't talk about, or maybe I just don't recall. When Adi asked Tia, she just shook her head like it hurt.

"*Una tragedia,*" she said. "Such a tragedy. My brother was a good man, and Isabella lost without him. Both gone so young. Una tragedia."

Following the pages of birth certificates is a small black and white picture with a dark-haired man that looks a lot like my recollection of Saint Pancras, only older. He's standing by a fire, holding a fish on a stick over the flames. There's a bench under a tree, and a book lays open next to a purse. Isabella's, most likely. She must be the one taking the picture.

Sitting on a blanket are two youngsters, a boy of about twelve, and a little girl of maybe four or five. The handwriting on the picture's rim states, "Pablo, with Manuel and Sofia."

The young girl is unquestionably Mama. I trace the outline of her face. If I were even half as lovely as she, maybe things would be different. Adeline is pretty, and identical or not, I missed out. I guess what's inside really does influence an individual's appearance.

The boy in the photograph must be Mama's brother. The brother that died. She spoke of him. Once.

Lower on the page is a picture of the same dark-haired man. A younger version, with his arms around a beaming woman. Isabella. Even in advanced pregnancy, my grandmother is gorgeous. Even more so than Mama, if that's possible.

Page after page of notes are scrawled neatly in the notebook, all in Adeline's precise script. Dates and names mostly. My eye lands on an old newspaper clipping. Beneath it, Adeline wrote, "Grandfather disappears."

"October 30, 1983: One week ago today, Mr. Pablo DeSantos, 32, was reported missing after spending the day fishing near Lazarus Springs State Park. His car and fishing equipment were abandoned on site. No sign of foul play. No body has been recovered. If you have any information regarding Mr. DeSantos, please contact the Kansas City Police Department."

Well, I'll be.

Taking the notebook with me, I go downstairs to the living room and curl up on the sofa. I turn the page.

Another newspaper clipping. This one made headline news.

"October 23, 1983. Suicide terrorist bomb kills 243 US personnel in Beirut."

Same day as our grandfather disappeared, but what does that have to do with anything?

A tiny clipping announces: "Isabella G. DeSanto, 36. Died August 5, 1991. Cause of death, accidental overdose. No foul play suspected."

The next few pages are filled with information I already know. There's the magazine clipping of Mama's first photo shoot, the one that caught Daddy's attention. She was eighteen. Six months later, there is the interview at Daddy's magazine, *International Family*. Mama is beaming at Daddy as he holds up her hand with the large diamond ring for the camera to see. They look so happy.

More magazine cutouts, a newborn picture of Adeline and me in the same bassinet, sleeping face to face. The magazine article quotes Mama as saying, "They cry when they are apart, so we decided to let them sleep in the same crib. They are happy this way." One of us has a chubby little hand sticking out from under her blanket grasping the blanket of the other.

I smile. Yup. That would be us.

The World Trade Center, before and after. The news clipping of Mama's disappearance. If not for the catastrophe that was on everyone's mind, it would have made headlines. She had quite the fan base from *International Family*. As it was, Mama's disappearance made it into a tiny hidden corner on page five. Fans are fickle.

The last page shows a picture of Daddy and a newspaper clipping. "October 20, 2002. Missing: Media Executive, Roger Johnson, owner of the high-end magazine, *International Family*, last seen on October 12, 2002. His wife, former model for *International Family*, disappeared one year ago. Mr. Johnson had been distraught over his wife's disappearance. The couple leave behind two daughters, twins, age eight."

I remember that day. The secretary said he was supposed to meet a client for lunch at the Petit Paris, a cozy restaurant across from the fountain at Lewis Park. It was one of his favorite places—close enough to walk and food worthy of the name. He never arrived.

A second news article.

"October 12, 2002. Terrorists explode two bombs in Bali's nightclub district, killing 202 and injuring 209, mostly foreign tourists."

Our personal tragedies always seemed to coincide with terrorist attacks. Hmm. I hear the Twilight Zone theme song in the back of my head. It's all very strange... and all coincidence. What was Adeline trying to prove?

I turn on my phone and type in August 21, 2013. I already know what it will say. I remember everything from that day.

"More than 1,400 killed in Syrian Chemical Attack."

SEPTEMBER 11

September 11, 2001

My whole world is decimated, and no one notices.

Adeline and I have settled into our first class. Music Appreciation. At precisely 8:10 Central Time, the door to the music room at Saint Vitus Classical School swings open. I, with the other twelve second grade children, cluster around our teacher in a room whose only decor includes posters of musical instruments and a music staff painted on the blackboard.

Maplewood recorders, fitted to our lips, are gripped with fingers still chubby enough to make covering those tiny holes a challenge. Intent on following the teacher's lead, at first I don't notice the intrusion.

Frère Jacques, Frère Jacques,

Dormez-vous, Dormez-vous?

The first recorder falls off sequence as the teacher lowers her instrument, turning her head toward the headmaster's frame, now filling the doorway.

Headmaster Henderson stands there, his normally rod-straight back drooping as though he has a bag of rocks on his shoulders. Deep wrinkles wind around his eyes and crease across his forehead. I hadn't noticed them before. Is it possible to age overnight? He has.

My spine tingles with foreboding as the headmaster looks straight over our heads toward our teacher. "A few minutes ago, another plane struck the South Tower. Classes are cancelled. Call the parents."

Adeline's fingers feel so tiny and cold as she reaches across the few inches separating us and grasps my own. Her dark eyes widen, growing darker still as her pupils expand. I squeeze, trying to give reassurance.

"Mama will be here soon. Don't worry," I say.

Mama always comes when there is a problem.

Sonnez les matines. Sonnez les matines.

Ding ding dong. Ding ding dong.

The initial cheer that rises from my classmates at the joy of finding an unexpected day off of school is short lived and quickly reabsorbed by stark walls, reflecting the somber attitude of the headmaster. Grown-ups rush through hallways past our class-room. Agitated whispers linger in the air. We silently follow the music teacher to our home room. At the rear of the line, Adeline holds me tight, and I do not resist.

One-by-one, our classmates leave as a parent or caregiver arrives to claim them. Mama does not come.

The bold-faced clock over the door reads 9:59 when an anguished cry comes from the teacher's lounge that sends cold fingers all the way down my back.

Teacher jumps to her feet, pointing at the few of us still in the room. "Don't move. I'll be right back."

We obey, rooted to our seats and watching the empty door, willing Teacher to return. Something is very wrong. I can feel it deep in my chest.

Staring at the sky through the spotless glass window, I expect black thunderclouds, heavy with rain. Instead, the sky is a deep, crystalline blue, a white cloudy line billowing behind a speck of a plane high above, its only imperfection. A gentle breeze lifts leaves on the tall oak. This is the kind of day Mama called "Baby Bear Days." Not too hot. Not too cold. Just right.

An eternity passes before Teacher's heels can be heard retracing the path she'd taken, the clicking on the tile a much slower rhythm than they played upon her exit. Her eyes are swollen, the ball of her nose red. A tissue is clasped tightly in the grip of her left hand. She nods at me, but I don't think she sees me.

Mama is not coming. I can feel it, just like a dream. The bad kind. I should have known sooner. Closing my eyes tight, I try to reach out and feel Mama like I feel my twin. I've tried this before, but it never works with anyone else. Just with Adeline. I shudder, feeling goosebumps rise on my forearms, and force myself to remain calm. I have to stay strong. Adeline needs me.

"Shall I read to you?" Without waiting for an answer, teacher pulls out a picture book and begins to read. She treats us all like babies, always bringing out picture books. Today I don't mind. The pictures are painted beautifully and take my mind off the sobbing I can hear from the teacher's lounge.

I'm quiet. Long ago I learned that if I stay quiet and listen, grown-ups forget I'm there and say things they wouldn't normally say around children. Today is no different. I hear whispers about fires and falling buildings, planes crashing and people jumping. New York, Virginia, Pennsylvania. These places are continents away from Saint Louis, and I try to figure out why everyone is so upset.

Glancing down, I realize I still hold tight to the recorder. I love my music class. It's the only class at school that makes me try hard to get it right. It's the only class that makes me forget.

Frère Jacques, Frère Jacques.

Round and round, the tune plays in my head. All movements

and whispers move to its dirge. I slip the recorder into my desk and glance up at the clock.

Twelve noon, then one o'clock passes. I nibble on my sandwich, wiping the crumbs into my lunchbox and staying quiet. Teacher is agitated and makes me give her a list of all the phone numbers I know. That isn't many. Daddy doesn't like Mama or us to be with other people. Teacher says he's busy with emergencies at work. His personal secretary reiterates that he knows about the girls, that Mama needs to get us. Mama does not answer her phone.

Mama isn't coming.

One forty-seven. We are the last to be retrieved. A much-relieved school secretary signs us over to Mona. I like Mona. She cooks and cleans for Mama and watches us when we're not at school. I love her manner of speaking. She's from this place near Russia and tells us stories about the cold winters and how she and her children would search the forest floor for twigs and branches to burn in their cookstove. She says the forests there are picked so clean, you would think they were a park.

Mona's face is full of wrinkles. Guess she never used any of the special creams Mama uses all the time, creams that keep old people from looking old. I like Mona's wrinkles. They turn up in all the nicest places and make her look like she's smiling all the time. Daddy thinks Mona's wrinkles are ugly. Mama says that's why she likes them. I think they're beautiful.

Hand in hand, Adeline and I march down the stone steps, out of the red brick building that houses Saint Vitus Classical School. We pass the rock lions standing guard at its base. Mama likes to wave at the lions. So I do too. At the curb is Mona's rusty car. It must've been one of the first cars ever made — that's how old it is.

Are you sleeping? Are you sleeping?

Brother John. Brother John.

The stillness of our house closes over me the moment we open the door. I really hoped Mama would be there, greeting us with her great big hug. I pretend not to like when she hugs me, but I do. She is soft and smells good.

As the day stretches to evening, Mona makes us do homework and won't turn on the television. She paces like she's caged in the room. She makes phone calls and speaks some language other than English. Out in the backyard, she smokes. I've never seen her do that before. When she comes back inside, her eyes are red.

"Why are you crying?" Adeline asks.

Mona wipes her eyes and smiles, cupping Adeline's face in her hands.

"Sweet child. I cry because so many died today."

"Our Mama?"

"Oh, no. Your Mama was far from where the people died."

Adeline is quiet for a long moment. "Why do you cry? Doesn't it mean all those people are with God now?"

A sob escapes Mona. "I hope so," she says. "God knows, I hope so."

Mama never comes home. Everyone talks about our "national tragedy," and no one is talking about Mama. Except for Daddy. He's mad. Really mad. I watch and listen but don't say much. I know why Mama doesn't come home. It's all my fault.

I'm sorry, Mama.

Tears threaten, and I swallow them back.

Frére Jacques. Frére Jacques.

Every time I see pictures of the Twin Towers collapsing, I think of Mama, and in the background, I hear recorders playing.

Sonnez les matines. Sonnez les matines.

Ding ding dong. Ding ding dong.

I never play the recorder again.

JETHRO

S LEEP ELUDES ME, AND just as I doze, I'm jerked back awake by the roar of a chainsaw outside my bedroom window. Leaping from my bed, I dash down the stairs and fling open the back door, ready to throttle the imbecile making the racket.

Across the expanse of the yard lies an enormous oak, a limb pressing down on Tia Lupe's climbing roses, the trellis split and sticking up like broken matchsticks between the limbs. The back fence leans in a drunken fashion out over the neighbor's property. Weeds choke flower beds and knee-high grass gives the once inviting patio a sense of abandonment.

Guilt. Such a familiar foe. Tia loved her yard. Why didn't I try harder to care for the place?

From where I stand, I can only see the backside of a man holding a chainsaw. Broad shoulders steady the machine as it gnaws through branches. I watch, torn between wanting to interrupt and ask who in the world he is and how he ended up in my backyard and letting him be, thankful that someone is taking care of the debris.

Maybe he senses me watching. Without warning, the machine's roar gives way to dead silence. Straightening up his large frame, he turns my way.

Oh, Lord! He's stalking me.

It's Jacob. Hand kissing, crazy man, Jacob.

"What are you doing here?" I ask.

Removing his safety glasses, he removes his hard hat, doing a slight bowing dip. Another odd mannerism.

"Well, good morning to you, Just Anna Marie." He smiles that wide, dimpled smile that could put him in Hollywood for lead in the next big romance movie. He's clean shaven, and even with hard-hat hair, he looks fantastic. My heart does this curious little flutter, and that aggravates me.

"What are you doing here?" I repeat. I don't care if I sound impolite.

"Cutting a tree. What did you presume I was doing?"

His smile is so big, I look away. I wish I hadn't mentioned shaving the mustache. Now that his dimple is unhindered, his smile is twice as charming. It's making me weak.

"You know what I mean."

"Seems I found employment, and you have work that needs doing."

"What about your arm?"

He flexes his muscles. Nice. *Good grief, get a grip on yourself, girl.*

"As I told you, it is just a flesh wound. I've had worse. Those anty-bee-otics got this healed up in no time."

Huh? Oh. Antibiotics. He's so strange.

"Who hired you?" I don't have sufficient funds in my account to pay for this.

He points to the logo on his hard hat. Manny's Lawn Care.

"My employer said to tell you not to be concerned about the fee. It is covered, though had I known it was for you I would have offered to do the work for free."

"Oh," I nod an acknowledgement, not wanting to give him the satisfaction of further conversation, or the realization that he's getting under my skin. Another mysterious benefactor or the same one?

"Would this be the same man who paid off my mortgage?"

Jacob looks confused.

"Yesterday, the letter you brought to work. Was it from the same person?"

"Ah, yes, my boss works for the man who sent the letter. So he paid your mortgage?"

"Yeah, and to tell the truth I'm feeling a little creeped out by that. I mean, that's a lot to give a stranger."

Jacob runs his fingers through his hair. The blond strands stand on edge. I almost miss the ponytail. Who'da thought he could look even better?

"I see what you are saying," Jacob says. "That is odd for a young woman like yourself to receive monetary gifts from an unknown person, unless it is a relative. Could it be from a family member?"

"No. I'm all that's left. The rest have all either died or disappeared." I wonder for a brief moment if it might be from my father. I dismiss the idea as soon as I think of it.

"I am very sorry to hear that, Just Anna Marie." Jacob looks so sad I almost laugh. "I will inquire from my boss and see if I can find any information. Perhaps that will put your mind at ease."

"Hey, thanks." I'm moved that he cares enough to bother, and I feel warm inside. I need to watch out with this guy. If I'm not careful I will end up all starry-eyed like some silly teenage girl straight out of a romance novel. I have to leave and collect the wits I have left.

"Hey, Thanks for taking care of this." I motion at the yard. "I guess I'll see you later."

I close the door, and leaning against the frame, I put a hand to my forehead. I'm amazed I'm not burning up with fever. This has got to be some flu. I'm not myself.

Laundry. That's what I need to do. Some menial task to get my mind off chainsaw man working just outside my window. Besides, I'm almost out of clothes.

Doing laundry isn't enough. Restlessness burns inside me, and like so many days over the past ten months, I'm drawn to get out. Lazarus Springs State Park beckons me, the last known location for my sister. And my mother. And my grandfather.

The morning air nips, so I slip a sweatshirt over my head, wiggle my feet into a pair of loafers, and snatch the keys to my car.

The drive hasn't changed in generations. Fields that will be covered in tall stalks of corn in another month or two flank the four-lane highway as it rolls up the hillsides and down the gentle valleys. It was probably the same a century ago, minus the paved road. Nothing in this part of the state ever changes. As I drive, I picture Jacob working on the back yard. Will he get all the chainsaw work done today, or will he be there again tomorrow?

Entering the park, I follow the circle around the campground and wind off to the side utility road, dodging ruts and washed out sections while curving along the river path until I reach the site. Mama brought us here often when we were little. She said the place chased away both heat and headaches and was her favorite getaway in all the world. Upon arrival, Mama would walk the clearing, caressing the old wood bench, now concealed among vines and sitting cock-eyed, its frame bent. She would rest a hand on the trunk of the tree like it was an ancient friend. Then she'd perch on the river's edge, dipping bare feet into the cool water and "wash away all but today."

My memories of Mama here are so vivid. I follow her footsteps, taking care not to tangle my fingers in the poison ivy that wants to claim the crooked old bench. I look at it with new eyes. Could this be the same bench in the photograph of Mama with her father and brother? The whole clearing takes on the sense of déjà vu as I gaze around with Mama's memories in mind.

The river has carved a beach of shallow, motionless water beneath the branches of Mama's tree. This is the tiny eddy where Adeline and I learned to swim. Did Mama also learn to swim here? What was her dad like? And her mother? Both dead so young. And her brother. I feel a tiny crumble in the armor of resentment I've built toward Mama over the years. She too lost everyone she loved.

As soon as the tender feelings rise, I reinforce the weak spot. If we were all she had left, why would she leave us?

But then, I know the answer to that. I resent her anyway.

Trees grow close to the river's edge, thick, leaf covered branches giving a canopy of shade over the narrow beach that last saw my sister.

Every place has its own feel, its own ambiance. This place, this river-bank feels like bass drums.

I drift to the water's edge. Rocky bluffs line the far shore, adding a postcard perfect backdrop to our shallow pool, protected from the central rush of the river's flow. Taking my shoes off, I relax and bury my head against my knees. Letting my feet slip into the cool, clear water, I listen. This is where I hear her best. Among the rhythm of bass drums come the clear, mellow tones of a cello. Adeline.

"Where are you?" I whisper, as I have every time I've come. There is no answer. There never is. Still, I have to try. "I'm searching, Adi. I'll never stop until I find you."

Time halts when the river flows by. I have no idea how long I linger, head bent and listening. Birdsongs, like piccolos, play in full chorus as the sun ascends higher in the sky. The morning chill gives way to a comforting warmth, but my feet are numb from the cold water when I rise to leave. Soft drum beats lure me, giving way to restless tension.

She's not here. I hear her, yet a heavy dread rises, telling me she's not coming back. I will not listen. I need to get home, back to my quest. Surely there's a rock I have yet to turn over.

I stop at the camp market where Tia brought us to splurge on root beer floats for special celebrations. Adeline loved this place, and I come here every chance I get. Bundles of firewood stand stacked along the storefront, ready for campers' fires. A bright orange soda machine glares out from the midst of them. Wind chimes hang from the overhanging soffits. There's little breeze, so they stand guard in silence. There is an odd dissonance in the air today, making me feel edgy. I glance around. Nothing is out of place. I've got to work on relaxing.

Inside is a tiny coffee shop, and Betsy makes a mean biscuit and gravy. When you have to live off your own mediocre cooking, Betsy's food is a welcome diversion.

The bell jingles as I enter, a pleasant tone in contrast to the rising tension in my head. Betsy looks up from where she's stacking cans on a shelf. She stands, wipes a strand of silver hair back from her face and beams at me. She's been running the place alone since her husband passed away a decade ago, and her slight frame belies a spine of steel.

A fellow tried to run off with her cash box two summers ago. He ended up in the emergency room having buckshot removed from his bum.

"Good morning, Anna." She stretches and straightens her back.

The radio blares from some back room. A country music singer is crying his heart out. Seems his love left him like all the ones before, and he's alone once more. That should be my theme song.

Betsy puts her hand on my shoulder. "It's good to see you. Missed you the past couple weeks."

"Yeah, been busy." No sense telling her I've been seeing my sister in a mirror and that I did an overnight at the local jail for almost stabbing a police sergeant.

"Your usual?"

"Please. You know I can't pass on your biscuits and gravy. I think I'll eat outside."

"Good idea. I hear the rain is moving this way in a few days. Catch the sun while you can.

She piles my plate high, and my mouth waters in anticipation.

"Enjoy." She passes me the plate, mounded a little higher than usual.

Stuffing a forkful into my mouth, I thrust open the door, step outside, and let the heavy door bang shut behind me. The picnic tables are along the side of the building, so I weave around the wood piles, past a pot of flowers, and turn the corner.

The air is punched out of me, and my food flies as I'm slammed face first against the siding. An arm is around my neck, and a hand yanks my hair in a death grip. A cacophony of sounds shriek in my ears.

"You!" A male voice growls, his breath hot puffs against my cheek. "I should have known you were part of this!"

"Wh—?" I try to speak, but the pressure on my throat increases. My mind is racing. What is happening to me? Who is this? What did I do?

"You think you're so fine. Too good for the likes of me. I be teaching you. Nobody says no to Jethro Tanner."

Jethro Tanner? I don't know a Jethro Tanner! He lets go of my hair, prying fingers following the curve of my hip as he presses his body full against mine. I struggle, try to call out, but he chuckles in my ear, pressing on my throat once more.

"Resist all you want, sweetheart." His rancid breath is hot on my cheek. "Makes it more entertainin'. Don'tcha think?"

His rough hand gropes under my sweatshirt. I try to pull away, but I'm pressed hard against the siding.

My eyes! Tears burn. I have to think. The pressure is building, and I feel like my eyes will explode out of my head. Air! I need air! My vision dims. My knees weaken. Jethro loosens his grip just long enough for me to fill my lungs. Sweet cold air sears my throat. Then he squeezes once more in a practiced vise. He will torture me, and then he will murder me. I know it. Shadows pull at the edge of my vision, expanding and receding. Is this what happened to Adeline?

No! She's not dead. She's not dead. She's not dead.

Maybe he has her? The thought fills me with fury.

I smash my foot down hard on his. He groans, then shoves me harder against the side of the building, giving me a moment to gasp for breath. I kick the wall, hard, and kick again, but his fingers are gripping my throat. Relentless. If I don't do something, I'll pass out.

If only I had a weapon! The only object I have is—" My eyes dart wildly around my restricted view. I tighten my grip on the only thing I have.

"You should ne'er had told me no, Adeline," he whispers. Spittle dampens my cheek.

I punch my fist backward into his face, still gripping fast to the stainless steel fork in my hand.

There's a roar, and I am free. Gulping air, wheezing, I turn and stumble for my car. Looking over my shoulder, I imagine Jethro reaching for me. But he's too busy writhing on the ground, bloody hands covering his face. Fumbling my keys, I unlock the door, dive in, slam and lock the door behind me.

"I will find you!" he shrieks. A few muffled cuss words follow.

My heart is in my throat, pounding so hard I think it will bruise my windpipe more than it already is. Air burns as I gulp it in. My hands are shaking, making it hard to get the key in the ignition.

"When I find you, I will kill you!" A bloody fist punches the air, aimed in my direction.

I reach for my phone, fumble, catch it, and fumble once more. I have to call someone. I have to call Betsy.

Just then, the front door to the store slams open, and out comes Betsy, the personification of Annie with her gun, shotgun high.

I have to warn her. "Go back! Lock the door!"

She can't hear me. My voice is hoarse, a cross between a wheeze and a cough. I'm astonished I can speak at all.

Call the cops. The phone is in my hand, my fingers hover over the keys.

"Anna? Where are you?" Betsy is looking for me as she steps toward Jethro, her shotgun at the ready, and her eyes sweeping the lawn.

"I'm in the car." No way she can hear me. I tap the horn.

Jethro rises from the ground, growling like some rabid beast, and stumbles in my direction. One hand covers his eye. I shudder. Is that where I stabbed him? Blood streams down his cheek. I don't recognize him, I've never seen him before. Would I recognize him if I had? But then, he thinks I'm Adeline.

I roll my window down a crack. "Lock the door! Get out of there!"

I slam my car into reverse, glancing in my rear-view mirror in time to see Betsy. She's standing her ground, shotgun level and aiming. I should have known she wouldn't listen.

"Boy! You stop right there!" she yells.

I brake. I need to help her. My breathing is coming easier, but my knees shake like Jell-O. My skin feels like a thousand small insects are crawling where he groped me.

He howls and turns to face Betsy. "What?"

"You heard me! And don't think I won't use this! I've used it before."

He tries to raise both hands, groans and clutches his injured eye.

I glance down. Splattered blood stains the back of my right hand. I fling open the door.

"Lie down on your belly," Betsy hollers.

He complies, bawling.

I run to the water spigot and, tugging up on the arm, shove my hand under. I've got to scour the blood off my skin.

"Mercy, ma'am! My eye! I'm injured!"

I scrub harder.

"Tell that to the sheriff," Betsy says.

I plunge my face under the water. My cheeks. I have to wash his breath off my cheeks. The side of my face that was smashed against the siding burns. The water soothes, burning away his touch from my skin. I want to tear my shirt off to wash all over, but I can't. Not while *he* can see me.

He's crying, and I want to throw up. The slime-ball. Then I recall what he said. *Adeline*. He called me Adeline. "You should never have told me no, Adeline."

He knows where my sister is.

I straighten myself up, blood surging to my face, and with balled fists run toward him. Throwing myself on his back, I grab him by the hair.

"Where's my sister?" I cry. "Where's Adeline?"

He screams like a girl. Somewhere, from far away, Betsy is yelling at me.

"Get away from him, Anna, get back!"

A police siren howls in the background. My ears are ringing that blasted dissonance, and I smash Jethro's face against the ground.

"Where do you have her, you monster?"

He goes limp. He doesn't even have the courtesy of remaining conscious long enough to answer my question. The ringing in my ears grows deafening, mimicking the siren of a police vehicle.

"Where's my sister? Where is she?"

I'm being dragged away, and I twist and turn, struggling to free myself. There's fire inside me. I'm going to erupt.

"He has my sister!" I scream as I'm tackled to the ground, my arms twisting behind me. With the cold click of handcuffs closing around my wrists, my strength leaves me, and I slump into the grass, exhausted.

"We got it, Miss." A man is speaking. "Calm down. Betsy's here with you. Will you be good if I leave you a moment to help my partner?"

I nod. The grass is cool against my bruised cheek. I breathe in the clean scent of it.

"He's got my sister."

"So, you never saw him before?" The sheriff asks me for the third time.

"No. But he thought I was Adeline."

"Your missing sister."

"Yes." How many times do I have to say the same thing? "We're twins."

He writes something on his notepad.

"You really should head to the ER and have that checked." He motions to my throat.

"No." No way. Jethro will be there. "I said I'm fine."

I am. My throat is sore, and so is the side of my head, but it's just some bruising, I'm sure. My breathing is easy. The day is young. "I'll go if I have trouble."

"You shouldn't be home alone."

I think of Jacob, cutting limbs in my backyard.

"I'm not." It's not really lying, is it? "A friend is there."

"Can she come get you?"

"Doesn't have a car. I'm fine. Really."

The sheriff and Betsy glance at each other.

"Alright." He doesn't sound convinced. He writes something in his notes, sighs, and closes his notepad. "Don't worry about Mr. Tanner. The police will accompany him while he's at the hospital. He'll be booked and not likely to get bail. The states' attorney's office will be contacting you soon."

NIGHTTIME VISITOR

TO MY CONSTERNATION, I'M disappointed to find Jacob gone when I get home. I circle the house, making sure every window is tight and the door is secured.

I take a lengthy, scalding hot shower, then crash on the bed. My muscles torque into knots. I shut my eyes for just one minute.

When I open them, I'm not certain if I'm awake or asleep. It's dark. A man sits on Adeline's bed, observing me from the shadows that obscure his face. I must be asleep because I don't startle. I don't scream. I lie there staring back. Even dreaming, I recognize who the shadow man is, and I'm glad he's here.

"You had a rough day," he says.

I reach a hand to my throat. "Yeah. Pretty bad. I'm okay. Now."

"I'm sorry. I shoulda had my men follow you. They'da killed that *sin verguenza*." The shameless one. Tia used that expression about people she didn't care for. "I got them watching now. You'll be secure."

"I stabbed him," I say. "With my fork. I jabbed him in the eye." I shudder.

Shadow man chuckles. "*Dios te bendiga.* You're so like your mother."

I don't respond. I don't remember her that way. I recall her on the floor, arms up to shield herself while my father kicked.

"I had to come check on you, make certain you not dead in your sleep."

I want to ask how he got in the house, but dreams are like that. In dreams, people walk through walls.

"You lucky."

"I don't feel very lucky."

"That Jethro, he won't bother you no more."

"Any more." Even in my sleep, bad grammar bothers me.

"*Que?*"

"Any more. You said it wrong. It's 'He won't bother you anymore,' not 'no more.' I know. The police have him."

"*Hija de tu madre.* You sound just like your mom, correcting my conversation." The man in the shadows chuckles. "About Jethro, the police, they don't just have him, they shot him."

"What?"

"Yes." His 'yes' sounds like 'jess.' Mama sometimes slipped and pronounced her yes that way too, especially when she got passionate about something. "He tried to grab the officer's pistol. They shot him. He's dead."

We are silent. I peer at the ceiling, wondering if Jethro is really dead. Shadows grow wide and wane as a car passes on the street, headlights reflecting off tree branches outside my window.

"What about my sister?" I ask.

"I haven't seen her."

The nuns taught us saints could see everywhere. I knew it was all fictitious.

"You think he had her?"

"He said no. My man believed him. My people, they can be convincing, and Jethro had no spine. He claimed to be a time traveler. *Muy loco,* that one."

"Do you think she disappeared because of me?" Even as I dream, I want to weep. *No. Please say no.*

"Why you say that? She loves you like her own self."

I shift and stare out the window. A tiny sliver of moon peeks out from behind a cloud covered sky.

"Mama said she loved me. That didn't stop her from leaving. It's my fault she's gone. I never told anybody, but it's true." If he's my saint, I may as well confess.

I roll back to face the shadow man. Even in my dream, I know it's my own Saint Pancras.

"No. That's not true."

"Sure it is."

"She was working to get you safe. Something happened. She'd never leave uncoerced."

Uncoerced. Big word for a guy with bad English. What language do they speak in Heaven?

"Yet she left," I say. There's a lengthy silence. "Why didn't you come sooner?"

"I've always been there, *Muñeca*." Doll. Tia called us that sometimes. "Watching, listening, searching." A ray of moonlight flickers across his face, giving me a glimpse of his eyes. They look like Mama's eyes. "It was safer you didn't know."

"Why?" A tear creeps down my cheek and across my nose. It's okay to cry, if only in my dreams.

"Shhh. Go back to sleep. Sometimes it's better no knowing."

Not knowing, I want to say, but I don't. "It was you, wasn't it?"

"What, *M'ija*?"

"You paid off the mortgage."

"It wouldn't do to have the house foreclosed. Tia wouldn't appreciate that."

"Can we meet?" He seemed like solid flesh the first time we met. "I'd like to meet you in person. Not just in my dreams."

Even as I say it, I wonder that I am so cognizant of my dreaming.

"Yes." I can hear him smile. "I'd like that. I'll send someone to pick you up."

"Okay. When?"

"Tomorrow. She'll call first. Her name is Alicia."

OF COFFEE AND HANGINGS

I LEAP FROM MY BED to the incessant ding-donging of the door-bell and cry out in sudden pain. I ache all over. Sunlight is streaming through the window. I swear I just fell asleep. I don't need a robe since I slept fully dressed.

I limp down the stairs. Who would have guessed fighting for your life could leave a person feeling like she'd run a marathon? I open the front door to find no one in sight. The doorbell ding-dongs once more. I groan. The back. The front door has chimes. "Ding-dongs" are the back door. I see Jacob peering in through the glass. He catches my eye and smiles.

"What?" If I could growl, I would. I push open the back door, ready to box someone's ears.

"Good morning, Just Anna Marie."

"It's seven in the morning!"

"Oh. My apologies for the late start, I became distracted on my way here. This is a marvelous city." He smiles, and the fight drains out of me.

I close my eyes and lean on the doorpost. It's too early for anyone to consider it a good morning, much less face it cheerfully and regard our little nowhere town to be a marvelous city.

"I found this amazing shop and thought I must share with you. Do you enjoy pastries? Seems your Mr. Buckster has incredible talent with cake, and the coffee is outstanding. You must try the coffee."

That's when I see the bag he carries, along with two Buckster's coffee cups prominently displaying their logo: Buckster's—Everyone's best friend! I love Buckster's. I raise a brow, motioning Jacob to come in.

He shakes his head. "The two of us alone? It is not proper." He blushes and hands me the bag and a coffee. "I will finish mine here, then be back to work."

"You're really weird." I follow him outside and gingerly ease myself down to sit on the step next to him.

He grins. When Jacob smiles, his whole face smiles. There's a tiny dimple on his left cheek. Or is it a scar? His face is all strong lines and edges. I want to ask about the scar along the base of his jaw. That one is definitely a scar, and while well healed, it doesn't look old. This mysterious, crazy man is intriguing. I find myself liking him, and that irritates me. Keeping my distance from people is a skill I've honed to perfection. The less I know, the less there is to miss when they leave.

"Enjoy your cake." Jacob nods, lifting his coffee in salute.

I pull out a muffin, a moist blueberry muffin—my favorite, except for pumpkin. But pumpkin is only available in the fall.

"Mmm." I take a bite, and what irritability remains vanishes as the sweet and tart melts in my mouth. "Thank you."

"You are most welcome, Just Anna Marie. A fine breakfast should never be taken in solitude."

He taps the chainsaw sitting on the step between us. "It is a fine day to be alive, and this current time includes some mighty fine tools avail—"

He halts mid speech, grimaces, scrunches his eyes together, and stares at me. Well, at my neck, to be more precise.

"Lord, have mercy! What happened?" He brushes my hair away from my neck.

My hand moves up and covers my throat. I forgot. How could I forget? The bruises must look even worse this morning.

"That was yesterday. A guy tried to strangle me."

Jacob looks way too concerned for my comfort level as he nudges my hand aside. For having such large, calloused hands, he has a gentle touch, and something shifts inside me, wanting to respond. I pull away and hurry to my feet.

He rises beside me.

"It's all right," I say. In my dream, Jethro is dead. This, however, is my life. I'm never that lucky. "The police got him."

"Are you well? Have you sustained injuries elsewhere?"

"No. I stopped him, okay? I'm fine. I don't want to talk about it."

Jacob raises his hands and steps back. His eyes don't leave mine.

"Were you here in your home? I should have remained to assure your safety before I left."

"I can take care of myself, thank you. Besides, it wasn't here. It was out by the river. Some crazy psychopath, calls himself Jethro Tanner. He thought I was my sister."

Jacob's back stiffens when I mention Jethro's name. His face pales. Turning his back to me, he strides to the fence, pacing back and forth along its length.

"Jacob?"

He doesn't respond. He marches the fence line like a sentry on duty, then halts, staring at some far-off position, talking to himself.

"Lord, did I cause this?" he mumbles. Then he removes his hat and roughs up his hair. Releasing his breath, he straightens and strides back.

"This man, Jethro, what did he look like?"

Ice is spreading up my spine. "Big, not as tall as you, but big. Thick arms and legs. Bad teeth. Dirty, like he hadn't bathed in months. I didn't get a great look at him. He grabbed me from behind."

Talking about Jethro brings back his smell. I want to spit. I can feel his hands on my belly. I pull my shirt lower around my hips.

"Continue."

The ice is supplanted by violent heat in the pit of my stomach. "That's about all. When I got away, I didn't get a good look at his face. It was all bloody. And I kind of went berserk once Betsy had him down on the ground. I don't remember much after that."

"Betsy? She was injured?"

I laugh. It's a bittersweet laugh. I picture petite, silvery-haired Betsy kicking open the front door with her shotgun aimed and ready.

"It would take a lot more than Jethro to get the best of Betsy. She's the store owner. She had her shotgun ready and him on the ground pleading for mercy."

Jacob doesn't laugh. He's examining my face like he's reading a book, like he realizes I'm holding it together by a thread. He nods. I look away.

"That is good," he says.

Silence hangs between us. Jacob reaches down and smooths my hair, tucking a stray strand behind my ear.

"You will be all right, Just Anna Marie. You are a strong woman." His voice is gruff, low, and full of some emotion I can't identify. It makes me feel all warm.

Our eyes meet. His blue eyes are dark.

I have this crazy urge to rush into his arms and let him hold me. I am *not* strong, despite what people think. I wrap my arms around myself and step closer to my door, further from Jacob.

"We must remain vigilant." He surveys the house. "Do you own a shotgun as well?"

"You know him, don't you?" A tremor raises the hair on my arms.

"I do. He is the one as shot me." Jacob studies the backyard, the house, the windows.

I shiver. "I don't think he had a weapon yesterday. This might have turned out a lot differently if he had."

Jacob's brow rises, and he nods. "Excellent. That is a good thing. Perhaps my gun didn't make it to this time. Listen, Anna Marie, Jethro is not a good man and generated considerable wrong in my time. I praise God you are well—and that he is with the police. Perhaps they will hang him."

I gasp and half choke. "*Your* time? Hang him?"

"He deserves no less for assaulting a woman."

"We don't hang people!" I don't know why this makes me angry. I should agree with him. All the warm feelings I had a moment ago vanish.

Jethro thought I was Adeline, and if he treated her the same way... I'd kill him with my bare hands. Still. Jacob speaks of lynching like it's the common rule of law, like he, Jacob, is from a different time. I close my eyes. All this talk of "my time" and "this time," it's delusional.

I think of Adeline in the mirror and the newspaper. None of it is possible. No. My brain is addled, and Jacob's strange mannerisms keep triggering odd ideas. I shake my head.

"Good grief, what planet are you from?" I back away, disgusted with myself for being open. Vulnerable.

"What planet? This same earth, Just Anna Marie, though I must admit being from another planet would be easier to accept. No, one day I was at the spring, the next found me one hundred fifty years into my future."

I take another step back, shaking my head. It is consistent with what he said the other night in jail. I thought I was dreaming. Just like I dreamed up saints visiting me in the middle of the night. My assumption that he's a bit looney is true. He's more than a bit looney. I feel oddly betrayed. I can't let myself get close to this man. He can't be right in the head. And neither am I. I'm a fool. A stupid, trusting fool.

MR. RODRIGUEZ AND THE DOG

THE PHONE IS RINGING when I step back into the house. Tia's old avocado green antique still works. Some things never die.

"Hello?" I hold the receiver to my ear. Why'd they make them so big?

"Hi, Anna! This is Alicia."

My brows shoot up. Alicia? She's real? Was my midnight visitor real as well? The hair on my arms stands on edge. I glance out the window to the front of the house. A blue sedan sits parked across the street, the tinted glass obscuring the face of a man relaxing in the driver's seat. One of "my saint's" people?

"I will be there to pick you up at 8:30. You need comfortable clothes and good running shoes."

"I don't have any good running shoes." It's true. The only tennis shoes I own are from the general store, and they're falling apart.

"Oh, don't worry." Alicia is way too chipper for this early in the morning. "Check out your closet. It's kinda like Christmas. My boss must have thought you needed an update. I'm surprised you didn't find them sooner. You'll want to eat breakfast. I understand there's a busy morning ahead of you."

With that, she hangs up. No waiting for questions. No waiting for affirmation. No hesitation on her part. It's like she expects I'll just do as she says.

I stand staring at the phone, not sure how irritated I should be. My mind is doing aerobics as I head up to my room. I throw open the closet door and gasp.

New clothes hang neat and organized according to color and function. Tags show they are not only expensive, but they're in my size. A row of shoes line the floor where my old worn-out clothes are normally piled. From a box in the corner, a familiar t-shirt is just visible under the folded flap. My old stuff. There goes the Twilight Zone theme song again.

I don't know who this Saint Pancras fellow is, but I don't appreciate him sneaking into my house and going through my stuff.

I pick through the box until I find my favorite jeans and grab the t-shirt off the top. My old tennis shoes are nowhere. Wearing my old shoes was like going barefoot—every rock poked through the soles as I ran. Still, I grumble something not very kind and reach for the new pair. The tag is still on them—$189.00. Wow. They fit like someone sneaked into my room one night and took a mold of my feet, then made these to fit. Maybe they did. A mental picture of The Shoemaker and the Elves comes to mind.

Should I meet with this man? What if he's a serial killer? What if he demands something I'm not eager to give?

If he meant me harm, he could've done some serious damage last night. He wants me safe. That's what he said. Safe from who or what, though? Jethro is in jail—or dead. I don't know what to believe.

Who is he? How does he know about my family? I need to meet him and find out what he wants. What he knows. Is he the key to finding Adeline? That last thought decides for me. I'm going.

Alicia is a cliché. She looks just like she sounds. Bouncy blonde with way too much energy and a body to die for. She rings my bell at 8:30. On the dot. I open the door and invite her in. I recognize her as the same girl who was waiting to give Jacob a ride from jail. Ah! Now I have two more mysteries to solve. Who is Jacob, and what connection does he have with my Saint Pancras?

"So, you work for my—" I almost say 'Saint,' but catch myself. That would be as weird as Jacob and his claims of time travel.

"Mr. Rodriguez," she answers. So that's what he calls himself. I guess Saint Pancras would be a little much.

Alicia smiles and rocks from her toes to her heels.

I point down at my amazing lightweight running shoes. "These fit perfectly."

Alicia beams as if she made them herself. "Of course!"

I follow her out to the Toyota parked on the street.

"I have a lot of questions."

When she smiles, I continue. "What do you know about—Mr. Rodriguez?"

"Sorry." She looks over at me with large eyes that really do look sorry. She opens the door and slides in. "I've never met him. He calls when he has work for me, and he pays well. Always cash."

"You don't find that suspicious?"

"Why? He's never asked me to do anything illegal."

Tax evasion, I think. That's breaking the law. Hate to pop her bubble.

"Just, you know, never meeting him? Him paying cash? Doesn't that suggest something not so honest?"

"Oh, no. I don't think so. My guess is he's some wealthy do-gooder who doesn't want the media on his tail. I bet his name isn't even Rodriguez. I respect that."

Breakfast doesn't sit so well when we take off on a winding country road that evolves from blacktop to washboard gravel to rutted dirt. Alicia could take me out here and kill me, and my stomach is so upset I wouldn't have the energy to stop her.

I glance behind us, expecting the blue sedan to be on our tail.

"No one's following," I say.

"No. They realize you're with me." So she knows I'm being watched. Interesting.

"And that's supposed to mean I'm safe?"

She nods and lifts the side of her blouse, exposing a holstered pistol. I've never been this close to a gun before. Who does she plan to use it on? I scoot as close to the door as I can get.

"Where to now?" I stare down the road at the never-ending depth of trees.

She bounces with enthusiasm. Guns don't shoot by being jiggled do they?

"We're almost at the crossroad," she says. "That's your drop point."

Drop point. The images that flash through my mind are all but reassuring. What would happen if I opened the door and jumped out now? I'm fast and in good shape. Could I outrun Miss Fitness here?

Just as my hand reaches for the handle, Alicia pulls to a stop. A dirt road criss-crosses ours. It's even narrower, if possible.

"This is as far as I go," she says. "You're supposed to wait here until a car comes for you."

"How do I know which one is for me?"

She gazes around, then levels her eyes on me, lips parting in a broad smile. "You'll be fine. I'm sure you'll figure it out."

Just a wee bit creepy. I almost refuse to get out.

"Don't worry. I'll be back in a few hours to pick you up. If Mr. Rodriguez wants you safe, no one will dare hurt you."

"Huh," I grunt. Without thinking, I reach a hand to my throat. It's still tender. "You'll be back to get me?"

"Yup!"

"Before dark?"

"You bet."

I climb out and watch as she turns and disappears in the direction we came from. My gut is tight.

"Mr. Rodriguez wants me safe." I holler at the woods surrounding me. "That's supposed to make me feel better?"

But I'm in the middle of nowhere, and it's miles to the closest house behind me. I'm crazier than I thought. The breeze carries the scent of pine and fresh turned earth. Birds sing, hidden among the overhanging branches. A frightened squirrel scurries out of sight. I'm alone. Totally alone.

Minutes pass, and I hear him well before I see his black Mercedes through the trees, maneuvering with care toward the crossroad where I stand. He brakes in front of me. A cloud of dust makes me cough as he leans across the passenger seat and opens the door.

When the dust settles, I recognize him. Saint Pancras. Mr. Rodriguez. Shadow man.

"*Buenos Dias*, Anna Maria. Glad you came."

I swallow hard as I clamber in and close my door. "It's you. You're real."

His smile displays perfect white teeth, and his black eyes sparkle. "*Por su puesto.* But of course. You look well, *M'ija.*"

It's the eyes that knock the wind out of me. Like déjà vu. I feel a tune similar to one I knew long ago echo deep in my chest, and every fiber of my being stretches with yearning.

"Who—who are you?"

He extends his hand to shake mine. Long, fine boned fingers grip mine. He isn't a large man, but his grip convinces me he's stronger than he looks. His nails are manicured, his hands smooth—like his voice. I grip back, staring him straight in the eyes. He can't learn how unnerved I am. Showing weakness is not an option. I don't know what he wants, but I don't trust him.

"I am known as Manuel Rodriguez, but the name of my birth is Manuel Xavier DeSanto. Your mother called me Chachi. So can you. I am her brother."

My hand is on the door latch. I need to run, but I can't pull the handle.

"No," I say, my voice flat. My heart pounds in my throat, and I have to swallow to continue speaking. "You died. A long time ago. I have no uncle."

A flash of emotion crosses his eyes. Then they go back to smooth. "Is that what Tia Lupe told you?"

"No. She never mentioned you."

"She was instructed not to."

"It was Mama. She said she used to have a brother, but she didn't talk about him. I figured you died. So that's you? The brother Mama wouldn't talk about?"

If Mama had been a man, this is what she would look like. Mama's hair was black like his. And shiny. Would hers have silver streaks now? His smile is Mama's as well, but most revealing are the eyes, so dark the pupils are indistinguishable from the rest. Where Mama's eyes laughed, Chachi's are hard, with an edge of sorrow.

"It was better that way. Your Mama's life was—complicated. Mine even worse. It was best if all believed I was gone."

"You let Mama think you were dead?"

"No! I would never do that to her! But she had to pretend. It was better that way."

"Why?"

"It's a long story. You be safer not knowing."

Who is this man? What has he done that endangers me by just knowing? A chill crawls up my back, and my stomach knots. I want to gag.

"Was it *your* fault? Did my parents disappear because of you? What about my sister?"

He puts his sunglasses on and begins maneuvering around the potholes and down the road through the canopy of trees. *"No creo.* I don't think so. If they were hurt because of me, my enemies would want me to know."

"Mira lo que haces! Look at this mess!"

I look around the floor, scattered with pages shredded from Mama's collection of magazines, and drop my hands to my side, scowling at my feet.

"Why did you do this?" Mama bends over and picks up the page nearest her.

"I didn't do nothing," I mumble under my breath. I hate those magazines. I hate the pictures inside. I hate that Mama displays them proudly where everyone has to see.

"Didn't do nothing? You didn't do nothing?" Mama's voice scolds my little girl self. "If you want to use words, use them correctly. You sound like my brother."

I am startled and forget my anger.

"You have a brother?"

"I did. I don't talk about him."

"Why? Is he dead?"

"I told you, I don't talk about him."

"We agreed it was safer if people didn't connect the two of us." Chachi's voice interrupts my thoughts.

"And that's changed? It's safe now?"

Manuel Xavier DeSanto, aka Chachi, shrugs. "It will never be safe. Hence the secret meeting place. No cameras, no one to see us together. But you're not a baby anymore."

"No." I eye his suit. Silk, I think. Definitely expensive. Fits his muscled shoulders like it was custom made. "I haven't been for a long time. We coulda used a rich uncle. Tia wasn't exactly rolling in dough, you know, and with extra mouths to feed on her retirement budget, no way it was easy."

"You telling me you didn't have no food? No clothes? Your house was cold?" My uncle's voice rises. I think I hit a nerve.

"Didn't have any," I correct him.

"What?"

"Didn't have any food. If you want to use words, use them properly."

Oh, my word. I sound just like Mama. He lets out a long breath and studies me. I get the impression he's hearing Mama too. I feel a tad bit guilty. Maybe he misses her as well.

"Sorry. That was a bit harsh. No, we were fine. No silk suits or fancy jewelry, but Tia always seemed to have enough. She said her angels took care of her—money was always there when she needed it. But still."

"Good." He's looking straight ahead, his expression lost behind his glasses.

"Where are you taking me?"

"To a guy I trust. He's a security expert. Let's say he owes me one. What happened to you yesterday should never happen again."

The woods part. Sunlight dazzles my eyes. Not a cloud is in sight. Overlooking a rolling meadow splashed with vibrant wildflowers worthy of Monet's attention, sits an A-frame house covered in solar panels. The early summer garden behind the house gives glimpses of trellised vines—tomatoes and what looks like squash. Chickens run loose, and a goat watches us from atop the skeleton of a rusted car. Oh, yeah. We're out in the boonies all right.

Announcing our arrival is the biggest German Shepherd I've ever seen. She approaches the car, hackles raised, her thunderous bark warning us not to get out.

A burly man emerges from the front door of the house. He must say something. I can't hear for all the barking. Whatever he says makes the dog sit and go quiet. The slow tapping of her tail beats to the rhythm of the man's approaching steps. He gestures with his hand, and she rises and rushes to the door, where I sit behind closed glass eyeing her. My mouth is dry, and my heart pounds hard. The dog's tail is wagging so hard, her back-end swings.

The man laughs, motions with his hand, and the dog sits, observing me with an expectant grin. Opening the door, the man extends his hand.

"You must be Anna Marie. I am Matthewson. Pleased to meet you."

I shake his hand, remaining frozen to my seat. That dog could swallow me whole.

My new-found uncle is exiting from the driver's door. The dog cocks her head to one side, glances at Chachi, taps her tail in acknowledgement, then ignores him. She has eyes only for me. I'm not sure what that means.

"That has got to be the biggest dog I've ever seen," I say. I wonder if she's part wolf.

"Sorry." Mr. Matthewson laughs again. My hand is still in his, and he tugs it gently, drawing me out of the car. "Where are my manners? Anna, this here is Bellona. Bellona, come meet your new owner."

The animal looks straight at me. Her tongue hangs out, and I swear she's smiling.

"She's mine?" I'm so confused. I rub my forearm in the exact place where Adeline bears her only scars. Adeline loved dogs. Me? Not so much.

"No Adi. It's a dirty dog. Besides, we're not allowed to cross the road by ourselves."

"But Anna, he's abandoned. I want to make sure he's alright."

She drops her lunchbox on the curb and dashes across the street. I'm in charge of protecting her, so I follow, but not too closely. I don't like dogs—we've never had one. What if it's wild or diseased?

When I catch up with her, Adeline is crouching, chatting in a soft voice to the growling, wiry-haired beast.

"See?" She looks into my eyes "It wants me."

Before I can stop her, she reaches to pet the mongrel, and the wiry monster jumps on her, sinking his teeth deep into her forearm. I yell, she hollers, and I kick as hard as I can, sending the little creature scurrying underneath a parked car.

"I don't need a dog," I say. "I don't like them much."

Bellona ignores my remark, and without sign of offense, wanders around me, sniffing first my knees and then my hands. She pauses in front of me and nuzzles my palm with her nose. It's cool and a bit damp.

"If it be any consolation, I have yet to determine if she will be yours." Mr. Matthewson has an odd way of speaking, kind of a cross between a Texas drawl with a bit of Harvard tucked in there for fun. "That's a lot of dog for the wrong person. Manny here thinks you can handle her. Come on in, Miss. Let's get better acquainted."

Bellona pads in behind me. I try to keep my distance. My uncle falls in step beside me.

We walk into a room with an open floor space and a vaulted ceiling. A sofa and chair face the rock fireplace dominating the far wall. It's flanked from floor to ceiling with bookshelves. A ladder leans against the far shelf, allowing access to the upper shelves. Mama used to read to us.

So did Tia. Despite her lack of formal education, Tia Lupe loved books, but most of hers came from the library. She couldn't afford to buy them.

"That was you, wasn't it?" Understanding hits me. I know—I'm slow. "Just like the mortgage."

"What?"

"Tia's 'angel.' You sent her money."

He shrugs. "Wasn't much. She wouldn't take no more."

I almost don't notice his grammatical error.

"You're no saint, are you." It's a statement, not a question.

Mr. Matthewson bursts out laughing.

"*Como?*" Chachi's black eyes glance at Mr. Matthewson and back at me. "What?"

"Saint Pancras. When we were kids, you told us you were Saint Pancras. That you were watching over us." I'm blushing. How naïve could I be? "Daddy was scared of you. What d'you do that made him so afraid?"

Chachi is chuckling. "I hoped you remembered. So, you thought I was a real saint?"

"We were seven. What were we supposed to think?"

His smile is perfect. Chachi could be on the cover of GQ magazine. I don't trust him one bit.

"He was your Mama's favorite. She prayed he would watch over her girls. Me? I don't believe in God or saints. I did the watching and protecting. As best I could."

"You didn't do a very good job." I don't know why I'm upset to find out this man is real, and that we're related.

The smile disappears.

"I know. I will never forgive myself. I'm sorry."

"I don't want sorry. I want my sister."

"I know, *M'ija*. Like I want mine." He rubs his hand through his hair and strides across the room, staring into the open fireplace.

"Sorry," I say. Two apologies in one day. The world must be coming to an end. "That was uncalled for."

"*Entiendo*. I understand what you feel. I feel the same. It's like they fell off the face of the earth. No matter how I look, *nada*. I'm talking with Fifi, your mother, one morning, and that same day, she's gone." He shakes his head. "That's why I agreed to meet you. You must learn some things about survival. Self-protection. That, and I want you to have the dog. She's trained to protect. But as her owner, you must also be trained to use her. Maybe if I'd done this for your mama, or Adeline…"

He's hurting. He may be the only person that gets what I'm going through. I turn my back to him and close my eyes. Why now? Why didn't he show up when Adeline first disappeared? I reach a hand to my neck. He waited until someone almost killed me. He should have come sooner. He can't be trusted.

Walking up to the wall of books, I glance over the titles. You can tell a lot about a person by the books he reads.

"This your place?"

My uncle shakes his head. "No. My friend here."

There are manuals. Mr. Matthewson must fix and maintain his own farm machinery. There are a bunch of gardening books, even one on herbal medicines. There are history books, some military manuals, and a load of paperback novels. A worn Bible, open on the coffee table, catches my eye.

"I wouldn't take you for a Bible reading man." I sit down on the couch and turn to the front of the Bible to see if any names are listed there.

Chachi paces. He glances at his watch.

"And what kind of man is a Bible reading kind?" Mr. Matthewson's eyes laugh, but he doesn't let it reach his lips.

I shrug. It's a good, non-committal answer. I'll have to use it more often.

"Unlike your uncle, I do believe in God. And I believe He has a hand in everything that happens in life."

Chachi removes his suit coat and hangs it over the back of a chair. "I leave you two to talk. Be back in a minute." He heads through a door to a back room.

"So, this God made my parents leave us? Made my sister disappear?"

"He may or may not have caused it, but He is in control."

"Sorry. I can't buy that."

We are silent. He doesn't argue with me.

Bellona sighs and lies down on the floor in front of me. I pull my feet up on the couch. She doesn't seem to notice.

"You Navy?" I nod at the picture on the wall.

"SEALs." Mr. Matthewson grins. "Those were the years."

"You two meet in the military?"

"No, in my job after I retired from the military. Government work."

"Really?" I can't picture my uncle doing government work. Not with his expensive taste in clothes. Unless he's corrupt.

"What kind of work was that?" I pretend not to be too interested. "I'll bet it was no desk job."

"If I told you, I'd have to shoot you. Is that what you think?"

I don't reply. He grins but doesn't give me an answer.

"So, tell me about my uncle. It's unsettling to have him pop up after all these years."

"I'm sure, but he had his reasons. I'll let Manny decide what to share. He's a good man, your uncle. I can tell you that much. I owe him my life."

That startles me. This man is every inch the Navy SEAL. My uncle isn't wimpy, but he is small framed. How could he have saved Matthewson's life?

"*Basta!*" Chachi strolls back into the living room, dressed in blue jeans and a black V-neck t-shirt. He looks a little less like mafia and more like an ex-soldier.

Bellona's head pops up, and she wags her tail.

Holding up his watch, Chachi points at the door. "Enough talking. Time to get to work. We got some skills to teach."

LIFE SKILLS

THESE SKILLS, I DISCOVER, are meant to instruct me on how to handle Bellona without getting myself mauled, eaten, or otherwise injured. I'm also told I need to know how to control *her* so she doesn't maul, eat, or otherwise injure someone undeserving of said treatment.

She is crazy smart, knows every command, and even anticipates some of my actions. I'm thinking she's not just a dog, but some intelligent alien in a dog's body. Hey, the Men in Black movies might be on to something.

We break for a late lunch consisting of BLTs on homemade bread. They're delicious. Bellona lies down behind my chair, her huge head resting on man-sized paws. Seems she has taken ownership of me, even if I haven't accepted her. Her eyes follow my hands as I raise sandwich to mouth. I break off a piece of bacon and slip it to her, half afraid she'll take my hand with the treat. She receives it, leaving my fingers untouched, a tap of the tail showing her appreciation. I think she's smiling. Maybe she's not so scary.

After lunch, we have a recap of the morning lesson. I'm catching on well enough that Mr. Matthewson leaves me alone with the large dog. I'm enjoying myself and don't even notice he's gone until he and Chachi come out of the house carrying a regular arsenal: a couple handguns, a shotgun, and a rifle. I eye them as they check the chambers.

"Bellona," I call.

She wags her tail and moves to stand beside me, nuzzling my hand. I scratch her ears the way Mr. Matthewson did, and she leans against my leg. She feels solid. Not that she'll be much protection if these people decide execution is my destiny.

"Handguns first," Chachi says. "What do you know about them?"

"Stay away from the hole in front?" I say.

"Excellent advice!" He laughs.

I can't help but smile. Smiling feels weird.

Safety first. We go through the handling of the weapons over and over, loading, unloading, chamber checks, keeping the muzzle pointed away at all times.

"Never muzzle anything—"

"—you don't intend to shoot." I finish the sentence. "I got it. You've only told me a dozen times. What I don't get is why I'm learning this. You know I'm too young to own a handgun."

Mr. Matthewson gives me a strange look. It's a lot like the teachers in grade school used to give me when I would come up with an illogical defense of a wrong answer.

"Life skills, young lady, life skills. There was a time when every man and woman in this country considered it normal to have a loaded gun in the house. Why should today be any different? Besides, my daddy was a Texan, where the second amendment is a way of living—and, your uncle insists. It's important you know how to defend yourself by any means available."

I nod, not sure how this will do me any good if I can't own one. I run through the scenario when Jethro attacked me. Would having a gun have helped? I don't think so. He attacked from behind. I never saw him coming. Still, this practice is invigorating, purposeful, empowering.

"Have a preference?" My uncle waves his hand over the collection of handguns. I remember Jacob discussing his revolver with Georgie and point at the only revolver in the bunch.

"Here, put these on." Chachi hands me some ear muffs and a pair of those awful looking safety glasses. He and Matthewson put on matching sets. "Now for the fun part. Let's see if you can work the weapon without shooting yourself or the people around you."

Behind the house is a mound of dirt built up with a target nestled at its base. Time to show off what I've learned.

"Focus, press—don't pull."

I'm way off.

"Try again."

And again. I have to reload so often I'm beginning to regret my choice in weapon.

I imagine Jethro in that piece of paper, with Adeline in his grip. *Bang, bang, bang.* Nice cluster right where I want them. Matthewson raises his brows while Chachi claps my back with enthusiasm.

"Did you know they all disappeared from the same place?" I blurt out while we stand, reloading. Yeah, I'm awkward and say things out of context. It's what's on my mind.

Chachi and Matthewson stare at me with raised brows, like, *where did that come from?*

"Your dad. Mama. Adeline…" I ignore their confused expressions. "They were all at the state park. I have no idea where my dad was."

Chachi frowns, finishes loading his magazine, and pops it back into his handgun. "I know, *M'ija.* Our family went fishing there all the time when Fifi and me were little. Papi loved it. So did your mother. We called it our *sanctuario.* Our sanctuary. Papi even made a little bench under a tree so our mother could sit and read while we were fishing. She didn't like sitting on the blanket. Was scared of *hormigas.* Ants."

"Fifi and I. Not Fifi and me."

Chachi rolls his eyes.

"This Fifi, you mean my mom?"

"Yeah. That's what we called her. Sofia was too fancy."

I nod, focus on my target, aim, then hesitate. "Did you know each one disappeared the same day as a major terrorist attack? Coincidence, but weird."

Chachi and Matthewson both freeze. Chachi's eyes darken, and his brows draw together. Matthewson stares at me.

"Wha' you sayin'?" Chachi's voice is so low, I struggle to hear him. His accent has turned thick, once again making his yous into jews.

I shrug. "Nothing. I just find it odd."

"I knew about your Mama. I left her by the river when I got the call about the towers. I shoulda made her leave first instead of letting her stay by herself."

"You were with her?"

"Yes. We met to discuss, well, some problems with your father."

I look down at my shoes. Problems with me, more like it. I know exactly what she was running from.

We go through the motions for another hour. The mood has shifted: Chachi's is dark. Matthewson's pensive. I'm disappointed. I think I was hoping they'd be able to come up with a theory that makes sense. I keep picturing my sister before the drops of water evaporated and took her image with it. The newspaper she held up. I say nothing about it.

There has to be a reasonable explanation.

I am a fast learner, or so they say. Chachi has me practice shooting the target while moving, stepping quickly to one side and then the other.

"It's all in the focus. Focus on your site. Line the site with your target."

It's kinda fun. I feel like a movie star.

We have a brief introduction on the use of the rifle before Chachi glances at his watch and announces that it's time to leave.

"Help Matthewson with these." He nods at the supplies laid neatly on a towel on the ground. "I gotta change."

We lug the equipment and boxed ammunition back to the house while Bellona trots back and forth, sniffing the ground.

"What's she doing?"

"Probably smelling where animals passed over. Got a nose on her, this one. She loves chasing squirrels."

By the time the guns are locked securely in Mr. Matthewson's safe, Chachi brings his now dust covered Mercedes to the front door. My uncle loads a huge bag of dog food into his trunk. When he opens the passenger door, he whistles. Bellona stops chasing phantom trails and comes running, jumping in the open door and squeezing into the space behind the seat. A dog that size looks out of place in this fancy car. I climb cautiously into the front. Chachi is back in his original attire: fancy suit, dark glasses hiding his eyes. He looks for all the world like some drug dealer or mafia boss. I shudder. Who is he, and what secrets does he hide?

"It's been a good day," I say. "I hate to ruin it, but I need to clear the air about one thing.

Chachi glances at me. His brows rise above the rim of his dark glasses. "*Que pasa?*"

"The clothes."

"You like them? I noticed you wore the same worn out clothes today."

"I don't like people going through my things without permission. It's creepy."

"*Entiendo.* I understand. Your stuff was so—old. You a pretty girl and should take better care how you look."

"You should've asked first."

"Would you have accepted?"

"Probably not."

"*Asi pense.* I thought so. Your mama would want me to help. She knew how to dress, your mama did. I shoulda done it sooner, but since you didn't know about me, that would have been worse."

"Don't do it again. Coming into my house without me knowing."

He smiles. He's so much like Mama, I have a hard time remaining irritated.

"No worries, *M'ija.* With Bellona there, it won't be possible."

He stops at the intersection where he picked me up, unloads the food and lays the bag on the side of the road. I hurry out before Bellona has time to scramble over me.

"Alicia will be here. She's about five minutes out." Chachi extends a hand.

I shake it. "I have so many questions."

"It's best that you know little about me, but, if you wish, we can discuss your mother next time."

"I'd like that." Maybe Chachi isn't such a bad guy after all.

"You did good work today, Anna. See you on Monday. You'll get to practice more target shooting, with the rifle next time—and we'll start hands on self-defense. In the meanwhile, keep Bellona with you. A dog can't protect you if she's not with you."

He leaves me. Standing there. Alone. Me and a dog the size of a dire wolf that could swallow me whole. Will she behave without Mr. Matthewson here to protect me?

She sits, her tongue lolling out one side in that silly smile. I reach with a cautious hand and pat the top of her head. She doesn't eat me. Her tail pats a rhythm in the dirt.

A moment later she stops grinning, and her body goes rigid. With a low growl, she stands, facing the road. A little gray Toyota comes bumping around the corner.

"It's Alicia," I say, relieved. Then I remember the commands I'm supposed to give to keep Bellona from unduly mauling the innocent.

"Relax." I do a hand motion, and Bellona's stiff stance relaxes. She sits, but her eyes follow the vehicle as it slows and stops beside me.

"I'm here!" Alicia rolls down her window. "Oh, wow! She's magnificent! Want to introduce us?"

This is weird. Introducing a dog I acquired through no desire of my own to a girl as secretive as my uncle.

Alicia sticks her hand out the window.

"Bellona, meet Alicia," I say, leading the dog to the outstretched hand.

Bellona sniffs Alicia's fingers, looks at me, and wags her tail. She seems to say, "That wasn't so hard, was it?"

When I open the car door, Bellona jumps in ahead of me. I'm not about to argue with a hundred pounds of animal with jaws strong enough to snap my bones in two. Alicia loads the bag of dog food into the trunk and pats Bellona through the open door.

We drive home in relative companionability with the first animal I've ever owned looking over my shoulder the whole ride. At least she doesn't drool.

I swear this dog knows where we're going. Before Alicia even stops, Bellona wags her tail, *thump, thump, thump,* and nuzzles the side of my head.

A blue sedan is parked across the street. The same car was there yesterday. I eye the driver as I get out of Alicia's vehicle. He looks familiar, I think. A lot like the fellow that lived one floor below mine at my college apartment. He's middle aged with thinning hair and is reading a book.

He glances up and nods. Yup. Same guy. A chill runs down my spine. Chachi's man? Has he been watching me for the past two years?

I've always been there, *Muñeca*, the shadow man said. Watching, listening, searching. How could I be so blind?

Inside the kitchen door, I find a large stainless-steel dog bowl filled with water and an empty dish beside it. Bellona walks straight to the water like she knew it was there and laps it up. This creeps me out. Someone is walking in and out of my place at will. I don't care how thoughtful they are about bringing me gifts. Gotta get the locks changed. Come to think about it, I'm glad to have Bellona with me.

Alicia lugs in the huge bag of dog food like she's superman or something.

"Did you bring these in here?" I point to the dog bowls.

She glances down. "Nope," she says. "Maybe the tree guy?"

"The door was locked," I say.

"Oh." She smiles. "Probably one of Mr. Rodriguez's people. You'll get used to it. Although," she pauses, considering the dog, "with this girl around, I doubt they'll be sneaking up on you anymore."

She glances around the room. "Need anything else?"

"No." The whole day I've felt like I'm sleep walking. My life has taken a strange new twist. "Thanks."

"See you Monday."

She leaves me alone. Again. With Bellona. I like the name, I decide, as I pat the large head with a little more confidence than earlier.

Bellona. Goddess of war.

In the living room I discover yet another gift. This one a box full of balls and odd chew toys. Bellona discovers them at the same time as I do, and starts rummaging in the box, tail swishing in eager anticipation. She comes out with a ball in her mouth and a smile curled up around it.

"You want to play?" I ask. Her answer is clear as she drops the moist ball in my palm. "I've never played with a dog before." I toss the ball across the floor and she dives after it, hurrying back to me with her recovered prize. She drops it by my feet. I laugh, picking it up to throw again. Having Bellona around may be more fun than I thought.

PROTECTOR

MY CELL PHONE RINGS. It's doubtless a wrong number, but I answer anyway.

"Hello?"

"Hello, Just Anna Marie!" Jacob's voice comes through the line. "I trust you found the patio to your liking?"

Clutching the phone to my ear, I lean to peer out the window. The oak no longer lays across the lawn. Stacked along a repaired fence line are logs cut to the proper size for Tia's fireplace. Mowed grass and roses tied to the trellis beg me to take off my shoes and tromp about.

"Wow! You and what army did all that?" I say. "It's amazing!"

Jacob chuckles. "I am overjoyed you like it. Tomorrow, I will clean the flower beds."

"Oh!" I'm all warm inside, pleased at the thought of having Jacob here again tomorrow. Ridiculous. "But tomorrow is Saturday."

"Is there something happening tomorrow?"

"No. It's just that it's the weekend."

"Yes, Just Anna Marie. Most Saturdays fall on the weekend."

"Yard crews don't work weekends. Is your employer paying you extra for this?"

"I will rest on the Lord's Day. Tomorrow I work, unless you prefer I did not."

"No. I mean, of course I don't mind. That'll be fine. It'll be good to have the yard finished so you can be done and not worry about it anymore, because I know you must have other jobs, like cutting up more trees and stuff. For someone else." I bang my forehead on the wall in front of me. There I go—non-stop, nervous run-on sentences again.

Bellona watches me with her head tilted to one side.

"I'm okay, girl," I whisper, covering the mouthpiece with my hand. She wags her tail once and tilts her head to the other side.

"You have a guest? My apologies, I should not be detaining you."

"No. It's just my dog, Bellona."

"I was unaware you had a dog. That is wonderful."

"Yes. Yes, it is. I just got her today, in fact. This house is too big for me by myself. I thought a dog would be good company and provide some protection since I'm here alone. I'll introduce you."

"I would like that." There's a long pause. Jacob coughs, then clears his throat. "Anna Marie, I understand that if a gentleman wishes to call on a young lady, it is common practice to take her to a dining establishment. I was wondering if you might care to accompany me to dinner tonight?"

I practically choke. Then I laugh. I'll never get used to his manner of speech. "Are you asking me out on a date?"

"Pardon me?" He sounds confused.

"A date."

"I believe it is June 6, in the year 2014."

"I know! Are you asking me to go to dinner with you? Like a date?"

"Ah! Yes. I am asking if you will go with me to dinner on a date, which I hope is tonight."

Granted I haven't dated a lot of guys, but this has to be the strangest date request I've ever received. I'd be nuts to go out with him.

But wait. We're both nuts.

"I'm supposed to keep the dog with me, and most restaurants aren't keen on dog hair wafting around their food, but I know this great pizza place that has outdoor seating. We can walk from my place. How about that?"

"Perfect. I will call on you in one hour."

My stomach flutters as I push "end" and stare at the phone a long while. I feel a smile spread across my face. "Bellona?"

She grins, tail tapping a rhythm on the floor.

"We got a date with Crazy Jacob."

The shower feels good on my aching muscles. Climbing out, I linger in front of the steamed up mirror. The tiny droplets reflect only shimmers of light. Wiping the moisture aside, I swallow and wish for one more glimpse of my sister, even if it's an imagined one. Tomorrow I'm going to the library. I have to look up the newspaper I saw in my hallucination. I know it's crazy, but this nagging won't settle until I prove it was all imagined.

I sort through the outfits lined up in my closet and shake my head. According to Alicia, 'Mr. Rodriguez' purchased them himself. The guy knows fashion. I choose a new pair of jeans and a fitted blouse with three-quarter sleeves. They fit perfectly. He even attached matching accessories to the blouse's hanger. I put them on. Wow. For a t-shirt and jeans kinda girl, this outfit makes me feel like Cinderella.

I dry my hair, slip on some shoes, and head downstairs just as the doorbell rings. Bellona barks, positioning herself between me and the door.

"Sit." I motion to her as I reach around to unlock the door. "Relax."

It's Jacob, in a newly pressed shirt and hair slicked back. He's carrying a bouquet of white daisies. No one has ever brought me flowers. My heart armor weakens.

"You are beautiful, Miss Anna Marie." He hands me the bouquet, and the look on his face says he believes what he says.

No one has ever looked at me that way. My armor is wax, Jacob the candle.

"Thank you." I turn so he can't see the heat rising in my cheeks. "I'll put these in water."

Bellona and Jacob are instant friends. Guess she likes crazy people. She immediately runs to the basket and gets her ball, returning to drop it at Jacob's feet.

There's a park down the block, so we decide to divert our trip so Bellona and Jacob can play fetch. It's a beautiful thing to watch, Jacob launching the ball with the movements of an athlete, Bellona, all muscle and gleaming gold and black fur, twisting and jumping to catch it. I get the impression they're both showing off—for me.

We're in high spirits when I put the leash back on Bellona and we head to the restaurant.

Having a dog along is a great conversation enabler. He tells me about his dog on the farm where he grew up. I tell him about my sister's encounter with the mangy beast. Jacob watches as I put Bellona through the moves Mr. Matthewson taught her.

He nods his approval. "That is a fine dog," he says, as we stroll down the sidewalk. "As fine a breed as I have ever seen. Is she part wolf?"

"German Shepherd."

"Yes, I imagine she does well around sheep."

I laugh. I'm proud, as if I had something to do with Bellona's training. "Well, I doubt she's ever been around sheep. Her trainer had a goat and some chickens, though. She ignored them, as far as I could tell."

We turn the block, and I see the restaurant a few blocks away. People are sitting outside at tables enjoying the mild weather.

"No sheep?"

"No. It's not that kind of farm. She's trained to protect people."

"Farms nowadays are strange places; however, it pleases me that you have a dog trained to protect. It is not proper for a young woman like yourself to be living alone."

"What's that supposed to mean?"

"How is a lady to be protected if she does not reside in her father's home? Or have brothers or a husband to guide her?"

I halt mid stride. My armor slams back into place, hardened steel, stronger than ever. There's one thing I learned from my father that has been reinforced by my uncle. Men will not and cannot be trusted to protect me. Life is no fairy tale. There is no Prince Charming. I take care of myself.

"You didn't just say that." Heat crawls up my neck and pushes up my cheeks.

"I said I am thankful you have the dog, since you have no man to protect you. Is that not why you purchased her?"

"I'll have you know that when my father left us, two little girls, abandoned—poof! Just like that! No goodbyes, no letter, no arranging for our care, *nada!* —it was an old woman who rescued us, raised us, protected us. We three females did just fine by ourselves with no male kin to protect us."

Jacob has taken a step away from me, bewilderment written all over his face.

I should stop, but I can't. "It was my father who beat Mama until she left, our father who left his accounts so protected that we had to live off the charity of an old lady. If he were proven dead, I'd be better off. At least I could access my inheritance."

Money. Daddy's one true love. If I had more, maybe I could find my sister.

"No. It was my great aunt who left me a small inheritance and a home."

Which I almost lost.

"No man in my life was ever worthy of the title, protector. And you can bet, no man will ever 'guide' me."

My voice is grating and loud, even to me. My heart, pounding like a war drum, makes my breaths come in rapid succession. A couple walking across the street glances our way, then picks up their pace and hurries around the corner. Bellona's ears are flat.

"Anna Marie." Jacob's eyes are wide. "I am sorry. I—"

"No, Jacob." Tears burn my throat. I can't cry. Tears are for the weak. I let my resentment burn them away.

My temper is a hot fire, and Jacob is fuel. I have to get out of here. I'm better off by myself.

"This was a mistake. This will never work. I'm sorry to disappoint you. I have a way of doing that. Enjoy your pizza." I twist the handle of the leash around my hand. "Bellona, to me."

I leave him standing there, and like Cinderella, I flee. Call it rude—I don't care. I can't. I have my dog: my new friend, companion, protector. I don't need a man. I need space. I need to breathe.

OLD NEWS

STARING UP AT THE building in front of me, I sigh. Its facade, covered with layers of river rock, is as familiar as home. The sign out front reads, Montview Public Library, 1908.

I left an unhappy Bellona at home with a bowl of food, water, and a bone to chew. Somehow, I don't believe the Montview Public Library will allow her inside. A sign on the door states, "Service dogs only," and I'm not sure which disability I could feign.

I just need to get back before she has to take a potty break. How often do dogs need to be let out? Jacob would know.

No. I'm not asking him, the jerk.

He was working out back when I left. I stepped over the cup of Buckster's coffee left like some offering to the gods on my doorstep. Retrieving my bike from the garage, I pumped the flattening tire and took off. The blue sedan trailed me, so I took a shortcut through the park. Let him try to follow me now. I did just fine without your protection up to now, Uncle Dearest. I can take care of myself.

I suppress the memory of Jethro. He can't hurt me anymore.

With the library looming over me, I secure my bike. My insides feel like jitterbugs.

"This is ridiculous," I mutter.

A blackbird, pecking at who knows what in the grass, cocks its head, listening. His eyes sparkle like polished onyx as he turns his head to see me better. I must not appear threatening, because he returns to his scavenging without further interest in my ramblings.

I called ahead, and the librarian said they were proud to have a complete collection of the Monroe Courier on microfiche. So here I am, following up on the insane notion that Adeline held up an old paper imploring me to look it up for some hidden clue about her whereabouts.

"Crazy is as crazy does." I bite my lip and force myself to walk up the sidewalk to the front doors.

Old book smell tickles my senses as soon as the door opens. I close my eyes and breathe it in. This is the scent of adventure, of questions asked and answered, of sweet escape.

"Oh! You're the young lady who called earlier!" The girl at the desk hardly qualifies to call me young lady. She doesn't look like she's finished high school. Maybe she's volunteering. "I pulled the paper you're looking for, as well as the microfiche for that entire month. You're lucky. I believe our library is the only one to have copied all the Monroe Couriers and kept them on microfiche. It's part of our local history! Come. Let me show you how it works."

I'm glad for the refresher. I used the microfiche for a research paper last year, but that's the extent of my experience with the ancient device.

"Thanks." I nod at the girl. "I shouldn't be long."

I take a deep breath, recalling Adeline's reflection, the circled date, and the carefully scripted message. Placing the plastic sheet labeled Monroe Courier, October 27, 1864 into the casing on the machine, I pull the glass cover until it locks in place and slide it under the lens.

This is nuts. *Focus.* I blink, wiggle the dial to enlarge the script below, and sharpen the image. My mouth is dry. Biting my lip, I blink again. The front page looks just like it did in my hallucination. *Blink.* That means nothing. All front pages looked alike in those days.

What am I talking about? In those days? No way Adeline is back in time. She just had some outlandish reason for holding up an antique paper. What am I doing here? It couldn't be Adeline in the mirror. That's ridiculous. Just me with a screw loose. Daydreaming. Wishing.

I keep arguing with myself, yet I continue scanning through the pages, looking for any section that appears to be the "Personals." That's what her message said. "Check Personals."

There it is. Huh. Just like that. "Personals" is typed in bold print at the head of the column. I scroll through, not sure what I'm looking for. Boy. They sure crammed a lot of writing into a small space.

The personals are full of short letters. Families, separated for various reasons, many torn apart by war, are trying to contact a loved one. There are also local announcements. Land, farm equipment, and other items for sale are interspersed among the "Mommy, I'm safe" notes.

Then there it is.

Letter for Anna Marie Johnson

My dearest sister, My greatest fear is that I may never see your sweet face again. Believe me when I say I would never have left if I had any other choice. I can't explain how I came to be here. Words would not suffice, and if they did, would require too many pages and Einstein's capacity to understand. One day I was vacationing by the river, and the next found me in the midst of a war-torn country side.

I arrived in September, 1864, just after the Battle of Fort Davidson. The news was replete with tales of Ewing's defense of the fort and his escape through enemy lines. Fifteen hundred men died. Many were from these parts. Things are different here, even their manner of speech. I must accommodate to the times, so I'm adapting. Know that I'm safe. I've found employment in the home of Samuel and Rebecca Dickerson of Monroe County. They have a large family, and Mrs. Dickerson is recovering from the recent birth of a healthy baby girl. Her husband has a withered leg but continues to farm the fields. They are grateful for the extra help.

There are two older girls close to my age and a whole herd of younger ones. Ten all together, so you see I am kept busy. Mr. Dickerson is a religious man. He owns no slaves and is a pacifist, determined not to bear arms. A combination of his withered leg and cooperation with governing parties has allowed him to maintain his farm.

I don't know how long I will be here. A local soldier has pined for my attention and didn't take kindly to my shunning his advances. I may seek employment elsewhere. I hope you are well. I worry about you since Aunt Lupe's passing. Being without you is like missing half of myself. Would that I could see you one last time.

Adeline.

Oh my word. I rub my eyes. This can't be right. I read the paragraph again. The wording is awkward. It doesn't sound like Adeline—it's way too old timey. Could it be a coincidence that someone by the name of Adeline back in 1864 had a dear sister with a name matching precisely my own? Was Einstein even born then?

It's a trick. A mean, insensitive April Fool's trick. Only it's not April. I look around the room expecting someone to jump out from a table, laughing and waving a box with the authentic Monroe Courier microfiche. "Joke's on you!"

But I'm alone, me and this buzzing antique machine that's telling me things that cannot be.

I reread the note, go to the hall for a drink, and return to see if it's disappeared or changed in the time I was gone.

It hasn't.

This is crazy. I lean in closer, reading everything I can from the top of the page to the end. I go on to the last page, then with newfound urgency, switch sheets to view the next day's paper, then the next. I can't stop myself. What if there's another letter? It's Adeline. Somehow, from somewhere not here, she's trying to reach me, telling me she's all right, telling me where to find her.

The clock clicking overhead means nothing. My phone buzzes. I ignore it. It dings to tell me I have voicemail. The librarian comes in and asks if I need any help. I don't think I answer. She leaves. I keep reading, searching.

Adeline. I can feel her, loud and clear. I keep reading, scanning for any words that might lead me to her: Anna, Adeline, Dickersons. Time travel.

Then I see it. The name Mr. Samuel Dickerson catches my eye, and my stomach rises to my throat.

November 2, 1864

Public Notice

Yesterday the home and adjacent barn belonging to Mr. Samuel Dickerson of Monroe County were confiscated and burned to the ground in accordance with General Order 11. This was done after the Union Army discovered the Dickersons were in possession of slaves and assisting rebel groups against our just Union cause. Fair warning was given to the Dickersons to evacuate prior to the destruction of their property. It has come to our attention that not all cooperated with the evacuation order, and some remained hiding on the premises. There has been loss of life, but the number of casualties is unknown.

Libraries have a rule about not speaking above a whisper. Never Miss Compliant, I seem to be breaking a lot of rules lately and haven't been making myself any good friends while I'm at it. A few days ago, they locked me up in the local jail. Today, I'm escorted out of the library, this time sans police.

I guess screaming is frowned upon.

I didn't mean to. Honestly. I rarely give in to hysteria. Neither do I usually read letters written to me by my twin sister over a hundred years before we were born, and then read on to find that the home my sister is—was—living in, is—was—(I'm so confused) burned to the ground by the 'good guys,' and an unknown number of people died in the fire. Could Adeline have been one of those victims?

How does this twin thing work anyway? Panic wants to push its way up and block my breathing. Technically, if Adeline really jumped to 1864, she would be dead by now whether or not she died in the fire.

But I still feel her.

Do You Know My Sister?

"**D**O YOU KNOW MY sister?"

I have no idea how I got home without killing myself or someone else as I tore through the park on my bike, tears blinding my vision. I drop the bike in the middle of the open gate and am standing there like Mr. Rochester's insane wife in Jane Eyre—my hair awry, and I'm sure, looking half mad.

Jacob is bent over the flower bed, sweat drenching his hairline. He jumps to his feet, and I lift a hand, warning him not to come closer.

"Anna Marie! What happened?"

"It's a simple question," I say. "You said you traveled through water. Over one hundred fifty years. Did you know my sister?"

He wipes the sweat from his forehead with the back of his hand, leaving a streak of mud. His brows squish together, and he frowns. "Do I know your sister?"

"Yes. Looks like me? Traveled back in time? My twin sister!" I stomp my foot and drop my hands to my side. Hot tears gather in my eyes and cascade down my cheeks, and my knees turn to jelly. "Just tell me. Did you know Adeline? Is—was she still alive?"

Somehow, he catches me as my knees give way, and I clutch Jacob's sweat-drenched shirt, burying my face in its folds. He holds me, making hushing sounds and smoothing my hair with rough, calloused fingers.

"Shh, Anna Marie. I have you. Shh," he says. "No, I did not know your sister. I wish I did."

Bellona is going insane, barking at the door. I hand Jacob the key, and forgetting propriety, he leads me inside and to the sofa. Bellona whines, climbing up beside me, licking my face and hands. I hear the faucet running in the kitchen, and Jacob returns with a glass of water. Placing the glass in my hands, he sits beside me. I lean into his shoulder.

My life is quicksand, and he's a solid rock. I grasp his hand and hold on for dear life.

"Talk to me, Just Anna Marie." He says, as my tears turn to hiccups. "Tell me what you found to upset you so. Tell me about your sister. Aside from what you said in the jail, I know very little."

And I talk.

August 22, 2013

Eight a.m. I'm drinking coffee and watching the morning show. The news anchors can talk of nothing but yesterday's horrific mass murder in Syria. Over 1400 civilians killed with chemical weapons.

My cell phone goes off. I expect it's Adeline calling to tell me all the details of her day on the river and the cookout last night. I know it disappointed her that I didn't go, but I had to practice. Tryouts for the symphony orchestra's new season are in a week, and I'm determined to make first violin.

I don't recognize the number. "Hello?"

"This is Sheriff Reed." A deep male voice speaks on the other end. "Is this Anna Johnson?"

"Yes, it is." My mind is racing. Do I have any unpaid parking tickets? Did I miss jury duty?

"Miss Johnson, do you know anything about your sister's whereabouts?"

I frown. Adeline never gets into trouble. Her idea of speeding is gunning the engine at a stoplight. "Yeah. She's camping at the river.

A group of them were going kayaking and camping this weekend. Is something wrong?"

"We don't know yet. Would it be all right if one of my men comes by to talk with you?"

"Yes. Yes, of course." I hang up and try Adeline's phone. It goes straight to voicemail.

"Adi," I say. "Where are you? Call me."

The Sheriff's man must have been just down the road, because I barely have time to throw on shorts and a t-shirt before the chimes ring. A uniformed officer holds his badge in front of the peep hole, Deputy something or other.

I open the door. "What happened?"

"We're still investigating, Miss Johnson. Your sister's friends called late last night when she neglected to show up at the campsite. We found her kayak, but your sister is missing. Would she have gone anywhere without telling her friends?"

I'm shaking my head and grabbing my purse. No way. She's nicknamed Steady Adi for a reason. No one is more dependable. "No. Something happened."

At the station I nod at Sergeant Bowman, relieved that he's here. He knows Adeline. We went to school with his children. The sheriff shows me pictures while his deputy takes notes. Yes, that's Adi's kayak. It's been dragged up onto the beach, the back end just touching the water's edge. Her backpack, wrapped in a waterproof bag, is neatly strapped in place. Her water bottle is in the holder. There are pictures of the kayak from various angles. Nothing looks out of place. Footprints lead from the boat to the water. None return.

"There's no sign of trouble. We're wondering if she got into someone

else's boat." He folds his hands and studies me. "There's also the possibil-
ity of drowning. We have men inspecting the river downstream."

"No." My voice is hoarse. "She's too good a swimmer. She
wouldn't drown."

"That's good to know. But we have to look at all possibilities."

It's happening again.

My head is dizzy, and the deputy looks at me like he's wondering if
I'll pass out.

"Someone took her," I say.

That's the only explanation. Mama might leave us because of
Daddy. Daddy would desert us in search of Mama. If he ever found
her, he probably killed her. But Adeline would never abandon me.
Not Adeline.

The deputy's brows shoot up. "Is there anyone that would want to
harm her?

"No. Not Adeline. Everyone loves Adeline."

"It's been ten months." I'm leaning on Jacob's shoulder, and he's resting
his cheek on my head. Bellona sits beside me. She watches me intensely,
sighing periodically. I swear she thinks she's human. "They say Adi
drowned. But she hasn't. They never found a body, so I don't know why
they keep insisting on that. I've contacted every missing persons agency,
even paid all I could to a private detective. Not a trace. It's like she vanished into thin air. Remember how I told you I saw her reflection in the
condensation on my bathroom mirror?"

Jacob nods.

"I thought I was looking at myself, but, as much as other people con-
fuse us, we really don't look the same. The last time I saw her, she held up
a newspaper—*The Monroe Courier.*"

"Yes, I know that one."

I peer up at him.

"The last issue of that paper was fifty years ago."

"Really? Go on."

"She circled the date. It said October 27, 1864. Under it, she wrote, 'See Personals.' I thought I was crazy. Delusional."

"And now you realize you are not."

"Yeah." I half laugh. "Sort of. At least not as insane as I thought."

It feels good to talk. It feels excellent to not be crazy. I close my eyes and reach out. Adeline. Music. She's still there. I take a deep, shaky breath.

"So, today you went in search of the Monroe Courier?"

Can this guy read my mind?

"Yes," I say. "I found it."

"They keep copies for this long?" Jacob rubs his chin.

"They have ways of making copies and storing them on tiny pieces of plastic. You need a special machine to read them."

"But you found it?" He sounds eager, almost excited.

"Yes. She wrote a note in the Personals, letting me know she was safe and how she found employment with a large family on a farm."

"Yes, yes. Many families communicated that way. That is good news, then. No?"

I pull away, "Are you crazy? That was 1864! This is 2014! Unless... unless...Jacob, do you know how I can get back to her?"

He stands and paces back and forth. It only takes a few of his strides to cover the width of the room. He rubs his forehead, his chin, his forehead again. Bellona lowers her head, ears angled forward. Jacob turns to me, his jaw set. "I do not know, Anna Marie. But she is there, and I am here, so there must be a way to get back and forth."

I look up at him, "I have to get there, Jacob. I need to know if she died in the fire."

"Fire?"

"Yes. I kept looking through the paper and found a small mention on November 2, a week after Adeline posted her note to me. The family she was living with, the Dickersons, were evicted under General Order 11 on November 1. Their property was burned, and not everyone escaped."

A shadow crosses Jacob's face. He stiffens and turns abruptly to face the window. His hand reaches out as though to steady himself.

My heart chills. "Jacob, did you know the Dickersons? Adeline's letter said Mr. Dickerson had a lame leg, and they had something like ten children. Did you know them?"

"Oh, God!" He groans like he's in pain.

"Jacob?" My heart is pounding. Bellona glances at me, then at Jacob, letting out a low whine.

He shakes his head, still staring out the window. "I did not know the Dickersons." His voice sounds forced, like he's choosing his words carefully. "But I know of these burnings. They were part of war, so we told ourselves, and thus could not be helped." He leans his head on the window frame. "They assigned one of these evictions to our unit about that time. I'm sure there were others. The Union was determined to remove any southern sympathizers from the region. I was not privy to the name of the family we removed. I tried to remain distant from the happenings."

His eyes have turned dark, like a man haunted by memories best avoided. "Many wicked things transpired in the name of war."

Movies and Music

J ACOB RETURNS TO SITTING beside me and grasps my hand. We talk and talk until we can say no more. His eyes have a sadness I didn't see there before, full of ghosts tormenting from his past. Some say war is kinder to its victims than to its survivors.

"There is much I would do differently," Jacob says. "I thought I was protecting my brother by remaining silent. In the end, I couldn't save him, and I lost myself. If it were not for a Bible given to me, I am sure I would not be here today."

I want to comfort, but I'm not very good at that.

"Your sister was with this family when the house burned?"

I nod. He cringes.

"I still feel her," I blurt out. That's what comforts me at the moment. "That has to mean something, right?"

He half smiles. "That *is* something."

This whole time-travel thing is still kinda weirding me out, so I jump up and start looking through Tia's stack of VHSes. Yeah. She never threw anything away, and right now I need a distraction.

"How about a movie?"

He raises a brow. "Movie?"

"On TV? Tell me you've watched TV."

"They had one at the big market store. I observed it for several hours before I was asked to leave. It is truly remarkable. Trying not to look the fool in this time is quite challenging, and I believe the man selling

televisions thought my questions rather bizarre. I do not have one. Is a movie what is on TV?"

"Some. There are all kinds of shows on television—that's what TV stands for, television. But movies are special because they're like reading a book through moving pictures. Here." I kneel in front of the shelf with Tia's collection. "Feel like something serious or something funny?"

"I could use a laugh."

"Me too."

I stick Princess Bride into the VCR, pick up the remote, and head to the couch. Jacob observes my every move. "This is an oldie but goodie. A classic."

Jacob leans forward and frowns. He stares at the screen as I fast forward through the trailers preceding the actual movie. When I stop fast forwarding and push play, he relaxes, leans back, and grins.

"Oh. This is better," he says with a sigh. "I was wondering how any story could be followed at such a quick pace."

Watching Jacob watching a movie is akin to watching a child on Christmas morning. Or so I imagine, seeing as I've never been around little kids. Bellona now lies on the floor in front of us, watching Jacob with as much curiosity as I do.

He nods his head with understanding when Westley leaves to find his fortune. "A man must be able to support a wife properly," he says.

Yeah, support her, but don't abandon her.

He shakes his head when Buttercup hears that Westley is dead.

"This is dreadful. Not funny at all." He reaches for the remote. I pull it out of reach.

"Just wait. He's not really dead."

Maybe movie watching is going to be too intense for this guy.

"No. Do not do it," he mumbles under his breath when Prince Humperdinck takes her to his castle to become his wife. Jacob slams his fist into the couch when Buttercup is kidnapped, grumbling under his breath. "A prince with no honor."

He cheers Fezzik when he rescues Buttercup from the water and later when he carries her up the cliff. He chuckles at Vizzini's logic and debates, and delights watching Westley and Inigo duel. He laughs as Westley conquers each man and rescues his very angry Buttercup.

"Can she not tell it is Westley? The mask does nothing to hide who he is."

"She thinks he's dead."

And so it goes, with Jacob alternatively sitting on the edge of his seat, quite literally, when the scenes are tense, to standing and cheering when Westley and his companions win against all odds. I'm laughing the whole time. Bellona jumps to her feet when Jacob stands, head tilted to one side, then lies back down when he sits. At one point she brings him a rag doll, drops it in his lap, and waits. He pets her head and she returns to her watchful position. A movie has never been so exhausting to watch.

"That was indeed a fine movie, Just Anna Marie," he says when it's over, getting up and looking through the videos on the shelf. "Let us watch another. Here…" His fingers linger over a handwritten title. "What is this one?"

I cringe. I don't like memories.

"No, that's not so good. Just a live recording of a concert. It's my favorite violinist, but the recording isn't so good. It's homemade."

Jacob isn't listening. He's removed the old VHS tape and sticks the new one in. "You are in this movie?" he asks. "The label says 'Anna Marie playing with Saint Louis Symphony.' What do you play?"

"Violin, but you can't really see much. I'm way in the back row."

He pushes play and comes to sit beside me. I close my eyes, but I can't shut out the music, and it crashes over me like a powerful wave, knocking me down and grinding my heart into the sand.

Jacob grins when Tia's shaky close up focuses on me sitting on the back row, concentrating on the music in front of me.

"You are a unique woman." Jacob's expression makes me squirm.

"What, you've never met a female violinist before?"

"Oh, I have known lots of people familiar with music. You are different, Anna. Not only are you beautiful, you think differently. Bull-headed and strong, yes, and I admit that has both its charms and complications, but you are a hidden trove of talents as well."

I'm speechless and blushing like a silly little girl. He thinks I'm beautiful. And talented. And bull-headed. And complicated.

If he only knew.

The camera pulls back to encompass the full orchestra, and the guest performer begins his solo. I watch, entranced and pulled back into the music complete with the memories and emotions of the day.

"Adeline! Look! They chose me as student musician!" I wave the paper proudly for my sister to see.

High school music students from all over the tristate region have sent in video auditions along with letters of recommendation for a chance to play with the Saint Louis Symphony Orchestra and a mystery master musician. I am one of five chosen.

I hug the letter tightly to my chest. "And look who the soloist is! Adeline! In my wildest dreams I would never believe I would meet him—much less play on the same stage!"

In preparation for the big day, I practice until my callouses blister and form new and tougher callouses. Then the hours of rehearsals begin, and at last, the final rehearsal with the maestro himself.

He is a short, stocky man of few words, but his eyes take in each and every one of us. His gaze lingers on the five of us in the back row of the violin section, the music honor students. I may as well be first violin, I am so proud to be here. And so nervous.

Then he lifts the violin to his shoulder, closes his eyes, and begins the opening line. The sound his violin produces fills me with a joy and longing I've never experienced before. All nerves cease as the music reaches to the deepest part of my soul, and there is nothing else. No maestro, no hall full of teachers and critics deciding on future music scholarships and acceptance into elite programs—just the music and me. The music is part of me.

"I want a man like that," I tell Adeline the next evening as we sip root beer floats in celebration of a successful concert.

Tia always marks special occasions with an outing to Betsy's camp store. The floats here are the best.

"The maestro?" Adeline wrinkles her nose. "He's so old!"

"No, not the maestro," I laugh, still a bit silly and giddy over the evening's event. "His violin. Have you ever heard such sound? It's a Stradivarius. Did you know that?"

"So, you want to marry a Stradivarius?" Tia smiles at me over her glasses.

"All the qualities in that violin are the qualities I want in a man." I feign swooning. "A magical depth of character that can't be explained, faithful, lasting, and gets better with age. Not to mention being downright gorgeous."

Adeline giggles. "I hear they can be temperamental."

"Not in the hands of the right person."

"And you are that person?"

I close my eyes, imagining holding such an instrument. I would take that over a man any day. I laugh. "One can dream."

"Not me," Adeline says. "I want a man who's rugged, likes the outdoors, and doesn't mind getting his hands dirty. You know, someone I can travel with and who isn't always doing things because it's practical—but wants to experience adventure with me. Oh, and he has to like animals. Chickens, goats, the whole shebang."

We're giggling like we used to when we were little girls, Tia along with us, our heads bent close over our floats.

I sigh. "You'll get your kind of man, Adeline. My dream man will never happen. I'm going to be single the rest of my life."

"Why do you say that?" Tia asks.

"Well, Adeline is that kind of person—outdoorsy, adventurous. Me? I'm not exactly a Stradivarius kind of girl."

"This is wonderful, just Anna Marie!" Jacob's voice pulls me back to the present. His eyes are moist as he stares at the television screen. "My father would have loved to listen to music like this. He played the violin. Did I tell you that? He was not as accomplished as this man, but he could make it sing. I did not know you played."

"I don't. Not anymore."

If only I had gone with her that weekend, she might not be gone—or I might be gone with her.

"Please, Anna," she begged. "You'll have fun. How do you expect to make friends if you never do anything but practice?"

"Once the auditions are over, then I'll do something with you."

I never made it to the audition.

I never had another chance to go camping with Adeline and her friends.

Jacob's eyes narrow as he turns and scrutinizes my face. "Why? It is obvious you loved it."

I shrug. "I lost interest. That's all. It takes a lot of work, you know?"

I don't tell him the music stopped when Adeline disappeared. I don't tell him that music is what life feels like, and I don't want to feel anything anymore.

His large hand closes over mine. It's warm and calloused. My eyes trace the rise of veins, the muscled forearms, the scattered freckles lost in deep tanned skin. I avoid his face. Jacob knows I'm not telling him the truth, but he doesn't push me to say more. The touch of his hand tells me he knows I'm hurting, and he's there for me.

Me? I do the strangest thing. I don't pull away.

CAIN AND ABEL

I HAVEN'T BEEN TO CHURCH since Tia Lupe's funeral, but when Jacob asks if I would attend with him today, I agree. I don't know if God exists, but I feel the need for a "cleansing of soul," a connection I'm missing. I'm restless, and church sounds like a good place to be. At least it sounds better than being home alone with the haunting melodies of my past.

I leave Bellona. She looks at me like she wants to scold me. I tell her to stay home and pray or do whatever dogs do when talking to their maker. I explain that I'm not sure God would appreciate her kind within the walls of a sanctuary, and I'm in no mood to be struck dead. You know, in case God is real. He and I haven't been on talking terms for a while.

"I came here last Lord's Day. Do you realize they have three services? I attended them all," Jacob says. "The preacher is excellent, and the music? It is unusual."

Adeline liked modern church music. She said it 'fed her soul.' I never got into that stuff, not so sure I have a soul that needs feeding. But it's church, so it can't be that intense.

We drive. The blue sedan follows. Guess a dose of holy won't hurt him either.

We're both quiet as we drive. A pensive melancholy that began last night still hangs in the air.

Everything differs greatly from any mass I attended with Tia. The place hardly looks like a church. The walls have no carved saints, no plaques marking donors.

A few banners hang on the walls with Bible verses on them. "For God so loved the world, that He gave His only begotten Son, that whosoever believeth in Him should not perish, but have everlasting life. John 3:16." KJV

"He that believeth and is baptized shall be saved; but he that believeth not shall be damned. Mark 16:16." KJV

"I am the way, the truth, and the life: No man cometh unto the Father, but by me. John 14:6." KJV

The verses sound familiar.

No pews fill the sanctuary, just padded chairs. Instead of an organ, there's a band. People greet me, shake my hand, give me a program. One man greets Jacob by name, patting his back like he's glad to see him.

Jacob leads me to a seat as the music starts, his hand gentle at the small of my back. Adeline used to listen to songs like this one. She was always more religious than me.

They project words on the screen, some song called "Come Thou Fount." Old fashioned words for an old-fashioned religion. The drum entry is anything but old fashioned. Everyone is standing. Some sing along, and some raise their hands. I look around, not sure what I'm supposed to do.

The band is pretty good. I prefer orchestral music, but these guys aren't bad.

My fingers itch, and I realize that for the first time since Adeline left, I want to play my violin. I rub my hands together and close my eyes. This piece would sound perfect with a violin accompaniment. The music swells, and I sway, letting it fill me. I interpose a flute, with a cello, expanding the deeper tones. They would complement the guitars and drums perfectly.

"Come, thou fount of every blessing. Tune my heart to sing thy grace."

The lyrics catch my attention. I wonder if the one who wrote them also perceived music the way I do.

"Streams of mercy, never ceasing, call for songs of loudest praise. Teach me some melodious sonnet, sung by flaming tongues above."

My mind wanders to grade school. I'm sitting in the chapel, and the songs of a choir surround me, but no choir is near. That must be different from what the song describes. I never saw flaming tongues. I shudder. Flaming tongues sounds like something from a horror movie. I hope I never see any.

"On Christ the solid rock I stand. All other ground is sinking sand. All other ground is sinking sand."

Sinking sand. That part I relate to. Adeline was my rock. It's been quicksand without her.

They move on to a livelier song. Something about forgiveness and being free. One of belonging. The lead singer's voice breaks with emotion. I feel nothing.

I glance at Jacob. His eyes are closed, his face raised to the ceiling. He's singing, and I like his voice. It's a deep, gentle baritone. It's full of a tranquility that matches the look on his face. It fits him perfectly.

Just when I think we might stand for the entire service, everyone sits. Jacob smiles and nudges me. "This is wonderful, isn't it?" he whispers. What does he expect me to say?

The preacher tells this strange story about some brothers. God asks for a sacrifice of sheep. Brother Abel, the youngest, is a shepherd, so he has plenty of sheep. He brings the best one he has and kills it on the altar. God seems to like this. I shiver. What kind of God wants us to kill an animal and spill the blood on an altar? What harm did that sheep cause anyone?

The older brother, Cain, is a gardener. He's good with the land and grows these amazing fruits and vegetables, so he picks the finest of his produce and brings it to God, placing them on the altar. I nod. I can relate to this one. He's bringing the best he has. Otherwise he would have had to buy a sheep from Abel, and isn't something from our own labor better?

Well, apparently God and I aren't on the same page, because God rejects Cain's offering. This makes him mad. It's like God doesn't think he's good enough and likes little brother better.

It makes Cain so mad, he begins plotting how to get his brother out of the picture. Maybe, if Abel is gone, God will see Cain's value. Despite this God and I not being on the same page, even I think this is a bit extreme.

Apparently, God gets wind of the plotting, and He decides to have a talk with the gardener. "Be careful," God says to him. "Sin is crouching at your door. It wants to take control of you, but you must rule over it." It's like God is saying, "Watch your temper, dude!"

It doesn't help. The unhappy brother sneaks up on shepherd boy, hits him over the head with a rock, and kills him. There's no one around. But that doesn't stop God from finding out.

"What have you done?" He says to the murderous brother.

God must have been angry, and I can imagine what God sounds like when He's mad. I'm thinking it's a lot like thunder.

"The blood of your brother is crying to me from the ground!"

And so, Cain is cursed with a brown thumb, made a fugitive for life, and no one lives happily ever after.

The preacher goes on about how God hates the shedding of innocent blood, and somewhere this gets carried into talking about abortions and war and all sorts of destruction of the innocent. He says God can forgive us for our past, but we have to confess our sins and come to the cross, and a whole bunch of religious jargon is thrown in there, so I have no idea what he's talking about.

My mind goes back to the bloody sheep and murdering brother story.

The sermon ends with the preacher claiming Jesus loves me so much he died for me, shed his blood like the sacrificial lamb, so I could live.

Maybe he can love other people, but not me. No one has ever loved me like that.

They pass out wafers and tiny cups of juice. Communion. I'm familiar with this, but the setup is different. We serve ourselves from a tray they pass around instead of the priest giving it to us. I'm not comfortable taking any. I was taught this is Jesus's actual flesh and blood. I didn't like it as a kid, and I don't want it now. It's weird, this bit about it being the body of Jesus broken for me and the blood spilled for me. Besides, I don't buy into this whole bit of one person's blood making good for someone else. What kind of justice would that be?

There's a few more songs. People go forward to be prayed over or something, and then we're dismissed.

Jacob's melancholy seems to be replaced by a peace of sorts. Mine, not so much. We both have a lot to think about though, and, like our ride here, we return home in silence.

"Can I drop you off at your place?" I realize I have no idea where he lives.

"No. I enjoy the walk." He smiles, that dimpled smile that makes my stomach do weird things. "If you have no plans, I would greatly enjoy watching more movies on the television this afternoon."

I respond with a smile of my own. "I'd like that." To my surprise, I mean it.

"Did you pray for me?" I ask Bellona as she greets me in wild excitement at the door. She acts like she expected me never to return. Maybe she was afraid God would strike me dead even without a dog in attendance.

I eat lunch, mostly healthy fare since that's what Alicia stocked my fridge with. Bellona taps her tail and smiles for me, so I give in and share bits with her. I laugh when she turns her nose up at the spinach. She's my kind of dog.

I decide we both need some exercise and slip the leash on her and wave at the blue sedan as we take off down the sidewalk in the direction of the park. My muscles have recovered from last week's workout session, and I feel the need to run.

Clouds are gathering to the west. Maybe it'll rain tonight.

Jacob is sitting on the doorstep when we return, a box of pizza beside him. He stands as I approach, grinning that smile that makes me feel like jelly inside. I think I'm beginning to really like this guy. From the way Bellona rushes up to him, back end in full happy swing, I think she likes him as much as I do.

"Hey." I'm still breathing hard from my run and glad for once that I'm flushed and sweaty. He won't be able to tell I'm blushing as well.

"The other night, I did not do so well when I wished to take you to dinner," he says. "Perhaps tonight I can provide us with dinner here?"

"It smells wonderful," I say. My stomach growls.

Jacob smiles. "Sounds like you are hungry."

My uncle must have gotten the cable TV going again, because when I turn on the set, a nature program is playing. It's a special on black holes, wormholes, and astrophysics.

An African-American astrophysicist is talking. "According to Einstein's theory of relativity, any presence of mass or energy will warp the fabric of space and time."

Jacob leans forward, eyes intent on the screen. He listens and follows the descriptions of time warps, rubbing his chin pensively. I watch Jacob as much as I watch the television. Not only is he amazing to look at, but he actually seems to understand what they're talking about! Finally, he interrupts, his voice soft as a prayer. "This negro man is a scientist?"

I nod. "Yes. One of the leaders in his field."

"This is astonishing. Freeing the slaves was more successful than I even imagined! This is proof, Just Anna Marie! Absolute proof!"

"Proof about what?" I giggle at his obvious wonder.

"This man is the equal of any white man, I am sure of it. Can you see? The war was not entirely in vain. This is indeed a marvelous time for mankind to live, with the negro and white man living in such harmony."

"Well, blacks and whites still have a lot to work on harmony-wise, but yes, the removal of slavery changed everything for the better."

The narrator talks about sunspots, galaxies, the speed of light, and about time. I always thought of time as something linear, starting over here and ending over there. But, according to this scientist, time is relative. It's bound to space in an inseparable union. Time-space, he says, warps and bends, with time slowing down or speeding up relative to the movements of other objects or places in space and the gravity fields that surround them. If that isn't confusing enough, there's this whole other area he calls quantum physics. Here, strange and, as yet, unexplained things occur. Weird stuff happens—so weird, Einstein referred to it as spooky.

Goosebumps raise on my arms. Far from being simple, the universe just keeps getting more and more complicated. For once, I wish I had taken more math and science classes. I don't understand half of what the guy is talking about. My brain hurts just trying to understand the terminology and the math he's using.

Jacob is all excited, waving his pizza slice in the air. "Yes! Yes! This is marvelous."

I get up to take a couple Tylenol and microwave some popcorn, wondering if any of this explains how Adeline fell back through time and Jacob came forward. Or are we all 'back in time' compared to some other time? Or am I in the future, Adeline and I having travelled here as infants, and she simply returned to where she came from while I got left behind—ahead? If we were close to a black hole, wouldn't everyone experience the identical time warp? If we can figure out the science of it, can we get back to Adeline?

I rub my temples. Nothing makes sense.

The Earth Cries Out

I DREAM OF A MAN, stealthily moving through the woods with a rock in his hand. Thunder booms from the sky. The man ignores the thunder. He's hunting, stalking. When I see the flock of sheep, it dawns on me who he's searching for.

"Don't!" I try to scream. "He's your brother!" But my warning is lost in the pattering of rain.

The drops of rain turn to blood, falling warm on my outstretched arms. I try to wipe it off, but it won't go away. The sticky residue smells like metal, and blood drips from my hands and onto the ground. My fingers close around something. I glance down. It's the rock—cold, hard, and covered in blood. No. No. I wouldn't do such a thing. The blood-soaked ground begins to writhe in pain, moving and groaning beneath my feet.

"Why?" It cries. "Why do you do this?"

I wake up, gasping. Thunder crashes outside, and rain pounds at my window. Bellona whines and licks my fingers. I lift trembling hands so I can see them in the pale light from the window. They are clean. Spotless. I release my breath. It was just a dream.

I scoot to the edge of my bed, and the dog climbs up next to me. She nuzzles my neck and places a paw over my shoulder as though to protect me. I stare into the darkness until the black night gives in to a gray dawn.

The rain continues all day Monday. We skip our visit to Mr. Matthewson's. Alicia says her Toyota is likely to get stuck in the mud. Instead, Bellona gets to go to the gym with us where she watches Alicia teach me some basic self-defense moves. I have to tell the dog to sit and stay several times before she relaxes. I don't think she likes it when Alicia grabs me in a choke hold, but she stays as directed. Bellona wags her tail and smiles when I succeed in throwing Alicia over my shoulders.

"Good job, human," I imagine her saying. "I knew you could do it."

More often than not, it's me on the ground, and she whines and growls her displeasure.

We break early. Alicia drops us off at home, and I settle down to read a good book. Bellona decides if I sit on the sofa, she can too. We rest, her giant head on my lap. She's great company, but she doesn't smell too good.

After a bit, I rise, call her upstairs, and wrestle her into the tub. You'd have thought I was killing her.

An hour and a dozen towels later, I finish drying the dog, myself, and all the surrounding bathroom fixtures. I'll have to ask Mr. Matthewson how he gives the dog a bath. She's not keen on the blow dryer either, but she seems to enjoy being brushed. By the time we're done, she smells like Herbs and Flowers Shampoo, and we're both worn out.

I crawl into bed, and let Bellona crawl in with me. Her warm back against my legs is reassuring.

I dream. I'm walking through the woods, and a rock is in my hand. Thunder rolls overhead. "No!" I cry. "I don't want to do this!"

I fall on my knees. What was it the preacher said? You must rule over it? But I can't. It's who I am. In front of me, there's the trunk of a tree. Blood is running down and through the bark. I am naked, exposed— Not even a robe to hide in. I curl into a ball, let my hair fall over me, and try to cover myself with my hands, but I only succeed in smearing blood over my whole body. Blood from the man on the tree. I did this. It's my fault he's up there. I can't look up. Instead, I stare at my hands. The rock is gone. The earth roils and moans. It cries out in agony as it's ripped and torn. A whirlpool of blackness opens up, and from its depths, it weeps.

"So many dead," it cries. "So many dead."

I awake with a pounding heart and Bellona licking my face. I push her away and swing my feet around to sit up. I'm breathing like I just ran a half marathon. I look at my hands, afraid of what I'll find, but like last night, they are clean.

The dream was so vivid, I expect the ground to move beneath my feet, groaning and crying, "So many dead!"

What was the verse the preacher used? "The blood of your brother is crying to me from the ground!"

I look around the room. The rain has stopped. Moonlight is shining through the window in a beam of light onto Adeline's bed.

My eyes fall on an object, partially hidden under my pillow. I freeze. Adeline's notebook.

So many dead! So many dead!

The blood of your brother is crying to me from the ground.

I grab Adeline's notebook and hurry past the pages of birth certificates. What was Adeline looking for? I skim through the pictures and newspaper clippings. Then I see it, and I can't believe I didn't see it before. My grandfather, Mama, Daddy, Adeline? All disappeared during man-caused slaughter of other people. Not coincidence. Adeline was connecting causal events.

I run to the kitchen, throw the notebook on the table, grab a pile of loose paper and a pen. The coffee pot has some day-old coffee in it. I pour it in a mug and place it in the microwave for a minute. When it dings, I rush back to the table. Bellona walks around sniffing the doors and furniture, then settles on the floor mat in front of her food bowl, watching me.

I begin writing, taking pages from Adeline's notebook and laying them out across the table to form a timeline.

October 23, 1983. Suicide terrorist bomb kills 243 US personnel in Beirut.

Below this I write, Mr. Pablo DeSantos—Grandfather—disappears at Lazarus Springs State Park.

September 11, 2001. 2,996 people dead, over 6,000 others injured in the attack on the World Trade Center in New York.

Mama disappears at Lazarus Springs State Park.

October 12, 2002. Terrorists explode two bombs in Bali's nightclub district killing 202 and injuring 209.

Father disappears. Location unknown.

August 21, 2013. More than 1,400 killed in Syrian Chemical Attack.

Adeline disappears at Lazarus Springs State Park.

I put my pen down and stare at the pages in front of me. Could it be? Could it be that Mama didn't plan to leave us? Father? The earth cries out, torn by the blood of innocent men. Could that anguish tear time as well?

I dial Jacob's phone.

He answers, his voice heavy with sleep. "Anna Marie?"

"What date did you fall forward in time?" I ask, not bothering to explain myself.

"What?"

"I said, what date was it when you fell forward in time?"

"April 27, 1865, I believe," he says. "Why?"

"I think I figured it out. The murders of so many—it tears time!" I hang up and type Jacob's date into my phone. April 27, 1865.

The steamboat Sultana, carrying 2,300 passengers, explodes and sinks in the Mississippi River, killing 1,800, mostly Union survivors of the Anderson Prison.

Throwing on a change of clothes, I grab my car keys and Bellona's leash.

I'm glad I parked my car on the street instead of the driveway. I don't feel like company right now. The blue sedan isn't there, but I imagine someone else is on watcher's duty. Instead of leaving through the front door, Bellona and I go around the side of the house and jump into the car. The moon is once again hidden by clouds. A heavy fog lies close to the ground, misting my windshield.

We drive through the still sleeping town to the highway. Knee high corn is covering the fields I pass, but none are visible through the haze. Sunrise is a vague glow behind me, trying to break through the mist, but the fog is too thick.

An hour later, I pull off where the road sign indicates "Lazarus Springs State Park."

This is the last place Mama and Adeline stood in our time, and I need to stand where they once stood, see what they last saw.

If only I could go as well.

I drive the circle around the park to the utility road and veer off near where they found Adeline's kayak, our swimming hole. Pulling off the road, I tuck the nose of my car in an opening between low bushes and trees. A large oak is at the river's edge, growing over a corner of the old wood bench. Poison ivy creeps over the splintered surface. I try to picture my grandmother sitting there, book in hand, while her children play at her feet and her husband tends the fire. Turning the wipers off, I sit in my car and study the surroundings, trying to take in every detail.

"You stay, Bellona," I say, opening my door. "It's all muddy, and you and I both know you don't want another bath."

She whines and smears her nose against the glass.

"Don't worry, I'm not going anywhere."

Bass drums. Does Bellona hear them as well? Adeline's song weaves in and out of the drumbeats. I walk to the rhythm in my head. I go first to Mama's tree. I rest a hand on its trunk, wishing it could tell me the stories of people gone from beneath its branches, reveal to me the mysteries of this place.

With just a few steps, I'm standing at the river's edge. My expensive running shoes soak up water and mud. A rusty fishing hook on a twisted line is tangled in the branches. I wade a few feet in, feeling the gliding pull of the water around my ankles. My eyes sweep over the muddy shoreline. Adeline's footprints have washed away long ago. There's nothing here. There never is.

Bellona barks, and an engine hums in the distance. The drumming is stronger, the pulse more intense. I turn to head back to the car, at once concerned about being alone and desiring to have this moment to myself. What was I expecting to find here anyway? It's not like I have control over events in history and can schedule a trip through the portal of time. Bellona keeps barking.

"I know you don't like being left in there. I'm coming."

She must not understand because her barking takes on a higher, more frantic pitch.

I take one last glance into the river as it moves gently around my feet. A small fragment of sunshine breaks through the mist and sparkles off the water. Drops from overhanging branches disturb the surface, rippling outward. My reflection appears, split into ringed images that scurry away. My reflection smiles.

I do not.

"Adi?" It's her. I know it is, smiling at me from that faraway place.

Bellona is going insane, trying to tear through the door. Tires crunch the gravel behind me. They stop. A man calls. A car door closes. The drumming has gained a fevered pitch.

"Anna Marie? Is everything well?"

I peek up. Jacob is opening the door for Bellona. I smile at him and nod. Tears blur my eyes.

I reach for the reflection. I reach for my sister with a longing that will split me apart. I miss her so much.

The boom of thunder crashes around me, and lightning strikes, knocking me backward. I fall, fall, and keep falling into a deep, cold blackness. I scream, trying to grab at anything to halt the dizzying descent, but my hands grasp emptiness, and my voice has no sound. Heat sears my innards, and I'm freezing cold. I feel the darkness crushing me, while at the same time slashing at my limbs. Death. Hell. Where is this?

"Oh, God!" My words have no substance. "Help me!"

1864

I COME TO, SHIVERING SO hard I think my teeth will shatter, tucked in a bed facing the biggest fireplace I have ever seen. Logs spit sparks and release smoke, most of which makes their way into the flue, but some smoke lingers in the room, causing my vision to blur.

Hanging from an iron hook over the flames is a black kettle even bigger than the one Tia Lupe boiled our school uniforms in when we came home with lice.

Weighing me down on the scratchy mattress is a mountain of quilts, several layers deep, smelling of mold and body odor. Once again, I think of lice. I wonder if I would be itching if I weren't shaking so. I should be sweating. Thick, heavy quilts compress me like an iron press, but the shivering shakes me from my teeth to the tips of my toes. I feel like a toy rattle in the grip of a giant infant.

Long shadows flicker through the dark room, and my eyes adapt to their surroundings.

The fireplace dominates my view. Gray log walls flank either side, the chinking smooth and thoroughly applied between each.

I close my eyes, trying to relax and will the shaking to stop. My heart is beating fast, and I feel a mingling of euphoria and hysteria.

It worked. I know it has.

"Anna? You awake?"

A soft voice calls me, and I open my eyes again. A woman with deep olive skin and slick black hair secured in a long braid is leaning over me.

Her eyes are so dark, I can't see her pupils. She smiles and tucks the blanket closer around my neck.

"What year is this?" I ask through chattering teeth. My throat feels like I've been yelling.

Her eyes widen. "You know what happened? That be a first. You arrived in 1864. October 30, 1864 to be precise."

"Adeline!" I try to rise but am shaking so much, I fall back onto the bed. "My sister! I have to find my sister."

"Adeline is well. She is with the Dickersons. I will take you as soon as your body adjusts. She believed you would come someday. We have heard much about you."

I'm trying hard to clear my thoughts. What was the date of the fire? November 2? No, that's when the article came out. November 1. Day after tomorrow.

"The fire," I push a blanket to the side and sit up. The room wobbles in circles around me, immersing me in waves of nausea. "I have to warn them," I say just before blackness engulfs me.

I awake again to the smell of meat roasting over the fire. The angle of the sun through the windows speaks of late afternoon. A young lady is tending to the fire. Slender hips and long bony limbs say she hasn't grown into her full height. I hear the chopping of knife against wood on the far side of the room.

"Where am I?" Something tells me I'm not in Kansas, and I don't see a yellow brick road. The chopping stops, and the younger lady turns toward me. She smiles a shy, curious smile that lights up her eyes.

"Mam, she's awake."

The same woman who tended me earlier approaches, wiping her hands on her apron.

"Anna." She places a calloused hand on my shoulder. Her fingers are long, and even with her gentle touch, I can tell they are strong. "You been sleepin' long. The shivering stopped a few hours ago, but I could not get ye to rise. I was concerned." She pats my shoulder. "Folk do not arrive with enough frequency to teach us what is normal."

The young woman sneaks up behind her, peering around her sleeve. The older lady draws her arm around the girl.

"I am Susanna. I found your mother when she arrived thirteen years ago. This is my daughter, Candace. She found Adeline when she arrived, and now she's found you."

"No, that couldn't be our mother. Mama has only been gone twelve years."

"Adeline said the same thing, but no. I reckon time doesn't flow in the same linear fashion from now to then. It was your mother, all right. She talked so much of her babies, she about drove my mama insane. She was desperate to get back to you. Lord knows she tried, but she never could."

My throat gets tight. Mama didn't leave us. Not on purpose.

"Is my mother here?"

"No." Susanna shakes her head. Her smile fades. "She remained but a few months. We believe she ended up in Arkansas. She said her father's people was from there, and she hoped to find some kin. Got one letter from her, way back. Said she'd gotten injured but was under the care of a physician and recovering well."

She moves to the fireplace and, using a long metal poker, turns the meat. "Have heard nothin' since then. What with the war and all, people are not easy to locate, and we live pretty isolated."

She folds her hands one over the other and glances at the closed door. "We keep mostly to ourselves. Folk around here do not take kindly to us native folk, much less one married to a negro." Then Susanna smiles so large it's like her face is all teeth. "And they likes even less when them natives and negroes can read as good as the best of them. Your mother, she taught us."

"Oh." I run my hand through my hair, trying to take it all in. Mama is alive. She's in Arkansas. She taught them to read. She was never one to follow traditional rules. "If you want to do well in life, you must be educated. You must read, read, read," she used to say whenever I grumbled about school.

"I read about that. About white folk not letting people of color learn to read. That changes, you know. Everyone goes to school in my time."

"That makes me glad."

My mind is doing the numbers.

"My sister—she's been gone for ten months. Are you sure it's only October 30?"

"Yes. She arrived on September 27, just over four weeks ago."

"Can I see her? I need to see her."

Susanna looks out the window. "You still have a few hours. If you hurry, it will give Candace a bit of time to play with the baby before you need to return. She loves that baby."

Susanna eyes her daughter. "Keep an eye on the time. You must not be in the woods after dark, and keep your rifle on you at all times. The wolves been getting mighty brave lately."

Candace nods, beaming.

"First, Miss Anna, see if them legs have settled in. Your sister had a terrible few hours adjusting before she could stand straight."

"Are you kidding me?" I throw my legs over the side of the makeshift bed. I'm steady as a rock. I feel like Princess Buttercup when she discovers her true love is not dead. "My sister is alive! If you wish, I could fly."

"That might draw the wrong sort of attention. Here." Susanna chuckles and strolls to the fire. She picks up a tin plate, grasps the meat with a large iron tong, and has Candace cut several slices.

"You girls eat first. You need the energy. Then you, Miss Anna, must change into proper clothing."

I look at my t-shirt and jeans, then over at Susanna and Candace. I do stick out as rather odd for the time and place. But Susanna is taller and fuller than me, Candace way too skinny.

"You have something in my size?"

Susanna laughs. "Oh, yes. I think we can manage. Eat first."

"I couldn't possibly eat. I'm so excited."

She hands me the plate, and I devour everything.

My heart is singing, and I feel more alive than I ever have in my life. I've found her. I've found my sister. If only I could tell Jacob. I've found my sister!

THE DICKERSONS

"WHAT DO YOU MEAN Adeline is gone?" I stand dumbfounded and ready to scream. "This isn't possible. You have no idea what I've gone through to get here!"

The edge of panic is working its way into my voice. The tightness in my chest grows, and it's not from having my torso all scrunched into this girdle like device.

"Please." Mary Elizabeth grasps my hand in both of hers. "Please, come inside, and we can talk more comfortably."

From what I gathered from Candace as we hiked over, Mary Elizabeth is the second oldest of the Dickersons. I'm guessing she's about my age, small, and slightly plump with a pleasant round face. She leads me to the parlor, where we join her mother and three other sisters.

The furnishings are made of richly carved mahogany and plush fabric upholstery. Heavy, corded drapes pull back from the windows, allowing the afternoon sunlight to cast friendly shadows across the room. In the corner, rising close to shoulder height, stands a harp. Its golden soundboard is inset with intricate Celtic carvings. The column is fluted and crowned with gold paint. It takes my breath away.

This house hums a sound I've not heard before. I glance around and realize it emanates from Mrs. Dickerson, and her music fills the home. Her song is a mixture of the light jingle of bells and the soothing rustle of a babbling brook.

"Mother, this is Anna Marie, Adeline's sister. Anna, my mother and my sisters, Martha, Nancy, and Margaret. Our younger sister, Susan, is helping Joseph with the chickens."

Where Mary Elizabeth is small and rounded, Martha, the eldest, is long and lean. Nancy blends in the background, stitching a piece of fabric. She glances up with a shy smile and returns to her work. While the older sisters are pleasant to look at, Margaret has the face of an angel. I nod, wondering if I'm supposed to curtsy, or bow or something. I stand, staring. I can't help but wonder who will die in the next couple days.

Mrs. Dickerson's hand flies to her bosom as she lets her breath relax.

"Thank heavens," she says. "I thought you were Adeline, poor dear, unable to get away! But of course, you are her twin. My, you really are identical!"

She holds an infant on her lap, swaddled in blankets so she resembles a bundle of clothes. Dark lashes rest against rosy, fat cheeks, and her tiny lips part in satisfied slumber.

"That's a beautiful child. Are you both well then? Adeline mentioned you were recovering from the delivery." I'm trying to be polite.

Mrs. Dickerson beams down at the sleeping babe. "Thank you, Anna. Yes, we are doing well."

I sink heavily into a stiff chair close to Mrs. Dickerson. The seat is padded, but the wood back hits square in the middle of mine and forces me to sit straight. I look around the room once more. I was never any good at small talk.

"I'm sorry." I don't know why I am apologizing.

Everyone is so polite and seem genuinely pleased to meet me. But it's my sister I want.

"My sister—you said she left? Where did she go? I need to catch up with her."

Margaret and Mary Elizabeth glance at each other, then cast their eyes to the floor.

"I fear that is unlikely," Mary Elizabeth says. "She left on the coach before dawn this morning, and the next coach won't be around for another week. Perhaps then?"

Candace strides over to Mrs. Dickerson and reaches out her arms. "May I?"

Mrs. Dickerson smiles and hands the child over. "Thank you. Fannie just ate, so she should sleep for a while."

With great tenderness, Candace carries the baby to the far end of the room, where she stands in the sunlight, gently swaying back and forth.

A door somewhere to the rear of the house pushes open then slams shut.

"Mother!" A boy's voice bellows through the house. "Mother! Is Adeline back? I will kill that Jethro Tanner if he done laid a hand on her!"

Mrs. Dickerson shakes her head. "Has laid a hand, William, *has*," she mutters softly.

I smile. Are all mothers grammar police?

Heavy footsteps rush down the hallway and into the parlor. A tall boy of about sixteen, with a mat of black curls poking from beneath a leather cap and hanging over bright blue eyes, halts in the door.

"Son," Mrs. Dickerson's voice is even softer than Mary Elizabeth's. "I would ask that you mind your manners when speaking in the house, and you know your father will not approve of you threatening any violence. Even against one as deserving as Mr. Tanner."

"But, Mother—" William looks at me, his eyes pleading.

I frown.

"Miss Adeline, are you well?" He snatches the cap off his head and holds it like a shield in front of himself.

"Did you say Jethro Tanner?" It must be a coincidence. But the Jethro in my time thought I was my sister—and he shot Jacob. "Is Adeline in danger?"

William's brows furrow together, and he blinks at me like I'm something strange.

"Anna Marie, may I introduce my oldest son, William. William, this is Adeline's sister, Anna Marie. Dear, forgive my son. He is fond of your sister, as we all are."

"Oh!" William grins. "You're her twin!"

I want to shake someone. Yes, yes, all the introductions are fine and nice and all, but what is happening to my sister?

"Please, can someone tell me what's going on? What happened to Adeline?"

"Mr. Tanner came to court her," William says, punching the inside of his cap, "but he is a crude, vile man."

"William." Mrs. Dickerson frowns at her son.

The teen nods at his mother, then continues. "He thinks 'cuz his Pa is high up in the army, he can do as he wishes, and when Adeline told him no, he got mad and started breakin' stuff. Father thought it best if Adeline were far away from here, so he sent her to our relations in Arkansas."

"Oh." My shoulders sag. My throat is burning and I want to go outside where I can breathe easier.

Mrs. Dickerson must notice my distress. She puts her finger to her lips and motions toward the door.

"Be gone with you, William. Miss Anna has much to consider without you causing her concern over her sister's well-being. Besides, your father will not be happy if your chores are incomplete when dinner is served."

William glances at me then his mother, slaps his hat back on his head, bobs my direction with a "Pleased to meet you," and hurries outside.

Mrs. Dickerson reaches an impossibly tiny hand over and rests it on my knee. Her skin is so translucent, I swear I can see the blood coursing through her veins.

"My dear." Her eyes are a deep blue, and there is a gentleness there that invites confidence. "You must be sorely disappointed. Your sister told me you live quite far away, and she misses you terribly. If we knew you were coming, we could have hidden her at Susanna's place. As it is, she was eager to go. She thinks perhaps you also have family in Arkansas?"

Mama. She's looking for Mama.

"Yes, that is the rumor. Will she be safe? Traveling alone?"

"As safe as can be in time of war. She accompanies friends of my husband. She will write and notify us of her new residence when she arrives."

"I need to find her."

I freeze and close my eyes. The fire. Am I messing with the future if I say something? Adeline isn't in danger, I can leave with Candace.

"Mrs. Dickerson, I can't explain how I know this, but your family is in danger." I can't hold it back.

The woman's brows rise. The girls all turn to look at me with similar expressions.

"Soldiers are going to burn your house down, day after tomorrow."

Mrs. Dickerson, with brows narrowed, smooths her already smooth hair.

"Why would anyone want to do that?"

"They say you have slaves. The Union Army plans to invoke General Order 11."

"That is ridiculous! Is that not true, Mother?" Margaret leans toward her mother. "Those are all lies. Everyone knows Father's conscience prohibits such a thing, and hasn't the mayor assured him our farm is safe? We provide so much extra grain for the people in the city."

"That is right, Margaret. Anna Marie, I will take your warning under advisement and inform my husband. It would be most helpful if you could divulge your source of knowledge."

"I read it. It is a credible source."

She frowns, a few age lines etching the side of her eyes. "Perhaps you misread. As my daughter explained, my husband has arrangements with the mayor, and we are quite protected."

"No. It's no mistake."

She pats my hand. "We will need to wait, and I will discuss this with Samuel. Meanwhile, please join us for tea."

As if on cue, a tall, black woman enters the room, carrying a tray.

"Thank you, Sarah." Mrs. Dickerson nods, and Sarah leaves the tray on the side table.

"Aunt Sarah!" Candace waves the woman over.

Could this be the slave mentioned in the paper?

At my curious glance, Mrs. Dickerson smiles. "Sarah is our cook, and we are very blessed to have her. She escaped from her slave owners before the war started and came here to be with her brother. We hired her a few years ago, but in truth, she is more like family than a hired hand."

"Oh."

Candace embraces her aunt, then approaches Mrs. Dickerson, handing her the still sleeping child. "I must be on my way before dark. Will Miss Anna be returning with me or staying here?"

"We have more room. Besides, Mr. Dickerson may want to ask her some questions," Mrs. Dickerson says.

Candace's face falls.

Mrs. Dickerson smiles, patting Candace on the arm. "If you have time, return tomorrow. Tomorrow is cheese making day, and I could use all the help available."

"Yes, ma'am!" Candace nods with enthusiasm, gathers up her skirt, and skips out the front door.

Mary Elizabeth pours the tea. Her mother hasn't risen from her seat once since I arrived. Her face is drawn as though she hasn't slept, her skin pale. Even her nail beds show no tinge of color. A fine powder covers her face, and dark circles under her eyes are carefully hidden beneath it. Classic signs of anemia. Maybe she has yet to fully recover from the birth of her last child.

I accept the tea cup and watch the others for cues on what I'm supposed to do next. I glance toward the door, and there, leaning against the frame, is the rifle.

I recall Suzanna's strict instructions before we left the house. Candace wasn't to travel without the rifle. Even the wolves were finding it difficult to find sufficient game in the war worn countryside, making it unwise for an unarmed person to travel alone.

"Oh, dear!" I rise, setting my cup on the side table. "Candace forgot the rifle! I need to run it out to her!"

Without waiting for a response, I pick up the rifle and dash out the door Candace took moments earlier. Cutting across the grass, I hasten toward the barn and the path beyond it, leading toward the canyon.

A muffled cry, a can being kicked, and a crash like something or someone falling in the barn stops me in my tracks. That may be a mighty upset cow, but somehow, I don't think so. With rifle in hand, I thrust open the door.

There, on the dirt floor, a man is straddling a struggling Candace. She cries out, and he slaps her face.

"Stop!" I aim the rifle in his direction, painfully aware that it isn't at all like the one my uncle had me use, and I have no idea how this thing works. *Pretend, pretend.*

The man looks up, his eyes fire, his face red.

"Jethro Tanner?" I almost drop the rifle before recovering my wits and aiming the muzzle directly on him. Candace is just a child! How dare he! I wish this rifle was equipped with a bayonet.

"Adeline!" He leaps to his feet and smiles a big, stupid, nasty-toothed smile. "I meant nothing by it. Just thought I would have a bit of fun scaring the negro. She should know better than walking around this place like she owns it."

"I thought you were in jail!" As soon as the words come out of my mouth, I realize I'm talking about the wrong time period.

"Like that will ever happen!" Spittle sprays from his lips as he laughs.

"Oh, but it will," I say. "Or maybe we can skip that and just send you to hell."

"Like you would shoot me. You have no idea what my pa would do to these people."

"You, you—monster!" It's lame, but I can't think of anything else to say, and I really don't know how to shoot this thing. "Get off this property!"

"Aw, Adeline. You know I come to see you. Some as told me you run off, and I was upset. Had to come see for myself." He stands with his hands up, glancing to the side. His holster belt and pistol lie on the far side of the shed.

"Candace, get his gun."

She hurries to comply.

"Out!" I want to shoot. Lord, I want to shoot, but if I don't work it right, he'll have the upper hand. "Or, as God is my witness, I will kill you."

Jethro's face darkens. The air is filled with a cacophony of emotion and strangling dissonance. I want to clasp my hands over my ears, instead, I grip the rifle tighter. He looks at Candace, now with pistol in hand, then at me. He spits. When he speaks, his voice is flat, clashingly cold. "I'm leaving, Adeline. Best watch your back. Nigger lovers have no place in these parts."

He leaves, and Candace runs to me, throwing her arms around my shoulders. I'm shaking so hard I can barely keep hold of the rifle.

"Here." I hand it to her. "I don't know how to use it. Are you alright?"

I remember Jacob's concern as he asked me that same question just a few days ago. *Jacob. If only he were here.* My heart tightens.

She nods. "Yes. Thank God you came."

"He is a vile, wicked man," I say, quoting William.

"Yes. And I fear he will seek vengeance. The Tanners are known for being prideful and won't easily let this slight go unnoticed."

"But he was attacking you!"

"It is his word against ours."

"I'll speak to the Dickersons."

They were right sending Adeline away. Now what will happen to Candace?

Cold dread presses in on me.

"Run home, Candace. Tell your folks. I'll tell the Dickersons what happened."

"I must go talk with his father." Mr. Dickerson is pacing the room as I tell them what occurred in the barn. "That boy has grown out of control."

"I will pray." Mrs. Dickerson rests a hand on her husband's arm. He stops pacing and looks down into her pale blue eyes. She smiles up at him. "Perhaps you can talk with Jethro again. He used to listen to you."

"I will try." He pats his wife's hand, and a look of understanding passes between them. These two have done a lot of life together, and it looks like it's brought them closer instead of tearing them apart. I don't think Daddy ever looked at Mama like that.

They look like the Mennonites from outside my town. Mr. Dickerson's beard lines his chin in a somber, almost severe, cut. His shirt is buttoned to the collar, and suspenders hold his baggy slacks up. When he reaches for his hat, the ensemble is complete. Maybe everyone dresses like this.

When he leaves, Mrs. Dickerson goes to the corner where the harp stands. She pulls over a small stool and sits. Closing her eyes, she leans her forehead on the wood.

"Come." Mary Elizabeth takes my hand and draws me toward the kitchen. "Mama likes to pray there. Let us leave her undisturbed.

Intrigued, I watch from the doorway and listen as her delicate fingers pluck the strings. I have never heard anything like this before. The sounds she plays echo her own song. She is literally pouring her self into the music. Her eyes remain closed, and there is more. A new sound joins in.

"Do you hear the singing?" I whisper to Mary Elizabeth.

She glances at me, one brow raised. "You mean the strings?"

I don't answer. Of course she doesn't hear. I shouldn't have asked. I stand, closing my own eyes, and I'm very still except for a perceptible flutter of my heart. The overtones of a choir can just be heard above the plucking of harp strings.

THE CAPTAIN

NOVEMBER 1, 1864

I've dozed sitting in the high back chair in the parlor of the Dickersons' home. I tried reasoning with Mr. Dickerson until late in the night, without success. He listened, stroking his beard as I spoke, his knuckles bulging with arthritis, his nails cracked from years of hard labor.

"At least have a gun ready, just in case." I plead.

Mr. Dickerson shakes his head, blue eyes piercing. "Nay. He who lives by the sword will die by the sword, Miss Anna. I have not refused to bear arms for my country during all these years, simply to rise up and kill for the sake of maintaining control of my own property. The Lord sees all. He will protect us."

Resolved to keep watch, I sit and wait as the night passes, knowing that at some time, a troupe of Union soldiers will arrive. I want to know the moment they step foot on Dickerson land. If Jacob were here, he could persuade the Dickersons to leave. He knows how General Order 11 works. He'd know what to say without sounding crazy.

The long hours of the night pass. Each swing of the pendulum on the large grandfather clock seems to take longer to complete its arc than the previous one. During the last hours before sunrise, I nod off, jerking awake as Sarah stokes up the wood stove in the kitchen.

Rising from my chair, I pick up the candle and trudge upstairs to the room I share with the girls. Nancy, Margaret, and Susan nestle together in one bed, Martha and Mary Elizabeth snuggle close in the other. A trundle is pulled out for my use, its blanket unruffled.

In the smaller room across the hall, I hear the clanking of boots against the wood floor. That would be the lads—William, James, and Joseph—preparing to milk the cows. Three-year-old Samuel Harvey, affectionately called "Harve," and baby Fannie sleep in the parents' room.

"Good morning, Anna Marie." Nancy yawns and stretches, then elbows Martha, who lies closest to her. "The night was uneventful?"

"Yes." I step toward the basin of water. Reaching inside, I splash the cool clear liquid over my face. My lids feel like they're made of sandpaper. The flickering candle casts long shadows against the wall. Sunrise is not far off, and the house is astir.

Horses. The sound of hooves beating against sod mingled with the murmur of men's voices drift through the silent yard. My heartbeat rises to match the rhythm. With trembling hands, I lift the curtain and peer out the window. Cast in moonlight, a line of men on horseback halt at the edge of the woods. Two horses break formation, their riders erect and moving with purpose.

"They're here!" I drop the curtain. What do I do? What do I do?

My heart is pounding so loud I can hear it. No, not my heart. There is actually someone pounding on the front door. I hear scrambling in the parents' room, then Mr. Dickerson's voice, calm but full of authority, outside our door.

"Girls, get dressed, and lock your door. Boys, Rebecca, girls, keep your doors locked, and do not come out unless I tell you!"

Footsteps descend the stairs.

More pounding, then a loud crash as the front door is kicked open.

"What is the meaning of this?" Mr. Dickerson's voice floats up to us.

The girls have scrambled from their beds and struggle to pull dresses on over their heads. I help Susan as she wrestles with hers.

"It's been reported that this residence is in sympathy with the enemy, owning slaves and providing food and supplies to the Quantrill gang." A voice booms through the house. The voice tickles a memory that is just out of reach, and it haunts me. "I hereby, under General Order 11, determine that this home and surrounding buildings must be burned to the ground!"

"Sir, those are false accusations on both accounts. Ask anyone in town. They can vouch for my good name."

There's a slamming door, a woman's cry.

"Mr. Dickerson! What is happening?" It's Sarah.

"See for yourself. They got themselves a slave woman." Jethro Tanner's voice rasps like nails on a chalkboard.

My head spins as it hits me. This is his revenge. The house burning— it's all my fault. I'm the cause of the event listed in tomorrow's paper. I should never have let Jethro go. My stomach lurches. Studying the faces of the young ladies clustered together, I wonder which of us dies today.

Men and horses stand in the shadows of the woods. We are surrounded. There's nowhere to hide. There is no escape.

"Jethro, of all people, you know—" Mr. Dickerson is interrupted by the thump of something hard against bone.

We hear him fall to the floor, and for a moment all is silent.

Sarah begins wailing. "What have you done? I am no slave!" She begs. "I am a free woman!"

"Save your tears, girl. The day is young."

The sisters huddle together, staring at the door in disbelief. Across the hall, a door opens, and William rushes out, slamming the door behind him.

"What did you do to my father?"

"Seems your father has broken the law, boy." The voice echoes deep like a long-forgotten dream. "Anyone else hiding upstairs?"

William doesn't answer. I hear boots coming our way.

"Sir, you must not—" William cries out as he is thrust hard against the wall and thump, thump, thumps down the stairs.

I listen for him to speak, to protest, to cry. But he is silent.

Jethro laughs.

"Oh, William!" A soft voice cries behind me.

I pray the boys locked the door behind him, that no one else is foolish enough to confront these men. If only Bellona were here.

There's a knock on our door, the handle moves, then a kick. The door breaks loose from the jam and swings wide. A tall, handsome, older man stands in the doorway, a smirk marring his fine features. His gaze takes in the sorry bunch of us huddled fearfully together. "Looks like we hit the Jackpot, Mr. Tanner."

I stand, staring. Lightning has struck the core of my being, rendering me powerless to move. I know the line of that jaw, the slant of those eyes, the cruel smile. I know that voice.

"Daddy?"

EVICTED

"**D**ADDY?" I REPEAT, REACHING behind me and grasping the bedpost for support.

There he is—older than I remember, but that's my father. Not as a ghost, but in the flesh. His powerful shoulders fill the doorway, and as he stoops to enter, his thick, blond hair brushes the top frame. Cold, gray-blue eyes peruse the room.

Always proud of his appearance, he cuts a handsome, polished figure in his Union Army uniform. Shiny black boots. Not a wrinkle anywhere. Not a speck of dirt. A pistol is holstered on one hip. Another, in hand, points directly at me. I scarcely notice.

My father is alive. My heart beats in tune to the rhythm of words inside me. My father is alive.

"I want this one," Jethro pushes past my father and grasps my arm. I twist, like Alicia taught me, and his grip breaks. He looks startled, then smiles his foul, black-toothed grin and reaches behind me, grasping young Susan. He thrusts her in front of me and puts his pistol to her head.

"I told you you would be sorry, Adeline. Now, if you do not behave and cooperate, it will be Susan that does the suffering."

"*No!*" Mary Elizabeth cries out, reaching for her sister.

Jethro presses the muzzle harder against Susan's temple. "Uh-uh-uh, Mary Elizabeth!" He shakes his head, clicks his tongue.

Susan stands still, eyes closed, almost as relaxed as in sleep. Her mouth moves slightly. Sweet, innocent girl.

"Jethro, please! You know us!" Someone is speaking from far, far behind me.

This can't be real. I'm dreaming. I shake my head, trying to clear it of the images I see. My father is undoing his belt.

"Daddy, no! It was me, not Adi." Anger explodes as I burst through the door.

Daddy's belt whips viciously across Adeline's legs, leaving a red welt in its wake. Adeline shakes her head, warning me back. Silent tears stream down her cheeks.

"You took it?" Daddy turns on me, and he looks every bit like the wolf in the National Geographic film Teacher played during quiet time—wild, head down, eyes fixed on his prey. "Did you give it to your mother? Is that what this is about? Where'd she go with it? It's your fault she's gone!"

I shake my head. I have no idea what Daddy is missing, but I can handle a whipping better than Adeline can.

The belt comes down hard. I'm too angry to cry.

"You!" He lashes out. Whip!

"Ever since you were born." Whip! *It stings so bad.*

"Nothing but trouble." Whip! *I almost cry out, but I can't. Crying is a sign of weakness.*

Adeline is pulling on Daddy's arm. He shoves her to the floor.

"I'll tell." My voice is barely above a whisper. I've had enough. "Saint Pancras will be mad."

Daddy's arm freezes midair. Do I imagine it, or does he go pale?

"This is all your fault." He's breathing hard, and the look he gives me makes me realize how much he despises me.

I never told good old Saint Pancras. I didn't know how. I never called for help. I wasn't convinced Saint Pancras would help some-one like me. Still, when Daddy returns from work early the next day, he's limping, and his lip is swollen. The hatred in his eyes tells me what words cannot.

Sometimes just speaking, I cause trouble.

"Daddy! Please! Don't do this!"

My father hesitates, peering at me with brows drawn. His belt is off, and he's fumbling with the drawstring on his britches.

God, help us! I pray. It feels like rusty words hitting a solid surface. God can't hear me.

"Ha!" Jethro Tanner laughs. "Very clever, Adeline. You don't even look like the Captain. 'Sides, his girls are babies, not whores like you. Sir, she's probably one of them come up from Texas."

"Daddy, it's me. Anna Marie. I travelled through the river at Lazarus Springs while looking for Adeline. All these years—I thought you were dead! Please, Daddy! Don't do this!"

He didn't abandon me! He may not have loved me, but he didn't abandon me. I want to throw myself into his arms, At the same time, I want to run as far from him as I can.

My father? Top dog in modern corporate America, he's with Jethro Tanner? It makes odd sense. This man kicked my mother until she could do nothing but curl in a corner and moan. All because he was angry at me. I wasn't good enough, not pretty enough. I couldn't keep a secret.

My fault! It's always been my fault! I press my hands to my temples and squeeze my eyes closed, struggling to halt the swell of tears, the flood of memories.

"Daddy! I'm so sorry I didn't obey. I'm sorry I caused so much trouble for you and Mama. I didn't know!" I'm crying now, oblivious to anything around me except for the man that stands in front of me. "I've tried to behave since you left—even got a music scholarship for college. I'm not very good at it being good, but Daddy—these folks have done nothing. It was my fault."

I beg like I wish I begged all those years ago. Back when it was Mama's life on the line. I was too scared to speak then, too scared of what would happen to me. I must speak now.

He stops fumbling with his britches and stares at me. His face is pale under the weathered tan. Reaching a trembling hand out to touch my face, he cups my chin and lifts it, looking into my eyes. He blinks hard and swallows. Deep creases wrinkle his once flawless skin. His blue eyes glisten.

"Anna Marie?"

I nod. He steps forward, arms open like he wants to hold me, then hesitates, straightens, and backs up.

"Your sister?" He considers the huddled figures behind me.

"Somewhere in this time. She went south—to get away from *him!*" I point and glare at Jethro.

A baby cries down the hall.

"Anna Marie, I'm so sorry—"

"Sir, the men will wonder what's taking so long. Can we get on with it?"

My father's head snaps up. His face darkens.

"Go wait outside, Mr. Tanner," he says.

"But, Sir—"

"That's an order, soldier!"

Jethro thrusts Susan hard against her sisters, gives me a long, cold look, then stomps away. Boots striking wood reverberate throughout the house.

"This ain't over, Adeline," he calls as he retreats.

"Isn't, you fool. Isn't," Daddy mutters.

I almost smile. A wave of relief rushes over me. For all the things my father has done in the past, he is *still* my father, and he's saved us. I throw my arms around him and grip him tight.

He trembles, then pulls away. "Forget about me, girl."

He steps out of my reach, secures his belt, and holsters his gun. His voice is thick, forced. "I'm sorry you had to see me this way. It's war, and I have my orders. I can give you an hour to grab what you can. Then we burn the place. I won't be responsible for any harm that happens after that."

Before I can process what he said, he's gone, and I'm left standing, staring into the empty hallway.

"Daddy!" I scream after him.

There's no reply.

Susan's small hand wraps around mine. "It's all right, Miss Anna. It will be all right. I prayed, and God told me they would not injure us. That's why I was not afraid."

The image of a child's face—eyes closed, at peace, lips moving in prayer—is seared into my soul. But she is just a child. I believed all kinds of things when I was a child. I stare at the place where my father stood. A familiar anger rises in my chest.

I *have* no father. That is my reality.

"Mary Elizabeth, tell the boys, and help them get ready to travel." Nancy steps forward and takes charge. "Margaret, check on William, Father, and Sarah. Martha, go to the kitchen and see what food we have that we can take. Be sure to get a pot to cook in and carry water. Anna Marie, help the children get on several layers of clothing. Be sure they have their best walking shoes and collect some quilts. I will help Mama. Hurry, we must be on the road within the hour."

James brings the cart to the back door, the two farm oxen harnessed in front, the milk cow tied behind.

Mr. Dickerson sits in a chair directing, a large gauze wrapped around his forehead where Margaret cleaned and tended to the gash on his head. I'm worried about William. He lies on the couch, unconscious. Sarah is crying while helping collect things in the kitchen.

I'm in a movie. This is a set. None of this is real.

"I wish you could come with us, Sarah," Margaret says. "But we must go south to our relations. It would not be safe for you there."

There's a scurry of feet as two younger children run past.

"I must bring my dolls!" Susan says.

"Margaret says only one, and you have to carry it." Joseph has Susan's hand, dragging her reluctant form behind him.

"Why do we have to wear so many clothes? I'm hot!"

"Joseph, be careful, and place the rifle along the wagon wall. We will need it to hunt."

I have to learn how to use the rifle.

"Someone check that William has shoes and a coat."

"Here, Nancy said to wear the jewelry under your clothes. She's heard folks steal what they can see."

Voices carry throughout the house, disconnected conversations tied together with a sense of urgency.

I walk from room to room, collecting quilts, coats. I am a ghost, weightless, without feeling. It's my fault. All this is my fault.

"No, Mother!" Nancy follows behind Mrs. Dickerson's tiny frame, Harvey clinging to his mother's skirts. "It will not fit in the wagon!"

"But it was my grandfather's—and they will steal it!"

"I know, Mother. But we need the space for blankets and food, and for you and the children to ride. Here. Take the picture of you and Father. Was this not taken just after you married? And the Bible. We must have the Bible."

"The harp! It came from Ireland!"

"We will pray someone who loves music will be blessed by it."

"All my books!"

"Maybe two or three."

"Oh, God curse them all!"

"Mother!"

The whole household rushes around completing various chores in stunned silence.

The rooster crows. *Betrayed. Betrayed,* he says.

The clock ticks, but time does not slow. Sunrise is in full bloom now. The row of horses at the tree line stomp their feet, impatient to be moving. We carry William and place him among the blankets. If he has a spinal injury, the jostling of the wagon will cause further harm. It can't be helped. One side of his mouth droops more than the other. I wish I knew what to do. At least his breathing is easy. I tuck quilts around him, creating a nest to protect his head and neck.

Mary Elizabeth snuggles baby Fannie in the blankets beside him. "Mother, you must ride with Harvey and hold onto Father. His head is still dizzy, so make sure he does not tumble off the back."

Sarah hugs Mrs. Dickerson and each of the children in turn. Tears run down her face.

"Be off with you now," Mr. Dickerson says, pressing some coins into her hand.

She shakes her head. "No, Sir. You will need every penny you have with you. Moses and Susanna will take care of me."

"But your wages—"

"When the war is over, you come home. You can pay me then."

With five minutes to spare, we leave. James leads the oxen and sets a pace that has the shorter legs scurrying to keep up. As full as our wagon appears, it is pitifully little for a party of thirteen to cross a state and begin a new life. There is so much we still need, so much left behind.

I look over my shoulder at the cluster of soldiers waiting at the wood's edge. Some have moved to the house. Scavenging. A bitter taste fills my mouth. I look for my father. Instead, my eye catches on another. No. My imagination is double timing it. So many of the soldiers look alike, I tell myself. But the tall one, standing with his hand on the shoulder of a skinny youth, reminds me so much of Jacob. Has he returned? No, if he did, he would do something. He wouldn't just stand there and watch. Not my Jacob.

I recall Jacob's voice, deep, rich and sad. *"I did not know the Dickersons,"* he told me. *"But I know of these burnings. They were part of war, so we told ourselves, and thus could not be helped."*

"You could stop this!" I scream to the specter of my memory. He must not hear me.

I stumble, and Margaret catches me.

"I am sorry about your father, Anna," she whispers, tucking her arm around my own. "But I thank God it was he, and not Jethro, who was in charge, and that you were there with us."

Tears burn my eyes, and I hurry my pace, matching my steps to hers. Don't look back, I tell myself. Don't look back.

We're alive. At least that's something. We are all alive. No one remains in the house. No one will die in that fire. Have I altered history?

We exit the drive, pass the boundary fence, and turn down the dirt road leading South. The wagon jerks as it takes the corner, and an anguished cry pierces the air. Mrs. Dickerson is pointing behind us, tears stream down her face. Furniture litters the lawn. The tall, ornately carved harp stands proud in the center. Two men struggle out the front door with a massive grandfather clock. Prized possessions that had been in the family for generations, lost forever.

As we watch, angry yellow and blue flames leap from an upstairs window. My heart lurches. I have entered many a home to rescue people, to extinguish fires. The fury of this one tells me it will not rest until every last bit is consumed.

ARKANSAS, HERE WE COME

"I'M THIRSTY!"

We've been walking for hours, and the sun is well above the trees. Joseph is lagging further and further behind the wagon.

"And I'm hot," eight-year-old Susan says. "So just stop whining and try to keep up." Her face is red, and sweat trickles down her cheeks.

We all look to Mr. Dickerson, who rides in silence, his head in his hands. He hasn't spoken since leaving his home. Mrs. Dickerson looks up from the nursing baby, her face drawn and eyes red from silent tears.

My fault. I should never have let Jethro get away.

It's James that decides our next move. He leads the oxen to the side of the road where the grass grows deep, and while the rest of us catch up, he goes to the wagon bed, lifts Harvey from his perch on the pile of goods, and lowers him to the ground.

"Here you go, little man." His voice catches in that awkward way boys have when hormones start to kick in. "Stretch your legs while we get something to eat. Father, are you well enough to stand?"

Mr. Dickerson looks up as if just aware that the wagon has stopped. He nods, scoots forward until his feet strike the ground, then turns toward his wife.

"Rebecca, are you well?"

Mrs. Dickerson gives a thin smile. "Yes, husband."

He stands, blinks hard, and pushes the hat back from his head. His eyes rest on William, who lies staring up at the cloudless sky.

"Son?"

William turns his head. "Fawther?" A line of drool drips from the drooping side of his mouth. He tries to sit up, one arm hanging loose at his side. Half his face draws tight. "Wha' happened?"

Mr. Dickerson cries out and rushes to where his son lies, clambering up next to him. He lifts William's head and cradles it like his wife cradles the baby.

"William! Oh, God forgive me for not seeing to you sooner. Do you hurt, boy?"

William shakes his head. "Mothaw, the giwls?" he asks, thick-tongued and slurred.

"They're fine. Mother is right here. The girls are following. James is taking good care of us. Everyone is fine."

"I tried. Tried to stop them."

"Yes, I heard. You were very brave. Nancy? Margaret? Is there anything can be done for your brother?"

"They hurt you." William lifts his good hand to touch his father's bandage.

"Just a scratch. More of a headache than anything else."

Because of my father.

I spread a quilt in the shade, and with Nancy's help Mr. Dickerson lifts his son and limps to where it's laid. His wife hands the baby to Susan, then climbs down after them.

"William." She kneels beside her oldest son, smoothing his hair away from his face. "My boy." She swallows hard, straightens her back, and smiles down at him. "You should have listened to your father and stayed put. Look at you. But don't worry. Now that you are awake, you will get better in no time. Do you agree, Samuel?"

Her husband looks away. "William is as strong as those oxen, and his will is stronger. I'm sure you are right, Rebecca. Let me see to getting some water and check on the others. He turns his back, wiping his face with the back of his hand.

Did my father ever cry over me? No, Daddy says tears are for the weak minded. Mr. Dickerson doesn't seem weak minded to me.

The milk can is dragged off the cart, and Martha hands out bread and sliced meat. We sit and eat, too tired to converse.

Mr. Dickerson returns carrying a bucket dripping with water.

"There is a creek not far." He motions. "Everyone drink. Then I need to get some to the animals.

"You're not going to boil it first?" I say without thinking. I often speak without thinking.

"It is for drinking, young lady, not to cook. We ate already."

"But, but—it might have germs."

He peers into the bucket and shakes his head. "Looks perfectly clear to me."

I've read about dirty water in these times. Didn't more soldiers die from cholera and typhoid than did of actual war injuries? Maybe I can make up for who I am by keeping them safe from the water.

"Sir, it doesn't matter what the water looks like. Germs that cause diarrhea and other illnesses are too small to see. If you boil the water, it kills them off. Trust me on this one."

He raises one brow and looks at me with a sidelong glance. "If they are too small to see, how would you know they are there?"

"I have been drinking water all my life and never boiled any of it." James stares down into the bucket.

"Water from wells is usually safe. It's the rivers and creeks that can be a problem. You can't know what is upstream, contaminating it."

Mr. Dickerson stares at me like I speak a foreign language.

I close my eyes in frustration. So, the germ theory hasn't become popular yet. How do I get them to understand? If only I had one of those fancy water filter gadgets Adeline used to take kayaking with her.

"Father," Mary Elizabeth's gentle voice breaks in, "perhaps Anna Marie is correct. She was right about the soldiers, and we paid her no heed then. Have you thought that perhaps God has given her the wisdom we need at this moment? Besides, the milk will spoil in this heat. Let us quench our thirst with that for now, and tonight we can boil water."

When Mr. Dickerson nods his agreement, I release my breath.

With the livestock hydrated, we reload the wagon and head on our way.

I'm trying to remember the last time I drove to Arkansas from Kansas City. It took me about three hours on modern highways. We're starting about an hour's drive northeast of Kansas City, so I'm guessing we have about 250 miles to the border, if we can go straight. How long will that take for thirteen people, most of us on foot?

The cold fingers of fear creep over me. I step around so I'm walking alongside Mr. Dickerson. He's opted to walk and ease the burden on the oxen for a while. His irregular gait doesn't slow him down at all as he keeps an eye on William, who is asleep once more.

"Sir, what do you know of the road we're taking? Does it extend all the way to Arkansas?"

He nods. "This is the same route we sent your sister on earlier this week."

My heart leaps. Adeline! I'm getting closer!

"The army uses it with regularity, so my understanding is it is fairly well maintained throughout the state of Missouri."

Oh, dear. More soldiers. As if we didn't have enough to worry about.

"Sir, if my memory serves, we have nearly two hundred fifty miles ahead of us. If we can make as much as twenty miles in a day, it's going to take at least twelve days." I glance at the wagon with the hastily gathered supplies and at the people trudging alongside. "Sir, we are going to run out of food."

He combs gnarled fingers through his beard. "I hear you, Miss Anna. We must not worry. If God can send ravens with food for Elijah to sustain him for four years, I reckon He can provide our needs for a few weeks."

"But—" Panic rises. Going hungry is not high on my bucket list. In fact, it ranks just below experiencing typhoid and cholera. Granted, any of these would be preferable to being assaulted and burned to death, but still.

Mr. Dickerson chuckles. "Your point is well taken, Miss Anna. We will need to do some hunting along the way. Perhaps God will sustain us with game instead of through ravens."

William is awake for longer periods of time as the day progresses. I think this is a good thing. To Mr. Dickerson's dismay, his wife insists on walking part of the time to allow Joseph and the younger girls to ride. I knew she was tiny but didn't realize how frail she is until now, as she holds her husband's arm and moves along, checking on one child and then another as we progress.

"Is your mother ill?" I ask Mary Elizabeth.

She and Margaret have been next to me, chatting companionably as we walk.

Her eyes cloud with concern. "Ever since our little brother died three years ago, mother has struggled with digestive issues. She was not fully recovered when she became pregnant with Fannie, and since Fannie's birth, mother remains weak. She has episodes of fainting when she exerts herself. The doctor bled her once, but it only made her spells worse. Father would not let him repeat it."

I shuddered. These were long ago barbaric practices only read about in books. They shouldn't be happening now.

"Smart man, your father," I say.

She smiles. "Yes. But when it comes to Mother, he is all fiddle headed. If something happens to her, God help him, but he will be completely lost. Did you know they met when he was ten and she only six? He says his heart has been in her hands since that day, and he never once looked at any other girl."

"As much as he loves his children," interjects Margaret, "I believe it is watching Mother grieve their loss that causes him the most distress."

"She's lost more than one?"

"Three. So far," she says softly.

"I'm so sorry." I rest my gaze on William.

Live, William. Please live.

"Our family has faired better than most, with ten children still living."

The countryside is flat, for the most part, woods filling land that, in my time, is planted thick with corn or soybeans. Even now, there are cleared areas, a few fields planted in various crops I don't recognize. More lay fallow. When men are at war, hunger haunts where abundance once grew.

Evening is coming, and my feet burn with fatigue. I refuse to be the only one over eight complaining, so I keep going without saying a word. My endurance would likely be little better than Mrs. Dickerson's if I hadn't pushed myself to run and exercise since Adeline disappeared. One foot in front of the other. We round a corner in the road and come to an abrupt halt.

Ahead, the road ends with a jagged gash, and two feet below, a river rushes past.

Rivers and Soldiers

S TUCK.

James lead the oxen down the washed-out banks of the river, and now the wagon wheels are to the hub in mud, and no amount of pulling will get us unstuck.

While James unhooks the large, gentle beasts, content to stand up to their forelocks in water and relax, the girls, Joseph, and I get to work unloading the piles of goods we so carefully loaded into the wagon.

Mrs. Dickerson, exhausted from the journey, rests on a good old-fashioned trunk and nurses Fannie. Actually, when I think about it, it's a pretty modern trunk she sits on, for this time at least. I don't think I'll ever get used to this memory paradox. Mr. Dickerson is tending to William, who can sit up on his own now and perches on a pile of quilts, leaning just a wee bit to one side.

Whatever fashion designer decided women should wear street-length skirts needs to be hanged. There is no way I can carry an armful of stuff and lift my skirts out of the mud at the same time. By the time I'm done, I don't know what's heavier—the black iron kettle or the hem of my skirt.

"Someone is coming." Joseph jumps off the tail of the wagon and trips in the mud. It doesn't bother him that he's splattered from head to toe.

We look where he points, and coming from the south is a cluster of men on horseback. Their tattered gray uniforms mark them as confederate soldiers. My heart produces an uneasy shudder as they cross the shallow waters and ride up beside us.

"A bit of a problem, there, I see." The man in the lead brings the group to a halt. Ribs protrude from the horses' sides. The men look hungry too.

"Yes, sir." Mr. Dickerson rises to meet them. "My son was leading and did not realize how deep the mud was until too late."

"You from around here?"

"From Monroe. About twenty miles north, sir. Refugees. They burned our home. We are headed to Arkansas."

"All these yours?"

"Yes, sir, and a family friend."

The soldier looks straight at me. I'm the only one not fair skinned and blue eyed. I'd hoped the fact that we all have dark hair might help me blend in but guess not.

"She mulatto?"

"Half Mexican." I speak up.

If I were half African American, would they take me as an escaped slave? I can't remember my history well enough.

The lead soldier sneers and spits on the ground.

He surveys our pile of belongings, eyes lingering longer than I like on the two oxen, then resting on the milk cow as she grazes a few yards downstream.

"You gentlemen in a quarrel?" He gestures toward the bandages on Mr. Dickerson's forehead and the bruise across William's.

"Union soldiers. My boy was unconscious half the day. He seems steadier now."

A flicker of something akin to concern crosses the soldier's eyes. "Me and my boys will get you unstuck." He looks away as he speaks, shoulders sagging. He looks exhausted.

One man has a shovel tied to his pack, and with the extra help, the wagon is out of the mud and on the southern bank in no time. One man returns to help carry William while Mr. Dickerson assists his wife across the shallows.

"I am much obliged." Mr. Dickerson limps forward and extends his hand to the one in charge.

attached. What I don't follow is how they can believe they are dead yet simultaneously alive and hidden in Christ.

I think of Adeline, how everyone thought her dead, but she was alive and hidden in time. I don't think this verse is talking about that.

Recalling the morning's events, a familiar wrath broils in the pit of my stomach. My father. I promise myself that someday he will pay for what he did today. If there is a hell, that would suit me fine. Hell cannot be hot enough for the likes of him and Jethro.

Mr. Dickerson reads on. "Forbearing one another, forgiving one another." Not a chance. I will never forgive him. I will move on, find Adeline, and find Mama. That is enough. Someday, I'll make my father pay. If I'm lucky, I'll make him set things right for these people.

"And let the peace of God rule in your hearts, to which also ye are called in one body; and be ye thankful. Colossians 3:12-16." (KJV)

And what does *that* mean?

He closes the Bible.

"Amen," Mrs. Dickerson says.

"Amen." The other voices join hers.

My voice is silent. I sit in the shadows and watch. There is no peace in my heart. I cannot be thankful for any of this.

Mr. Dickerson assigns us to team up for night watch duty. Mary Elizabeth asks to join me, and he nods. We get first watch.

Mrs. Dickerson makes her rounds, checking on each of us, tucking the blankets closer around the younger children. When she comes our way, she kneels in front of us.

"Are you girls holding up well?"

"Yes, Mother." Mary Elizabeth leans forward and places a kiss on her mother's cheek. "You better rest. We will be fine."

Then she turns to me. Her eyes are gentle as she searches my face. A ripple of bells, and the gurgling sound of water wafts over me.

"It has been a difficult day for you, dear Anna." Her tiny hand rests on my knee. My knee feels strangely warm beneath her cool fingers. How can she concern herself with me after all that has happened to them today? "I thank you for warning us. You are not at fault that we did not heed you. I am grateful you are with us."

Does she know it was my father who tore them from her home? She must not. She thinks I'm innocent. Rising, she rests her hand on my head. It reminds me of when the priests would bless us when we were children.

Returning to the wagon, she hovers over William, placing a hand on his chest. Head bent over him, she closes her eyes. Her lips move, but I can't hear what she says. Her hand rises and falls with his breathing. Opening her eyes, she gazes at her son. A tear glistens in the moonlight.

"Be well, sweet William," she whispers, then moves to the side of the wagon where her husband lies. She lifts the quilt and snuggles close to him.

I look away. Nestled with our back against a cluster of River Birch, a quilt pulled around us and insulating our body heat against the encroaching coolness, Mary Elizabeth and I can see both the road and the river. Little by little, the gentle chatter around the fire dies down, and all appear to sleep.

"It must be amazing to have such a big family—and everyone gets along."

"It is never boring." My companion laughs, a quiet chuckle so she doesn't wake anyone. "And we *mostly* get along. James and Joseph get to manhandling each other at times, but mother says it is the way of boys. Not William, though. He was born protecting us all, I think."

"Martha is the eldest, right? How close in age are you?"

"Martha just turned twenty-one. She is eighteen months older than I, Nancy a year younger. Margaret is seventeen, William sixteen."

I remember when I first met the Dickersons, and William came rushing in, worried Jethro had hurt my sister. "William sure had Jethro pegged."

"William is not patient with men like Jethro. They have had words in the past. Jethro once was keen on Margaret. She may be the prettiest of us girls, but she has more spunk than most and dealt with Jethro just fine. Still, William had a prolonged conversation with Jethro about respect and the proper channels for courtship. Then when Adeline came around, Jethro took after her like one obsessed. Only he said since she was no proper lady, he did not need to follow proper channels. You can imagine what William had to say about that!"

"Jethro is a dreadful person." I'm really good at stating the obvious.

Mary Elizabeth sighs. "He was not always so bad. Their farm borders our own, and he used to love to hang around with Father and Mother when he was younger. His home—well, it never was a place of peace. He asked Father if he could live with us, way back before everything happened. Father said no, his family needed him. Father often wonders if he did the right thing, but he had no way of knowing. Jethro has had to live through things most people can only imagine." Mary Elizabeth stares off into the darkness.

I'm thinking it doesn't matter what kind of home you grew up in, that doesn't excuse the things he's done.

"When Jethro was ten years old, his ma gave birth to twins, a boy and a girl. They were tiny and cried all the time. So did she. She was never a happy woman, mind you, but the twins took the life right out of her. She stopped bathing, neglected the other children, would hardly eat. One day Jethro came in from working out in the field with his father and found his ma sitting by a washtub full of water, swaying and moaning. The babies were in the tub. She had drowned them both."

"No!" A sudden surge of sorrow wells up and threatens to choke me.

"Yes. He nearly strangled his mother right then, likely would have had not his father stopped him. She went mad, and Jethro helped care for her until she died three years later. She threw herself off the bluffs south of our place, or so he says. There were rumors, but considering what she did, no one questioned him. He only grows angrier and more belligerent with time."

"I see." Despite myself, I feel a tad sorry for the guy. Just a tad, though. That's all I can spare.

"Mother and Father care deeply for him. I think they feel guilty that they did little to help after Mrs. Tanner gave birth, Mother lost a baby of her own at the time. Still, knowing what Jethro has been through, do you understand why I must forgive him for his involvement this morning? For all his threats, I do not believe he would have hurt us, not us."

I shudder and shake my head. "You're wrong." I can still see the newspaper announcement reporting the fire, unknown number dead. "I'm glad we're away from him."

"What of your father? That must have been difficult to find him in that manner. Adeline said he left your family when you were little girls."

My eyes narrow, and I feel the muscles in my jaw tighten. "Yeah. I don't want to talk about him."

"Forgive him, Anna."

"After what he did? You wouldn't say that if he'd killed William."

"He is broken, like Jethro."

"No. He's just an arrogant, selfish man who never loved anyone. He doesn't deserve forgiveness."

"None of us do."

I don't answer. She's exactly right. I've brought trouble with me wherever I go. I'm as unlovable and unforgivable as my father. It's in the blood.

"We cannot live angry, Anna Marie. It is like wood rotting from the inside. As tough and strong as we may be on the outside, anger will destroy us in the core. Peace comes only with forgiveness."

"I hope he dies." I pull the quilt tighter over my shoulder, retreating into what warmth it provides against the ice in my heart. "I expect I'll never see him again, so it doesn't matter."

Mary Elizabeth's hand reaches for mine and pulls it onto her lap under the quilt, drawing me close. She rests her head on mine. Adeline used to comfort me like this. And Mama did too. Then, there was Jacob.

"It matters, sweet girl. It matters. But all will come in God's time."

What matters to me is that we make it to Arkansas, and that I find my sister.

BUSHWHACKERS

THIS IS SO MUCH harder than I imagined. We are on the fifth day of our journey, and I've nicknamed the remaining ox 'Snail.' That's the pace we seem to take. The landscape is crisscrossed with creeks and small rivers. The worst are the swampy areas where we have to detour wide off the path to find ground dry enough to pull the wagon. We can cross some creek beds easy enough. Others drop off for several feet where the soil has washed away. For these, we have to unload the wagon and push and pull to prevent our wheels getting stuck in the mud again.

Mrs. Dickerson tunes in to our discouragement and tries to cheer us by singing lively tunes. The rest of us join as best we can until we need to save our breath for the exertion of walking, and walking, and walking.

Game is scarce, and our supplies run low. I think of Bellona, with her nose to the ground picking up the scent of squirrels.

I don't think we've reached the halfway mark yet. We hope to make it to Nevada, Missouri soon. Maybe we can purchase more food there.

William walks more each day. His limp mimics his father's as they tread arm in arm, each adding support to the other. I made a makeshift brace for William, using sticks and a petticoat torn into strips. It keeps his knee from buckling, and he concentrates hard to move the leg forward. He's sullen and doesn't sing along. It's probably too hard to both walk and sing. When he walks, we have to move slower, but Snail can use the break. Mrs. Dickerson gets short of breath when she walks for more than a half hour at a time, so she rides more often.

It's time to break. James leads Snail off the side of the road to the grass. She's eager to eat. I don't think she's getting enough either. The verdant green grass of summer has changed to pale yellow. The warm weather will be gone soon.

My stomach growls loud enough to be heard in Kansas City as Nancy ladles out some stew from last night's meal. There's one corn cake each left from breakfast. There are small chunks of rabbit in the thin broth. She serves James first. He eats quickly, then heads to the woods with his rifle, hoping to find a squirrel or two.

Our meal is far from filling. I've never been this hungry in my life. Mr. Dickerson bows his head and thanks God for providing for our needs.

I see some tiny mushrooms, wrinkled brown umbrella shapes poking up from the soil next to where I sit. "These safe to eat?" I ask Martha, who has settled next to me.

She glances at them and shakes her head. "I wish they were. Even a small amount will cause dreadful cramping, diarrhea, and even paralysis."

But they look so good.

Little Harvey cries and begs his mother for more corn cakes. Mary Elizabeth wipes his cheeks and gives him a bone from the big pot to chew on.

"Well, look at this!" Men and horses step out of the woods.

I jump. Mary Elizabeth nearly drops her bowl, and Susan cries. None of us heard them approach.

The men remind me of some of the street gangs in my time, with red bandanas secured around their necks identifying what group they're with. "We arrived just in time for dinner!"

"We will be glad to share what little we have left." Mr. Dickerson rises and extends his bowl to the first man approaching. Long, oily, yellow hair hangs limp to his shoulders, and a thick mustache is stained brown. A wad of tobacco puffs out one cheek. His leather vest and ruffled shirt speak of a love for finer things, fine things now covered in filth. A pistol hangs from each hip.

"Bushwhackers!" Martha whispers, pulling Joseph and Susan to herself.

A waft of body odor floods the previously pleasant space as the man approaches. He slaps the bowl away, splashing the precious little nourishment on the ground.

"We ate." His lips curl in a smile that looks like a snarling dog.

Bellona smiles better. How I wish she were here right now.

"But you never know when need arises. We will see what else you have."

Mrs. Dickerson, grasping Fannie to her chest, moves away from the wagon as they approach. William stands in front of the wagon.

"We have no extra," he says, a slight slur to his speech.

"William, it will be all right." Mr. Dickerson's eyes plead with his son to back down.

"It is wrong, Father."

With lightning speed the man punches William on the side of the head, then laughs as he staggers, grabs for the side of the wagon, and slides to the ground.

"I decide what's right and what's wrong."

Both parents cry out and rush to William's side.

I act without thinking. Grasping a handful of mushrooms, I crush them into tiny bits in my hand, and stroll to the wagon. I only wish I could crush these men as easily. Today, however, I am not powerless. Not completely. I will make them pay.

I lift the tin with dried meats Mr. Dickerson has been saving for when we are truly desperate, open it and hold it close to my chest

"Take what you need. Just please, leave us the venison." Reaching into the tin, I rub the mushrooms into the dried pieces, pretending to smell the contents. I know bullies. As much as I hate to give up the meats, they'll take them no matter what we say.

A coarse laugh and a few lewd comments, and he jerks the tin from my hand.

I squint up one eye, and glare at the offender.

"May it inflame your gut and freeze your limbs," I mutter low, so only those close by can hear. "And worse to any who bother us after you."

He eyes me suspiciously before spitting out his chew and reaching in the tin. He makes a show of taking out a chunk, filling his mouth, and chewing.

"Delicious." He licks his lips.

I continue with the evil eye, or what I imagine an evil eye looks like to them. He laughs, too loudly. He reminds me of Georgie in grade school. Another bully, and Adeline his victim. Trying to scare him, I proclaimed a 'curse' on his food when he passed me in the cafeteria. Luck would have it, he had a bout of severe diarrhea that afternoon, and I got blamed for it. Luck would have nothing to do with the misery to come on this thug.

There are four of them, each dressed alike, except for some variation in hat style or color. They poke through our stuff, removing and tossing blankets and cookware carelessly aside. Opening the wood chest, they chuckle as they remove Mrs. Dickerson's prized serving plate and silverware.

"The silver will be easy to sell. Oops!" He opens his hand and the platter falls to the ground and breaks into pieces. "Well, that's sad. It was likely worth something."

"Stop right there!" My heart sinks as James steps out from behind a tree, his rifle aimed at the man closest to him.

Quicker than in the movies, eight pistols are directed at James.

"James, no!" Mr. Dickerson's voice rings out.

James's rifle wavers, and in that moment of indecision, it's snatched from his grasp, his arm is twisted behind his back, and he's thrown to the ground. I pray he doesn't resist.

He doesn't.

Piece-by-piece they rummage through the family's belongings. Everything of value that can be carried is taken. Even Mrs. Dickerson's books, except for her Bible. I sigh, relieved that they leave the wagon and Snail.

The men mount their horses and prepare to ride off. The lead halts and turns abruptly.

"I changed my mind," he says. "We might be getting hungry." And with his gun pointing directly at James, he grasps the lead on Snail's neck and pulls her away.

The Shadow of Death

THE MOON IS FULL tonight, illuminating the earth as if it were day. During the third watch of the night, the first seizure hits.

"Mother!" From her place in the wagon alongside her brother, Susan's voice pierces through the night, silencing the songs of frogs and crickets. "Something is wrong with William!"

With a flurry of quilts tossed to the side, we rise from our sleeping places, surrounding the wagon and peering over the sides at the young man. William's body convulses in rhythmic spasms, contracting and relaxing in turn with increasing frequency. His neck arches, and his eyes roll back so the whites alone are showing. Drool puddles at the corners of his mouth. His chest jerks, trying to draw breath. No cloudy mist comes from his mouth, like the ones from the rest of us.

I pull myself into the wagon, ignoring the splinters that tear at my palm, turn William on his side, and cradle his head to keep him from banging against the wood floor. The jerking movements nearly pull his head from my lap. I'm trying to remember my training.

Protect the patient. Turn on his side. Wait it out.

"What do I do?" Mrs. Dickerson breathes hard, her eyes wide.

"Keep him from hurting himself." I glance around me.

Eleven pairs of eyes stare from ashen faces.

I hope I'm right. "Here, keep him away from the sideboards. Make sure he doesn't hurt himself. And you—" I motion to Mr. Dickerson who has climbed up next to his wife. "Tend to the other side. Don't hold too tight. The seizure should stop soon."

They nod.

"What about us?" Nancy asks.

"He needs room, best stay back for now."

An eternity passes in the minutes that creep by until the seizure subsides. William makes a gurgling sound as he relaxes. With caution, I slip my finger in his mouth to make sure his tongue isn't blocking his throat. There's a gasp, a groan, and then normal breathing ensues.

"William!" Mrs. Dickerson shakes his shoulders. "William! Wake up!"

I still her hand. "He will sleep for a while. Don't move him."

Wringing her hands, she leans back, closing her eyes. Her lips move, but I can't hear what she's saying.

"Those men. They did this." Mr. Dickerson leans over his son.

A cloud of breath appears where William exhales. These men only finished what my father started.

"I suspect he had some swelling in his brain from the incident at the farm," I say, remembering the left sided weakness and slurred speech. Things seemed so much better. "The punch in the face must have aggravated it. I don't know. I'm no doctor."

James stands at a distance with slumped shoulders, his hands stuffed into his pockets. Tears stream down his face. When our eyes connect, he turns and hurries away.

The pale glow of moonlight gives way to the stronger rays of sun and much welcome warmth. We don't break camp, fearing to move William. His mother tends to him, wiping his forehead and dripping water into his mouth while speaking soft words only he can hear. Once or twice, his lashes flutter. He does not wake up.

Wandering up and down the creek bed, Mr. Dickerson and the older girls search for onions and frogs, non-poisonous mushrooms, or anything else to satisfy our appetites.

"James?" I lift my skirt as I step over fallen branches and walk around trees in the direction the boy took this morning.

I find him, curled against a rotting log, his face smudged black, tear streaks cutting paths through the grime. He sits up, pulling at his shirt and running a hand across his nose when he sees me.

"Hey, there," I say. "You all right?"

"Well enough." He scoots to the side, clearing a place for me to rest. "How is William?"

"Not so good." I lower myself beside him. "He hasn't awakened."

"I shoulda been there. Yesterday. I'da heard them coming. Father says I have the keenest ears of anyone he knows. I had the rifle. I should have stopped them."

I smile at the twelve-year-old man who had been a boy just a few days before. "Even if you heard the men coming, I don't think your one rifle could have stood up to the eight pistols they carried. Nothing we did would have stopped them."

"I'll track them down and kill them." His eyes narrow, and he sets his lips firm and straight. He looks just like William. "You wait and see."

"Not so sure your father will appreciate that," I say. "Isn't he against violence of any kind?"

"I do not care. They gotta be stopped."

I know how he feels. This lean, lanky boy, all knees and elbows, has tried so hard to be a man, to help where William normally did. He's fought to remain cheerful, to lighten the worry for the rest of the family. He hasn't complained. Not once.

"Can I trust you with a secret?" I ask.

He nods.

"Do you remember what I said to the leader? When I begged him not to take the tin of meats?

James's eyes narrow. "You cursed him. Are you a *witch?*"

"No." I chuckle to myself. "But I sure hope he thinks I am."

"Why?"

"If what I said happens, the ones who follow him will be scared to death of me and will spread the word to leave us alone."

"How is anything going to happen?

"I rubbed poison mushrooms all over the dried meats." I let what I said soak in.

James's eyes grow wide and his grin is wider. "Those worthless vermin are likely sick as death right now."

"I hope so, James. I hope so."

The Bible says God wants vengeance for Himself, I am told. Today, it is mine.

The second seizure hits mid-morning. William jerks and spasms until his lips are blue. The effort of keeping him from thrashing against the sides of the wagon leaves us exhausted. He doesn't wake up. When I pull back his lids, I notice his pupils are large and fixed, despite the brightness of day.

We wander around the trampled remains of our campsite, distracting ourselves with simple tasks, trying to keep busy, while remaining close at hand.

When Mr. Dickerson comes back into camp with no food to show for his searching, I take him aside, my heart heavy. "Go, talk with him." I squeeze his arm. "He hears you. The hearing is the last thing lost."

It's weird how they take my word for things. No one questions me.

James stands by his brother but manages only a few words before he hurries off. The sisters huddle together, ever watchful.

Sitting close to his oldest son, Mr. Dickerson leans into his wife for comfort. He reads from the only book not taken from them—the large family Bible.

"The Lord is my shepherd; I shall not want."

I look around me. Here is a God-fearing family that never did anything to hurt anyone. *You could do better than this, at least for them*, my thoughts scream at whatever God might be listening.

"He maketh me to lie down in green pastures: he leadeth me beside the still waters."

Not much on the green grass, but the creek is slow moving. You did that much at least. But it's not enough. Unlike sheep, we can't eat grass. Green or otherwise.

"He restoreth my soul:"

Maybe for them. My soul is past restoration. Were these Bible verses meant only for good people, like the Dickersons? How can they love a God like the one they worship? Why would God take everything from them, yet promise to restore their souls?

"He leadeth me in the paths of righteousness for his name's sake."

Agitation stirs in my gut. *God, these people are righteous already. If you're so powerful, why don't you stand up for them?*

"Yea, though I walk through the valley of the shadow of death—" Mr. Dickerson's deep voice breaks. He buries his face in his hands, and great sobs shake his frame. "I will fear...no...evil: for thou art with me." (Psalm 23:1-4, KJV) With a groan, he closes the Bible.

"Oh, Rebecca, Rebecca. Forgive me. I cannot bear it."

His wife covers his massive gnarled hands with her tiny ones, bringing her face close to his so their foreheads touch, and with tears glistening on her cheeks, she whispers something only he can hear.

Great sobs break loose as Mr. Dickerson clings to his wife. She holds him like she's comforting a small child. Then she sings. It is soft, but it carries over the camp and stills us all. It breaks me. I am witness to something I cannot explain. While my soul screams at God, her sweet, clear soprano voice is a soothing salve over the sorrow in our hearts.

"God moves in a mysterious way, His wonders to perform; He plants His footsteps in the sea and rides upon the storm." With one arm soothing her husband, she reaches with the other to smooth William's dark hair from his brow and tucks the blanket around his shoulder.

"Deep in unfathomable mines of never failing skill, He treasures up His bright designs and works His sovereign will."

A broken baritone joins hers, and together, father and mother weep and sing over their son.

"My times of sorrow and of joy, Great God, are in Thy hand. My choicest comforts come from Thee, and go at Thy command."

I cannot bear to watch and retreat to the far corner of camp. I am too angry to rest and too weary to cry.

The third seizure comes as night falls, and when it is gone, so is William.

BROKEN AND HUNGRY

WE CANNOT LINGER.

Hunger gnaws, and we have no remedy with our supplies gone and our only rifle taken from us. With great effort, we summon up sufficient energy to dig a grave, placing it far enough from the creek bed so when floods come, his body will remain on solid ground. I have no idea how far it needs to be to avoid contaminating the water itself, and frankly, I can't think about it.

Wrapped in his favorite quilt, we lower William into the earth. Mr. Dickerson reads from his Bible. Then, together, we push the soil back in place.

I do the sign of the cross, for the first time missing the necklace with the delicate silver crucifix Tia Lupe gave me and insisted I wear over the years. It hangs on my headrest back home, placed there the day Tia was buried.

As the last clump of dirt is pressed into place, Mrs. Dickerson falls to her knees, one hand on the freshly packed soil, the other over her heart. Silent sobs rack her frail frame. Martha, Mary Elizabeth, Nancy, and Susan cling to each other, clustered tightly beside their father. Margaret leans on him, Fannie's tight curls nestled under her chin. Joseph grips his father's hand. His face gaunt and chin trembling, Mr. Dickerson stares, his eyes void.

"Mama! Hold me!" Harvey pulls on his mother's skirt.

Like me, James stands alone, his expression dark and eyes red from crying.

Desolation. Total desolation weighs down on us so heavy, it takes effort to breathe. Despondency. Annihilated. Abandoned.

"God," I whisper. "How much more?"

In silence we disassemble the wagon of all but it's bare bones, and Mr. Dickerson adapts the halter so two people can pull in place of the ox. We leave the wood chest over the grave, along with the iron pot and a few farm items. Perhaps William won't feel so abandoned with memories of home close by.

Mr. Dickerson says William is no longer here, so leaving these things near him serves no such purpose. Still, since we can't carry them anymore, we leave them guarding the site.

The water bucket is secured in the corner of our altered wagon, the Bible and wedding portrait wrapped with care and placed among the folds of quilts.

The vacant space on the wagon floor is a stark reminder of what is lost.

For a long moment, Mr. Dickerson gazes at his son's final resting place. With a sigh, he pulls the halter over his shoulder, James takes up the other, and we begin to walk south once more.

One step and then another. Two hours later, we stop, and Mary Elizabeth and I insist on taking a turn.

"You are girls!" Mr. Dickerson protests, shaking his head. "The boys and I will handle this."

In my day, those are fighting words. Mary Elizabeth responds with a tired laugh.

"Do not be silly. We know we are girls." Her drawn face shows concern for her father as she removes the straps from his shoulders. "You raised us strong, Father, but we need you not to kill yourself. And seeing as Joseph cannot carry this load, we must help."

He doesn't argue. Fatigue lines his face, and his shoulders droop. James hands over his harness without a word. Mr. Dickerson checks on his wife, who lies asleep in the wagon bed, her small body curled around her infant child.

Hours pass. We stop only to rest, drink from our diminishing store of water, and to switch turns pulling the wagon. Mrs. Dickerson walks intermittently, holding and kissing each of her children as she moves between them. They cling to each other.

All but James. He walks apart. Silent.

"I'm hungry!" Susan drags on Nancy's arm. "I'm tired. Why does Father not stop so we may eat?"

"Be quiet, little girl." Nancy doesn't say much. Of all the sisters, she is the one I know the least. She seems so much older than her eighteen years. She melts into the background and watches. "God will provide. We must be patient."

The emptiness in my stomach has reached the point of physical pain. But at least it distracts from the ache in my heart. My head pounds, and I'm long past the point of breaking out in a hunger sweat.

"What I would give for a slice of pizza right now?" I say.

"What is pizza?" asks Susan.

"It's my favorite food—it's Italian."

She scrunches her nose and looks up at me. "Are you Italian? I thought you told the soldier you were half Mexican. I do not know any Italian people."

"I am half Mexican, but where I come from, there is an Italian restaurant near my house, and they have the best pizza." I think of Jacob, startled and stepping back in response to my angry outburst during our one and only date.

"What is a restaurant?" Margaret speaks up. It appears my talk of food is drawing an interested crowd.

"It is an eating establishment," Nancy answers. "Mostly providing soups, from what I have read. They are popular in France and in some big cities like New York and Boston. Is that right, Anna? Are you from a big city?"

"Where I'm from, restaurants provide all kinds of food, like an Inn or diner. It's where you go to eat if you can't eat at home."

"Oh!" Susan's brows draw together. "Do you think there might be a restaurant in Nevada?"

"I will be happy with a general goods store!" Mary Elizabeth says. "Or a bakery!"

"I would be grateful for some kind person sharing a bowl of porridge with us," says Margaret.

"Tell me about the pizza," James' eyes are large, expectant.

"It's delicious." I close my eyes, seeing Jacob, sitting on my doorstep with a box of fresh, hot pizza, that quirky half smile lighting his face. I don't remember if I ever thanked him. My mouth waters and I rub my rumbling stomach. "They make a dough and toss it in the air over and over to form a thin disc about yea big." I motion with my hands. "Then it's put on a large flat pan, covered with a special tomato sauce—"

"Eww! Tomatoes?"

"Hush, Susan." Nancy places a restraining hand on her little sister's shoulder.

"Tomatoes make the best sauce," I say. "After the dough is covered with a layer of tomato sauce, it is covered with lots and lots of cheese, then baked until the dough is cooked and the cheese turns golden at the edges."

James is licking his lips. I swallow. The smell of garlic and cheese lingers heavy on my memory.

"My favorite food is corn mush with honey." Susan takes my hand in hers. "Mother always makes that for my birthday."

"Fried bacon." Mary Elizabeth smiles. "Cooked so the ends are all curled and crisp."

"Sarah's apple crisps," Margaret says.

The food talk continues, and somehow, our fatigue is more tolerable and our hunger pangs less intense.

"Daddy will be angry. You can't do that, Adeline!"

"But she's cold. I have another coat at home. Daddy won't know."

"I'll tell."

"No, you won't. I'll get spanked if you do." She shrugs off her brand-new coat.

I look over at the mother watching her two little girls on the swing set. Her face is drawn tight, and dark circles line the otherwise pretty eyes. Their clothes are washed of color, and their sweaters are so thin in places, their shirts show through.

"Daddy doesn't want us talking to people like them."

"I've played with Mattie before. She's nice. She doesn't have a daddy, just her mommy. That makes her like us—except we have a daddy and no mommy."

The park is two blocks away from our house, and most of the children who play here come with their nannies or their mothers. Mama has been gone for four months now, and we come alone. With the bicycles Daddy gave us for our birthday, we ride to the park by ourselves while Mona gets dinner ready. We're always careful to be home before Daddy gets there.

Mattie's lips are blue, and her little sister, Emma, shivers as well.

"Fine. Then Emma can have mine." I shrug off my own.

Adeline looks at me with wide eyes. "Really?" She jumps with excitement and wraps her arms tight around my neck. "This is so much fun! Let's go!"

She grabs my hand and dashes across to the swings. "Mattie, Emma, would you like these? We have more coats at home, And you look cold."

The girls' excitement matches Adeline's as they ooh and aah over the plush colorful coats, still warm with our body heat. Their mother cries and kisses the tops of our heads. I don't like that so much but shrug it off. Adeline and I laugh, get on our bikes, and hurry home before we freeze.

"Daddy can't know," Adeline says. "He'll make us take them back. Promise you won't tell."

I promise.

I haven't had such a good time in a long while.

Daddy is home and at the table when we rush inside. Adeline's cheeks shine rosy red, and we are both shivering to the core. Maybe Daddy won't notice.

"Where are your coats?"

My heart sinks at the first words to come out of his mouth. "Coats?" I ask stupidly.

"Yes, coats, like the things you wear in the cold, the ones we bought last week?"

Adeline stands silently, looking at her feet.

"Oh. Those," I say. "I don't know."

"You don't know?" Daddy's face turns as red as Adeline's, but I don't think it's from the cold.

"Um, I think we lost them."

"You lost them. Where might you have both lost your coats?"

"School?" My mind is racing, trying to think of a story Daddy will believe that won't earn us a spanking.

Adeline kicks gently at the leg of the table, tears brimming in her eyes. She won't look at Daddy or at me.

"Mona, did the girls have their coats when you picked them up from school?"

"Yes sir."

Daddy looks at me, then Adeline, then back at me. He knows we're hiding something.

"Go to your room." He stands and points his finger at our door.

We obey. As we walk, I can feel my backside burning already.

"People who are careless with their belongings end up being poor." Daddy walks past us to our bedroom window. "If you are poor, you don't have the comfort of a warm house or decent food." He raises the window pane. A blast of cold air makes the curtain puff inward. "Tonight you will sleep with the window open and go to bed without your supper. See if you like it. And then think long and hard about taking better care of your things."

He closes our door firmly behind him and leaves us standing there.

We stare after him in shock that we got off so easily. I rub my backside. "Whew! That was close."

We laugh and rush to the window, leaning out to watch people as they pass.

Soon our laughter gives place to chattering teeth, and we move away from the open window and crawl into our beds, pulling the blankets up around our necks.

The aroma of warm food somehow permeates the room despite the closed door, and my stomach growls. I've never skipped a meal before, and being hungry is not an experience I care for. Tossing and turning in bed, I look out the window and watch as the sky turns from blue to pink to black.

"Adeline?"

"Uh, huh?"

I jump across to Adeline's bed, dragging my blanket with me and spread it over hers. I crawl in next to my sister and snuggle close.

"I'm starving," she says.

"Me too."

"Do you wish we didn't do it?"

"No. I'm glad."

"Me too."

We lay, giggling at the rumbles of each other's stomachs.

"Thank you for not telling, Anna." Adeline smiles at me and clasps my hand.

"Yeah," I say. "But tomorrow, I'm asking Mona to make us pizza."

Gravemounds and Respite

"LOOKS LIKE THE ARMY camped here recently." Mr. Dickerson drops his harness, letting the wagon tongue dip into the ground. "It's as good a place to rest as any."

In the gathering dusk, lights flicker on the rise just south and east of us. The night air has a chill to it, different from others this week. We've been fortunate the warmth has lasted this long. A ring circles the moon tonight. I think that means something, but I don't remember what it is. I am utterly and hopelessly ignorant. Despite the layers of clothing we wear, I hope it doesn't portend snow.

"That would be Nevada." Mary Elizabeth sighs, gesturing at the lights in the distance as she removes Joseph from her shoulders and rubs her neck. "It's not much of a city anymore. The Union burned it two years back. We hear they have restored the mill and a few other necessities, so perhaps they have food for purchase. We should make it there mid-morning."

Mrs. Dickerson scoots off the wagon and massages her lower back. "Children, let us investigate and see if the soldiers left anything behind that may be of value. Samuel, if you could fetch us some water, I am very thirsty. Our supply is depleted."

Discarded fire pits dot the clearing, and the freshly trampled ground tells a tale of many feet and hooves residing here. A broken chair leans against a tree, and a crutch is tossed aside into tall grass.

A cry of excitement brings us running to find Martha holding high a cracked saddle bag. Inside is a soldier's ration pack, containing a handful of rice, peas, and dried beans, along with three rolls of hardtack and a small pouch containing salt. For all the turkeys slaughtered on the first Thanksgiving Day, the pilgrims could not have been more thankful than we are tonight. This is a feast.

While Martha runs to deliver the food to her mother, the rest of us explore through the oncoming dark, scouring the clearing with renewed enthusiasm.

Soldiers are filthy creatures. It's obvious none of these men were trained in the Boy Scouts, taught to dig trenches for their latrines or to cover their messes. The woods here are full of hazardous deposits, and the stench of excrement and rotting leaves permeates the air.

Hurrying back toward the clearing, I trip, falling face first atop of a mound of earth. As I look up through the dark shadows, the shape of a cross looms over me. I scramble to my feet, brushing the dirt from my hands and skirt. To my left is another mound, to my right four more. Each marked with a cross or a stone.

Did these men die in battle, or was there illness in the camp? I rack my brain, trying to remember my Missouri Civil War history, and can't remember anything. Why didn't I pay better attention in class? What I see frightens me.

"I'm not so sure we should remain here," I say when I return to camp.

"Why do you say that?" Martha asks.

"There was sickness, I think. The men, their bowels were loose. The stench by the water is pretty bad, and I found some fresh graves. There's not been any battle here recently that you know of, has there?"

"I think we are not able to walk any further tonight. We will be gone first thing tomorrow." Mr. Dickerson looks around at the faces staring up at him.

"Okay, well, just be extra careful about what you eat and drink."

Several people glance at each other, and my stomach feels like it's pushed its way into my shoes.

"Don't tell me you drank the water before boiling."

"Just a bit," Mrs. Dickerson replies. "We are fine. Still, we will be more careful hence."

Around the fire, the family carries on in a tired, sedate manner, the memories of the theft of belongings and the death of a brother are a heavy weight tucked aside so we have strength to survive the present. The water bucket, on the fire with the contents from the soldier's rations, fills us with hope for tomorrow.

As I do every night, I miss Bellona's warmth curled against my legs. Fatigue has its benefits, and we sleep hard, awakening chilled but ready to be on our way.

Like Mary Elizabeth predicted, we arrive at Nevada, Missouri mid-morning. I wonder if Adeline passed this way.

A cluster of houses nestle close to the water mill, making up what was once a thriving city. Blackened skeletons of homes dot the landscape and line the street. A church, its whitewashed siding stained black on one side where the fire failed to burn through, stands at the corner of a square that at one time was lined with fine shops and the mayor's office. No shops are standing. Perhaps the mill has supplies.

A young man walking across a pasture pauses, then hurries to the farmhouse overlooking the mill. A sheep on the end of a rope follows behind him.

As we approach the house, a grandmotherly figure comes out the front door, rifle in hand.

"Who are you, and what are you needing?" She asks. She holds her rifle down at her side, a precaution, not a threat.

"I am Samuel Dickerson, and this is my family. We come from Monroe County, up north."

She squints at him. "What you northerners doin' down here? You Union boys?"

"No ma'am. I do not believe in killing. I will not take sides in this unjust war."

"Ha!" Her laugh is coarse. "So they burned you out, did they? Them's can't tolerate someone as not sides with them."

"Yes ma'am. That is exactly what happened."

"Got some place to go?" Her lips pucker up over the vacant space where teeth should be.

"Family in Arkansas."

"And you lookin' for food and shelter?"

"We can pay."

"Good. Not as money does much good in these parts, but it's better than beggars. Road was full o' them all summer. You folks running late. Come on in, the sorry bunch of you. Y'all need to share beds—'twill be tight, but the place is warm and dry. Best get yourselves in. A storm be comin'."

I look at the clear blue sky. Gusts of warm air is blustering, causing ripples in the uncut grass. The branches of the only unburned oak in front of the house sway back and forth, rustling the few remaining leaves.

"They call me Granny Gray." She pats each one of us on the shoulder as we pass in front of her to enter the house. When it's my turn to enter, she rests her hand on my arm, bringing me to a halt.

"I seen you look up at that there sky like I was a crazy woman. Look. You see how the wind blows them branches? That means the cold air be coming, and cold and hot care none for each other. They fight for which gets to stay. My bones be telling me the cold is gonna win this one. You be seeing. I ain't no crazy woman. When your bones get old as mine, they be telling you stuff too."

I like Granny. Her wrinkles remind me of Mona. Her eyes remind me of Tia.

Granny Gray knows the needs of travelers and soon has water pumped from the well and heating over a large iron stove.

"Get your aching bones washed clean, then your clothes. Lord have mercy, but from the looks of you, I think you be needing a bit o' nourishment."

She retreats to the fireplace. A pot similar to the one we left with William hangs over the flames. The scent of meat makes my mouth water as we go about washing while waiting for the stew to cook.

When I think my stomach will eat itself from being so empty, we are called to eat. Steaming bowls line the pine table, and we nearly forget our manners in our eagerness.

"This is amazing," I say.

The thick, brown broth warms its way down my throat and into the heart of my soul. Chewy chunks of fibrous meat float among carrots and potatoes.

"Have I died and gone to Heaven?"

Mrs. Dickerson blanches, and I remember William. Me and my big mouth.

"That there's bear meat." Granny nods at our bowls. "My boy is a good hunter."

Over dinner, Granny Gray fills us in on the news for these parts.

"Union passed by a month back but didn't bother coming this way. Figure they done took all as worth anything anyway. Them Bushwhackers come by once or twice, but we just give em some grain, and they done leave us alone. We pretty good at hiding our livestock."

Grandma Gray motions out the window. "My son be getting here late this evening, I 'spect. He be makin' sure the mill secure with the storm comin' on. That be his boy you saw coming in. My daughter and her young'uns live across the way, so we's got ourselves all close here. Most of the townsfolk as survived moved out after the fire."

"We are grateful to you for sharing what you have." Mrs. Dickerson's voice is soft. "I pray we are not a burden to you. I know times are hard for everyone."

"My husband, God rest his soul, was a trapper." Granny Gray grins wide. "Afore we had young'uns, I ran the trail with him. We knows how to keep soul connected to the bones."

"We have much to learn." Mr. Dickerson sighs. "Any help you can extend our way, well, it might save the rest of the family."

Grandma Gray's eyes draw close, and her puckered lips frown.

"This war's taken more from us as we is willing to give. God be the great equalizer. Them's as acts gracious, He will reward. Thems as not, so help them, but God will make things right. I help where's I can. I know this country like it was my own backyard. I be teaching you some things if'n you listen."

We listen. As we do, clouds darken the sky.

PROMISES AND ANGEL CHOIRS

"IT BE MADNESS LEAVING with winter setting in." Granny Gray putts around her kitchen, wrapping the last bits of supplies for us to carry.

"We thank you for the reprieve." Mary Elizabeth takes the sack from her. "But our surest move is to hurry on our way and pray we arrive before the worst of the winter months hit. Our numbers would deplete your stores much too quickly."

"Pish, posh!" Grandma Gray waves a hand, but she has to know it's true. She hugs Mrs. Dickerson, places a kiss on Fannie's forehead, and shakes James's hand as we head out the door.

"God bless you for your kindness." Mr. Dickerson's deep voice trembles. "It was an honor spending Thanksgiving with you and your family."

We look quite different from the company that straggled in nearly two weeks earlier, haggard cheeks quickly filled with abundant food. Costumed in an array of worn furs the old woman rustled up, we could pass for a band of Native Americans. Pale, blue-eyed natives. Except for me. I fit the part.

"Betwixt here and Jasper is bushwhacker territory. Blend in the woods where's you can, and keep alert. I marked on the map where my man set his lean-tos. 'Less they been raided, they got you some basics there and some shelter. Set yourself the trap of an evening, and with luck you'll have meat by mornin'. Save the shootin' for emergencies. You want no one knowing your whereabouts if'n you can help it."

She surveys our ragtag group, nodding with satisfaction. "James and

Margaret, you two remember what my boy taught you about them traps? Keep sure they's greased regular-like so as not to lock up with rust. A rusty trap ain't no good to nobody."

With the assistance of Grandma Gray's son and grandson, they have converted our wagon into a glorified, backward facing wheelchair. It won't carry much in the way of supplies, but we don't have enough of those to worry about. The new "carriage," as Susan calls it, is light, easy to maneuver, and just large enough for Mrs. Dickerson to ride with one small child nestled alongside her. I'm expecting her teeth will be shaken out of her head before we get two miles down the road, but it's better than having her pass out on the way.

The quilts bundle around the rations, and what belongings we have remaining are tied to our backs like large, lumpy backpacks.

As the sun rises, we're on our way, pushing forward, anxious to make shelter before nightfall.

No one crosses our path. We stop for a quick lunch of biscuits and dried bear meat.

Mrs. Dickerson nibbles on the biscuit, shakes her head, and hands the meat to her husband. "I am not hungry." she says, rubbing her temples. There's a flush to her cheeks.

We make good time, finding the shelter before dark, just as snowflakes begin to fall. If Grandma Gray was correct, we made just under thirty miles today. At this pace, and if the weather cooperates, we should make it to Arkansas in three to four days.

The lean-to hides the opening to a long narrow cave. As promised, a few pieces of cookware are stashed in the back along with split wood and blankets over moldy straw. James and I are famished. Everyone else is too tired to eat and collapses on the floor, ready to sleep.

"Does your head ache you, Rebecca?" Mr. Dickerson kneels before his wife as she nurses little Fannie.

"A bit, husband. I am sure it is nothing a good night's rest cannot cure."

"My head has been aching as well," Martha leans over to whisper to me. "I pray we are not getting the ague."

I awaken to hear Mrs. Dickerson rush out the entrance of the lean-to, gripping her stomach. When she returns, she lingers close to the mouth of the cave, moaning.

By morning she shivers with fever and begins retching. Mr. Dickerson rises, rubbing his temples. Beads of sweat stand out on his forehead despite the cool temperature of the cave. Martha coughs. James stokes the fire and turns wide eyes toward me, eyes reflecting the fear and concern I feel as well. I don't know what's going on, but it doesn't look good.

"Does anyone else feel sick?" I make my way to Mrs. Dickerson and place a hand on her forehead. "Mrs. Dickerson, you're burning up!"

Mr. Dickerson is hot to the touch. Martha says her head hurts, and her bones ache. I look all around me, suppressing the urge to bolt. I remember the mounds at the soldiers' camp, the crosses, the stones, the filth in the woods beside the creek, and my hands go clammy.

"Oh, no." I lean against the wall of the cave, nails digging into the cool, dirt-caked rocks.

"Who drank the water at the last camp? The one before Granny Gray's?"

"Mother, Father, Martha, and me. The rest of you were searching for supplies at the time, and we had the soup going by the time you arrived," Mary Elizabeth says. "We were so thirsty but did not drink much. Do you think it had those 'germs?'"

I pace, thinking. I'm too young for this. What to do. What to do. If I ever make it back to my time, I'll see they teach paramedics how to deal with nineteenth century illnesses.

"All right. Anyone who is feeling ill, let's bring your bedding to the back of the cave. Susan, can you be a big girl and keep the Harve and Fannie in the lean to? We want to keep them away, and maybe that will keep them from getting sick. James, Margaret, we need to fill every container with water and set it to heat."

"What about me?" Mary Elizabeth asks. "I am not ill, simply tired."

I look her over. She's pale. But that might be from the lack of good lighting.

"Rest. We're going to need it."

Once we have every pail, pan, and bucket full of water, I give a lesson in hand washing.

"Imagine that there are evil creatures all over our skin that are causing us to get sick," I say. "They are so tiny we can't see them. They call these bacteria."

James snickers but stops when Margaret glares at him.

"Lucky for us, these bacteria don't like hot water. They also float away when we pour clean water over them and scrub with soap." I raise the bar of lye soap Grandma Gray stuck in Father's pack.

To keep from spreading these bad bacteria, we have to wash our hands after each time we take care of someone who is ill. Whatever you do, don't touch your face with your dirty hands. Use the soap, and pour just enough water over them to rinse them clean. Don't reuse the water once it's contaminated. Does that make sense? James, can you check on the trap your father set last night and reset it? I will need you to be our guard and water boy today. Joseph, please help."

James nods and, without a word, leaves us.

Nancy sits at her mother's side, rinsing her forehead with a cool cloth. At first Mr. Dickerson paces but soon tires and sits beside his wife. By evening he is curled up beside her, huddled under a blanket, his teeth chattering. We force them to drink sips of water. I'm wishing for some Coca Cola or ginger ale. A good dose of antibiotics would save the day. By nightfall, Mary Elizabeth has the fever. The rest of us take turns sleeping and caring for the sick.

Morning comes, and our patients are no better. The day is long as we tend to our sick, and the night even longer. We work in shifts, catching a few hours of sleep, one person at a time, before rising to apply cool, wet rags to fevered foreheads and be sure the younger children are fed and cared for. Despite our attempts, we see no improvement. Mrs. Dickerson's lips are cracked, her stomach swollen. Her milk is dry. Margaret prepares some rice to feed the baby.

"God sent you." Mrs. Dickerson's soft voice interrupts my worried thoughts.

I'm leaning over her with a spoon of salted water. She reaches up to touch my cheek. "You have been an angel sent from Heaven for our time of greatest need." She smiles, and a drop of blood forms where her lips crack.

"No." I shake my head, blinking back tears. A tear escapes and drips down my cheek. "I brought trouble. I always bring trouble."

"None would be alive today, were it not for you."

I see Jethro in the barn, attacking Candace. I should have shot him dead right then and there. But I didn't know how to use the old rifle. My weakness gave him the opportunity for revenge.

"It was my fault. Jethro—" My throat closes, and I can't speak.

"No. I could take the blame. I did not help when Jethro needed it the most. But ultimately, it was Jethro's doing."

"My father—" I hesitate. Does she realize the captain is my father?

"I know." She places a hand over mine. Her fingers are cold. "I know about your father. But you are not your father."

She sighs. Her breathing comes in short tight breaths. The music that is her is growing louder in my ears.

"Thank you, Anna. I am at peace knowing my children have you with them. See that they make it to my brother. He will care for them."

I am crying and not ashamed to let my tears fall.

"Samuel?" She turns her head toward her husband. From where he sits keeping vigil over his wife, Mr. Dickerson reaches for her hand. His eyes are glassy, and spots of red dot the high points of his cheekbones.

"I am here, Rebecca."

"You have been a good husband, Samuel. A good father. I am happy I chose you."

He takes her hand and brings it to his parched lips. Tears stream down his cheeks, and he moans, pain etched across his face.

"No, Rebecca. Stay with me."

"My children?" She looks at me.

I meet her eyes and leave to call the younger ones inside.

"I am so proud." Her voice is a hoarse whisper. A feeble hand reaches and rests on the bowed heads of each of her children in turn. "May God's blessing be on you. I will always love you."

Her hand falls to her side, and she rests her head back on the roll and dozes. Her breathing becomes labored. A rattle from her lungs becomes more pronounced. I feel her hand tap my own, and when I look, she is gazing upward.

A smile breaks out on her face, and her eyes focus on some distant point on the cracked rock ceiling. The light jingle of bells and the soothing rustle of a babbling brook are fully absorbed into a choir of voices.

"Oh! Look, Samuel!" She gasps and points into the blackness above. "Look, Samuel! It is so beautiful!"

That is all. The swell of music fades. Her soul leaves, a smile marking her last goodbye.

Samuel lies beside her, wrapping long arms around her tiny body, and draws her close. Margaret puts her hand on his shoulder. Silent sobs wrack his frame.

"Oh, my Rebecca," he whispers into his wife's unhearing ear. "Light of my life. How will we go on without you?"

Martha is the next to leave us. She departs as she lived, softly, without a word. Never a complaint. One minute she thanked us for the water. The next she was gone.

Mr. Dickerson falls into delirium soon after midnight. We are grateful when he sleeps, but even his dreams cause him to cry. His hands search the blanket beside him as he calls his wife's name, then sobs and calls for William. He settles into a calm sleep as morning approaches, and we slip outside to see where we may bury our dead.

The ground is muddy from the melting snow. Water drips from the leafless branches overhead. The sun does not shine. The forest and sky have no color. Even the birds are silent.

We dig. We are too tired to dig deep, so we use rock from the hillside for the rest.

The children need tending. Susan's eyes are red and swollen. Fannie is crying. Margaret takes Joseph and Fannie outside for a walk while Nancy makes something to eat. I lower myself by Mary Elizabeth's bedroll.

She smiles and tries to sit up, but the effort is too much for her. "Did you hear about the wealthy man and the angel of death?"

"No." How can she joke right now?

"The man begs the angel to let him bring just one thing with him. The angel agrees, and the rich man runs into his closet and sticks a bar of gold into his bag. He drags it with him all the way to the Pearly Gates."

"Then what?"

"Saint Peter demands to see what is in the bag that he worked so hard to bring with him. When the rich man opens his bag, Saint Peter looks at him in astonishment. 'You brought paving stones?'"

She laughs. Dry coughs interrupt her laughing, and she gasps for breath. I hurry and bring a cup of water to her mouth.

"Do you see?" She says once she can breathe again. "The things that seem so important to us, they are not so important. Losing our home, not so bad. It is the people that count. You are my dear friend, Anna."

"William?" Mr. Dickerson cries out in the corner. "William, is that you?"

Margaret rushes to her father's side. "Father, I am here."

He looks at her but does not see her, staring blankly into the shadows. "Oh, William. You look so well."

Margaret begins to cry.

"No, Father, please. Not you too."

He mumbles, pats her hand, closes his eyes, and sighs heavily.

Mary Elizabeth squeezes my hand. Her palm burns against my own. "Father will leave us soon." A tear rises to the top of her lashes and runs across her nose. "Watch over James. It will be hardest on him. He blames himself. As God forgives, he must learn to forgive, both himself and others. Teach him this."

I nod, but it is a promise I can't keep.

"Anna?" Mary Elizabeth's eyes hold mine.

"Yes?"

"Do you recall that first day when you asked if I could hear the singing?"

I nod.

"I did, but thought I was imagining it. Today, when Mama died, I heard them. Anna, it was glorious. I will sing with them soon. Do not weep for me."

By that night, Mr. Dickerson and Mary Elizabeth have parted.

In the morning we bury our dead. One grave, four bodies.

We wash our supplies as best we can, burn the lean-to, the straw bedding, the scattered wood and brush inside the cave. I will not risk Granny

Gray's son coming to this spot and contracting whatever the Dickersons had, if we haven't left death in our wake already.

The mound of dirt and rock, with two sticks tied together to form a rough cross, are the only explanation we leave behind.

I want to sit right here, let the cold take over my bones, and die. I am weary beyond words.

First, I have to find Mrs. Dickerson's brother like I promised. Then I have to find Adeline.

My mind reaches. The events of the last few days have silenced all thoughts not immediate to the moment. I long for my sister, and there is solace when her music plays.

In the crisp wintry air, I bring a shaky hand to my forehead and look around. Nancy nods. Her shoulders droop, and tears shine in her eyes. She carries Fannie, tucked in a strap of cloth and secured to her like a modern baby wrap. Margaret places Harvey and our precious water can into the tiny carriage, and we walk.

One step follows another. I move on.

Eighty miles. On foot. With a six-month-old infant, a three-year old boy, four of us girls, and two boys, not yet teenagers, to protect us. We have enough food to last two days. One rifle, and a small trap. I'm dragging my gold bar to the Pearly Gates.

HE'S BACK!

THE RUGGED TERRAIN OF the Arkansas Ozarks has kept the populations isolated, and makes it a challenge to locate Mrs. Dickerson's family, the Hollidays. As luck would have it, we stumble across a boy carrying two large rabbits slung over his shoulder.

"The Hollidays?" His eyes sparkle in response to our query. "Don't know them personally, but my cousin might. He exchanged a prized pig for some lumber fine cut at the sawmill so as he could build his German bride a fancy house, city style."

"Was the owner of the mill a Holliday?"

"Oh, Heavens, no. Everybody knows the O'Brian's run the mill. It's while my kin was at the mill, another fellow as was there decided he would buy the pig. Seems he had himself a sow, but they ate the boar, and then they regretted it, there being no male around from which to propagate."

"He was a Holliday?"

"Shucks, no. He was the cooper. His pa has the still."

"Do you even know about the Holliday clan?" I ask, thinking perhaps this boy got into the whiskey maker's stock.

"That be what I was tryin' to explain. While's they was talking, and the wood was being cut, the miller mentions hows his wife is keen to get herself a piano, and he been trying to figure who in these parts could obtain such a fancy piece. That be when the cooper says as he tried to court this Holliday lass whose father makes musical instruments outta wood. My kin thought it comical that if the whiskey man and the music man joined clans they could all have a holiday!"

Oh, brother.

We drag our weary selves up the hill to the "fine" one room cabin where this boy's kinsman resides. He directs us to the miller, who has a general idea where the cooper lives but warns us that if we wander off the path and fall upon the still, we will get shot. Managing to avoid assassination, we locate said cooper who is still sweet on the Holliday girl, but heartbroken because she doesn't reciprocate.

The Hollidays own their own patch of mountain peaks and valleys, a day's hike from the mill. Reaction to our arrival is what I imagine the modern reaction would be to a space alien ship landing at the Saint Louis Arch. First, everyone scatters into the cluster of log cabins, slamming doors and barring them shut behind them. This feat is followed closely by muzzles of rifles and shotguns pointing out the windows, all carefully aimed in our direction.

"What is going on?" James raises his hands and nearly drops Harvey, who's riding piggyback.

I look at our scraggly group, covered in furs. "Look at us. We look like a bunch of hostiles ready to ambush."

I let my fur fall, as do the others, and we now appear to be what we are. Dirty, tired, hungry white folk, mostly children.

James calls out, "I am James Dickerson. Does Ian Holliday reside here? We are his family. My mother was his sister, Rebecca."

We proceed to be engulfed in an overwhelming amount of hugs and slaps on the back as relative after relative pours from their cabins to welcome us. We've arrived just before Christmas.

It's the beginning of March now. Blustery winds blow warm from the valley, and our little family has settled in the tiny "old house" or two-room cabin behind Uncle Ian's "big house," the new three-room cabin. There's a shared cook house between the two residences. It's tight, but the relatives promise as soon as the planting is done, they'll help build another room where there is now a porch. I've seen their gardens. Shouldn't take long to plant. Rocky, steep terrain isn't conducive to planting large crops.

Most of their nourishment comes from the free-range pigs, chickens, and even a wandering cow or two. I have no idea how they keep track of them. It's the gardens, not the animals that are fenced in. Guess it keeps the livestock out. The goats get tied and moved throughout the day. Uncle Ian says they keep the grounds clear of poison ivy and brush.

Fannie is thriving on goat's milk and porridge. She sports four teeth, two on top and two on the bottom, and clings to Nancy as if she were her mother. Guess she may as well be.

A fine Swiss fellow has been calling on Nancy, and she behaves all flighty and acts like a young teenager when he's around. At nineteen, she is the eldest now.

Margaret has been in communication with Granny Gray's grandson, blushing and running to her corner of the room whenever a letter arrives. I didn't realize they had hit it off so well during our short stay. I'm guessing she learned more than trapping during their lessons together. I am relieved no one in the Gray household contracted the fever.

Susan and Harvey are enthralled with all the attention they receive from the many aunts and cousins.

Joseph is learning how to carve pretty patterns in wood. He says someday he'll make a harp like the one his mother left behind. He works for hours in the shed with Uncle Ian, sanding and carving and bending the wood, joining it just so to make an instrument that looks an awful lot like the dulcimer. When Uncle Ian plays, he can make the music that comes out of those gentle strings laugh, sing, or cry. I picked it up once, but playing makes me feel things, and I'm not ready to do that.

James remains detached, bordering on rude. The only mingling he does is when the older boys take him out for target practice or hunting. He spends hours trailing through the mountain forests. Sometimes returning with deer, sometimes squirrel. When mention of his parents or William arises, James leaves the room. His Uncle Ian says he needs more time.

As my restlessness grows, I join James on his pilgrimages through the woods. I can now load the rifle and shoot, hitting my target at least seven out of ten times. We talk of weather, animals, the plant life. He never speaks of what we've been through, except for once when he aimed at a blue jay, muttering about cursed Yankees under his breath. Actually, he used words more colorful than that, but if Mama taught me anything, it was that the words we use matter, so I won't repeat them.

Now that the weather is tolerable, we head into the valley on Sundays to join the rest of the mountain folk at the white planked church in the middle of town. Because of the distance travelled to get there, we make a day of it, and it becomes almost as festive as going to the fair, with picnic baskets and blankets and old friends greeting and mingling. I make few friends. My need to leave is growing. I have to move on. Find my own relatives. Find Adeline.

Last Sunday, Ezra came to our spread. He's tall, kinda like Jacob, with strawberry blonde hair, kinda like Jacob, and a twinkle in his blue eyes. Just like Jacob. I think he's come for Margaret—most men do—but he gives her only a cursory acknowledgement and turns his attention on me.

He even speaks like Jacob. My heartbeat picks up a pace, and I move away, relieving Nancy of caring for baby Fannie and grabbing Harvey by the hand and pretending they need more food and tending to.

This week I am wary, and sure enough, Ezra stands tall at the back of the church, watching the door as we come marching in. He does this half bowing motion, just like Jacob does, and our eyes meet.

My throat constricts.

"I'll be back in a moment." I squeeze Margaret's hand and sneak outside.

The church is too small to hold me and my memories at the same time.

I hurry down the sloping hill, past the horses and carriages lined by the dirt road, past the minister's home, and I keep going. Overwhelming homesickness hits me. I want to be back in Tia's house, wearing my blue jeans and a sweatshirt. I want pizza and muffins and good coffee. I miss Jacob's blasted good moods and booming laughter. I even miss his over-zealous protectiveness. It's ridiculous. I take deep breaths, willing myself to relax.

A deer path meanders through the woodlands, and I follow. Birds sing overhead, and a squirrel scurries up a tree, scolding me loudly as I pass. I am agitated. Dissonance pulls me, hurting my ears. Still I walk. A tree has fallen across the path, and unlike the deer, I can't leap over it, so instead I sit and close my eyes, breathe deep, relax, and dream of home.

Of Adeline. Of Mama. Anything but Jacob—oh crud. There I go thinking about him again.

There's a rustle of leaves behind me. I turn. My head bursts with a cacophony of mismatched sounds. Behind me looms an altogether too familiar person—greasy haired, red eyed, rotten toothed.

Jethro.

"Hello, Adeline. You thought I wouldn't find you." He sneers as only he can. "I told you this was not over. It took a while tracking you, but you will find I do not take no for an answer."

"You're insane!" I scream. "Leave me alone!"

I scramble to my feet, half stumbling as I swing my legs over the fallen timber. My skirt catches, and I yank it, leaving a fragment of fabric behind. I run.

So does he.

We crash through the woods. Branches tear at my face and pull my hair. I have to keep going. *Oh, God! Can You hear me? Please help!* I didn't make it this far to fall prey to this man!

I'm fast. The boys in grade school could never outrun me, and most of the fellows in junior high saw nothing but my back side when I did track. I'm fast, but so is Jethro. I dodge an outcropping of stone, duck a low branch. I hear his feet pounding the earth behind me and getting closer.

A root catches the toe of my boot, and I fall. I go down, arms flailing, powerless to catch myself as I crash face-first into a heap of muck and leaves. A stick pokes from the ground inches from my eye. My cheek burns as I jerk away. Frantic, I grasp at the earth, struggling to propel myself up and forward. My feet tangle in a web of fabric as my skirt tangles around my legs. Jethro lands on top of me, knocking the wind from my lungs. I claw, scratch, grab a handful of leaves and fling them into his face. He shoves me down, jerking my arms behind me. I eat dirt, taste blood.

"No!" I scream, kicking and twisting, but he's too strong.

There's barking and the sound of feet running my way.

"Help!" I shout.

Jethro slaps me and thrusts my face back into the wet leaves, muffling my cry.

The barking gets closer and is replaced by a deep ominous growl. Jethro loosens his grip, and I snatch my arms free just as a giant wolf dog leaps at Jethro's face. He raises his arms, and I hear the crunch of bone and a terrified cry as massive jaws close over Jethro's forearm.

I force myself up and flee. I need a tree to climb, a rock to throw, a club to swing.

"Anna Marie! Stop!"

I stop so abruptly, I almost fall over my own feet. My heart pauses mid beat.

"Jacob?"

He runs to me, engulfing me in a bear hug, and I wrap my arms around him and hold tight, crying and laughing and being totally nonsensical, and I'm sure snot is running down my face and mixing with the tears as I smear it all into his thick flannel shirt. I bury my face in his chest. He's solid. He is real.

Jacob is here. Everything will be all right.

Pulling back, Jacob sweeps my hair away from my eyes, then wipes the tears from my cheeks. He turns my head one way, then the other, running a finger over my cheek. His finger comes away with a streak of blood.

"Anna Marie! Are you injured?" His voice quivers.

I shake my head, unable to say anything but a squeaky, "Jacob?"

Jethro hollers. A dog growls.

"Jacob! Adeline! For God's sake, help me!"

Jacob turns to face the man who moments before wrestled me to the ground. His cheeks redden, and with a deep guttural noise he turns and rushes the man on the ground. A fist crashes into the side of Jethro's face.

"You worthless vermin!" Jacob raises his fist to strike again.

The dog's hackles are raised, and she shakes her head, the broken arm still in her grip. Jethro screams.

It's Bellona! Bellona is here!

"Stop!" I cry out.

Jacob doesn't hear me. He's going to kill Jethro.

I hurry to them and grab the back of his collar. "Stop!"

This is *my* revenge, my fight.

Jacob falls back. His whole body quakes, and it's not from fear. His blood covered fist is balled tight.

Bellona's tail stands straight and stiff behind her. Her jaws remain clamped around Jethro's arm.

"Please," Jethro begs. "Please help me!"

I draw his revolver from his side and aim it at his forehead.

"Release."

Bellona drops her hold on Jethro's arm and sits back, eyes never moving from the man at my feet. She growls as if daring him to move.

He cries and draws his injured arm close. "I am sorry, Adeline. I promise I won't do nothing bad again. Just let me go. You have my word!"

My finger is on the trigger. My aim is spot on.

"He is dear to my parents. He was not always this way."

"Your word? Is that supposed to mean something?" My hand is shaking as sweat pours down my forehead and drips into my eye.

"Do you understand why I must forgive him?"

I squeeze my eyes shut, trying to get Mary Elizabeth out of my head. I picture Jethro as a young boy, finding his twin siblings at the bottom of the washtub. A broken, pathetic little boy.

I can't shoot.

"They loved you, you know?"

"Who—what?" Jethro stares at me, eyes wild.

"The Dickersons. They're dead. Did you know? Because of you! Because of your lies!"

"What? How?"

"William died from his head injury. Were you the one who hit him? The others died from Typhoid, I think."

He has the decency to look stricken.

"Mary Elizabeth forgave you. Just before she died. How does that make you feel?" I'm crying. Yet the pistol doesn't waver.

Jethro begins to weep. "I am sorry. I am so sorry."

"Got some rope?" I ask Jacob.

He nods, lowering a pack from his back and pulling out a length of twine.

"Tie him to the tree."

"But I need a doctor!" Jethro cries.

"Yes. You do." I tuck his revolver into the folds of my skirt and check him for more weapons. Bellona hovers at my side. I can feel her muscles tense and ready to attack. I remove a dirty knife from his boot. "Maybe if the good Lord feels kind, someone will find you before the wolves do."

"Mercy. Reddington, please. You and me, we been through a lot together. You are like a brother to me."

Jacob jerks the knot tight. He leans close to Jethro's face. I've never seen him angry before.

"If you ever touch her again, you are a dead man. Do you hear me? Dead."

Tears run down Jethro's cheeks. "I won't. I promise. I won't. Let me go. Please!"

"The only reason you are still alive, Jethro Tanner, is because Mary Elizabeth forgave you. She challenged me to forgive you too." I stand, exhaustion hitting me like a heat wave. All the fight drains out of me. "I can't."

Once Jethro is secure, Bellona leaps on me, tail wagging so hard her back end resembles a belly dancer. I kneel, hugging her massive head and running my fingers through the thick gold and black of her coat. If animals cry for joy, she is. Any remnants of tears or blood left on my face are washed away in an abundance of doggy kisses, and I am so happy to see her, I almost kiss her back. Almost.

Jacob is staring at his hands as if they belong to someone else and he's wondering where they came from. Our eyes meet. His are moist.

Reaching down, he traces my jaw with the back of his hand. "I have never—it is like I lost my mind. To think, if we had not arrived when we did."

"It's okay, Jacob. I'm okay." I reach for his hand and hold it to my cheek.

A smile spreads across his face, accenting his dimple. "Oh, Just Anna Marie. Am I dreaming, or have we actually found you?"

Taking his hand, I rise. I'm shaking all over. "We must be dreaming the same dream."

He tucks my fingers in the crook of his arm. I can feel the steady beat of his heart. He draws me up the path, the way I came. Bellona is so close, I almost trip over her as I walk.

"There is much to tell you." He squeezes my arm.

"You cannot leave me here!" Jethro cries as we depart. "I'm injured! Red! Adeline! Please!"

Jacob looks over his shoulder, his hand lingering on the grip of his handgun. With a sigh, he keeps moving. "We best call on the lawman and see that Jethro is taken into custody."

"Let him rot where he is." My fleeting feelings of charity are over.

"It is what he deserves. But he may get away. Let us get the lawman."

REPUTATIONS AND PROPOSALS

"WHAT ARE YOU DOING here?"

"Would you rather I leave?" Jacob glances at me sideways, that dimple showing beside a lopsided grin.

"No, never!" I hug his arm and laugh. My breathing has returned to normal, and my legs no longer want to give out as we stumble up the hillside toward the church.

"And Bellona!" I feel like I'm soaring through Neverland. "I didn't think I'd see either of you ever again!"

"It has not been easy. We've been tracking you for the past few weeks. Sarah told me where you were heading but did not know the precise location of the Dickerson relatives. Do you know how hard it is to get straight directions from folks in these parts?"

I laugh again. I am so happy to see this man, I can hardly stand it.

"Yes. Someone's kin knows of a fellow with a mill who knows of a fellow with a pig, who knows a fellow who makes musical instruments, who has a daughter of the last name Holliday. Yeah. I know."

"When I arrived at the Holliday's, an old man informed me they had left for church. I was ecstatic to be so close, but as we approached the church, Bellona must have heard you. She went insane, barking and tearing off through the woods. I followed."

"Just in time." I shudder. Maybe God did smile on me once in a while.

We walk in quiet. I can't believe I'm not dreaming.

Jacob looks at me sideways. "Makes musical instruments, eh?"

I feel myself go all dreamy. Music. I still can't play, but listening has been a salve over deep wounds. It's the emotional lifeline that keeps me from going insane. Closing my eyes, I hear Adeline's melody, reassuring me that she is alive, and for the first time in a long time, my life feels intact. I long to play once more.

"Did you say he makes instruments?"

"Yes! The most beautiful lap harps and dulcimers, although that's not what he calls them. That's what they're going to be called. In the future. Wow, this is so weird, actually being able to talk to someone who knows what I'm saying!"

"You used to think *I* was crazy."

"Yes, I did. So, tell me, Mr. Time-traveling,"—in my head I add hand-kissing nutcase—"crazy-man, Jacob. How did you get here? I mean, back in this time."

"Remember you telephoned me? I knew something was amiss when you made that call, and I hurried to your house. The door was locked, and your car and dog gone." He glances at me sideways. "How did you get past the guard anyway? He never saw you leave. What is the use of hiring a guard if you do not let them know where you are going?"

"You mean the security guy outside? It was raining, plus I'm sneaky. Besides, I didn't hire him. My uncle did."

"Uncle?"

"Yeah—Manny's Lawn Care? Never mind. It's a long story. Go on."

"We broke in, found your notes all over the counter, and I knew right away where you were going. We jumped in the security man's car and followed you."

"Oh… the car. I heard a car drive up just before. And someone called my name—was that you?" I vaguely remember seeing Jacob with his hand on the door of my car, calling my name. It was Adeline that had my full attention.

"Yes. You had the strangest expression on your face." Jacob glances my direction and smiles. "Lord have mercy, but you nearly gave the fellow who was with me apoplexy when you vanished into thin air!" He laughs again. "I wonder but he has not gone mad entirely after Bellona and I vanished right after you."

"That doesn't explain how you got here."

"Bellona was having a fit. As soon as I opened the door, she flew out. I grabbed at her leash, and she yanked me straight into the water. It felt like I was being torn apart and dragged through some black hole. I awoke in the middle of a creek bed, with that beast of an animal licking my face." Jacob reaches around me and scratches Bellona's ears.

"Oddly enough, even though we departed moments after you did, I arrived several months later. You and the Dickersons had long escaped. Who would have thought time travel was not linear?"

"Who'd believe it was even possible!"

"I am thankful, Just Anna Marie, thankful for being taken from my time and brought back again."

"Really?"

Just Anna Marie. He has called me that from day one. It's weird, but I like the nickname. Even if it does remind me of my hometown jail.

"It has taught me many things, but most importantly, I met you."

"Oh," I flush with warmth.

I need time to digest what he said, but at the moment, I'm feeling right giddy that he's here. I have to be careful. I can't let my feelings grow. Not now. Time travel, or not, there's one thing experience has taught me. Life is not safe. No one can be held too close.

He pauses at the forest edge where three horses graze. "Meet Dark Matter, Sunspots, and Steady Eddie."

I laugh. They are beautiful animals. Dark Matter lives up to his name. He's so black, he'd be invisible on a moonless night. Sunspots is a dappled gray. Steady Eddie, a thick-necked, glossy, silver.

"So, Dark Matter and Sunspots are from the astronomy program we watched. What's with the Steady Eddie?" A twinge of nostalgia hits. Adeline's friends called her Steady Adi.

"He started off as Andromeda, but I soon discovered he is all muscle and no speed. Without constant prodding, he knows but one pace. Steady. Steady Eddie was the nickname Johnny and I always used for horses like this. He will make a good horse for pulling a wagon or a plow." He leads them toward the church's fence, where other attendees have secured their mounts.

"Stay." I motion to Bellona.

She gives me a disapproving look, whines, but complies.

I turn to Jacob. "I suppose we should head inside. Everyone is there, including the lawman."

He smiles, giving me his arm, and winks. "As you wish."

Once inside the church, we find the congregation still worshipping, and we slip into the back pew. My clothes are a mess, and my hair is a shambles. I didn't even think about it until the dark looks come my way from a couple ladies sitting close.

I smother a laugh.

"What?" Jacob leans toward me.

"I was just thinking how bad it must look, me coming to service late, with you, and my clothes like this!"

Jacob doesn't laugh. His cheeks go red, and the horror on his face makes me want to laugh harder.

"I am sorry, Anna Marie. I did not consider that. Your reputation—"

"Shh." I poke his side, noting the elder moving our direction with a frown on his face. "Behavior police." I stifle a laugh again.

I catch bits and pieces of the sermon. Seems the preacher doesn't approve of the 'devil's music' that is prevalent in the Ozarks. That toe-tapping rhythm only riles up the emotions and leads to 'debauchery and carnal lust.' That explains the number of children in the congregation. I blush when I see the preacher is looking straight at me.

After the service, we hurry to find Uncle Ian. James and Marga-ret join us. I notice Margaret eyeing Jacob. I want to say, "Remember Grandma Gray's grandson," but I don't because Jacob and I aren't a thing, and she has just as much right to be interested in him. Wait. More right, because I'm not really interested, so I have no reason to feel jealous. Not one bit.

"Mr. Holliday, uh, Uncle Ian." I'm still trying to get used to calling him Uncle. "This is a friend from back home—Jacob Reddington. Jacob, this is Mr. Holliday."

"Sir, is there a lawman in attendance in your congregation?" Jacob extends his hand to shake Uncle Ian's.

Returning the greeting, Uncle Ian rubs his chin and frowns, looking from Jacob to me.

"Sir, remember the man responsible for burning the Dickerson's place? He tracked me here, and, well, Jacob got here just in time." I shudder.

"Sir," Jacob says, "we left Jethro tied to a tree. He is injured and not likely to escape. However, we need to report this to the law."

"Well, I say so!" Veins are bulging in Uncle Ian's temples, and his eyes spit fire. "Sheriff O'Dell! Get your rifle, and get over here! This man is going to lead you to a killer!" He grabs Jacob by the arm and strides across the lawn to a surprised cluster of men.

"He needs to die! I am going to kill that Jethro!" James yells after his uncle.

"Hush, James." Margaret smacks her brother's arm. "We are in front of God's house. You cannot speak like that!"

"I will speak as I wish!"

Uncle Ian turns around and points a finger at his nephew. "Son, you take the women and children and get them back safe to the house. No arguing. Be on your way, now. The men will take care of this."

It's Margaret that does the taking of women and children home, and she practically has to tie James to the wagon to do so.

"He was still there, blubbering and crying like the fool he is," Jacob says.

Jacob and I sit on the veranda. The night air is crisp and cool. I pull my shawl tighter around my shoulders.

"The sheriff has him locked up, good and secure. The circuit judge will be notified. I suspect that is the last he will be bothering anyone."

"Jacob?"

"Yes?"

"Do you think this is the Jethro before he time travelled, or after? I mean, if this is before—that means he gets away from here. If it is Jethro after—that means he didn't die and he got away from there. Or do you think we just changed history, and he never makes it to my time?" My brain hurts thinking about it.

Jacob's brows go up as he ponders what I said. He rubs his forehead, then his chin, then his forehead again.

"Lord, have mercy." He shakes his head. "I have no idea."

Then I recall the attack outside Betsy's camp store. I remember the give of flesh and the hot blood as I stab my fork into his eye. I shudder.

"It's before."

"What?"

"Jethro. It's him before. He still has both eyes."

A piano melody flits in and out through the evening air. It's a beginning of a song, mixed with lost and wandering chords. I tilt my head to soak it in and wonder. No one has a piano in this village.

We sit for a long time, Bellona at our feet. The moon rises, dimming the brightness of the stars. A fiddle sings a lively dance tune from a home down the street. The preacher would not approve. I want to hold Jacob's hand. I want him to hold me in the street and dance to the music. Instead, I work my fingers through Bellona's thick fur.

Jacob keeps glancing at me with that sideways look he does when he's thinking about something and not sure what to say. He plucks at the peeling spindle from the rail next to him, scratches his cheek, cleans his fingernail with a sliver of wood.

"Good, grief, Jacob. You're antsier than James on a bad day. Just say what you're thinking. It can't be all that awful."

He inhales, long and slow, then exhales. "Just Anna Marie, I got to thinking, and I spoke with Uncle Ian, and he thinks this would be wise as well…"

"Go on."

"I saw the looks the folks at the church gave you, and even though we explained what happened, I think most of them still hold us suspect. I believe, for the sake of protecting your reputation, that we—that we—"

I'm staring at him in disbelief. My jaw is hanging open, and I just about choke. No way is he about to say what I think he's going to say.

"I believe we should get married."

He's done it.

"You *are* crazy, Jacob!"

"No, I am sincere! I would be right proud if you married me."

"No way. Absolutely not. Not a chance! I don't care about my reputation! I know what happened, and so does anyone that counts!" I'm standing up and screaming now.

The music goes still. A head pokes out a window down the street, and a door opens at the neighbors'.

"I don't care what you think!" I yell at the eavesdroppers. "I will marry for love, not to protect my reputation!"

With that, I lift my skirts and flee inside.

TRAGEDY AT THE WATER HOLE

"TIA SAID HER PEOPLE settled near an Indian reservation close to the border into Arkansas. Her folks moved north to work the fields when she was a baby. We know Adeline was heading to Arkansas. She must have gone searching for family there."

Uncle Ian rubs his chin and nods. "I understand how that may be. Still, I do not like the two of you taking off by yourselves. It ain't proper. Plus there be them bushwhackers as are still troubling these parts."

I listen, amazed that this large, ill-grammared man can be brother to the tiny, soft spoken, articulate Rebecca Dickerson.

"That is what I told her. I can travel quickly by myself and search for Adeline's whereabouts. An unmarried man and woman on the road alone, it is not right."

I bristle. "Don't be ridiculous. I trust you with my life. Besides, we won't be alone. Bellona will be with us. Just like old times."

The two men stare at the large dog, asleep at my feet, and frown.

"If you don't take me," I throw my arms up in the air, "I'm going alone. And none of you can stop me.

"You are the most pig-headed woman I have ever known, Anna Marie." Jacob pounds a fist on the table. I glare at him.

Bellona paces toward the open doorway. A low growl emanates from her throat, followed by a huff, like she's ready to bark.

"Quiet, girl." I point to the floor, instructing my dog to sit and be still. She ignores me. "You should know, Jacob. I didn't come this far to sit and twiddle my fingers when I know my sister is somewhere out there. I've got to find her. Please. I have to."

"That is why I—"

"Uncle! Uncle Ian! Miss Anna! Come quickly!" James's cry jerks us from where we stand leaning over the table and studying a rough sketched map. Bellona lunges out the doorway.

In the distance, I hear screaming. I know that voice.

"Joseph!" I rush outside. "James! Where is Joseph?"

James runs to me, grasps my hand, and drags me with him toward the cries. Tears stream down his cheeks.

"I did not mean to! Hurry, Anna! Hurry!"

It is unseasonably warm for the middle of March, and James is shirtless and barefoot. His hair is wet.

"Hurry! He's at the water hole!"

And hurry we do, driven faster by the frantic barking and shrill cries coming from the pool below.

"We're coming, Joseph!" James's voice cracks. "I have Miss Anna! I'm coming."

Writhing on the ground by the edge of the pool, Joseph wails. My stomach lurches. His hands cover his face, and blood drips through his fingers.

"No!" I scream and run to his side, pulling his hand away.

In memory, I see Jethro, hands covered in blood. On the ground beside Joseph lies not a fork but a long, pointed stick—a gooey, bloody mass stuck on the end.

"I'm so sorry, Joseph. I did not intend to hurt you. Be well. Please be well!" James sobs as Jacob lifts Joseph into his arms and carries him up the hill to the house. The screaming stops, and Joseph goes limp, pain eased for the moment by a loss of consciousness.

Once inside, we clear the map aside and lay Joseph across the table.

"What happened?" Nancy runs through the door, gasping for breath, Fannie on her hip. "I heard James crying!"

"Joseph!" Margaret barges through the door behind her older sister.

They gape at Joseph's long, thin frame, his feet, too large to match the rest of him, hanging over the edge of the table. His eyelid sags over a pool of blood that oozes from the place where once his eye had been. Nancy backs out the door and retches into the flower bed.

"What do we do?" Margaret looks at me.

Everyone looks at me. Like I know what to do with an amputated eyeball?

"Clean rags. I need clean rags and hot water." I figure clean rags and clean water can't do more damage. But the damage done can in no way be undone.

I peek at James. He has retreated into the corner, his arms wrapped tightly around himself, and he rocks, great sobs racking his shoulders. All the pent-up tears of the months before pour down his face.

"James!" I say, a little louder than I intended.

His head jerks up.

"I need you to fetch a bottle of your uncle's whiskey. I think you know where he hides it. Hurry. I need to clean this before Joseph wakes up. And I need some kind of tool—with a long narrow grip that can pick out splinters and such."

Knocking the chair over in his haste, James rushes out back to his uncle's work shed.

I brush Joseph's hair back. My hands are shaking.

"No one here understands what needs doing better than you do." Jacob takes my hand in his, turns it over, and rubs my palm with his thumb. "Your guess is better than ours. Your former employment trained you for such things. Trust God to direct these hands."

I jerk my hand back. I am *not* trained for this, and God has yet to help me out. "God hasn't bothered to direct these hands before, Jacob. Everyone else I cared for has ended up dead. I'll leave the praying to you."

Problem is, I can't stand by and do nothing. Jacob is right about one thing. I am better qualified than anybody else in this town. Good grief, people still practice bleeding to get out 'bad humours' in this time. At least I know about germs and hygiene.

I glance at Uncle Ian's large hands and shudder.

"Go wash your hands." I shoo him away from the table. "You probably still have pig slime on them from feeding time. Go! And use soap.

You too." I point at Jacob. "And take the dog outside. She's getting in the way.

The two leave the room, with Bellona at Jacob's heals. Uncle Ian studies his hands, turning them from side to side. "What is wrong with my hands?" I hear him ask as they head to the well. "They be clean."

I go to the basin in the kitchen and scrub my own.

"Water is ready." Margaret motions at the stove. "I will wash as well. Then I can assist you."

By the time the men return, and James comes running in with an open bottle of Uncle Ian's finest, we've washed the blood from Joseph's face. He moans, And James's face goes pale.

"Here." I take the whiskey and an instrument that looks a lot like needle-nosed pliers from James. I drop the pliers into a shallow bowl and pour some of the whiskey over them.

James is shaking and pale.

I motion to him. "I think you better go outside."

I dip some hot water into a bowl and mix in a liberal amount of the alcohol. Soaking a rag in the mixture, I nod at the two men. "Hold him down. He may wake up."

Beads of sweat line Jacob's brow as he lowers himself over the boy's chest. Uncle Ian takes one look at me, grabs the whiskey bottle and takes a long swig, then places his hands on either side of Joseph's head, immobilizing it.

Margaret is my assistant, holding the water and handing me rags. The girl has a stomach of steel. She might get a bit pale, but she never flinches.

First, I lay the soaked rag over the angry red mass of flesh that once held an intact eyeball. Joseph moans but doesn't move. Gently, I pull the lid up and back so I can see better. I'm praying I'm not damaging things any worse than they are already, but how do you clear a wound of bacteria in this time? I also need to make sure there are no remnants of the stick still in the socket.

When the first drops of fluid touch the inner eyelid, Joseph jerks and cries out, kicking his legs, then goes limp once more. Uncle Ian trembles and looks longingly at the remaining whiskey.

"Don't even think about it, Joseph is gonna need some of that for the pain. He's not going to stay asleep much longer." I peer under the lid. "There! There's a piece."

Using the pliers, I remove the splinter. Blood-tinged fluid oozes out. The whole socket looks like tenderized raw meat, but at least it's clean.

Satisfied that no debris remains to fester, I do a final rinse, then place a dry bandage over the injury. "I think that's all we can do."

Jacob relaxes and selects a clean length of dry cloth, wrapping it around the boy's head to secure the bandage.

"No matter how often I see something like that, it is never easy." He studies me a moment, like he's just figuring out something new. "You did right well, Just Anna Marie. You did right well."

The look in his eyes makes me all warm inside. I glance away. "It won't give him his sight back."

"No. Nothing this side of Heaven can do that."

"Right." I look around for something to do.

Margaret has cleared the water and soiled cloths. Joseph is moaning softly.

"Do you mind staying and watching for a while? If he wakes in a lot of pain, I think a sip of whiskey will help. Don't let Uncle Ian finish it. He doesn't look like he handles blood well." Without explanation, I leave. I need to find James.

I find him sitting on the front steps, picking at slivers of wood poking from the plank he sits on and staring ahead. At the rate the men around here pick on the wood, the whole structure will be dismantled before long.

James has grown so much this winter. His pants expose his ankles and a swath of lower calf muscle. The hair on his leg is thick and dark.

"Hey." I sit next to him and have to look up to see into his face. He stares at me with eyes empty of emotion.

"He'll be all right," I say.

James flicks a speck of wood into the air, returning his focus to the empty space in front of him.

"I got it cleaned out, and the bleeding stopped. He's strong. He'll learn to work with one good eye. People do it all the time."

James blinks in slow motion. His mind is somewhere far, far from me.

"Watch over James. It will be hardest on him. He blames himself."

I close my eyes and lean on the handrail. I feel like I've done a workout with Alicia. Bellona comes padding alongside me, sits by our feet, and lays her head on James's lap. She rolls her eyes at me and sighs, as if she was the one who did all the work.

"You lazy dog," I say, scratching her between the ears.

She opens one eye, looks at me, then sighs again.

James lifts a hand and rubs it across her back, his gaze fixed on the unknown point ahead.

"He didn't want to play."

I almost jump when James speaks.

"I wanted to play like the sticks were swords, but he didn't. He said Father would not approve."

James turns and looks into my face. "I told him not to be a ninny. I told him if Father had stood up and fought like a man, we could have licked those bushwhackers. I told him if he didn't pick up the stick and learn to defend himself, I was gonna teach him a lesson."

Tears flow fast, and I reach for James, pulling his head to my shoulder and wrapping my arms around him. He pounds a feeble fist on my shoulder.

"I didn't mean to hurt him. I went for his chest, but he moved. He moved, and I couldn't stop!"

I hold him. For all his growing up and all his height, he's just a boy right now. Just a broken and hurting boy. And we both cry. We cry until there's nothing left in us to cry.

"It was an accident, James," I say.

"No." He shakes his head. "No. It was my fault. There's more. It was me. I killed William."

CONFESSIONS

"YOU WHAT?"

"I killed William."

"No. No. No! What are you talking about? I was there!" I pull away, and James's shoulders slump. I have to lean closer to hear him.

"Back at the house, when those men came, William wanted to go help Father. He said if we all worked together, we could keep them from hurting anyone. I wouldn't let him go."

"Your father told you to keep the door locked and stay in your room."

"That is what I said. William would not listen. He said if something happened to Father, it was on me for not helping. I was a ninny. I was too scared. He pushed past me, saying it was my last chance to do the right thing. I locked the door and did not leave, even when we heard them break down your door."

"But you didn't hurt William!"

"Do you not understand? William was right! If we had gone together, it would have turned out differently—but I would not do it. And now William is dead."

"Oh, James!" I want to cry all over again, but tears take effort, and we are both spent. "You were doing the right thing by obeying your Father. Did you see the soldiers out there? No matter how hard we fought, they would have won. There were, like, twenty of them, all armed and ready to fight."

James sags against me. I turn his face so he can see me. His face is so close to mine, I think my eyes cross.

"I'm glad you didn't open your door."

His brows meet in the middle, and his nose scrunches. "Why?"

"Then you would have known what really happened, and you wouldn't want anything to do with me again. You still might not."

"What do you mean?"

My heart is pounding, and my hands go clammy. I love this boy, and now I'm going to lose him too. But it's better than him blaming himself.

"What? Know what?"

"It was my father, James. My dad hurt William and kicked your family out of the house, and because of that, all the awful things happened. My dad is the Yankee captain responsible. I think about it every single day, and I can hardly live with myself. My own blasted father!" I'm shaking. "If I never came, none of this would have happened."

Now it's James that's holding me, and we rock and somehow find more tears to cry.

He doesn't pull away in disgust. He doesn't call the sheriff and report the Yankee sympathizer hiding in their midst. He doesn't rail me with curses. He doesn't even shoot me. He rocks with me and cries and tells me it's okay. He forgives me for being the daughter of a bastard.

I have no idea how long we sit there, but the chickens head to the trees to roost, and my stomach starts growling. We've had enough emotional turmoil for one day, and it's time to check on the patient.

Jacob spread a bedroll in front of the unlit fireplace, and Joseph is lying there, all curled up like a baby. His one good eye is puffy and red but follows me as I walk in.

"How are you feeling?" I kneel on the floor beside him, putting a hand to his forehead. It is cool to touch.

"I am all right." He gives me a thin smile. "Jacob gave me some whiskey. Stuff is nasty."

"Yeah, I'll bet. Does it help?"

"A bit. As long as I do not move my head."

"Good."

Jacob is standing there, hands in his pockets. He shrugs.

"I figured there would be no dinner if Joseph remained on the table.

Besides, he cannot fall off the floor. Do you think giving a ten-year-old whisky seems a bit of a risk?"

"I'm sure it is. Not my first choice either."

"Surely someone has some laudanum."

I hadn't even thought of that. Laudanum. Isn't that what Poe used that drove him to madness? The thought of Joseph having such nightmares makes me shake inside. "No. I don't know much about drugs, thank goodness, but a bit of drink in small amounts should be safe."

There's pulled pork for dinner, sent over by one of the many aunts or cousins or some Holliday kin that heard about today's disaster. I think about the "kinsman" that killed his only hog and smile.

Music floats through the open window. Someone plays what sounds like a guitar. A fiddle joins in. My fingers ache, but I tuck them into fists and ignore them. From another home, I hear the sounds of laughter.

I look around at the people who have taken me in, family crammed together around the large table, talking in quiet tones. Nancy sits closest to Joseph, watching over him as he sleeps on the floor. There are dark circles under her eyes. She pats Susan's hand, thanking her for helping fill in with chores without being asked.

Susan beams. "I helped Auntie Siobhan knead the bread."

Fannie has butter all over her face, having decided the bread is optional. This is what family is about.

TURN FOR THE WORSE

I AWAKE WITH A START as some crazy rooster cock-a-doodle-doos outside my window. I'm thinking rooster and dumplings sounds really good right now. I groan and roll over, then bolt upright.

"Joseph!"

I intended to remain by his side through the night in case he needed me. What am I doing in bed? I toss off the quilt.

Margaret blinks at me and rubs her eyes. "Morning," she whispers.

"I have to check on Joseph."

Hints of sunlight dance on the morning haze, warming the large multipurpose room that serves as bedroom for the guys by night, dining and living room by day. I find Joseph sleeping where I last saw him. A low fire burns in the fireplace, and someone took the effort of placing bricks in a line so Joseph can't roll too close to the flames. Bellona lies with her head across his chest. Her eyes follow me as I near. A tap of the tail the only movement she makes. In the rocking chair where I planned to keep my vigil, Jacob sits. He must have carried me to my bed and sat watch in my place.

A red stubble shadows his chin. A strange emotion grips me as I gaze at him and marvel at the fine line of his jaw, the solid build of his frame. He looks amazing, even if he drools in his sleep. My eyes travel down the line of his torso. His quilt has fallen off one shoulder, exposing the outlines of well-shaped muscles. He's got biceps Alicia could appreciate, and I'm not even saying anything about those pecs. I remember the solid feel of him as I cried against his chest the day he found me. I don't think there's an ounce of flab anywhere on this guy. He's a good man too. He'll make some girl a very lucky bride.

Oh, good grief. Someone needs to get a shirt back on this guy.

My gaze rests on his hands. That's safer. Hands. Large, capable, gentle. I recall how they trembled when I asked him to help with Joseph last night and how they steadied as he gritted his teeth and buckled down to do what needed to be done. Those hands would have killed Jethro for my sake. I recall how they felt as they held mine during that joyous hike back to the church. Warm and work worn. Not sweaty—I hate sweaty hands. Those hands have soothed strong horses and calmed my fear on more than one occasion.

Closing my eyes, I let out a long breath and fan myself with my hand. What is wrong with me? I've never reacted to anyone like this, and I don't care to begin now.

When I open my eyes, Jacob is watching me. A sideways grin plays mischief on his face. I blush. Someone, please tell me he didn't see me gawking.

Stretching, he tightens his biceps and grins wider. Yep. He saw. I need a hole to crawl into.

"Thanks for taking me to my room."

"You were worn. I figured I could watch for you."

I glance at Jacob and have to look away. He's still grinning at me.

"Looking good. Joseph looks really good." I nod at our ward on the floor.

"Yes, he does."

"James too." I glance to where James sleeps.

Little Harvey, who has taken to sleeping with 'de big bwoys,' is snuggled close. "He looks good too."

"Yes."

"Strong. Look at those muscles." Good grief. I'm just digging myself in deeper and deeper. "Need to have the boys keep their shirts on at night. Still a bit cold, don't you think?"

He grins, fingering the quilt that hangs loosely around one shoulder. "I was thinking it a bit warm."

I blush and nod at James. "He tries hard, watches out for all of us."

"He has character," Jacob says. "The boy will give his life to take care of the people he loves."

Our eyes meet, and my throat gets that weird tight feeling again.

"Yes, he would. That's what I love about him."

Jacob tilts his head to the side, holding my gaze. One brow goes up, and he squints questioningly at me.

Yes, I'm talking about you, I want to say. But I can't.

Maybe he senses the tension in the room. Whatever the case, I'm relieved when James yawns and opens his eyes. He runs his fingers through his hair, causing the black curls to stand up straight off his head. It makes me smile.

"Good morning, James." I am much too cheery in my greeting.

He rubs his eyes, blinks, and wipes them again. "Morning, Miss Anna, Jacob. How is Joseph?"

That's the end of a calm, peaceful morning.

Harvey, in typical Harvey fashion, rolls over fully awake, and runs across the room, throwing himself on Jacob's lap, wrapping chubby little arms around his neck. "Morning! I's wake!"

He proceeds on to me, "Morning! I's wake!"

I stop him before he throws himself on top of Joseph.

Tearing free from my grasp, he runs to perform the same morning ritual in the girls' room, waving his arms and crying, "Morning! I's wake!"

Joseph can sit up and eats a bit of morning gruel. Gruel is a good name for it. I have no idea what all is in this mush we eat. I think its contents vary from day to day, and with its varying contents, the quality of the flavor. But it's warm, and after days of going hungry, I will never turn my nose up at a meal again.

By the midday meal, Joseph says he's not hungry. He asks for a sip of whiskey and lies down on the bed Margaret and I share each night. I change his bandage. I'm not sure what a wound like this is supposed to look like, but this makes me nervous. The swelling is increasing, and there's angry red in with the purple bruising.

By nightfall, his cheeks are flushed, his skin burns, and my heart sinks. An odor comes from the drainage that wasn't there earlier.

"Jacob?" I call him inside, trying not to alarm the people coming and going. "What do you think of this?" I show him the eye, lifting the bandage for inspection. I know he's seen lots of wounds out on the field. Maybe he has a better idea of what to expect.

He sniffs, touches Joseph's cheeks, and grunts.

"Well?" I don't like the sound of the grunt.

Jacob rubs his forehead, then his chin, then his forehead again. "I think it might be ready to fester," he says. "It is hard to predict. Some wounds will get angry but clear up with time. Others get bad and do not get better. If only we had some anty-bi-otics."

"Well, we don't."

"Am I going to be all right?" Joseph looks up at me with his one good eye. It is also red and inflamed. "I ache all over."

"Auntie Siobhan says she heard about a doctor down in the city that's rumored to heal folk better than most doctors." James' voice comes from behind us. "People around here are scared of her. They say she is a witch. They say she speaks odd, and no one but a witch can heal like she does."

"James, I didn't realize you were standing there." I wonder how much he overheard.

"What if she is not a witch, but really good at what she does? Just because she speaks odd and is able to heal, does not mean she is evil. You speak odd, and you are no witch.

"My Mama's a witch, and she taught me how to make curses. I hope the food makes you so sick, you wish you're dead."

I was seven years old and already knew that when dealing with bullies, you had to make them scared of you.

Georgie Walker was the school bully. His victim of choice, my sister. Adeline trusted everyone, even Georgie. When she didn't do so well on her spelling, Georgie persuaded her that eating blue playdough would make her smarter. She got sick as a dog. He ran around school making fun of her, so I beat him up. Did a pretty good job of it too. I smile at the memory.

Luck would have it, Georgie did get sick that day after his meal. I think, deep down, he was a chicken, and I freaked him out. He never bothered us again.

But I got Mama in trouble.

For all my good intentions, I cause trouble wherever I go.

"Miss Anna, are you listening?" James interrupts my recollections. "What do you think?"

"About?"

"About taking Joseph to the lady doctor."

I look at Jacob. He nods. "I will take you."

"I'm going with you." James's eyes shine. "Besides, Uncle says it's not proper for unmarried people to travel alone."

I look at James and frown. "What else has your uncle been saying?"

James shrugs. "He thinks you should marry Jacob, and have it done with."

"Oh, really?"

"He says the two of you remind him of a couple of—"

Jacob clears his throat. "We have the dog, that will be supervision enough. I need to get supplies for a few days. I do not know how long it will take. James, come with me. I need to ask your uncle's approval." He glances at me, and his cheeks redden. "About taking Joseph."

LADY DOCTOR

T HE NIGHT IS SHORT. Rising before the rooster, we saddle the horses, loading our packs and Jacob's bundles behind us. Jacob has his two horses. Dark Matter will carry both him and Joseph. I ride Sunspot, the dappled gray. She nuzzles Bellona like they are old friends.

"Didn't you have three horses?" I ask.

"I sold Steady Eddie. We needed supplies."

I feel a pang of guilt. He's a good guy, spending his resources, helping us with nothing to gain from it. Even after I turned down his proposal of marriage.

"Godspeed." Margaret gives me a hug, then kisses her brother.

James scowls, despondent that his uncle won't let him join us. The new school teacher is coming and wants to meet his students.

Nancy tucks a scarf around Joseph's neck, rests a hand on his feverish face, and smiles up at him. "You be strong and fight this, Joseph. I cannot bear to lose you."

"I will." His voice is shaky.

"And obey Miss Anna and Mr. Reddington. Don't give me any reason to worry, do you hear?"

By the first hints of sun, we are on our way. The rooster crows as we turn onto the road. Bellona zig zags ahead of us, tearing off into the woods with her nose to the ground, returning moments later with her silly grin and nothing to show for her chase. Jacob takes the lead. Joseph leans back into the curve of his arms and dozes off. Jacob is so careful with the lad. He will make an excellent father someday.

I wonder what *his* father was like.

"Have you been home since returning?" I pull my mare up so we ride side by side. "I just realized, I don't even know where you live."

In fact, I know very little about him.

"My place is just south of Saint Louis." He stares straight ahead. "On a farm, not far from the river. And no. I cannot return home. Besides, I needed to know you were safe."

"Oh. Are your folks still living?"

"Mother lives. My father died many years ago." He rubs his forehead then his jaw and looks at me with an odd gleam in his eye.

"I had a younger brother. Johnny. He survived the war and died returning home. I swore to protect him, to never attempt to return home without him, but in the end, I could do nothing." Jacob's eyes widen, and he runs his hand over his face. "Mercy, Anna! I just realized—this time thing has me not thinking straight—the war is still going. Johnny is alive! He has not yet been killed. Good, Lord, he is still alive!"

And he kicks his horse and takes off.

Joseph grasps at the horse's mane and cries out.

Jacob jerks back on the reigns, and the black horse slows so quickly, it throws the boy forward. Jacob grabs to steady him.

"Sorry, son. I was not thinking! I just realized, my brother is alive!"

The pace is faster, and Jacob is so excited, it becomes contagious. Even Joseph seems brighter and more alert. A light drizzle falls, and Jacob stops long enough to draw his wool blanket from his pack and cover Joseph. I pull out the oiled skins, wrap myself, and we move on. Droplets form on Jacob's hat, pooling together until enough mass has gathered to form a stream and drip from the rim onto his shoulder. He ignores it. I blink away mist that collects on my lashes.

We stop for lunch beneath the overhang of a rocky outcropping, a temporary reprieve from the steady drizzle. Bellona eats her portion in two gulps and takes a nap while we talk.

"How much farther?" I ask.

"I am thinking about five miles to the outside of the city. We should skirt around the north edge, and if Mrs. Holliday's gossip was correct, we should come on the doctor's house on that side of town."

"My backside feels like I've had a whipping."

"Did you get many of those as a girl?" Jacob is grinning at me.

"More than I deserved." I glare at him.

His smile vanishes. "I am truly sorry to hear that."

"Yeah, well. What doesn't kill you makes you stronger."

"Your Pa?"

I shrug and encourage Joseph to eat some cheese and to drink. I decide he could use a sip of whiskey. The jostling of the horse ride must be agony for him, but he doesn't complain.

"Somehow I get the feeling I would not care much for your father if I had the chance to meet him."

"I don't suspect you would." The memory of my father rises like a wound bursting open. I don't want to talk about him.

"I wish you could have met mine," Jacob says. "He would have liked you."

I can't imagine why Jacob thinks his dad would like me, but I'm cold, and my backside hurts, and I need a distraction.

"Tell me about him."

"I look like him. Johnny takes after my mother's people. I take after my Pa—except his hair was as red as it gets. Folks always said it was easy to remember his name, they just had to remember what he looked like."

I smile. Jacob's beard is coming in, and it is most definitely red.

"He trained horses, bred some of the finest in the valley and would take them to the big city—Saint Louis—and sell some when we had need of cash. He had a way with animals and people alike. Folks looked to him for advice, and he always had a word of encouragement. That's what I remember most about him. He had a kind word for everyone. He played the fiddle. Only he called it a violin. He could make it sing in ways that preacher could only imagine in his worst nightmares."

We both laugh.

It's time to move on. We collect our supplies and climb back onto the horses. Joseph is quiet, huddled beneath the blanket.

"What happened to him? To your father?" I ask once we've settled in at a comfortable pace.

"We lived near the big river and knew never to go into the water except where the sandbar formed quiet pools. But one day Pa's brother came visiting. We went picnicking by the river, and my uncle wanted to swim. He said he swam better than Pa and could handle the current. It was but a few moments before he realized the danger he was in. Pa went in after him, got him back to the sandbar just as a tree rolled past in the current. A branch caught Pa's foot and dragged him under."

"That's awful."

Jacob's jaw works. "I thought so too. One thing I have come to realize over the years though, is my Pa died like he lived. Laying his life down for his brother. If I can be half the man he was, my life would not be lived in vain."

We ride, not speaking for a long while. The road widens, and the terrain flattens. We are entering the plains. The city isn't far. Jacob is lost in thought.

"Anna Marie?" His voice catches my attention. "Do you think we can change the past? You know, if we can relive it? I mean, did not the news clipping say there were fatalities in the Dickerson fire? Yet Sarah told me you all survived. Do you think you changed history by being there?"

"I don't know," I say. "I think so, but maybe we just alter it a bit. No one died in the fire, but we had so many die on the way south. Perhaps they were the ones who would have died anyway."

Jacob rubs his whiskers. His eyes are focusing on a distant memory. "But if it were your sister that died, and you could go back and warn her, would you?"

"Absolutely." I'm beginning to understand. "Is this about your brother?"

Jacob looks at me, his face drawn and jaw clenched. His fists tighten and loosen. "We are ambushed on the way home. My brother will be killed ten days hence."

We ride around the curve on the road, and ahead of us is the first house we've seen all day. More houses line up in the distance. Daylight is fast waning.

"Looks like we've reached Fayetteville." I say, studying Joseph who has awakened but looks miserable. He is pale except for the red swelling showing from the edge of his bandage. "I hope we find the doctor soon."

We skirt the houses, keeping to the road north of town. At one point, Jacob stops at the baker's shop to inquire. He returns with a smile spread across his face and a large parcel in his arms.

"He knows the doctor well. Says she saved his wife's life. Insisted on sending some of his breads and cake to her since we were going that way." Jacob climbs back onto his horse's back behind Joseph. "Big two-story colonial on the right."

The equivalent of a city block, and we are there. Jacob lowers Joseph to the ground. I slide from my saddle and almost collapse.

"Good grief! My traitorous legs!" I giggle. My legs are spaghetti. Very painful spaghetti.

Jacob laughs. "I would be happy to carry you, Just Anna Marie, but it seems Joseph needs me more."

A sign on the door states: Medical Clinic, Dr. T. Easton, Dr. S. Johnson.

"We share a last name." I point at the sign. "Wonder which one is the magical healer." I look for the doorbell, shake my head, and go for the knocker.

A shadow moves inside, and a candle flickers and moves in our direction. The door opens, and a young woman wearing a starched white apron opens the door.

"Good evening, ma'am." Jacob removes his hat. "We have need of a doctor. Is one of them home?"

She nods, opening the door wide.

"Clean your feet before coming in, if you please, and the dog may remain on the porch. I'll let the doctor know she has a patient."

A wide wooden staircase lines one side of the foyer. The walls are covered in floral wallpaper. Opposite the stairs is a narrow table holding two lamps, the light made brighter by the strategic placement of an ornate, gold-framed mirror.

Hanging his wet blanket on a coat stand, Jacob motions for me to do the same with my oiled skin. Joseph is pale and shivering. Jacob puts his arm around him, and I wonder if he sees his own brother in this lean, lanky boy.

Footsteps echo from the hall behind the staircase. A slender woman, with thick dark hair gently streaked with gray and tied back casually at the nape of her neck comes around the corner. She leans lightly on a cane. Her head is down, a mild limp breaking an otherwise elegant bearing. As she approaches, she looks up and smiles. A jagged scar runs from the corner of her mouth up across her cheek and extends into her hairline above her ear, giving her smile a puckered and crooked twist. One eyelid droops, but the eyes are what I see. So dark, the pupil is almost hidden—deep, kind, and gentle eyes, eyes a lot like Tio Manuel's.

My heart stops. Time stops. Breathing stops.

It can't be.

I gasp. "Mama?"

"Mrs. Powers?" Jacob bursts out at the same time.

MAMA MIA

How would you like to have your very own photo shoot?" Daddy
is walking me down the hallway of his office. The cubicles along
the side are all empty. Everyone has gone home except for Daddy,
Mia (Daddy's secretary,) and a photographer I don't know.
Mama is with Adeline at the second-grade school play rehearsal. I
don't have a part, so I'm with Daddy.

"Really? Like Mama?"

"Yes."

"Can I have my hair done and makeup and everything?"

"Of course. But this has to be our secret. Mama wouldn't be
happy to see you wearing makeup. She doesn't realize how grown
up and how beautiful you are."

I beam. It's not often Daddy tells me I'm pretty.

As we enter the set, the photographer looks up. "She's still
not here."

"No problem. My daughter will stand in this once. Mia, can
you do her hair and makeup?"

Mia's brows go up. Then she walks over to me and extends
her hand. "C'mon, sweetie. First, let's get you out of those
school clothes."

She tosses a silky robe at me. I nod. I've seen Mama's photo shoots. She always wears a robe during makeup.

Mia puts the eyeliner on really thick and a lot of rouge and lipstick. When she's done, I don't recognize myself. When it's time to select a gown, we pass the dressing room and head back to the studio.

I'm confused. "What about my outfit?"

Mia laughs. "We don't have kids' clothes, honey. You'll be taking pictures like that."

Suddenly the softness of the robe feels uncomfortable. I pull it tighter around me.

The photographer has me sit on a bench and positions me really awkwardly. I look at Daddy. He nods. Then the photographer loosens the robe so it falls around my shoulders.

"There you go, gorgeous," he says. "Smile for me."

I try, but this isn't what I expected. The camera flashes. The lights are blinding.

"Here, now without the robe." He's taking the robe off my shoulders, and his hand lingers at my waist. He leans too close and runs his hand across my chest and to my stomach. I don't like this at all.

"Keep your hands off her, Ramon," Daddy says. "She's my daughter! A bit of respect."

I close my eyes. I'm being silly. It must be all right if Daddy says it is. Still, Mama says we're supposed to keep these places private. Goosebumps are rising on my arms. I pull the robe back up.

"Leave that down! You're ruining the pictures!" Ramon is angry.

Tears blur my vision. "I'm cold, Daddy. I don't like this."

"*Stop that crying. Tears are for the weak, so don't embarrass me.*"

Now Daddy is mad at me too. I ruin everything. Tears fall harder. Ramon is still taking pictures. Daddy walks up to me and slaps my face.

"*Enough!*" *His voice is cold.*

"*That's good,*" *Ramon says, the camera flashing.* "*She's perfect.*"

I sniff and swallow, trying to stop the tears.

"*Forget it. This won't work. I don't know what I was thinking. She's all wrong for this. She's too young.*" *Daddy graps my arm and jerks me off the bench..*

"*She's no younger than the rest,*" *Ramon says.*

I hate how he stares at me—like I'm some kind of pastry, and he's hungry.

Daddy shoves me toward Mia. "*Clean her up, she's a mess.*"

Mia takes me back to the makeup room and helps me rinse my face clean and get back into my school clothes. She doesn't say anything. She must be disappointed in me too.

"*You can't tell your mom any of this,*" *Daddy says as we drive home.* "*She will be very angry and disappointed in you. She might even leave us. If word got out how poorly you did, it could ruin her career. This has to be kept a secret. Do you understand?*"

I nod, fighting back tears. Daddy hates when I'm weak. My stomach is all yucky feeling, like it gets when I eat cooked spinach.

Weeks pass. I keep silent. It is the one thing I will not share with Adeline. I'm ugly and dirty, and everyone makes me mad. I get in trouble at school.

Mama picks us up. When we get home, she motions to Adeline to wait in the living room.

"I need to talk with your sister," she says, and leads me to our room.

"What's bothering you, mi amor? You've been acting very strange lately."

My stomach still has that yucky, too-much-spinach feeling. I look at Mama. She is beautiful, even without being all made up.

"Do you ever take off your clothes for your pictures?" I can't help myself. It slips out of my mouth before I can swallow the words.

"Of course not!" Mama says. "That's not the kind of magazine we have."

My stomach twists tighter. I should be relieved, and I am. I hate the thought of Mama taking pictures that way.

Mama goes still, like the stone lions at school. She takes my chin and makes me look at her. I try to look away.

"What happened?" There's a dangerous edge to her voice I've never heard before, and it scares me.

"Daddy said not to tell you, that you would get mad and leave us."

"Well, now you have me curious." I can see her trying to collect herself, restraining her temper. "I insist you tell me. I won't get mad at you, I promise. And I will never leave you." She grasps my chin tighter. She may be trying to hide her anger, but I feel it. "Has your father touched you?"

I squint up at Mama. What a weird question. "Sure, he holds my hand sometimes, and sometimes he hugs me. Why?"

"Just tell me what is upsetting you. Tell me everything."

I've never been good at keeping secrets. I tell Mama

everything. She is very quiet. The room is cold. She says she isn't mad at me, but I think she is.

When Daddy gets home, they fight. He knocks her down, kicks her. I want to run out and stop him, but I'm scared. Adi and I cling to each other on the floor of our room. I pull the pillow over my head and pretend music is playing really loud so it will block the noise.

Daddy was right. Mama leaves us. All because I couldn't keep a secret.

Mama blinks, eyes drawn in question as she studies first me, then Jacob, then me again.

"I'm sorry. I'm Mrs. Johnson. You must have me mistaken with someone else."

"Mama?" My knees wobble. My voice trembles and breaks. "It's me. Anna Marie."

My hand betrays me and reaches for her, but I catch myself and jerk it back, crossing my arms across my chest. This can't be real. It's a dream. I can hardly breathe.

Mama turns her head to one side and frowns. "Anna Maria?"

I nod. For once, words won't come.

"My Anna? Is it you?" Now *she* is reaching, and her hands shake as she touches my cheek, brushing the hair away from my face. "*Dios mío, no puede ser!*"

"Yes, Mama. It's me!"

Tears are falling down both our cheeks, and we reach for one another. I hug her tight. I will never let her go. Not ever and ever.

She's thinner than in my memory, but still soft. So soft and warm. As I bury my face in her hair, the scent of her engulfs me.

She pulls back, holding me at arm's length, running her hands over my hair, my face, my shoulders. Then she pulls me tight again.

"*Gracias, Padre nuestro.* My daughter is returned to me. *Mi Anna*

Maria. Thank you, Father God! Anna. I never dreamed I would see you again. And your sister? Is Adeline with you?"

"No." I shake my head and draw a hand across my eyes to clear my vision. "I hoped she was with you."

Mama frowns. "With me? Here? No." Her eyes widen with understanding. "Did she disappear as well?"

"Yes, last year—but she *is* here. In this time. I haven't found her yet, but I can feel her."

Mama holds my face in her hands, gazing at me with shining eyes. "Both my girls are here? *Que maravillo!* Amazing! Look at you. You are a beautiful woman, my Anna. I've missed so much."

There's a bump behind me as Joseph stumbles backward. Jacob grabs him and lowers him to the floor.

"Pardon the intrusion, Doctor, ma'am." An edge of panic laces Jacob's voice. "But the lad is not well."

A flurry of activity ensues. Jacob carries Joseph to Mama's exam room and lays him on a raised table. Mama removes the bandages. Her nose crinkles, and she bites her lip.

"How did this happen?" Agile fingers skim the swollen skin surrounding the empty orbit.

"A stick in the eye." Jacob doesn't enhance the explanation.

"What have you done for it?" She holds her palm over Joseph's forehead.

"I didn't know what to do, so I diluted some whiskey in clean water and rinsed it as best I could. I cleaned under the lid. I don't think there was any debris left."

Mama's brows raise as I speak. "That must have been terribly painful."

"He was unconscious, thank God," I say. "Did I do wrong?"

"No. It was important to get the wound cleaned. Son, what is your name?"

"Joseph, ma'am."

"Does it hurt terribly?"

"They give me sips of whiskey when it pains too much."

She laughs. It is the laugh that fills every happy childhood memory—deep, beautiful, unchanged. "I see. Well, young man, how about another sip. I need to clean your eye again, and it may burn. Not so much as the whiskey, I'm thinking, but things are pretty raw. First, I'll need to get my supplies."

Joseph nods, accepts a sip, and braces himself. His good eye is watering, and he bites down on his lower lip. Jacob grasps his hand.

Mama places a hand on my shoulder on her way out of the room. "You did well, Anna. Remarkably well."

When she returns, she carries a pile of bleached white cotton rags and is followed by the maid, carrying a large basin of water. Steam rises from the water's surface in thin wispy fingers. They remind me of the incense burned by the priest at Tia's church—fingers of prayer rising to Heaven—and I find myself praying as well.

Thank you, God. Thank you for bringing us to Mama. Now, please, if you don't mind, help Joseph get better.

"I have found that a saltwater solution is most effective for cleaning infected wounds." She soaks several of the rags in the warm water. She touches her elbow to the water and nods. "The temperature is good. We want it warm to draw out any pus but not so hot it will cause further damage."

She squeezes the excess water into a second basin, then cleans the angry red skin. Joseph clenches his jaws but does not cry out. He grasps Jacob's hand so tight, his knuckles turn white. Bit by bit, as Mama's gentle hands move in slow circles, Joseph relaxes.

"That wasn't so bad." Mama smiles down at him. "That's the worst of it. The first water burns, but then the wound adjusts. Now, son, we're going to soak your wound for a while. You may actually find this to be soothing."

Placing some dry rags below Joseph's head, she applies a soaked roll of cotton over the injured eyelid, covers it with a layer of dry cloths, and wraps a bandage to hold it in place.

She dries her hands and smiles that crooked smile.

"Now we rest and let his body and the good Lord do the rest. Meanwhile, we have some catching up to do. My experience here can fill a whole book, and I'm sure yours can as well."

We talk until the candle flickers and dies. Jacob refuses to leave Joseph. He sleeps on a cot, one hand resting on the boy's arm. Bellona wanders between us, not sure where she needs to be. Mama and I sit close, our hands clasped together, afraid to fall asleep lest we wake up to find this is all a dream.

"I thought you left—because of what I did." I pick at a loose thread poking out of my skirt.

"What are you talking about, *mi amor?*"

"The pictures. Daddy. I knew you were mad. I thought that was why you left."

Mama's face grows hard. "That *sin verguenza*, your father. No shame. I would have killed him that night if I were stronger. I planned to leave, yes, but *never* without my girls. I needed proof of what he was doing so he couldn't take you away from me. I found it too, on a flash drive in his computer. I was going to turn it in—but it made the trip with me. Lots of good it did here! I would have destroyed his life."

"Then 9/11 happened," I murmur.

Mama is crying. "Yes. I tried to get back to you. I was so scared—leaving you alone—with *him*. Did he hurt you?"

I shake my head. "No. Chachi made sure of that. Daddy was scared of him."

Mama smiles. "My brother? He came? I knew he would."

My curiosity piques. "What's his story, anyway? He kinda freaked me out. Is he like mafia or a drug lord or something?"

"His story is a tragic one, it could fill a book. We will talk of it later. Your uncle is a good man and he promised to watch out for you. He was the only reason I had any peace at all." Mama smiles.

When Mama smiles, her scar pulls her cheek on one side, making it look almost like a grimace.

"What happened?" I cringe as I run a finger along the scar that mars her face. I remember the magazine pictures, the advertisements—her exotic features and unique beauty.

She looks away, reaching her hand to cover her cheek. "A man beat me and left me for dead. I tried to defend myself, but he took my knife, and—" She makes a slashing motion across her cheek. "I thought I was going to die. I was alone in the woods, bleeding, my leg broken. Thomas found me, brought me here to his mother's home and nursed me back to health."

I gasp. "Oh, Mama. That's awful!"

"I thought so as well, but it has been the best thing that ever happened to me."

I frown. "How can that be good?"

"My beauty was my crutch, and it drew the wrong men into my life. Without it, I have been free to develop parts of me I never knew existed. Thomas and his mother encouraged me and gave me the safe place I needed to do just that. Mrs. Easton changed my life. She led me to God, *mi amor*. I became—well, for lack of a better description—I became a new person. I was even able to forgive your father."

I go cold. "Well, I haven't."

Mama nods, rests her hands on my arm. "It isn't always easy, even after it's been done."

"Is Thomas's mother still alive?"

"Yes, but she's bed bound. She had a stroke and can no longer speak. We read to her, tend to her physical needs, but she is a shell of who she used to be." Mama glances at the ceiling above us and smiles. "She was a lot like you, both in her love of music and her lack of fear about breaking the rules and pushing boundaries. She is the one who saw my interest in medicine and encouraged Thomas to teach me."

"So you went from being a model to being a doctor." I grin. "I would never believe it."

"It's a lot easier in this time, believe me! No years and years of advanced education required! My knowledge of germs and general cleanliness puts me light years ahead of half the physicians. I also remembered Tia's passion about her herbs. She knew just what to use for which ailment and talked about it all the time. Then Susanna taught me a few Indian cures. A bit of this and that and with our combined knowledge, Thomas and I have a lot of success."

"Rumor has it you're a witch."

Mama rolls her eyes. "*Dios mio*. That again. People don't like a woman being a doctor, but they respect Thomas, so they keep their peace."

When we can no longer force ourselves to stay awake, we check on

Joseph one more time. Jacob is leaning over so his head is resting on the crook of his arm on Joseph's raised bed. Both are asleep. We go to Mama's room, and I crawl into bed beside her. I am a little girl once again, snuggled safe in my mother's arms.

"This Thomas…" I arouse from near sleep. "He knows you're not from this time?"

"Yes."

"He believed you? He didn't think you were crazy?"

"It took time. At first, he thought it was the fever—after the beating. But yes. He believes me."

I stare at the ceiling. It is high, with thick crown molding edging the walls. The window is open, and a cool breeze blows through. I glance around the room. A vase with a dry flower sits on the table beside Mama's journal and open Bible. A brush and hand mirror lie beside the water basin. There are no signs that a man sleeps here. I find that reassuring. I just found my mother, I'm not sure I'm ready to share her yet.

"Will I meet him tomorrow? What's he like?" He doesn't sound like my father or most men I know. Maybe he's like Jacob.

Mama doesn't answer. Her breathing is deep and relaxed. Her melody is back, playing with my memory, but it is different somehow. Calmer, more fluid. It sounds peaceful. I listen to her song and the rhythm of her breathing and let them lull me to sleep.

JACOB THE DECEIVER

WHEN I AWAKE, MAMA is gone.

With a cry, I rush down the stairs with my heart pounding hard. Was it a dream?

I find her in Joseph's room.

"His wound is looking much better." She smiles up at me, unaware of the panic I felt finding her gone. "The swelling is down, and it smells much better. You brought him here just in time."

"It feels better." Joseph touches the clean bandage over his eye. "My eye—is it gone?"

"Yes, Joseph. I'm afraid you lost that one. I'm very sorry." Mama manages to deliver the bad news with a gentle touch.

He nods. His good eye blinks in quick succession. "Does it look dreadful?"

"It doesn't look great right now, but it will get better. Did you ever see sketches of pirates?"

"Yes."

"You'll get to wear a patch just like some of the most famous pirates. What do you think about that?"

"Could I choose what color to make my patch?"

"Of course."

"Can I still read?"

"Yes, you will do most things just the same. You still have one good eye."

A thin smile spreads on Joseph's face. His chin quivers. "Then I suppose I shall be fine."

A cough at the door, and we look up to see Jacob standing there watching us. He holds a package in his hand.

"Mrs. Powers?"

I frown. "You called her that yesterday. That's not her name."

Mama's face goes pale. She rests a hand on my arm. "That's the name your father uses. Johnson was too common for him. Powers suited him better." She turns to Jacob. "Do I know you from somewhere, son?"

"Daddy?" Ice rushes to the pit of my stomach. "You know my father?"

"Yes, Anna. I know your father." He turns to Mama. "and we have met—but our meeting has not happened for you yet. We will meet less than two weeks hence."

"You know my father?" I stand. I vaguely remember the man holding the horses in the woods outside of the Dickerson's home. The tall soldier speaking with the teen boy.

"What are you talking about, Mr.—?" Mama squints. Her scarred face pulls to one side.

"Reddington. Jacob Reddington. Please, call me Jacob."

"You! You were there! You burned their house!" I want to scream, but my voice comes out in a harsh whisper.

"I was. I was there." Jacob's shoulders stoop. His eyes plead with me to listen.

"I saw you. With my father's men. How could you? I trusted you!"

"What meeting, Jacob? How do you know me?" Mama is holding my arm, trying to get me to sit.

I shrug off her grip. "Why didn't you tell me? You tricked me. All this time. You knew I would despise you if I knew you worked with Daddy. What else did you do in the name of war, huh? Go around burning, thieving, and raping? How many, Jacob?"

"I did not know he was your father. I swear, Anna. You have different surnames!"

He shoves the parcel into Mama's arms. "Here, you gave this to me. You told me to return it to you again someday. I have carried it with me at all times since then, aside from my night in jail. They took it from me then. Ma'am, you giving me that book changed my life."

Mama studies the leather wrapped parcel, turning it over in her hands. Brows drawn, she unties the water-stained ribbon that secures it. Unfolding the wrap with care, she exposes a small, well-worn Bible and a thick, leather journal. They look like the ones on her desk upstairs. Her hands begin to shake, and she looks up at Jacob.

"These are mine! My life, my story is in these pages. How did you get them?"

"I think that is best explained by your own writing, ma'am. You also gave me your brother's phone number and a letter to give him. After some—interrogations—," Jacob pauses and rubs the back of his neck, "he was persuaded that your letter was authentic. He was of great assistance to Anna and myself, and very relieved to know you were well."

"My brother? Chachi?"

"I understood his name to be Manuel."

"Yes, it is. I gave you his number?"

"Made me memorize it and burn the paper."

Mama's eyes narrow. "Repeat the number."

Jacob repeats the same number Chachi made me learn. I stand frozen in shock.

"You never told me any of this," I say.

"I did not know he was your uncle."

Jacob flips through the journal and opens it toward the back. A small picture falls to the floor. Mama bends to pick it up.

"Oh!" She exclaims. "Where did this come from? I love this picture!"

"It was your husband's."

I know the picture. It's Adeline's favorite. Mama stands with shallow waves swirling around her legs, holding three-year-old Adeline and me each by the hand. She's laughing, and so are we.

"You!" I am rage. "You came looking for us. Did Daddy send you?" I snatch the photo from Mama's grasp.

My head is reeling, and the heat of my anger chills my very bones. Jacob. He is not who I thought he was. He lied to me. Tricked me. I am a fool.

"Anna, I did not know who you were. Please let me explain."

"You've said more than enough!" I turn to leave, but Jacob grabs my arm.

"Anna Marie—"

"Don't ever speak to me again, Mr. Reddington." I break his grip and stomp away. I can feel his eyes on my back. I will not turn around.

I am rock. I am ice. I will not feel.

Mama and Jacob spend ages in the next room. I will not be part of Jacob's plans, or listen to the lies he spreads. Instead, I put on my shawl, call Bellona to follow, and go off to explore. If I were home, I would put on my tennis shoes and go running.

No town we have traveled through is untouched by war. Fayetteville is no exception. The streets are dotted with burned-out buildings. An occasional log cabin and small shacks serve as temporary residences where grand houses once stood. A mill, newly constructed, turns its wheel round and round as the flow of the river passes below it. Random houses remain of the once wealth infused city. Most are of brick, but others of white wood siding and gabled rooflines.

Rutted and muddy streets form an organized grid, replete with puddles quick to hide potholes and rocks. Bellona zig zags with her nose to the ground, eager to inspect every post and sidewalk. I'm not sure how she can stand it. The smell isn't the most pleasant. I think people still have no qualms emptying their chamber pots into the gutters. Once that part dawns on me, I'm careful to avoid any standing water and shoo my canine companion away when she wants to splash through them.

Gaunt figures work in small garden patches, cleaning debris, or repairing a building. They pause and watch, unsmiling, as we pass. Some cast admiring glances at Bellona. One whistles to her. She ignores him. From what I gather, this town has been occupied by both North and South and harassed by roaming gangs of bushwhackers. I wouldn't welcome a stranger either, were I in their shoes.

Orchards of apple trees line the outskirts of town. A soft cloud of buds beginning to bloom draws swarms of honey bees. Perhaps this summer will bring happier times to the people living here.

In front of the dry goods store, a boy sits on a step.

"Paper, Miss?"

I glance down, longing to take the paper and turn to the personals. But I have no money. The headlines speak of the siege of Petersburg. The Union has recaptured the fort, successfully thwarting the confederate advancement.

I know what they don't. The war will be over soon.

Today's date is April 1, 1865. At home, in my own time, young people and grown-ups alike are playing pranks on each other. I pull my shawl tighter around me. It doesn't have to be April for me to be played the fool.

Having walked full circle, I find myself once again standing in front of the two-story house that holds Mama's clinic. A wide porch lined by elegant columns beckons the occupants to sit and watch the passersby, but the porch is vacant. The sign on the gate mirrors the one on the door. Medical Clinic, Dr. T. Easton and Dr. S. Johnson. A small thrill of pride runs through me despite my anger at Jacob and my irritation with myself. My Mama, the doctor.

"Anna!" Mama hugs me as I enter her clinic room. "I can't believe you're truly here."

Joseph sleeps. His color is much improved.

"Jacob is looking for you. He wants to talk before he leaves." Mama takes my shawl, folding it neatly.

"I have nothing to say to him."

"But if you just listen, you might understand."

"No. He's lied to me, not only in the last week, but in the months I knew him before all this stuff happened. I'm not interested in anything he has to say. Tell him I wish him the best, thanks for saving me from Jethro, and I hope he can save his brother. I mean that. The last part. About his brother. I'm guessing that's where he's headed?"

Mama's eyes darken, and she looks like she's in pain. I harden myself. I will not be manipulated.

"Don't look so sad, Mama." I touch the side of her face. "He's not my type."

"How would you know if you don't give him a chance?"

Heat rises.

"Trust me. I know my type a lot better than you ever could."

Mama sucks in air, covering her mouth with her hand. Brother. Me and my words. People are better off without me around to add prickles to their pain. I don't *mean* to be insensitive. I just am.

Trying to maintain a sense of self control, which really is silly since I've lost that already, I turn and leave, proceeding to the room I shared with Mama last night. I close the door and turn the key. Seems the walk didn't give me the alone time I needed after all. I throw myself on the bed, pull the pillow over my head, and block out the world.

An hour passes. Maybe more. Who cares when time isn't relevant anyway? There's a knock on the door. It's a solid door, made of dark stained wood with a pattern much like open books paneling its face. The handle wiggles, but the lock remains secure.

"Anna Marie?" It's Jacob. His voice is gentle.

Pain courses through my chest.

"I am sorry for deceiving you."

At least he can admit it. Now he can go away and leave me alone.

"You are right. I have done unforgivable things. It took me many months to forgive myself, so I cannot blame you for not extending forgiveness."

There's a long pause. I can picture him standing on the other side, rubbing his chin, then his forehead like he does when he's not sure of what to say, and I have the urge to run to the door and let him in, but that is not about to happen.

"I did not know the captain was your father. I am sorry, Anna."

I close my eyes, hugging the pillow hard to my chest. I will not cry. Nothing Jacob says can move me. I am a rock.

A slip of paper slides under the door. I turn over and cover my head again.

When something upsets me, I obsess, and today is no different. I need to turn off my brain. Stop thinking.

I'm totally spent. If I curled up in this bed and slept for a week, it wouldn't be enough. But sleep eludes me. I need a distraction. I never could lie around and do nothing while the sun is shining. This would be the perfect time for watching a movie or listening to the radio. To lose myself in mindless entertainment. If only.

I glance out the window at the backyard, where a flock of chickens peck at the grass. Somehow, I don't think they'll provide the distraction I need. A book would be nice. There are some in the den, but that would require me exiting my room and risking running into someone who wants to speak. I am not in the speaking mood.

There, on the floor, one corner under the door, is a folded piece of paper.

It must be a letter. From him. I'm ignoring it.

But it refuses to be ignored. The thing, once noticed, cannot be unseen, and my eyes keep wandering to where it lies. So I walk to the door, pick it up, crumple it in my hand, and toss it in the corner out of sight.

HE'S GONE

I WATCH OUT MY WINDOW as Jacob's horse exits the stable. He pauses and peers up at my window. He can't see me, but nevertheless, he tips his hat. He sits tall and straight. Man and horse move as one.

There's something about him that captivates me, and I hate myself for it. I can't tell when Jacob nudges his mare to move forward, but she does. I watch as they ride slowly down the road, picking up pace as he moves away from the houses. I watch as horse and rider become smaller and smaller against the sloping horizon. I watch until he's out of sight, and I feel empty.

Downstairs I find Joseph sitting up and eating his breakfast. I meander toward the kitchen.

"Can I help?" I ask the cook. She studies me, no doubt dubious of my skills. I wasn't much of a cook using modern conveniences, so I'm not sure how I will do anything here besides hinder. "At least I can wash dishes. I need to keep busy."

Her eyes widen with understanding, and she points me at a butter churn. "Work on that for a while," she says.

There's a knock on the door. My heart does this little jerking thing, and I wonder if Jacob forgot something. The cook sighs, wipes her hands on a towel, and goes to answer the door.

"Doctor Easton has returned!" Cook returns, all smiles. "Go, he will be eager to meet you."

I find him in the parlor, seated across from Mama. Her hands fly as she speaks. If you tied Mama's hands, I swear she'd go mute. He listens to every word she says, leaning forward and beaming at her animated expressions. When I enter, he rises to his feet, takes a slight bow, and reaches a hand to shake mine.

"This is indeed a marvelous phenomenon, having you in my home, Anna Marie." He means it, I think. His grip is firm, his eyes steady as they meet my own. "I am Thomas Easton. I have the privilege of being your mother's partner here at the clinic. She has taught me much over the years. Please, sit. I am anxious to hear of your travels."

He is easy to talk to. As we sit, I almost forget about Jacob. I retell the story of my arrival, the encounter with father, the burning. I cry telling them about William's death.

"A brain bleed," Mama says. Thomas nods.

Mama holds me as I describe the days of hunger, the cold, the creek with the graves. Her eyes sparkle when I tell them about Grandma Gray's murdering the English language, her knowledge of the outdoors, her generosity, giving from the little she had.

Dr. Easton's eyes get moist as I relive the days in the cave—our desperate struggle to care for Mother Dickerson, her husband, Martha, and Mary Elizabeth, and our inability to dig a grave deep enough and how we piled rocks over their shallow grave in our attempt to keep wolves and other wild beasts from devouring their remains.

They laugh as I describe my frustration at the meandering tales and difficulty getting directions once we neared the Dickerson's home. They smile at my description of the home we made, the closeness of the family, the music that filled the mountainside.

"You always loved music." Mama rubs my hand. "My mother did as well. I have so few memories of her—before. The good ones are full of singing. Tell me, do you still hear people as melodies?"

I nod, touched that Mama remembers. "Some. Some are music, and some have sounds all their own."

Thomas grows angry when I recount the story of Jethro chasing me through the woods, relieved when Jacob finds me.

"That is the young man I told you about, the one who left this morning," Mama says.

"The one who informed you about Roger?" Thomas's eyes cloud over. He frowns.

Mama pats his arm but doesn't answer.

Thomas grins when I describe Bellona lunging at Jethro and clamping down so hard on his arm the bone shatters.

"As a physician, I should not enjoy that story so well," he says. "But I cannot help myself."

"If you like that, you'll appreciate this one more." I tell them about my struggle with Jethro outside the camp store, culminating with me stabbing him in the eye with the only weapon I had.

"What weapon was that?" Mama is breathless, sitting on the edge of her chair.

I glance down, concerned she may fall to the floor. "My fork." I shudder.

So does she. "Speaking of eye injuries!" Mama almost knocks over the vase of flowers on the table beside her, she rises with such haste. "I forgot Joseph! His dressing needs to be changed!"

Thomas rises and takes Mama's arm. She leans on him, her limp barely noticeable.

She removes the bandage, and Thomas leans over to inspect the injury. He sniffs the drainage and smiles. I relax the moment I see his response.

He pats Joseph's shoulder. "How does it feel?"

"I hardly notice it anymore, except if I move too fast or bump it on the pillow."

"That's good. You are well on your way to not needing a doctor."

After dinner, I help with the dishes. At least I can do that much to earn my keep. The cook isn't quite sure what to make of me but enjoys the company and chit chats about Mrs. Easton, the neighbors, and the latest gossip about the war. Finishing my chore, I dry my hands and head back to the main house.

"I do not understand why you must go." I hear Thomas's voice as I come around the corner.

I pause, not sure if I should interrupt the conversation.

"He's dying, Thomas."

"That is a good thing."

"He's still my husband."

"Even after what he did to you? You still feel an obligation to him? What of me? Of this practice?"

"I'm coming back. My place is here. Working with you."

"Then do not leave."

"Please try to understand. Roger is my husband. And he is lost. I have been forgiven of so much. The least I can do is offer forgiveness of my own. I have to talk with him."

There's a long silence. Daddy is dying? He deserves it. Mama should know that. He deserves to die, alone and miserable. Mama has done nothing that needs forgiveness. I don't understand her drive to reach out to my father.

I'm feeling guilty for eavesdropping, but it would be even worse to walk in now, so I remain where I stand and continue to listen. Footsteps pace the floor, steady and even. I picture Thomas walking back and forth while Mama sits watching.

"Very well." The pacing stops. "But I am going with you."

Mama sighs, relief, I think. "Thank you, Thomas. In a few days, Joseph should be well enough to return home. We can leave then."

I need to be alone. I return to our room, sit on the edge of the bed, and look out the window, down the road, across the valley. I wonder how far Jacob traveled today.

The crumpled paper lies in the corner, inches from my foot. I lean down, pick it up, and smooth it on my lap. Jacob's handwriting is elegant and smooth. I didn't expect that from someone with hands as large as his. Each letter is constructed with care, even and firm, like the man who made them. A smudge of ink is the only imperfection on the page. I sigh, giving in to a sudden need to know what he says.

DEAR ANNA MARIE

My Dear Anna Marie,

It is true, over the years of the war, I have done things no man should ever do. I have killed and wounded many a man who did nothing wrong except be born on the opposite side of the country from myself. I took part in the destruction of homes and cities, all in the name of war. I have turned my back and ignored worse things to protect myself and my brother. In the long run, I protected neither.

Back in your time, when you spoke of the Dickersons and the fire, I was not straightforward. While I did not know for sure theirs was the home I remembered, not knowing the name of the family, your description sounded too much like the family whose home I witnessed burn to the ground. Children were still inside. I tried to save them, but my fellow soldiers restrained me. Their cries haunt me still. I could not bear to tell you when you asked. I feared knowing, you would despise me. I longed for your trust then, and my not telling all cost me your trust today.

It took me many months before I came to peace with God over my sins. Many tears were shed before I understood the largeness of His forgiveness and the grace extended to transform such a wretch as myself into a child of his. When your mother gave me her Bible, she saved my life. For in its pages, I found a reason to live.

I realize, however, that despite receiving God's pardon, I am not free from the consequences for what I have done. I understand how my participation under your father's leadership will make me utterly repulsive to you. Please believe me when I say I am sorry. I never intended to hurt you or to hide who I was from you. I could never imagine that a woman such as yourself could in any way be associated with a man such as my captain.

Would you believe me if I told you I saw you first in my dreams, many months before we met? Would you believe me if I told you I loved you even then? It is true. You can imagine my shock when I saw you in the jail. I so often had seen your face in my dreams, and then to realize you were real.

As we became better acquainted, my heart became yours unreservedly and without regret. It will remain yours as long as I draw breath. I do not understand God's purpose for bringing our lives together, but I know I am a better man because of you.

And now I must leave you. When my brother, Johnny, ran away to join me in the war, I made a promise to my mother to bring him home safely. I was unable to keep that promise. Perhaps, if God allows, I may be able to do so now.

Is it possible to change history, or does God put events in motion that are unalterable? I do not know, but perhaps for this, I was allowed to survive and return to this time.

As I write, the strangest thought occurs to me: there may be another me along that road. A Jacob who has not seen the death of his brother, a Jacob who has yet to travel to your time. A Jacob without you in his life. How will I affect my own history? My future? By doing this, will I never meet you? Will that other me dream of you as I have? Will he love you and pursue you as I have? Can I be jealous of my own self? My brain aches with pondering such thoughts, so I joke with myself and say, may the better man win. I must trust that the Lord has this under His control.

I take my leave, thankful that you have returned to your mother and are in a safe place. I pray your search for Adeline is successful and that your life from here forward is a blessed one, surrounded by those you love.

I could not bear to leave with so much unsaid. Perhaps one day, we will meet again, and perhaps then you will find it in your heart to forgive me.

With all my love,

Jacob

JACOB IS IN DANGER

MOBY DICK. ALTHOUGH UNRECOGNIZED in this era for the genius it is, there's a reason it's a classic. Joseph bites his nails and leans toward me, listening to every word. We laugh when Fleece preaches to the sharks, urging them to overcome their voracious nature. We shiver at the descriptions of harpoons piercing the flesh of "innocent" whales and marvel at Ahab's infectious drive for revenge. Right as the giant white whale rushes the whaling ship, there's a dreadful pounding on the door.

Bellona's bark erupts, loud and threatening. I nearly drop the book, and I swear Joseph rises three feet from his chair.

"Miss Anna!" I hear the anxious voice the moment the maid opens the door.

"I must speak to Miss Anna!"

It's James, and my heart beats hard in my chest. Something is wrong. I rise, nearly tripping over the crazy skirt that inevitably wants to tangle around my ankles whenever I hurry.

"James! What's wrong?"

"I have terrible news! Jethro Tanner escaped from jail. Old Pete and his gang broke him out, and he left this note."

He hands me a paper, sullied with coffee and tobacco stains. My hands shake as I open it.

"As the Lord is my witness, them who put me here will surely die. Beware, Jacob Reddington. I will find you and all them with you."

My hand flies to my mouth and suppresses a cry.

"When did this happen?" I sink back into my chair. "When did he get away?" My mind is racing, trying to calculate how quickly Jacob will travel and my chances of catching up with him.

"The sheriff found him missing late last night. I came as soon as we heard."

"Is someone ill?" Mama rushes into the room. "I heard the door."

Her eyes light on James, and her brows furrow. "What's wrong, son?"

I can see why she would think him sick. He is flushed and breathing hard. I can only imagine how his horse must look after making the trip in half a day, one that took Jacob and me all day to ride.

"Mama, this is James, Joseph's older brother. He brought bad news." I fidget with the note, then hand it to her. "Remember the man I told you about who assaulted me near home and again in the mountains?"

James stares at Mama. He looks confused.

"Yes." Mama takes the paper. "You said the judge was to arrive this week. They have him in custody."

"This is your mother?" James continues to gawk.

"He got away," I answer my mother.

"Your mother is the lady doctor, and you didn't know?"

"Oh, dear." Mama skims over the note, pauses, and reads it again. Her brows shoot up. "It's a good thing Jacob left. They'll have no idea where he is."

"He has gone?" James's voice breaks. "He ain't here with you still?"

"Isn't. No. He isn't here. He left two days ago," Mama says.

"Where to? Are you really Miss Anna's mother?"

"Yes, I am. Jacob headed to Missouri to find his regiment."

James squeezes his eyes tight and slams a fist into his palm. He says a word that has Mama on the verge of scolding him.

"That's where they're headed. One of the other prisoners said he overheard Jethro telling Old Pete his captain had stashed a good bit of gold and jewels stolen from the homes they burned out. They were headed north to Missouri, following the army." James swipes a lock of hair away from his eyes. "Wow. I did not know Miss Anna had a mother."

Mama looks at me. I look at her. We nod.

"Let me get Thomas. We need to leave right away," she says.

I pat James on the shoulder. "Mama and I were separated many years ago. Except for Joseph's injury, I wouldn't have found her."

Once again, James protests being left behind. "I made it all the way here by myself—in half a day. I can do it!"

We're in the stable, placing the last of our hastily gathered supplies into the saddle bags.

"Yes, no doubt you *are* able, but your horse isn't, and we don't have one to spare. Besides, someone has to take care of Joseph. It's too soon for him to be moved," Mama says.

James pouts. "Miss Anna can stay, I can use *her* horse."

"Not a chance." Wrapping my bedroll around a change of clothes, a tin plate, and a small canvas, I secure it with twine and tie it to the back of my saddle.

"He has a point," Thomas says.

"I'm going." I glare at both of them, checking my food sack.

Thomas shrugs and grins. "Sorry, James. See that expression? It is just like her mother's, and it means you have a better chance of snow in July than you have of dissuading her."

"He could move to the southern hemisphere," I quip.

"You are sure you can change the bandages, just as I instructed you?" Mama asks.

"Yes, ma'am."

"Three times a day. And be sure to wash your hands thoroughly with soap after you remove the old dressing and before you handle the clean one."

"Yes, ma'am."

"He's healing well. The infection is clearing. It should be safe to return home by the end of the week, as long as he has minimal discomfort."

"Yes, ma'am."

"Whatever you do, don't let Doctor Williams touch him."

Thomas snorts a laugh.

James scrunches his nose. "Huh?"

"What are you laughing at, Thomas Easton? You wouldn't let that man near your horse, much less your child!"

Thomas raises one brow, winks at James, then returns to his work.

"Do not let her frighten you, boy. She simply has a difficult time surrendering control. You will manage. Tis no hard thing she asks, and she is right. She is always right."

Mama smacks Thomas's shoulder. "Remember you said that." The look that passes between them speaks volumes. There's a lot more to this friendship than collegial respect. "It's time. *Vamonos!*"

Hiking up her skirt, revealing a pair of men's slacks beneath, Mama sticks a foot into the stirrup and pulls herself up and in place with such ease, it amazes me. I forget she's lived this life for over a decade.

James blushes and turns away.

"Try galloping in a skirt some time, James." Mama chuckles. "Trust me, the slacks are more decent and a whole lot safer."

"Don't look at me!" I laugh, raising my skirt to reveal my own slacks beneath. Poor James is likely traumatized for life. Grasping the horn of the saddle, I attempt to pull myself up. Epic fail. I, unlike my mother, require assistance getting onto the horse's back. So much for youthful athleticism. Bellona whines, standing on her back legs and pawing at my legs. She is staying with the boys. It eases my conscience about leaving them alone. She'll keep them safe. Thomas carries his gun, and I conceal Jethro's pistol in my skirt. We'll be fine.

Missouri, here we come.

The Ozarks have a rugged beauty about them, with stunning vistas, rivers, lakes, and waterfalls crisscrossing the mountainous terrain. It's a grand place to vacation. In the twenty-first century, by car. While I can appreciate the untarnished beauty of the nineteenth century, my thighs and backside rebel.

Almost plunging headlong down steep ravines, splashing through ice cold rivers, and ascending mud-soaked hillsides, we move on and on at breakneck speeds. In truth, I am the only one in danger of breaking my neck, one minute holding the horn to keep from sliding off the back, the next moment clasping the cantle so as not to flip over my horse's neck. No one notices. If they do, they are too polite to mention it. I have a feeling they find this humorous or maybe they're making me pay for insisting on coming along.

We rise each morning with the sun, stopping only for what bodily functions are required. Each night we collapse on our bedrolls to sleep, most nights without the luxury of a fire. Thomas says we don't want to signal our location to any who would harm us.

After two days, and we emerge into hill country. We are back in my home state. We skirt cities and towns that I'm familiar with, but they look nothing like what I know. Mostly, we keep our distance from the towns. More and more, we find remnants of recent campsites soldiers have occupied.

The morning of April 9 dawns with clear skies. At the courthouse in Appomattox, Lee and Grant are sitting together to work out the conditions of surrender, marking the beginning of the end to this war. It is strange to be living on the cusp of history and know what cannot be known to any around us. I want to yell the news into the wind! *Go home! It's over!*

We cut a path toward Cedar Creek, hoping to cut Jacob off on his search for his regiment. This is the road his people take, according to what he told Mama. On this road, his brother dies. That will happen tomorrow, if Jacob's quest is unsuccessful. My stomach churns, and we spur our horses on faster.

I wonder how his troupe knew about Appomattox so soon. The news could not travel this far west from Virginia overnight. Then it dawns on me. They knew for the same reason we do. Daddy knows his history.

Eminence is north of us when the sky turns black and thunder begins to rumble. We seek shelter under a rock overhang and wait out the passing storm. I toss, turn, and stare. Clouds scurry past brilliant stars, giving way to a clear night sky. Thomas rises to check the horses. Mama lies motionless beside me, but I can tell from her breathing she doesn't sleep either.

I rise to the sound of unease. I pat the pocket of my skirt. The revolver I took from Jethro is secure in its depth. We break camp before sunrise, a renewed sense of urgency burning deep. Today we find out if history can change.

"We're getting close," Mama says. "I believe Jacob stated they were ambushed a mile or two down this road."

I hear a familiar dissonance. My bones are on edge.

My horse favors her foot. Oh, crud. Tell me she hasn't thrown a shoe.

I halt my horse, dismount. Thomas sees what I'm looking at and dismounts as well.

The sound is louder, too familiar. My stomach tightens as I recognize the cacophony.

"Jethro," I whisper. "Mama, Jethro is close. I can feel him."

Hoofbeats echo on the path we just took. We exchange glances, shifting our feet and searching our surroundings. Do we try and hide, or do we stand our ground and hope for the best? It sounds like a solo rider.

My horse whinnies, lifting her head and sniffing the air with excitement. She tosses her mane, paws the ground, and whinnies again. The coming horse whinnies a reply. Too late to hide. Whoever it is knows we're here.

I see the black horse first. Then I see her rider.

"Jacob!"

I want to rush over and hug him and tell him I'm so glad to find him and I'm sorry I judged him and that I don't want Jethro to find him, or us for that matter, because I really like the idea of there being an "us".

So I stand... and say nothing, holding the reins to my horse and staring stupidly as he approaches. He swings off his horse, glances at me, and looks away. I stiffen. Maybe he's not as happy to see me as I am to see him. Not that I blame him.

"Mrs. Johnson, Doc, Miss Anna. What a surprise."

"You're in danger!" I want to kick myself. No, 'I'm sorry I was mean,' no 'are you all right?' I'm such a jerk.

His brows furrow, and he turns a questioning look toward Mama. "Ma'am, you know my intent."

"We came to warn you," Mama says. "Jethro escaped and is heading this direction, Anna thinks he's close. He's looking for you."

"And my father. He thinks my father has a bunch of money, and Jethro lured the gang to come steal it, and he swears to come after you and all who are with you, so we came. To warn you. Because, because...

I needed to." All right. Now I know I'm an idiot. I bite my lip to keep from saying any more.

"That makes sense. It was likely he who attacked our group." Jacob runs a hand across his forehead, then rubs his chin. The stubble of a beard is growing in, some of the hair is blond, but most is red. The red compliments his blue eyes.

He glances down at Sunspots's hoof. I want to warn him that we all need to get moving. Jethro is near. I stand like an idiot and watch as he dismounts and kneels to check my horse's shoe, lifts the hoof, and removes a stone. She nuzzles his hair. Then her head snaps up, and she snorts.

Jacob stiffens, his hand goes to his gun.

He's too late.

Someone else's hand reaches his pistol first. It's Jethro. His rotten-toothed sneer spreads across his face as Jacob freezes.

NO GREATER LOVE

"WELL, WELL. IT SEEMS only right that if you take my gun, I should have yours. Wouldn't you say?" Jethro spits at the ground. "Such a pretty little party. Never took you to be the deserting kind, Jacob. Why are you not with your unit? Something happen to that wee brother of yours?"

"I would never desert!"

"Ah, so says the man of honor. Yet here he stands. You and me, we ain't so different."

He shoves Jacob, and he falls on the ground in front of me. "Down to falling for the same gal. But I wasn't good enough for you, was I, Adeline?"

I don't answer. I see Thomas move out of the corner of my eye.

"Uh, uh, do not touch your gun, good sir, or I shoot both the ladies. You wouldn't care to have that on your conscience, now would you?"

Thomas moves in front of Mama. "We have a small amount of cash, son, if that's what you are after."

"Thank you for telling me. I'll tend to that later. Miss Adeline, seems you got my men scared off. They took one look at you through them trees and rode the other way. They's be saying you's a witch. Said you done cursed their leader, and he died in his own mess. I says, witches must die."

"You made a promise," Jacob says. "You said you would not harm her."

"What good is a promise when it be coerced? Coerced, see? I can speak fancy like, just like you and the lovely lady. But I done decided. If I cannot have her, I ain't leaving her for you."

"Jethro, you do not have to do this." Jacob raises his hands.

"Oh, but I had plenty of time to think this one out. Time in that jail, with my arm all in pain. You ever been to jail, Jacob? Well, the beauty of my plan is this—I am going to shoot you with your own gun. Ain't that ironical? Shot with your own bullet?"

"Will not be the first time," Jacob mutters.

"What?" Jethro frowns. "Do not try and distract me. I am preparing to shoot you, but before I do that, I thought I'd shoot the lovely Adeline. How many bullets is this thing holdin' anyway? Enough to put one in each of your friends? Can't leave witnesses, see? Might tarnish my reputation. But if you, the deserter, killed all these fine folk, then killed yourself, well that would just be a tragedy. Ain't that a mastermind?"

I step forward.

"Your beef's with me, not with them. Please don't hurt them. I could've killed you, but I didn't. Please Jethro, consider that." My heart is pounding so loud I'm sure Jethro can hear it.

"Not so brave without your dog around, are you?"

"She wouldn't have hurt you if you hadn't been trying to strangle me." So much for trying to appease him.

"Beg," he says. "I liked the way that sounded."

"Never." Blood rises in my cheeks, and my vision turns red. I feel the cold steel in the folds of my skirt. This time I will not hesitate.

He pulls back the hammer of Jacob's gun. The click reverberates through the woods. In my pocket, my hand closes around the revolver. In one smooth motion, I pull it from my skirt and aim.

"No!" Jacob leaps toward me and shoves me, throwing himself in the path of Jethro's bullet. Everything is slow motion, like in the movies. I never take my eyes off Jethro, and I shoot as the flash leaves his gun. If I die, he goes with me. There's a second shot. Jethro's head snaps back, and I feel warm blood splatter my face as I hit the ground. I must be shot. I wait for the pain, but it doesn't come.

Then I see him. Jacob is falling. A blossom of blood stains his chest.

I try to catch him as he collapses to the ground, but he falls just out of my reach.

Jethro collapses and lays motionless. Cries and voices are calling around me, somewhere in some far-off place. What has happened? I cannot understand.

"*No!*" Tears pour down my cheeks. I'm wild and desperate, crawling to Jacob. I grasp him to me, cradling him in my arms. "Not you! You can't die! I need you!"

I hold him. This man who has been so strong lies limp in my arms, and I pull him close. Mama is beside me, leaning over him, trying to stop the bleeding.

"Anna Marie." Jacob raises a hand to caress my face. His fingers are cold. "Did he hurt you?"

Yes! I want to say. He has torn my heart. He has taken what I love most. I sob, shaking my head. "No. I am untouched."

He smiles. "Thank you, Lord." His eyes close, then flicker open. "How did you learn to shoot like that?"

I shrug. "I got mad."

"Ah, yes. I know that temper." His laugh turns to a cough. Blood trickles from his mouth.

I wipe it away.

"You are worth it." He blinks as though trying to focus. His breathing is coming in short shallow gasps. "My life, to keep you safe, is worth it. I love you, Just Anna Marie. I always have." His eyes meet mine. His face is a blur through my tears, but I swear he grins that mischievous grin of his. "Methinks...you like me...as well!"

"I love you, Jacob." Why did it take me so long to realize this? I kiss his forehead, his cheeks, his lips. They are cool. I kiss him again.

He kisses me back. Salty tears wash down my face and cover his.

"Am I...dead? Is this...Heaven?" His voice is soft. He coughs. Then he is still.

"No! No!" I lay him on the ground, placing my hands over his heart and begin compressions. "Mama! Do something! Help me!" Blood trickles from his wound. I feel for a pulse. Nothing.

I begin again. "Please, please. You can't leave me Jacob. You can't! Oh, God! Please! A miracle!"

I feel a hand gently pushing mine away.

"He's gone, *M'ija.*" Mama's voice breaks through my prayer. "Let him go."

His blood covers my hands, soaks my dress. I did this. This is all my fault. I'm the one who deserves to die. I bury my face in his neck and I weep. I am empty. Grief is all that's left.

We bury him along the side of the road, where the shade of a tall oak cools the ground. The oak reminds me of Jacob, steady and strong, not easily swayed. Tall and beautiful.

We leave Jethro for the animals to scavenge.

Mama says Jacob pushed me away, Jethro's bullet striking him instead of me. Thomas's shot went off just after mine. We both struck our target. Two men are gone. The world is better for the loss of one, but that can never make up for the loss of the other.

Few men have ever lived, or will ever live, like my Jacob.

We stop at a cabin in the woods to ask directions. Mama says she must go to the camp where my Father is dying. I can't bear the thought of moving further, so I remain behind. The lady of the house is about my age but looks much older. A toddler clings to her legs, and a baby sleeps in a cradle. She lacks several teeth, but her smile is sweet, and her hands gentle as she washes the blood from my hands.

I resist at first. This is all I have left of Jacob—this blood on my hands and dress. I was supposed to die. It should be my blood soaking the ground. My body buried beneath the oak. Why hasn't the earth opened up to swallow me?

I am too tired to resist anymore. I give in and let the water wash me clean. If only it could wash the blackness off my soul.

I Once Was Lost

BEFORE, I THOUGHT OF myself as a rock. Now I am shale, hard to the touch, but unable to hold the weight of the most casual grip, flaking off into pulverized pieces. I thought myself cold as ice. I am more like the glacier, breaking under the weight of the deposits layered one over the other throughout the years. Deep cracks and porous surfaces form as I slide ever closer to being absorbed into the sea.

Mama is quiet when she picks me up at the cabin. ""Your father is gone. He was crushed by his horse, just as before."

I shudder. I was not privy to what happened before. I don't want to know. All I knew was my father, Jacob, and Johnny travelled together with a group from their regiment, and most were killed.

"Before he died, he said to tell you he was sorry. He loved you in his own broken way."

It means nothing.

Later, as we ride through the forest, she pulls her horse beside mine. "History is changed. Johnny is alive."

I look up at her, tears swimming in my eyes.

"Tell me."

"They were ambushed, but this time by fewer men, so they were able to defend themselves."

"Jethro and his group weren't there."

"That must be what happened." Tears shimmer in her eyes.

"How is Johnny?"

"He was shot in the leg, shattering the bone. Jacob made a tourniquet. It controlled the bleeding, but he could do nothing to save the leg. Thomas and I had to amputate. He will live."

"Jacob? He is well?" I see him, lying in my arms, cold, lifeless, a hint of a smile across his face.

"He is unharmed." Mama studies me for a long minute. "Anna, this Jacob is not the same as the one we knew. His future is also changed. I didn't send him to the spring like he said I did before. I didn't share any of the things he told me to. I didn't give him my journal. He will most likely not fall to our time. He won't find you." She reaches a hand toward me like somehow her touch can ease my pain.

It doesn't.

My heart is imploding. I nod. I know it's better this way. I only hurt the ones I love.

"This Jacob has a family that needs him, *M'hija*. His brother has to learn to survive this post war tragedy with only one leg. His mother depends on him. It would not be fair."

I think she's trying to persuade herself.

She's right. This is the other Jacob. The one my Jacob wondered about. The one who has yet to find peace and forgiveness for the things suffered through the war. I swallow hard, but the lump remains lodged in my throat.

"Your Bible. Did you give him your Bible?" I can't look at Mama. The road in front of me is a blur.

"Yes. I had to do that much."

I blink hard. My nose drips. I run my sleeve over it. "Thank you."

James and Joseph are gone when we return, and I'm glad. How do I explain that the man who did so much for all of us lies cold under an unmarked grave, a tall oak the only reminder of his last resting place?

I spend my days doing little meaningless things around the house. Bellona shadows me everywhere I go.

On April 15, the news of Lincoln's assassination has the nation in an uproar. To me, it makes little difference. I continue my pointless existence.

When I can put words to paper, I write. I send a letter to Margaret and tell her of Jacob's passing and inquiring after Joseph's health and James' well-being. Most often I retreat to Mrs. Easton's room. She has a large, well-worn Bible, and I read aloud to her. She follows me with her eyes, blinks an acknowledgement of my presence, and the non-droopy side of her mouth smiles ever so little. She listens and finds meaning in what I read. This book brought my Jacob peace and a reason to live again. I read to connect somehow with him. It soothes the ache in my chest enough that I can breathe a little.

I feel closer to Jacob. This is what he read to find forgiveness. I wonder if the other Jacob is finding it as well. I don't deserve to be forgiven, so I don't search for it. I seek to understand.

I tell Mrs. Easton stories of my childhood, the things I have done. I tell her about my Father. A tear runs down her cheek. She blinks but doesn't look away. Her eyes are kind. Little by little I find my anger toward my father changes to pity. I mourn, not so much for him, but for what could have been.

A pianoforte sits against the wall of Mrs. Easton's room. Mama says she played it well before the stroke. I tinker and figure the melody that is my sister. Someday, I will search for her. I can't right now. Not yet. I tell Mrs. Easton about Adeline and describe her music. I learn the deep melancholy tones that cover my soul. As time passes, a few notes work their way in. Not quite a melody, but something besides the clash of chords.

The dreams come again. The same ones I had in that other life. I run through the woods, thunder claps overhead, and rain begins to fall. Only it isn't rain. My hands are covered with blood. I fall, naked and ashamed, at the base of a tree. Crimson liquid runs down, soaking the bark and the ground below. It smells metallic, the smell of a life leaking out. I will not look up. This time the ground doesn't open its angry mouth. And it doesn't cry, but a voice cries from high up in the tree.

"Why?" It moans. "So many dead. I died to save them all."

I tell Mrs. Easton my dreams. She's easy to talk to. Maybe because she can't voice any blame. While I speak, her own music comes through— soft, so very soft I can barely perceive it. I play it for her as best I can. Her eyes smile.

Margaret writes. Joseph is well, playing with his cousins and improving his carvings under his uncle's tutelage. Nancy is engaged. Granny Gray and her grandson came to visit. James is staying after school taking extra lessons with the new schoolmaster. They want me to visit first chance I get.

Days pass, then weeks. The summer is almost gone. Sunday morning, I tuck Mrs. Easton comfortably in a chair next to a window so she can watch the birds and the clouds, and I leave with Mama and Thomas to attend the service. There's a visiting preacher today, so the church will be full.

Thomas walks close to Mama, and her hand lingers on his longer than usual. I smile. She deserves a man like him.

The church is packed as we grab the last few seats on the back pew. I remember Jacob's horror when I pointed out my messed-up hair and dress and the dirty looks the women gave me. My heart aches when I recall his awkward proposal and my harsh response to it.

There's a new tune in the building today. I haven't heard it here before, but I *have* heard it elsewhere. It sounds like distant choral voices, singing without words. My spine tingles.

The preacher is missing his hand, amputated halfway between elbow and wrist. Like so many veterans, his life has been permanently altered by the war. His smile is warm, genuine, and there is a gentleness to his voice. I strain to hear.

He speaks of men dying to save their brothers out on the field of battle. "Greater love has no man than this, that a man lay down his life for his friends."

Jesus said that, about Himself. That's what the preacher says. We, though undeserving, wicked, and worthless people, have been saved because our Lord loved us and laid down His life so that we could be with Him in paradise.

I listen, drinking in the words.

"He died for you," the preacher says, his eyes resting on me. "He loves you that much."

Could this be true? My heart beats faster.

I've experienced love like this. Jacob loved me. He died to save my life, even when I rejected him. Is this what Jesus did? Could God love me like that? I think I'm beginning to understand, and I'm in awe. Could it be true that the creator of the universe, the One who keeps the tiniest atoms in place and organizes the movements of all things seen and unseen, loves me enough to die, like Jacob did, for me?

I remember Jacob's blood covering my hands, soaking my clothes. It should have been my blood spilled. I remember my dreams, me falling at the foot of the tree, my hands covered with the blood of the one hanging there.

He died because of me. Because He loves me that much. But he didn't stay dead. He rose again.

I understand.

I go to the altar when the food and wine is offered. I can't reject Him anymore.

Tears stream down my face, and when the preacher asks if there are any who wish to be baptized, I raise my hand.

We walk to the river, singing a hymn that will echo for always in my heart.

"I hear the Savior say, thy strength indeed is small; child of weakness, watch and pray. Find in Me thine all in all."

We've reached the river's bank. The preacher reaches for my hand. I take his and step into the cool water, feeling the tug at my skirt.

"Jesus paid it all, all to Him I owe; sin had left a crimson stain. He washed it white as snow."

I am plunged beneath the surface. Above me, the sun glimmers through the shimmer of water. The current pulls and flows past me, taking my old life with it. My hair comes undone and swirls around my face. Then the preacher's strong arm lifts me out into the summer air.

"Lord, now indeed I find Thy pow'r and Thine alone can change the leper's spots and melt the heart of stone."

I am clean. When I come out of the water, Mama rushes to me and wraps her arms around my drenched shoulders, kissing my cheeks.

I grab her around the waist and lift her, twirling in a circle. "Mama!"

I throw my head back, close my eyes, and take in deep breaths of good clean air. "Mama, I understand! I finally understand!"

"All to Him I owe. Sin had left a crimson stain. He washed it white as snow."

For the first time in my life, I am clean. The lightness that fills me is indescribable. I feel like a person who has been buried alive, spending years breathing through a straw, unable to do more than gasp for breath. But now the dirt has been lifted, and I rise to fill my lungs with air for the first time.

We walk the few blocks home, my skirt clings to my legs, but I don't care. I skip and spread my arms like a bird in flight. I want to run. People give me strange looks.

"I've been baptized!" I wave as I pass. Some smile. Others scurry faster along. The sun is brilliant, reflecting off the first gold and red leaves indicating the changing season.

There's a woman pacing on the front porch when we arrive. From the looks of her, she's been there a while. She practically falls on Thomas when she sees us.

"Thank God!" She clasps his hands, wringing them in her own. "I'm Lydia Brown. My brother's wife is in labor. He sent me to get you!"

Thomas looks at Mama.

She nods. "That is something you do better than I. Let me get your bag."

"May I go with you?" I have always wanted to see a delivery.

Mama laughs.

Thomas shrugs. "I can pass on the family knowledge," he says. "Best put on some work clothes."

He turns to the young lady. She's staring at me with the strangest look on her face.

"Oh, sorry. I don't always look like this." I wave a hand across my soggy attire. "I was just baptized—in the river."

She still stares at me like I'm some kind of ghost. I have this urge to jump and yell "boo!" but I restrain myself.

"To what address do you want us to call?"

"Our homestead is east of here, sir. About ten miles, maybe a few more. I will lead the way."

She's anxious to get moving, so we prepare quickly.

Bellona greets me with her usual enthusiasm, back end wagging with the joy of one who thought I was gone forever and finally returned home. When she calms down enough, she circles my skirts, sniffing curiously at the damp fabric, giving an intermittent wave of the tail before turning to dash up the stairs ahead of me to Mrs. Easton's room. I surprise her when I place a kiss on her cheek and hug her close.

"I understand!" I say. "I was baptized today!"

Mama thrusts a couple of sandwiches into our hands and bids us Godspeed.

Lydia leads, and Thomas follows, asking questions as he goes. "Is this the lady's first child?"

"Oh, yes."

I take the rear. Bellona dashes back and forth through the woods with her nose to the ground and tail wagging behind her, returning frequently to check on me. Often, she brings me a stick or a leaf, or some other odd object clenched between her teeth, grinning her silly smile as she drops it on the ground ahead of me and takes off in search of more treasure.

We veer off the main road, down a trail that is no more than a footpath. The going is rough.

"Is the baby full term or early to come?"

"As far as I know, it is due to come."

Branches rub against my boots as we ride. Down the mountainside, across a creek, up the other side. I want to sing "The Bear Went Over the Mountain" but don't want to freak Lydia out entirely. She glances back at me, shakes her head, and keeps going.

"Any problems with the pregnancy?"

Lydia shakes her head.

We traverse the mountain top. The view is breathtaking. The valley below is dark green in fields ready for harvest. The sun is warm on our backs as we ride on.

"How old is your brother's wife?"

Lydia scrunches her nose and turns to look directly at me. "How old are you?"

She's a strange one.

"Almost twenty-one," I answer. "Why?"

Lydia turns her gaze back to Thomas. "She would be almost twenty-one."

So, we're about the same age.

The big river snakes back and forth in the distance. If we followed that river east to the Mississippi, then continued north from there, we would end up in Saint Louis. Somewhere along the river's path, we would pass Jacob's home farm. I wonder if his family still lives there. If they still raise horses.

Our shadows are beginning to stretch long in front of us. My canine companion now travels at a steady pace behind me. I hope we get there soon. There are still wolves in these mountains.

"This way."

We branch back down hill and come upon a clearing. A knoll surrounded by trees on three sides and cleared on the fourth, allowing for an unhindered view of the valley below. Most people leave the trees for a wind block. The couple here must prefer the scenery to weather protection. I smile.

The view is breathtaking. No debris litters the front yard. A small vegetable and herb garden is fenced off to protect it from the cow that grazes below. Chickens run free. A rose vine climbs a trellis at the corner of the porch. The flowers are the same color as Tia's climbing roses.

Lydia is the first to dismount and runs up the steps to the house. As I slide off my horse, and motion Bellona to sit, stay.

A short, broad-shouldered young man throws open the door.

"Did you find the doctor?" He peers out in our direction.

"I did," she says. "And I'm not saying who else I found."

And he stares at me just like she did. I look at my dress, run a hand across my face, and smooth my hair. I look behind me. Maybe they're staring at something over there. Nope. Just me.

"Hi!" I wave my hand, not knowing what else to do. "I'm Anna Marie. I was baptized today." Yes. That's really what I say. Because I'm awkward that way, blurting out something totally inane to a man whose wife is in labor. I'm smiling and feeling really stupid and am totally not prepared for what happens next.

"Lord have mercy!" Lydia's brother whoops, leaps off the porch, and rushes down to where I stand with my mouth hanging wide open.

I thought *I* was awkward.

He swoops me up in his arms, twirls me in a circle, and yells. "Adeline! Your sister is here!"

ADELINE

P RACTICALLY CLAWING MY WAY free, I fly into the house. I
really do fly, I swear, because I didn't once feel the ground touch
my feet. Hey, I can travel through time—what's a little thing
like flying?

There, in the middle of the spacious room that serves as bedroom,
kitchen and living space lies my sister. Her face is rounder, perhaps a tad
bit puffy. Her hair rests across her pillow in a long braid. Beads of sweat
stand on her brow. Her beautiful dark eyes are round and have this mixed
expression of shock and pain. And she is very pregnant, like, majorly.

"Oh, my word! You're huge!" I blurt out and throw myself at her. She
is the most beautiful woman I have ever seen.

She cries out, and I jerk back. "I'm sorry!" I didn't mean to hurt her.

Her face draws up in a grimace, and I think I can feel her pain.

Maybe not.

The pain is all in my hand. She has it in a death grip and pulls me
down next to her, so our faces are inches apart. She squeezes till my bones
overlap, and she's breathing hard, panting like a dog. I panic and look to
Thomas, who is just entering the house.

"Do something!" I cry. "She's dying!"

He chuckles, moving calmly to stand by my side, and places a hand
over Adeline's bulging middle.

"She is not dying, Anna Marie. She's in labor."

The contraction eases, and so does her grip on my hand. She rests her head and gazes at me. "Anna? Am I dreaming again?" A tear escapes and runs down her cheek.

I wipe it away and kiss her hand. I'm crying too. "I'm here, Adeline. I got your message! I've been looking for you for so long!"

She smiles. Dark rings form crescents under her eyes. She motions to her husband. "Branson—did you see? My sister is here!"

He sits on the side of the bed beside her, smoothing her hair, then leans over to kiss her forehead.

"I knew you'd come." Her eyes haven't left mine. "Didn't I, husband?"

"That you did!"

I become aware of Bellona, now at my side, peering at me then Adeline, confusion clear on her face. She whines, and I grasp her large head and hug her to me.

"Bellona, meet my sister!" I'm laughing through my tears.

Adeline responds with a gasp.

"Sorry I won't be much of a hostess today." She groans and grasps my hand again. "I-really-am-happy—oh, crud! Here it comes again!"

In my head, a full symphony breaks out, not unlike Beethoven's fifth. Some family reunion.

In the wee hours of the next morning, baby Sarah Anne makes her appearance. She's all wrinkled and red and covered with this slimy white stuff. She waves her little fingers wildly like she's lecturing the whole lot of us and is downright mad. The tiny thing screams louder than any little set of lungs should be able to scream. Adeline is crying something about how beautiful she is and reaching for her.

My brow raises as I inspect the child. Beautiful isn't how I would describe her. I keep my mouth shut.

Thomas lays the messy little creature across Adeline's chest, and the most amazing thing happens. Sarah Anne stops screaming, opens her eyes, and gazes right into her mother's face.

I think my opinion is changing. This little one, eyes intent on taking in her mama for the first time, is the loveliest little person I've ever seen.

Branson is crying as well, and with one arm under Adeline's head, the other pulls her and the child close. He inspects Sarah Ann's fingers, her toes, her tiny mouth, and pulls a blanket over the two of them. Then he kisses my sister full on the lips.

Thomas heads home alone. No way I'm leaving.

"Hey, I just became an aunt!" I shoo him off. "I've got bonding to do." Then I turn to Adeline. "He'll be back tonight."

"That won't be necessary." Adeline gazes at me, then at her daughter who is nursing with vigor. "I'm fine. And with you here, I'm better than fine."

"He won't have a choice. You see, four hours across that valley and up toward Fayetteville, there's a lady who's dying to see you."

Her eyes narrow. "Who?"

"Mama."

"Mama is here? Just ten miles from here?"

"Yep."

Our eyes fill with tears. We're being way too emotional, and we hug each other for the twentieth time.

"Tell me." I settle in beside Adeline, drawing her head to my shoulder. "Tell me everything since you left home."

And she does, beginning that day at Lazarus Springs.

She waved for her friends to go on without her.

"We were just around the corner from the spring and the little eddy where Mama taught us to swim. You remember that place?"

I nod.

"The water flowed past, like a living thing, crystal clear. It always seemed to call out to me. I loved that place."

I can picture it like it was yesterday. A sand bank creating a protected pool, the perfect swimming hole or fishing corner.

"I paddled around the eddy, rammed my kayak up on the shore, then got out and pulled it up onto the bank. It was such a pretty, little clearing. Did you know Mama's parents used to go fishing there?"

"I found the news articles you clipped. I never knew about them."

Adeline closed her eyes and sighed. "The dirt road, overgrown with small plants and vines came close. A bench, the wood peeling and splintered, nestled in the underbrush at the base of a large tree whose branches shaded the beach. I could picture Mama standing there, watching and laughing as we splashed in the shallows."

"I stood there for a while, just looking around and wondering what happened to Mama and her father. They both went missing, right there."

"During a terrorist attack."

"That was the weirdest thing. Did something happen that day, when I disappeared?"

"Yes." I grasp Adeline's hand and kiss it. "More than 1,400 killed in a Syrian chemical attack."

Adeline lets out a slow whistle. Bellona, who has been sleeping by front of the door, lifts her head and studies us.

"Wow. That explains it. Sort of. I decided to go swimming. It was hot, and the water looked good. As I waded out, I saw the strangest reflection shimmering on the water's surface, strange because it wasn't mine. It was the reflection of a woman, her hands covering her face. I wished her hands would move, and for a moment they did. She looked just like Mama, except older, and her face was distorted—like she'd been cut. Reaching out, I touched the reflection. Oh, Anna, it was the most frightening thing that ever happened to me."

Candace found Adeline at the creek, dazed and freezing. "When she tried to tell me where and *when* I was, I couldn't believe it at first, but when her mother told me about Mama so many years earlier, what she looked like, her sassy manner, and even how she flipped her hair away from her face when she talked. I knew it had to be true."

The Dickersons hired Adeline on to help with the little ones. "I was grateful they took me in. Everyone was talking about the Battle at Fort Davidson and Ewing's escape, and few were inclined to be friendly toward strangers. It's so hard for a woman to survive alone in this time, and I was penniless, homeless, and friendless."

It was at the old water trough that Adeline first saw Anna's reflection.

"I thought I was imagining things, but then it happened again, and well, I knew it was you and I had to communicate somehow. I got William to place the ad, and then I carried the paper with me everywhere, trekking out to the trough multiple times a day until you reappeared."

Jethro came calling. This upset William. He said Jethro had a reputation and shouldn't be trusted. The night after Adeline saw Anna the last time, Jethro got pushy about his intentions. When she asked him to leave, he began throwing things. Mr. Dickerson told him to go home and get cooled off.

Next day, Mr. and Mrs. Brown were heading south on a coach. Mr. Dickerson feared Jethro's intentions, so asked if Adeline could ride with them.

"I intended to move on further south toward the Indian reservation. Mama's folks lived there once, and I wondered if Mama might have gone that way. But I had no money, and I was alone. Then I met Branson. I wrote the Dickersons, telling them the news." Adeline glances up at me with a sheepish grin. "We got married three weeks later. We planned to travel, search for Mama, but then," she pulls her baby close, "I found out we were expecting, and Branson insisted on staying put until the baby was old enough to travel. We stayed with his parents until this place was finished. Moved here in time to plant a garden and get settled before the baby was due."

I squeeze Adeline's hand and lean close to her. "Do you love him, Adi? Is he the outdoorsy, adventure-loving guy you used to say you wanted? Or did you decide 'animal loving' was enough? I saw those chickens and the cow outside."

Adeline's eyes sparkle. "He's all that and more. Anna, God has given me the best man in the world. I have so much to tell you, and I can't wait for you two to get to know each other."

I stand up, pat her hand, and move to better see out the window. Branson is throwing scraps out for the chickens, and they flock toward him from all directions.

"As you can tell, I have a dog now." I turn to find Adeline watching me.

"She's beautiful."

"She's a trained guard dog. Chachi got her for me. That would be our uncle. Did you know Mama had a brother?"

She nods. "Yes, I found his picture when I was doing our family history. I thought he died. Wasn't his name Manuel?"

"His father nicknamed him Chachi. Short for *muchacho*. I never found out what he was involved in, but it must have been pretty bad. He faked his own death. Even after that, he was afraid someone would find out he was alive and hurt one of us to get at him, so he kept hidden."

"That's terrible. Mama must miss him dreadfully."

I never thought of it like that. It would be terrible not being able to see your brother, especially while you lived in the same "time zone."

"So, did you ever find your 'Stradivarius?'" Adeline pushes off the quilt and picks up a fan from her bedside table.

"My Stradivarius?"

"Yes. Don't you remember? I said I wanted to marry an outdoorsy guy. You said you wanted to marry a violin."

We laugh, and my heart constricts. I look back out the window.

"So, no one special?"

"I found the perfect Stradivarius." My voice is low, my throat tight. I cough to clear the restriction. "I was just too stubborn to realize it until he was gone."

"Gone?"

"He died saving my life."

I face my sister. The joy that beamed on her face moments earlier is replaced by a deep pain, reflecting my own. Memories flood back. I miss him so much.

"You would have loved him." I know she would. She would have seen immediately what I saw too late.

She reaches for me, and I fall on my knees beside her, burying my head on her lap. I let her hold me as I cry.

NOT MY JACOB

MY SOUL IS AT peace. I don't know when I have ever felt this way.

It began when I rose from being washed in the river. Now, returning to Mama's home after our reunion with Adeline, music washes over me, and I am complete. I know who I am.

I go upstairs to Mrs. Easton's room, gently close the door behind me, and sit at her side, holding her hand as I speak.

Her skin is pale, nearly as translucent as Mrs. Dickerson's had been, with fine blue veins visible beneath the surface. Her nails are yellow, with lines and cracks showing the years of hard work. Thomas files them to keep them from getting thick and broken. Brown spots freckle the back of her hand, but her palms are pure white.

"I never understood, before," I say to my aged friend.

Her eyes watch me, intent and expectant.

"One priest talked about God being a loving father. That never meant anything to me. I didn't want another father. The bishop who came to the school talked about God being a just God, and warned us to 'be good lest you come under His wrath.' I tried to be good. It never worked."

I laugh, pat her hand and stand. "I came to the conclusion that there either was no God, or He didn't like me much. It wasn't until Jacob— when he died... I never knew anyone could love me like that."

Mrs. Easton's eyes glimmer. It must be so hard not being able to speak. But then, a new thought comes to me. Maybe she's been speaking on my behalf for these many months.

I sit back on the side of her bed and stare into her face. "You've been praying for me, haven't you? All this time! You couldn't speak to me, so you spoke to Him!"

She blinks, and a wedge of a smile plays with the corner of her mouth, and tears shimmer in her eyes. I hug her.

"I have to show you something. I haven't shown anyone else. Listen! I found my song."

I rise and go to the pianoforte, take a deep breath, and close my eyes. The music flows, fluid and free. I finally know who I am.

Summer ends too soon, and brilliant reds, golds, and yellows cover the mountains. We travel through the mountains to witness Nancy's wedding. She's beautiful. Everyone hugs me, and mutter condolences about Jacob. Everyone lost someone dear during the war. They understand, but I still have trouble talking about him.

Joseph comes running to greet me, looking for all the world like an overgrown puppy with a pirate patch. James stands as tall as Thomas. He's still long and gangly, but his smile is ready and the tilt of his head confident. I hug him tight.

"I'm going to be a preacher someday, Miss Anna." He grins and his blue eyes sparkle. "Would you believe it? I been helping the teacher at school, and he thinks I have a gift for oratory."

"Your father would be so proud!"

The leaves fall and the air turns crisp and cool. Bellona and I travel the path back and forth between Adeline's and the big house so often, I think the path actually gets wider. Mama comes every chance she has, but the clinic is busy and demands much of her time. She's teaching me how to mix herbs and make medicinal teas, and I observe as she and Thomas inspect and attempt to diagnose various ailments. I'm busier and more content than I've ever been.

The week before Christmas, a carriage arrives carrying Lydia, Branson, Adeline, and the baby. We meet at the courthouse and witness as Mama and Thomas exchange their vows.

Adeline leans on Branson's arm. Her face glows. I love seeing her this way, so complete, so happy. This is one thing I will never experience. I lost that chance when I rejected Jacob's proposal. I won't let myself think about what could have been.

Men come to court. I'm flattered but cannot accept any of them. It isn't fair to them, always competing with the memory of another and always falling short. It's okay. I'm content. My life is full.

I bury my face in my niece's curls, breathing the sweetness in. She giggles and pulls my hair. My life is good.

February brings cold winds and snow. We don't leave the house very often. As winter thaws and gives way to spring, we bury Mrs. Easton. I grieve her passing. Though she never spoke a word to me, somehow I know she loved me as much as I grew to love her.

"We're planning a road trip," Mama announces shortly after May Day.

We're enjoying a picnic lunch in the shade of an apple tree. Adeline's family has come for the day. I relish these moments when we're all together.

Sarah Ann crawls off and picks up what looks like a pebble, except it has legs. Branson brushes it from her hand. She arches her back and wails. Adeline looks at me and shrugs. "She likes bugs. What can I say?"

"A trip? That sounds wonderful. Where to?" Branson says.

"Springfield. There's an Agriculture and Modern Machinery Fair next month. There will also be a group of physicians meeting to discuss advancements in medicine. They've invited Thomas to attend.

"You're not invited?" This bothers me. I will never get used to how they push women to the periphery, no matter how skilled they are.

Mama regards me. One corner of her mouth turns up ever so slightly.

"Yeah, right. Wrong century, sweetheart. But don't worry. I've taught Thomas everything I know."

"Anna should come with us," Thomas says. "The two of you could explore the fair while I'm in meetings."

"I don't know. Adeline might need help." Thinking of traveling far from my sister makes cold shivers go up my spine.

"Oh, no you don't." Adeline gives me a knowing look. "You can't stay around here forever. Go with Mama. It'll be fun. Besides, Lydia is plenty of help. Just promise me, both of you, that if you see someone's reflection in the water, you won't go touching it."

I laugh. "Not even my own."

"Is that how this time travel thing works?" Thomas asks. "By touching the reflection of someone reflecting from other side?"

"We can't be sure, but it seems to be the case—but it only happens when there is some catastrophic killing event. The three of us—and Mama's father—all fell through at the same place."

Mama nods. "It was this isolated swimming hole. Papa used to go fishing there all the time, and I used to take the girls swimming in the same place. We figure that spot must be a vulnerable location—like a weak spot on the time continuum."

"Daddy fell through somewhere else, so there must be more than one place this happens."

Thomas is staring at his hands. "Do you miss it?" He doesn't look up. "Do you want to go back?"

"No!" We all three respond at the same time, and I'm surprised to realize it's true.

"My place is here. With you." Mama reaches for Thomas' hand.

Adeline grins at Branson. "And I'm staying with you."

My time has nothing for me. Everyone I love is here.

It's a beautiful day when we leave the place that has become more home to me than anyplace I've lived. I glance back at the house as our buggy pulls away. We should be back in two weeks, but it's like I'm saying goodbye to an old friend and not sure when I will see her again.

We hitch Dark Matter and Sunspots to the buggy. Jacob knew horses well. These two are a perfect match. Bellona wears her happy face, anticipating a new adventure, I suspect. She is my ever-present shadow, to the point where I wouldn't be surprised if she starts diagnosing patients before I do. She gets bored with my long days at the house, and I find her to be ever enthusiastic when the horses come out. Horses mean running and opportunity for chasing squirrels and rabbits.

We stop in little towns along the way. The war may be over, but the roving gangs are still a problem, and camping is less desirable. Midway through the third day, we arrive in Springfield.

The city is bustling with life. We pass a steam mill by the river. The sounds of an engine clanking and the cloud of vapor coming from the chimney tell me it's in full operation. A brick factory is not far, the yard full of bricks laid out in a herringbone pattern with enough space between to allow air to circulate and aid in drying. Men and boys are busy turning the bricks.

As we get closer to the center of town, I see people of varying nationalities hurrying through the streets: some Black, a few Chinese, even a handful of Mexicans. My untrained ear picks up accents from the broad sounds of Britain, clipped gutturals of Germans, and lilting sing song of the Irish. We don't even draw a second glance.

Near the city center, my heart thrills to see a library. The sign says "Open to the Public." I nudge Mama, and her eyes light up. Books. I want to crawl out of the buggy right now and immerse myself in whatever adventures the shelves present. Do the libraries of this time smell of old books like those in my time?

"See those stables over there?" Thomas points across the road. "That's where Wild Bill shot David Tutt. I met Mr. Hickok during the war. The fellow has a fondness for drink and a restless temper. They'll get him killed someday.

Mama and I gawk. They'll be talking about this and making movies about Wild Bill a hundred years from now.

We stay at a hotel not quite as famous as Hickok's gambling establishment, but ours is quiet and "more respectable." We have the last room.

"I'm sorry. It is all we have left, but it has a sitting room attached. I can have a cot brought up for the young lady," the gentleman at the counter informs us.

We take it. The fair starts tomorrow, and rooms are at a premium.

The first day of the Agriculture and Modern Machinery Fair arrives, and I'm champing at the bit to go exploring. I have to sit through an interminable breakfast of tea and scones before the livery man arrives with the horses and buggy.

We step out onto cobblestone streets as the last of the night lanterns are being removed from their hooks on the posts. It feels like a movie set. I glance around, half expecting to see cameras and powerful lights.

Their absence is a reality check, although the pungent odors of unwashed humans and livestock is reality enough.

Mama chuckles as I trip over myself trying to get into the buggy, forgetting the cumbersome skirt that tangles around my feet. I hear that in the "wild" west, ladies are getting away with wearing trousers. I'm also told that women who try to do that in the civilized regions of these United States are likely to be thrown in jail. It seems "all men are created equal" wasn't yet intended to include women. Meanwhile, it's lift the skirt or drag the dirt home with you.

On the far side of town, vendors have set up tents to draw in gawkers and buyers alike. Horse powered versus man powered farm equipment is proudly displayed: planters, rakes, and stackers, as well as new models of plows touted to be more durable than any of their predecessors. Posters show a single man leisurely holding the reins to a team of horses while a young boy tags along pouring seed from a pouch or just smiling up at his father. It's the revolution of the single-family farm.

Sewing machines and mechanized looms are in their own section. Mama pulls the buggy up along the side and gets down to inspect. I follow, keen on getting a close-up view. There's a carnival atmosphere to the whole affair.

But it's not the sewing machines that catch my eye. It's the horses, clustered together in a pen opposite the "domestics" tent. A young man is brushing down a silky chestnut while showing the horse to an interested customer. William would be about his age had he lived. Tall and lean, this boy has a shock of red hair and a wispy mustache that clings to his upper lip. As he circles the horse, his gait is uneven. When he moves into full view, I see his peg leg. Another war casualty. And he's so young.

"Gentle, reliable." His voice carries my direction. I lean on the fence to watch more closely. "She will not win any races, but she is a real Steady Eddie."

My heart does a pinch. Steady Eddie. I've heard that phrase before.

"Are those your horses, Miss?" A voice calls behind me. Then, "Whoa! You're a friendly pup!"

I turn, not sure if it's me being addressed. A tall, blond man is kneeling next to Dark Matter. She nickers and nuzzles his hair. Sunspots is not to be left out and butts his side, bobbing her head up and down like she does when she's happy to see me. She's not that way with most people. But it's Bellona that surprises me the most. She's all over the fellow, with her backend wagging so wildly, it's likely to break apart.

"Bellona, down!" I walk toward where the gentleman squats on the ground. "I'm so sorry. I don't know what got into her. She's not usually so affectionate toward stra—" My words strangle in my throat as he straightens and turns toward me.

Bellona sits, doing that doggy grin of hers as her tail pounds its rapid rhythm on the ground.

"Oh!" My hand flies to my chest. "It's you."

He's talking to me. His speech is all muffled like it's echoing from far, far away. He smiles. A dimple flashes beside his bushy, handlebar mustache. Oh, that thing has to go.

I'm having trouble breathing. Mist settles over me. Music is everywhere. I blink, trying to focus on his face. His smile wavers, and a cloud of concern darkens his blue eyes. Those eyes. The same color as the sky.

And I'm lying on my backside staring up at the cloudless sky, trying to catch my breath while Bellona whines and licks my cheek and Jacob leans over me, waving a sheet of paper in front of my face.

"Miss! Are you all right?"

I've died and gone to Heaven, I want to say. I long to reach up and touch his cheek. I want to grab his face and plant a big kiss right on those lips. I want to slap him and ask him why he did such a stupid thing as go and get himself killed in the first place. I close my eyes.

"Yes. I'm fine," I say.

This isn't the Jacob of my past. This is the Jacob from before. After. Whatever.

"Sorry about that." I apologize for the second time. "Call me Grace."

I laugh. My voice is shaky, and so am I as I struggle to get back up. My feet catch on my skirt, and I plop back down.

"See what I mean?"

He chuckles, that same low chuckle I remember, and takes my elbow, helping me to rise. "I see you live up to your name."

"Oh, that's not my name." I brush dirt from my skirt. My face is burning. I'm making a total buffoon of myself. "Sarcasm. I was being sarcastic, you know, seeing as I am anything but graceful, just falling over my feet for no good reason. 'Cuz you standing there with my horses and my dog acting like you're her long lost best friend is no reason for me to fall over like some fool woman." There I go with the idiotic, nonstop, run-on sentences again.

He's not my Jacob. He's not my Jacob. I close my eyes, wishing for a deep dark hole to hide in.

When I open my eyes, he's gazing at me with his head cocked to one side and one brow raised.

"Never mind me." I straighten myself and walk to my horses.

"Have we met?" he asks.

I freeze. My back is to him, and I'm glad he can't see my face.

Yes! I want to say. You proposed to me once. You died saving my life. But he's not my Jacob.

"I don't believe we've met." I'm breathing nice, slow breaths, forcing myself to relax.

"Name is Reddington. Jacob Reddington."

I know. Oh, help me, I know. I feel him come close. This Jacob's presence is every bit as large as the one of my memory. He extends his hand as I turn to face him.

"I'm Anna Marie Johnson. Just Anna Marie is fine."

"Pleased to make your acquaintance, Just Anna Marie Johnson." He grins. It's daggers to my heart. "That is quite the dog you have. Not sure I have seen one like that. Is she part wolf?"

"German Shepherd."

"Oh. Sheep dog?"

"No, guard dog. For personal protection."

He's patting her head, and her tongue is hanging out with her silly happy smile.

"Oh." He looks dubious. "Guard dog, eh? Bellona, did you call her? Is that not some ancient war god?"

"Yes. She's not usually this friendly. You must remind her of someone."

"I will take your word for that. Do your mares have names? They look to be about the finest pair of horses I have seen in these parts. Nearly as friendly as your shepherd." He's rubbing the black's nose. She snorts and flicks her lips, looking for a treat.

My heart tugs.

"Thank you, Mr. Reddington. They used to belong to a fine horseman and dear friend. That one is Dark Matter. I call her Matt for short. The other is Sunspots."

"Peculiar names."

"Yes, my friend was intrigued by space and time as well as by horses."

"Was? Is he no longer intrigued by such things?"

"He died."

Awkward silence. I kick the dirt and look over my shoulders for Mama. What's taking her so long? I avoid looking at Jacob's face. I'm afraid I can never look away if I do, and he thinks I'm nuts already.

"I am sorry. I should not have probed."

"Those your horses?" I ask, pointing at the pen.

"Indeed." His eyes sparkle. "Would you care to see them?"

He extends his arm, and I can't help but take it. He's solid, not as lean as last I held him, but still solid.

"Are you certain we have not met? You look familiar."

Is he flirting with me? I release his arm. I can't do this. I can't pretend he's a stranger. Every word, every gesture is familiar to me. *This is not my Jacob.*

"Maybe you met my sister. We're twins."

"Maybe." His brows pull close as he rubs his forehead, then his chin. So much like my Jacob. He frowns, then shakes his head.

"You know, I gotta go." I feel a tightening inside, and I have to move. I have to get away. "Thanks for picking me up off the ground, and I'm really happy Johnny's okay. Have a good life, Jacob."

I pick up my skirts and flee down the street, away from my horses, away from Mama, away from Jacob. I run all the way to our hotel, Bellona by my side. She thinks this is some new kind of game.

I don't look back. I can't.

I'm breathing hard. My heart is pounding well on the high end of my target rate for exercise when I barge into our room, which is blessedly vacant. I throw myself on my cot and cry until I fall asleep.

It's Music

"PRECIOSA, WAKE UP." MAMA is rubbing my back. I groan, grab the pillow, and cover my head.

"I heard of your morning. You met Jacob—and left quite an impression, I think." Mama tugs at my pillow.

I grip it tighter. "Leave me alone." Even to my self-pitying ears, I sound like a child. "I want to die."

"You need to rise, *mi amor*. We are invited to dinner."

"Where?" I peek out from under my pillow. I haven't eaten since breakfast, and my stomach rumbles. I'll save the dying for another day.

"It seems Mrs. Reddington insists on meeting the doctors that saved her son's life—and Jacob asked if you could join us. We're going to their house."

"They live in Saint Louis. It will take days to get there. I'm not interested. I'll eat here."

"Silly. They moved. They have a farm just east of here. Come, now. Let's make you presentable." She combs my tangled hair. She used to do that, when I was little. It soothed me then.

Tension eases from my shoulders. "Mama, I don't know if I can bear it."

"I know." She lays a hand on my shoulder. "Who knows? Maybe once you get to know him, he won't be your type. But then, perhaps it wasn't chance you ran into him today. One thing is sure, he is intrigued. He asked many questions and even asked permission to call on you."

Someone has wrapped a steel strap around my chest and yanked it tight. "Oh, Mama." I lean on her shoulder. "It's too much to hope for."

Thomas pulls the buggy up at six o'clock sharp. We squeeze on the bench beside him. Bellona rides on the luggage shelf, all proud and regal. People watch with keen interest, pointing curiously as we ride past.

I'm so nervous, the crowds no longer intrigue me. We ride past the library, and I don't look its direction. Thomas is chatting with Mama about the meeting. He speaks quickly, and his hands carve the air in animated gestures. Mama is smiling.

Leaving town, the road is well-packed and smooth. Matt and Sunspots pick up their pace. Neat farms lie on either side of the road. The landscape rolls in a peaceful fashion, perfect for the corn and wheat that grows thick in the dark fertile soil. Mountains rise to the north. The Reddington farm looms ahead. Somehow, I know that's their home. It fits everything I imagined.

Horses lift their heads to watch as we approach. Green pastures, enclosed by split rail fencing, circle a sturdy barn. On a small rise is a farmhouse. Not too large, but welcoming. A porch wraps around the entire place. Daisies bloom in the flowerbed. Jacob's favorites.

Mrs. Reddington is a tall woman, lean and straight. Her hair, a dark blond, is streaked with silver. She does not look like Jacob until she smiles. They share the dimple.

She rushes to greet us, drawing Mama into a giant hug. Tears glisten in her eyes.

"Please! Come in. Our home is your home. We owe you everything."

"Not to us," Mama replies. "To God."

"Yes." Mrs. Reddington holds Mama's hands, gazing at them as she turns them palm up. "And these were His hands."

As I cross to the porch, Mrs. Reddington grasps my arm. Her gaze is gentle but curious and assessing. I should be used to people looking at me like I've grown an extra body part, but I have no idea why I get that reaction. I wish I did.

She looks me over from head to toe. Her brow rises. Her eyes are a caramel brown, not blue like Jacob's. "You must be the young lady Jacob told me about, the one with the horses."

So, that explains the thorough inspection. What did she hear?

"Yes. They are out there, with the buggy. And my dog." I glance back.

Bellona lies on the ground near the horses, right where I commanded her to stay. She catches my eye, and her ears perk forward.

"You have a lovely home." I don't know what else to say. It's polite small talk, I know. But I mean it.

"Thank you." She looks over my shoulder and smiles. "It is Jacob's, all paid for. I add a much needed woman's touch."

"And she keeps Johnny and me from starving on our own cooking." Jacob's deep voice is soft behind me.

My heart does that little jumping thing. Coming beside me, he half bows, and my breath catches. Every movement is so familiar.

"Jacob, perhaps you can take the young lady and show her some of your horses, since she is so fond of animals. Dinner is not quite ready. I shall be happy to entertain the good doctors. Could you send Johnny in if you see him?"

He grins at me, a sparkle in his eyes. "I would love to. Just Anna Marie, I am pleased you came." He wraps my arm around his. "I was afraid I frightened you off permanently. You have no idea my delight when your mother came looking for you. To see her again was wonderful and then to find out you were her daughter!" He leans down and whispers, his face inches from mine. "Your mother is quite a remarkable woman. I owe her much. Perhaps you will allow me to tell you about it."

I nod. I can't speak. My heart is blocking my vocal chords.

Bellona whines. I call her, and she joyously rushes Jacob. He laughs, squats down, and wrestles with her playfully, scratching behind her large ears.

"Guard dog, did you say?"

I shrug. "She has been known to break a man's arm."

"Huh." Jacob stands and peers down at Bellona with renewed interest. "What did he do?"

"Attacked me." I give him a coquettish smile.

"Oh!" His brows knit together as he looks at me then pats my dog. "Well, good. I can see why she travels with you."

He shows me the stables, taking obvious pride in his accomplishments. He built them himself, with the help of an uncle and his younger brother.

"I thought you lived near Saint Louis," I say, forgetting myself.

He gives me a quick glance.

"Yes, we did." His brows narrow. "I do not recall us talking about that."

"Just something I heard. So, what brought you south?" I want to kick myself.

"My mother's brother owns a mill in town. Saint Louis is getting crowded, so we sold our place there, and with that and the money I earned during the war, we purchased twice the acres, with the house, some good breeding horses, and have some extra to live off. I figure the way of the future is in horses. Horses and steam. But for farming, more and more of the equipment is designed to be horse powered. It is one way to use knowledge I already have and make a living off it."

We are quiet a long time. I keep watching him when I think he's not looking. I want to pinch myself, struggling to believe he's real. He's a bit awkward himself. I catch him looking at me like he's got some big questions, but he's trying to be discreet.

"May I ask you an odd question without you thinking me inappropriate? I would hate to frighten you." He grins. "It is a far run back to town."

"Oooh-kay, I think." I do have an urge to run.

"Your mother may have told you I served in your father's regiment."

I cringe. Here comes the 'your father was a monster, so you must be a terrible person; it was nice to meet you, but goodbye' speech. But he doesn't drop my arm, and we keep walking.

"The war is a separate matter," he says. Maybe he sees me cringe. "Best save that discussion for another day. It is just, when your father was dying, he said some very strange things."

He pauses.

"Your father, well, please do not think me rude, but did he suffer from mental illness?"

That was not what I expected.

"No!" I say, without hesitation. "Well, I don't really know. He didn't raise us. I only saw him once after he disappeared. I was eight when he left and didn't see him again until last year, and I would rather not talk about that. Was he a terrible person? Yeah. But crazy? I don't think so."

"He disappeared?" He releases my arm.

I keep walking.

"Why? Do you know why he disappeared?" he asks.

"You don't want to know."

"I do."

"Nope. You'd think *I* was the crazy person."

"Try me."

"No."

He rubs his forehead, then his chin.

"You ought to shave that mustache," I say and want to kick myself. Again. "It would show off your dimple—and your smile. You have a great smile."

He must be thinking about something else. He's looking at me with that look he gets when he wants to say something but isn't sure he should.

"Alrighty. You may think me insane, but here it is. When your father was dying, he kept begging me to take him home. To his family. He said they had advanced treatment there and could heal his back. He said… He said he came from the year 2002."

"Oh." I keep walking. What can I say? I'm not going to lie to him, and I sure am not going to tell him the truth.

He grips my arm, forcing me to stop, then turns me toward him.

"Your mother had the same reaction when I told her, back at the hospital. I would not have thought anything more about it, except, well, your father gave me his purse. He intended to bribe me into taking him home, but he was so far gone, no bribery could make a difference even if I was inclined to accept. It was what I found inside his purse that is so astonishing."

He pulls an old black bifold wallet from his pocket, opens it, and pulls out Daddy's driver's license. His picture, address, and birthdate are clearly visible. "First, I found this. I would be inclined to believe it was some practical joke, although I find the material intriguing. Still, it was the other item he carried that astonished me."

Jacob removes a photo, the one of Mama holding Adeline with one hand and me with the other. The beach picture, still colorful and lifelike after all these years. The one I caught in the other Jacob's possession and refused to allow him to explain. I reach for it. Tears fill my eyes, and I have to blink hard.

"I have never seen a photograph like this before. Would that be you? It is your mother—of that I am certain. And you told me you have a twin."

I gaze at the picture—Adeline's favorite. A picture from a time our family was happy and intact. Before all the leaving.

"Yes. I'm that one." I point to the my three year old self, head thrown back and shrieking with joy.

"It is true, then. Did you also come from the year 2002?"

I smile, shaking my head. "No. 2014."

He rubs his forehead, his chin, his forehead. Just like my Jacob. His head tilts a bit to the side, and a half smile, half look of awe fills his face. "This is most amazing. It does, however, explain much."

"How so?"

"Captain Powers seemed to know many things that no one should know. When battles would occur and where to position his men so they always experienced fewer casualties than most units. He even knew the war ended before other leaders were aware."

"My dad knew his history," I muse.

"And you, Just Anna Marie, do you know our history?" His smile is tentative, the tilt of his mustache suggesting there's more to his question than what's on the surface.

When I don't reply, he tucks my hand in the crook of his elbow. We turn and walk toward the house.

He believes me. I don't know what to say, and I'm so afraid of saying the wrong thing.

"Just Anna Marie?" He grins sideways at me. My heart pinches. How alike they are. "Do you believe that God brings people together for a purpose?"

"Oh, yes!" I think of Tia, of the Dickersons, Granny Gray, of my Jacob.

"Do you think God has someone in mind for you, someone to be your companion through life, and He works out ways to bring you together?"

I stop walking. I'm shaking, but I can't explain why. "I think so, but I don't know."

"Anna Marie, please forgive me if I sound bold, but would you believe me if I told you...?" He stops and looks at me really weird.

I know I haven't grown an extra head, and I know I don't look any different than I did ten minutes ago.

"Go on," I say.

"Do you recall how I kept asking if we had met? This morning, when I said you looked familiar."

"Yeah."

"Would you believe me if I said I have been having dreams about you for the past year?"

My knees go weak, and before they can give out I lower myself to the ground. I could blame my dizziness on a corset, but I refuse to wear one. So I sit, awkward and unladylike, with my knees drawn up and my forehead buried in a fold of my skirt.

Breathe, I tell myself. *Nice deep breaths.* Bellona is licking my face, and Jacob leans over me.

My Jacob's voice echoes in my memory, repeating words written in his letter. *Will that other me dream of you as I have? Will he love you and pursue you as I have? Can I be jealous of my own self?*

"Well, I do seem to have a rather potent effect on you!" he says through a smile.

I smile back. "That you do, Jacob Reddington." I'm blushing again. "But before you say any more, there are a few things I need to tell you. Please don't say anything until I finish—no matter how crazy I sound."

He nods.

I tell him about meeting him—another him—at the small jail in my home town, of our growing friendship and fights in my time, about my falling through at the river, the disaster at the Dickerson's. I tell him about my father, how I saw Jacob and his brother in the trees.

He shakes his head, his eyes filled with sorrow. "I remember that house. They fared better than most Captain Powers and his lieutenant encountered. The things we did were inexcusable, war or no. But your father was a different man when he came out of that home."

"Different?"

"Yes, less—how shall I explain it?—less cocky, more pensive. The home raids ended after that."

"Oh." I ponder this idea. I wonder if encountering me there changed my father. A deep sorrow fills me, an ache to know what he was like in his last days.

I describe the heart wrenching journey south, the loss of dear friends and of making new. I tell him about my encounter with Jethro and how Jacob and Bellona found me just in time.

"Jethro Tanner did you say? He was in our regiment, your father's lieutenant. He deserted about a month before the war ended. I wondered what happened to him."

Just thinking about him makes me shiver and look around.

I tell him about Joseph's accident and our trip to find the doctor and finding my mother. How Jacob determined to save his brother.

"What happened to Johnny?"

I tell him what the other Jacob recounted. About the large band of men ambushing their group and he and my father being the only survivors.

"But that is not what happened. Three men ambushed our party, and we chased them off. Only one of ours died. Several were injured—your father and Johnny were the worst."

"I know," I say. "But that isn't what happened the first time."

He looks at me like I've a screw loose.

"I'm just telling you what you—what the other Jacob—told me. I know it's a lot to take in. Mama and I believe Jethro was responsible for the attack, but when I killed him, the battle swung in your favor."

"So, you're telling me Jethro died? That you killed him?" Jacob steps back and looks me over. "You are so small. Was it your dog that killed him?"

"No. She only broke his arm. On the previous encounter. I never should have, but I left her behind with James when we went to warn you—I mean, the other you."

Jacob looks totally confused. "But, he was in jail."

"Yes, yes. I know. He escaped."

I tell him about Jethro's threat, how Thomas, Mama, and I took off to warn Jacob. I tell him how he—no, the other Jacob—pushed me away, taking the bullet that should have ended my life. I tell how I shot Jethro as I fell.

I choke with emotion when I recall burying him under the tall oak, with no marker because we had no way to make one.

I do not tell him about his proposal. I do not tell him about our one and only kiss. Those are memories I cannot share.

And I'm crying, and Jacob is holding me.

"Me thinks you cared very much for this Jacob," he says.

I cry harder and hold tight to his neck. "More than he ever knew."

It is dark when we return to the house. We walk hand in hand, and even if this is not my Jacob, it feels right. Bellona trots alongside, grinning around a large stick in her mouth. I signal her to stay and she drops her stick. With a sigh, she sits and watches as we make our way up the steps and into the house. The table is set for two. The other plates have been cleared.

"I'm sorry!" I exclaim, blushing. "I—we didn't hear you call!"

"Never you mind." Mrs. Reddington glances at Mama, and they both smile. "You two appeared to be having a good discussion, and we decided not to interfere. You will have to put up with cold food, however. Jacob knows I do not go out of my way to warm it up if he's not here when he ought to be."

Johnny is standing near his mother, twisting his hat in his hand.

"Good evening, Johnny." I extend my hand. His grip is firm, his eyes steady. His smile is like his brother's. "Jacob has told me much about you."

He reminds me of William, the same overgrown arms and legs. The same stance of a young man turning from boy to man and pulling himself to stand tall.

His smile is shy. "It is good to finally meet you, Miss Anna."

As if drawn by a powerful magnet, my attention falls on an object hanging on the wall behind Johnny, on a special hook.

I walk over, glance at Jacob, and swallow. "May I?"

He nods. "It was my Father's. Do you play?"

I pick it up. Its deep shine and rich stain show years of dedicated care. I turn it over and admire the fine craftsmanship. I pick the strings, one by one, tightening until it's tuned to perfection. The richness of tone even in tuning sets my heart on fire. I glance inside the casing and gasp.

"Mama!" I point inside.

Stamped in blurry black ink inside, it reads: "Antonius Stradivarius Cremonensis, Faciebat Anno 1721."

My eyes meet Jacob's. With trembling hands, I lift the violin to my chin and begin to play.

THE END

ACKNOWLEDGEMENTS

James Dickerson was my husband's great-grandfather. Granddaddy, my husband's grandfather, loved to tell the story of James' escape during the Civil War. His family was wrongly accused of owning a slave, having an African-American woman working in their home. A troupe of Union soldiers forced the Dickersons from their home with only the few belongings they could hurriedly throw into a wagon. As they fled, their home was set on fire.

Along the way to Arkansas, according to Granddaddy, both parents died of typhoid fever. Eight children, including a baby girl, made the rest of the journey alone.

While doing some family tree research, I not only found registration and birth records for the Dickerson family with names, ages, and pictures of the parents, but I also found records of their deaths. To my surprise, I found records of the deaths of two older daughters: Mary Elizabeth and Martha. With these two, the total number of children evicted with their parents was ten. Mary Elizabeth and Martha both died within days of their parents, so I assume they also contracted typhoid. An older son, William, died the same year, but the records didn't give a date. There were also records of three children who died in infancy prior to the events in my story.

Since all able-bodied men were forced to join one side or the other, I had to invent a reason that would excuse Samuel Dickerson from fighting and allow him to remain at home. Hence the lame leg.

Independent military gangs, known as Bushwhackers or Jayhawkers roamed the state, raiding the military as well as ambushing local individuals and families, coercing them for supplies, or murdering them on site. The most famous of the Missouri gangs were the Quantrill gang. The Union set into law General Order 11 in an attempt to prevent local people from 'supporting' these men, as well as a way of forcing southern sympathizers out of the territory. This order forced people to leave their homes and their property was burned to the ground.

Another family story Granddaddy shared was about two of the brothers getting into a fight while at a swimming hole. The fight came to an abrupt halt when one brother punctured the other one's eye out with a stick. Since photos of James as an older man shows him with both eyes intact, I must assume he was not the one injured.

James Dickerson lived well into his eighties, and made his living selling religious books. He was known as a man of faith.

These few details of family history inspired the Dickerson part of my story. As far as Anna Marie and her family are concerned, they are entirely fictitious and if any character looks or sounds familiar, that would be total coincidence.

Being familiar with the Latino culture, I opted to include some of that in my story. The part of falling through time? I had the coolest dream during which I saw my reflection in the condensation on a wine glass, and when I went to wipe the drops away, I "fell" to another time. I woke up and said, "Now that's a story!"

As I wrote Anna's story, Sofia and Jacob drew me into their lives. They need their story to be told, along with a peek into the mysterious Chachi. I am working on those!

And yes, I own a German Shepherd. Her name is Belle.

Thank you for reading. I hope you had fun. I did!

Made in the USA
Middletown, DE
10 October 2023

40566184R00170